The only tradition which binds these stories together is that of literary excellence. Each, in its separate and extremely disparate way, is a story which moves the reader, which excites, titillates, amuses, horrifies, or otherwise brings about an emotional reaction. In a (much overused) word, these stories communicate.

And it doesn't matter a damn whether the style is traditional, or new wave, or unique.

Read and enjoy.

Books by Robert Silverberg

DIMENSION THIRTEEN
MOONFERNS AND STARSONGS
NEEDLE IN A TIMESTACK
SON OF MAN
THE MASKS OF TIME
THORNS
TO OPEN THE SKY
UP THE LINE

Edited by Robert Silverberg

ALPHA ONE
ALPHA TWO
DARK STARS
GREAT SHORT NOVELS OF SCIENCE FICTION

ALPHA TWO

Edited by

Robert Silverberg

BALLANTINE BOOKS • NEW YORK
An Intext Publisher

SBN 345-02419-2-095

First Printing: November, 1971

Printed in the United States of America

Cover art by Larry Kresek

BALLANTINE BOOKS, INC.
101 Fifth Avenue, New York, N. Y. 10003

Table of Contents

INTRODUCTION

The series of anthologies under the *Alpha* heading has no particular thematic axe to grind. Lately we have seen science fiction collections designed to open people's eyes to the menace of pollution, collections of stories all of which deal with voyages to the moon, a book of stories set in the year 2000, and assorted other specialized enterprises. Our net is wider here. The sole purpose of the *Alpha* anthologies is to bring together science fiction of high literary merit—stories that break from the unlamented Buck Rogers era of ray-guns and loathsome monsters and provide entertainment and stimulation for an adult audience. In their way, I suppose, the *Alpha* volumes are guilty of special pleading, even as are the antipollution anthologies: the goal here is to show what a supple, variegated, dynamic, and sophisticated literary mode science fiction can be when it is at its best.

Whatever else these stories may be doing, they all explore the interplay between human beings and the technological society man has created for himself. Good science fiction simultaneously peers into remote realms of space and time and holds a mirror to the contemporary moment; and if the reflection in that mirror is somewhat distorted, so be it. Blame not the messenger for bearing bad tidings. Herewith ten stories which demonstrate the unsettling kinds of insights that science fiction alone can offer. More are on the way.

ROBERT SILVERBERG

ALPHA TWO

CALL ME JOE

Poul Anderson

When we go to Jupiter, we will have to explore it by proxy, for that vast planet is notably inhospitable to the fragile bodies of human beings. The challenge of Jupiter has called forth some splendid science fiction—I think particularly of Clifford Simak's "Desertion" and James Blish's "Bridge"—but a special place in the Jovian literature must be reserved for this turbulent, shattering story, perhaps the most powerful of all Poul Anderson's innumerable tales.

The wind came whooping out of eastern darkness, driving a lash of ammonia dust before it. In minutes, Edward Anglesey was blinded.

He clawed all four feet into the broken shards which were soil, hunched down, and groped for his little smelter. The wind was an idiot bassoon in his skull. Something whipped across his back, drawing blood, a tree yanked up by the roots and spat a hundred miles. Lightning cracked, immensely far overhead where clouds boiled with night.

As if to reply, thunder toned in the ice mountains and a red gout of flame jumped and a hillside came booming down, spilling itself across the valley. The earth shivered.

Sodium explosion, thought Anglesey in the drumbeat

noise. The fire and the lightning gave him enough illumination to find his apparatus. He picked up tools in muscular hands, his tail gripped the trough, and he battered his way to the tunnel and thus to his dugout.

It had walls and roof of water, frozen by sun-remoteness and compressed by tons of atmosphere jammed onto every square inch. Ventilated by a tiny smokehole, a lamp of tree oil burning in hydrogen made a dull light for the single room.

Anglesey sprawled his slate-blue form on the floor, panting. It was no use to swear at the storm. These ammonia gales often came at sunset, and there was nothing to do but wait them out. He was tired anyway.

It would be morning in five hours or so. He had hoped to cast an axehead, his first, this evening, but maybe it was better to do the job by daylight.

He pulled a decapod body off a shelf and ate the meat raw, pausing for long gulps of liquid methane from a jug. Things would improve once he had proper tools; so far, everything had been painfully grubbed and hacked to shape with teeth, claws, chance icicles, and what detestably weak and crumbling fragments remained of the spaceship. Give him a few years and he'd be living as a man should.

He sighed, stretched, and lay down to sleep.

Somewhat more than one hundred and twelve thousand miles away, Edward Anglesey took off his helmet.

He looked around, blinking. After the Jovian surface, it was always a little unreal to find himself here again, in the clean quiet orderliness of the control room.

His muscles ached. They shouldn't. He had not really been fighting a gale of several hundred miles an hour, under three gravities and a temperature of 140 Absolute. He had been here, in the almost nonexistent pull of Jupiter V, breathing oxynitrogen. It was Joe who lived down there and filled his lungs with hydrogen and helium at a pressure which could still only be estimated because it broke aneroids and deranged piezoelectrics.

Nevertheless, his body felt worn and beaten. Tension, no doubt—psychosomatics—after all, for a good many hours now he had, in a sense, been Joe, and Joe had been working hard.

With the helmet off, Anglesey held only a thread of identification. The esprojector was still tuned to Joe's brain but no longer focused on his own. Somewhere in the back of his mind, he knew an indescribable feeling of sleep. Now and then, vague forms or colors drifted in the soft black—dreams? Not impossible, that Joe's brain should dream a little when Anglesey's mind wasn't using it.

A light flickered red on the esprojector panel, and a bell whined electronic fear. Anglesey cursed. Thin fingers danced over the controls of his chair, he slued around and shot across to the bank of dials. Yes—there—K-tube oscillating again! The circuit blew out. He wrenched the faceplate off with one hand and fumbled in a drawer with the other.

Inside his mind he could feel the contact with Joe fading. If he once lost it entirely, he wasn't sure he could regain it. And Joe was an investment of several million dollars and quite a few highly skilled man-years.

Anglesey pulled the offending K-tube from its socket and threw it on the floor. Glass exploded. It eased his temper a bit, just enough so he could find a replacement, plug it in, switch on the current again—as the machine warmed up, once again amplifying, the Joeness in the back alleys of his brain strengthened.

Slowly, then, the man in the electric wheelchair rolled out of the room, into the hall. Let somebody else sweep up the broken tube. To hell with it. To hell with everybody.

Jan Cornelius had never been farther from Earth than some comfortable Lunar resort. He felt much put upon that the Psionics Corporation should tap him for a thirteen-month exile. The fact that he knew as much about esprojectors and their cranky innards as any other man alive was no excuse. Why send anyone at all? Who cared?

Obviously the Federation Science Authority did. It had seemingly given those bearded hermits a blank check on the taxpayer's account.

Thus did Cornelius grumble to himself, all the long hyperbolic path to Jupiter. Then the shifting accelerations of approach to its tiny inner satellite left him too wretched for further complaint.

And when he finally, just prior to disembarkation, went up to the greenhouse for a look at Jupiter, he said not a word. Nobody does, the first time.

Arne Viken waited patiently while Cornelius stared. *It still gets me, too,* he remembered. *By the throat. Sometimes I'm afraid to look.*

At length Cornelius turned around. He had a faintly Jovian appearance himself, being a large man with an imposing girth. "I had no idea," he whispered. "I never thought . . . I had seen pictures, but—"

Viken nodded. "Sure, Dr. Cornelius. Pictures don't convey it."

Where they stood, they could see the dark broken rock of the satellite, jumbled for a short way beyond the landing slip and then chopped off sheer. This moon was scarcely even a platform, it seemed, and cold constellations went streaming past it, around it. Jupiter lay across a fifth of that sky, softly ambrous, banded with colors, spotted with the shadows of planet-sized moons and with whirlwinds as broad as Earth. If there had been any gravity to speak of, Cornelius would have thought, instinctively, that the great planet was falling on him. As it was, he felt as if sucked upward;

his hands were still sore where he had grabbed a rail to hold on.

"You live here . . . all alone . . . with this?" He spoke feebly.

"Oh, well, there are some fifty of us all told, pretty congenial," said Viken. "It's not so bad. You sign up for four-cycle hitches—four ship arrivals—and believe it or not, Dr. Cornelius, this is my third enlistment."

The newcomer forbore to inquire more deeply. There was something not quite understandable about the men on Jupiter V. They were mostly bearded, though otherwise careful to remain neat; their low-gravity movements were somehow dreamlike to watch; they hoarded their conversation, as if to stretch it through the year and month between ships. Their monkish existence had changed them—or did they take what amounted to vows of poverty, chastity, and obedience, because they had never felt quite at home on green Earth?

Thirteen months! Cornelius shuddered. It was going to be a long cold wait, and the pay and bonuses accumulating for him were scant comfort now, four hundred and eighty million miles from the sun.

"Wonderful place to do research," continued Viken. "All the facilities, hand-picked colleagues, no distractions . . . and of course—" He jerked his thumb at the planet and turned to leave.

Cornelius followed, wallowing awkwardly. "It is very interesting, no doubt," he puffed. "Fascinating. But really, Dr. Viken, to drag me way out here and make me spend a year plus waiting for the next ship . . . to do a job which may take me a few weeks—"

"Are you sure it's that simple?" asked Viken gently. His face swiveled around, and there was something in his eyes that silenced Cornelius. "After all my time here, I've yet to see any problem, however complicated, which when you looked at it the right way didn't become still more complicated."

They went through the ship's air lock and the tube joining it to the station entrance. Nearly everything was underground. Rooms, laboratories, even halls had a degree of luxuriousness—why, there was a fireplace with a real fire in the common room! God alone knew what *that* cost!

Thinking of the huge chill emptiness where the king planet laired, and of his own year's sentence, Cornelius decided that such luxuries were, in truth, biological necessities.

Viken showed him to a pleasantly furnished chamber which would be his own. "We'll fetch your luggage soon and unload your psionic stuff. Right now, everybody's either talking to the ship's crew or reading his mail."

Cornelius nodded absently and sat down. The chair, like all low-gee furniture, was a mere spidery skeleton, but it held his bulk comfortably enough. He felt in his tunic hoping to bribe the other man into keeping him company for a while. "Cigar? I brought some from Amsterdam."

"Thanks." Viken accepted with disappointing casualness, crossed long thin legs, and blew grayish clouds.

"Ah . . . are you in charge here?"

"Not exactly. No one is. We do have one administrator, the cook, to handle what little work of that type may come up. Don't forget, this is a research station, first, last, and always."

"What is your field, then?"

Viken frowned. "Don't question anyone else so bluntly, Dr. Cornelius," he warned. "They'd rather spin the gossip out as long as possible with each newcomer. It's a rare treat to have someone whose every last conceivable reaction hasn't been— No, no apologies to me. 'S all right. I'm a physicist, specializing in the solid state at ultrahigh pressures." He nodded at the wall. "Plenty of it to be observed—there!"

"I see." Cornelius smoked quietly for a while. Then:

"I'm supposed to be the psionics expert, but frankly, at present, I've no idea why your machine should misbehave as reported."

"You mean those, uh, K-tubes have a stable output on Earth?"

"And on Luna, Mars, Venus . . . everywhere, apparently, but here." Cornelius shrugged. "Of course, psi-beams are always pernickety, and sometimes you get an unwanted feedback when— No. I'll get the facts before I theorize. Who are your psimen?"

"Just Anglesey, who's not a formally trained esman at all. But he took it up after he was crippled, and showed such a natural aptitude that he was shipped out here when he volunteered. It's so hard to get anyone for Jupiter V that we aren't fussy about degrees. At that, Ed seems to be operating Joe as well as a Ps.D. could."

"Ah, yes. Your pseudojovian. I'll have to examine that angle pretty carefully too," said Cornelius. In spite of himself, he was getting interested. "Maybe the trouble comes from something in Joe's biochemistry. Who knows? I'll let you into a carefully guarded little secret, Dr. Viken: psionics is not an exact science."

"Neither is physics," grinned the other man. After a moment, he added more soberly: "Not my brand of physics, anyway. I hope to make it exact. That's why I'm here, you know. It's the reason we're all here."

Edward Anglesey was a bit of a shock, the first time. He was a head, a pair of arms, and a disconcertingly intense blue stare. The rest of him was mere detail, enclosed in a wheeled machine.

"Biophysicist originally," Viken had told Cornelius. "Studying atmospheric spores at Earth Station when he was still a young man—accident crushed him up, nothing below his chest will ever work again. Snappish type, you have to go slow with him."

Seated on a wisp of stool in the esprojector control

room, Cornelius realized that Viken had been soft-pedaling the truth.

Anglesey ate as he talked, gracelessly, letting the chair's tentacles wipe up after him. "Got to," he explained. "This stupid place is officially on Earth time, GMT. Jupiter isn't. I've got to be here whenever Joe wakes, ready to take him over."

"Couldn't you have someone spell you?" asked Cornelius.

"Bah!" Anglesey stabbed a piece of prot and waggled it at the other man. Since it was native to him, he could spit out English, the common language of the station, with unmeasured ferocity. "Look here. You ever done therapeutic esping? Not just listening in, or even communication, but actual pedagogic control?"

"No, not I. It requires a certain natural talent, like yours." Cornelius smiled. His ingratiating little phrase was swallowed without being noticed by the scored face opposite him. "I take it you mean cases like, oh, reeducating the nervous system of a palsied child?"

"Yes, yes. Good enough example. Has anyone ever tried to suppress the child's personality, take him over in the most literal sense?"

"Good God, no!"

"Even as a scientific experiment?" Anglesey grinned. "Has any esprojector operative ever poured on the juice and swamped the child's brain with his own thoughts? Come on, Cornelius, I won't snitch on you."

"Well . . . it's out of my line, you understand." The psionicist looked carefully away, found a bland meter face, and screwed his eyes to that. "I have, uh, heard something about . . . well, yes, there were attempts made in some pathological cases to, uh, bull through . . . break down the patient's delusions by sheer force—"

"And it didn't work," said Anglesey. He laughed. "It *can't* work, not even on a child, let alone an adult with a fully developed personality. Why, it took a decade of refinement, didn't it, before the machine was debugged to the point where a psychiatrist could even 'listen in' without the normal variation between his pattern of thought and the patient's . . . without that variation setting up an interference scrambling the very thing he wanted to study. The machine has to make automatic compensations for the differences between individuals. We still can't bridge the differences between species.

"If someone else is willing to cooperate, you can very gently guide his thinking. And that's all. If you try to seize control of another brain, a brain with its own background of experience, its own ego—you risk your very sanity. The other brain will fight back, instinctively. A fully developed, matured, hardened human personality is just too complex for outside control. It has too many resources, too much hell the subconscious can call to its defense if its integrity is threatened. Blazes, man, we can't even master our own minds, let alone anyone else's!"

Anglesey's cracked-voice tirade broke off. He sat brooding at the instrument panel, tapping the console of his mechanical mother.

"Well?" said Cornelius after a while.

He should not, perhaps, have spoken. But he found it hard to remain mute. There was too much silence—half a billion miles of it, from here to the sun. If you closed your mouth five minutes at a time, the silence began creeping in like a fog.

"Well," gibed Anglesey. "So our pseudojovian, Joe, has a physically adult brain. The only reason I can control him is that his brain has never been given a chance to develop its own ego. I *am* Joe. From the moment he was 'born' into consciousness, I have been there. The psibeam sends me all his sense data and sends him back my motor-nerve impulses. But nevertheless, he has that excellent brain, and its cells are recording every trace of experience, even as yours and mine; his synapses have assumed the topography which is my 'personality pattern.'

"Anyone else, taking him over from me, would find it was like an attempt to oust me myself from my own brain. It couldn't be done. To be sure, he doubtless has only a rudimentary set of Anglesey memories—I do not, for instance, repeat trigonometric theorems while controlling him—but he has enough to be, potentially, a distinct personality.

"As a matter of fact, whenever he wakes up from sleep—there's usually a lag of a few minutes, while I sense the change through my normal psi faculties and get the amplifying helmet adjusted—I have a bit of a struggle. I feel almost a . . . a resistance . . . until I've brought his mental currents completely into phase with mine. Merely dreaming has been enough of a different experience to—"

Anglesey didn't bother to finish the sentence.

"I see," murmured Cornelius. "Yes, it's clear enough. In fact, it's astonishing that you can have such total contact with a being of such alien metabolism."

"I won't for much longer," said the esman sarcastically, "unless you can correct whatever is burning out those K-tubes. I don't have an unlimited supply of spares."

"I have some working hypotheses," said Cornelius, "but there's so little known about psibeam transmission—is the velocity infinite or merely very great, is the beam strength actually independent of distance? How about the possible effects of transmission . . . oh, through the degenerate matter in the Jovian core? Good Lord, a planet where water is a heavy mineral and hydrogen is a metal? What do we know?"

"We're supposed to find out," snapped Anglesey. "That's what this whole project is for. Knowledge. Bull!" Almost, he spat on the floor. "Apparently what little we have learned doesn't even get through to people. Hydrogen is still a gas where Joe lives. He'd have to dig down a few miles to reach the solid phase. And I'm expected to make a scientific analysis of Jovian conditions!"

Cornelius waited it out, letting Anglesey storm on while he himself turned over the problem of K-tube oscillation.

"They don't understand back on Earth. Even here they don't. Sometimes I think they refuse to understand. Joe's down there without much more than his bare hands. He, I, we started with no more knowledge than that he could probably eat the local life. He has to spend nearly all his time hunting for food. It's a miracle he's come as far as he has in these few weeks—made a shelter, grown familiar with the immediate region, begun on metallurgy, hydrurgy, whatever you want to call it. What more do they want me to do, for crying in the beer?"

"Yes, yes—" mumbled Cornelius. "Yes, I—"

Anglesey raised his white bony face. Something filmed over in his eyes.

"What—?" began Cornelius.

"Shut up!" Anglesey whipped the chair around, groped for the helmet, slapped it down over his skull. "Joe's waking. Get out of here."

"But if you'll only let me work while he sleeps, how can I—"

Anglesey snarled and threw a wrench at him. It was a feeble toss, even in low-gee. Cornelius backed toward the door. Anglesey was tuning in the esprojector. Suddenly he jerked.

"Cornelius!"

"Whatisit?" The psionicist tried to run back, overdid it, and skidded in a heap to end up against the panel.

"K-tube again." Anglesey yanked off the helmet. It must have hurt like blazes, having a mental squeal build up uncontrolled and amplified in your own brain, but he said merely: "Change it for me. Fast. And then get out and leave me alone. Joe didn't wake up of himself.

Something crawled into the dugout with me—I'm in trouble down there!"

It had been a hard day's work, and Joe slept heavily. He did not wake until the hands closed on his throat.

For a moment, then, he knew only a crazy smothering wave of panic. He thought he was back on Earth Station, floating in null-gee at the end of a cable while a thousand frosty stars haloed the planet before him. He thought the great I-beam had broken from its moorings and started toward him, slowly, but with all the inertia of its cold tons, spinning and shimmering in the Earth light, and the only sound himself screaming and screaming in his helmet trying to break from the cable the beam nudged him ever so gently but it kept on moving he moved with it he was crushed against the station wall nuzzled into it his mangled suit frothed as it tried to seal its wounded self there was blood mingled with the foam his blood *Joe roared.*

His convulsive reaction tore the hands off his neck and sent a black shape spinning across the dugout. It struck the wall, thunderously, and the lamp fell to the floor and went out.

Joe stood in darkness, breathing hard, aware in a vague fashion that the wind had died from a shriek to a low snarling while he slept.

The thing he had tossed away mumbled in pain and crawled along the wall. Joe felt through lightlessness after his club.

Something else scrabbled. The tunnel! They were coming through the tunnel! Joe groped blindly to meet them. His heart drummed thickly and his nose drank an alien stench.

The thing that emerged, as Joe's hands closed on it, was only about half his size, but it had six monstrously taloned feet and a pair of three-fingered hands that reached after his eyes. Joe cursed, lifted it while it writhed, and dashed it to the floor. It screamed, and he heard bones splinter.

"Come on, then!" Joe arched his back and spat at them, like a tiger menaced by giant caterpillars.

They flowed through his tunnel and into the room, a dozen of them entered while he wrestled one that had curled around his shoulders and anchored its sinuous body with claws. They pulled at his legs, trying to crawl up on his back. He struck out with claws of his own, with his tail, rolled over and went down beneath a heap of them and stood up with the heap still clinging to him.

They swayed in darkness. The legged seething of them struck the dugout wall. It shivered, a rafter cracked, the roof came down. Anglesey stood in a pit, among broken ice plates, under the wan light of a sinking Ganymede.

He could see, now, that the monsters were black in color and that they had heads big enough to accommodate some brains, less than human but probably more than apes. There were a score of them or so; they struggled from beneath the wreckage and flowed at him with the same shrieking malice.

Why?

Baboon reaction, though Anglesey somewhere in the back of himself. See the stranger, fear the stranger, hate the stranger, kill the stranger. His chest heaved, pumping air through a raw throat. He yanked a whole rafter to him, snapped it in half, and twirled the iron-hard wood.

The nearest creature got its head bashed in. The next had its back broken. The third was hurled with shattered ribs into a fourth; they went down together. Joe began to laugh. It was getting to be fun.

"Yeeė-ow! Ti-i-i-iger!" He ran across the icy ground, toward the pack. They scattered, howling. He hunted them until the last one had vanished into the forest.

Panting, Joe looked at the dead. He himself was bleeding, he ached, he was cold and hungry, and his shelter had been wrecked . . . but, he'd whipped them! He had a sudden impulse to beat his chest and howl. For a moment, he hesitated—why not? Anglesey threw back his head and bayed victory at the dim shield of Ganymede.

Thereafter he went to work. First build a fire, in the lee of the spaceship—which was little more by now than a hill of corrosion. The monster pack cried in darkness and the broken ground; they had not given up on him, they would return.

He tore a haunch off one of the slain and took a bite. Pretty good. Better yet if properly cooked. Heh! They'd made a big mistake in calling his attention to their existence! He finished breakfast while Ganymede slipped under the western ice mountains. It would be morning soon. The air was almost still, and a flock of pancake-shaped skyskimmers, as Anglesey called them, went overhead, burnished copper color in the first pale dawn-streaks.

Joe rummaged in the ruins of his hut until he had recovered the water-smelting equipment. It wasn't harmed. That was the first order of business, melt some ice and cast it in the molds of ax, knife, saw, hammer he had painfully prepared. Under Jovian conditions, methane was a liquid that you drank and water was a dense hard mineral. It would make good tools. Later on he would try alloying it with other materials.

Next—yes. To hell with the dugout; he could sleep in the open again for a while. Make a bow, set traps, be ready to massacre the black caterpillars when they attacked him again. There was a chasm not far from here, going down a long way toward the bitter cold of the metallic-hydrogen strata: a natural icebox, a place to store the several weeks' worth of meat his enemies would supply. This would give him leisure to— Oh, a hell of a lot!

Joe laughed, exultantly, and lay down to watch the sunrise.

It struck him afresh how lovely a place this was. See how the small brilliant spark of the sun swam up out of eastern fogbanks colored dusky purple and veined with rose and gold; see how the light strengthened until the great hollow arch of the sky became one shout of radiance; see how the light spilled warm and living over a broad fair land, the million square miles of rustling low forests and wave-blinking lakes and feather-plumed hydrogen geysers; and see, see, see how the ice mountains of the west flashed like blued steel!

Anglesey drew the wild morning wind deep into his lungs and shouted with a boy's joy.

"I'm not a biologist myself," said Viken carefully. "But maybe for that reason I can better give you the general picture. Then Lopez or Matsumoto can answer any questions of detail."

"Excellent," nodded Cornelius. "Why don't you assume I am totally ignorant of this project? I very nearly am, you know."

"If you wish," laughed Viken.

They stood in an outer office of the xenobiology section. No one else was around for the station's clocks said 1730 GMT and there was only one shift. No point in having more, until Anglesey's half of the enterprise had actually begun gathering quantitative data.

The physicist bent over and took a paperweight off a desk. "One of the boys made this for fun," he said, "but it's a pretty good model of Joe. He stands about five feet tall at the head."

Cornelius turned the plastic image over in his hands. If you could imagine such a thing as a feline centaur with a thick prehensile tail— The torso was squat, long-armed, immensely muscular; the hairless head was round, wide-nosed, with big deep-set eyes and heavy jaws, but it was really quite a human face. The overall color was bluish gray.

"Male, I see," he remarked.

"Of course. Perhaps you don't understand. Joe is the complete pseudojovian: as far as we can tell, the final model, with all the bugs worked out. He's the answer to a research question that took fifty years to ask." Viken looked sideways at Cornelius. "So you realize the importance of your job, don't you?"

"I'll do my best," said the psionicist. "But if . . . well, let's say that tube failure or something causes you to lose Joe before I've solved the oscillation problem. You do have other pseudos in reserve, don't you?"

"Oh, yes," said Viken moodily. "But the cost— We're not on an unlimited budget. We do go through a lot of money, because it's expensive to stand up and sneeze this far from Earth. But for that same reason our margin is slim."

He jammed hands in pockets and slouched toward the inner door, the laboratories, head down and talking in a low, hurried voice:

"Perhaps you don't realize what a nightmare planet Jupiter is. Not just the surface gravity—a shade under three gees, what's that? But the gravitational potential, ten times Earth's. The temperature. The pressure . . . above all, the atmosphere, and the storms, and the darkness!

"When a spaceship goes down to the Jovian surface, it's a radio-controlled job; it leaks like a sieve, to equalize pressure, but otherwise it's the sturdiest, most utterly powerful model ever designed; it's loaded with every instrument, every servomechanism, every safety device the human mind has yet thought up to protect a million-dollar hunk of precision equipment.

"And what happens? Half the ships never reach the surface at all. A storm snatches them and throws them away, or they collide with a floating chunk of Ice VII—small version of the Red Spot—or, so help me, what passes for a flock of *birds* rams one and stoves it in!

"As for the fifty percent which does land, it's a one-way trip. We don't even try to bring them back. If the stresses coming down haven't sprung something, the corrosion has doomed them anyway. Hydrogen at Jovian pressure does funny things to metals.

"It cost a total of—about five million dollars—to set Joe, one pseudo, down there. Each pseudo to follow will cost, if we're lucky, a couple of million more."

Viken kicked open the door and led the way through. Beyond was a big room, low-ceilinged, coldly lit, and murmurous with ventilators. It reminded Cornelius of a nucleonics lab; for a moment he wasn't sure why, then recognized the intricacies of remote control, remote observation, walls enclosing forces which could destroy the entire moon.

"These are required by the pressure, of course," said Viken, pointing to a row of shields. "And the cold. And the hydrogen itself, as a minor hazard. We have units here duplicating conditions in the Jovian, uh, stratosphere. This is where the whole project really began."

"I've heard something about that," nodded Cornelius, "Didn't you scoop up airborne spores?"

"Not I." Viken chuckled. "Totti's crew did, about fifty years ago. Proved there was life on Jupiter. A life using liquid methane as its basic solvent, solid ammonia as a starting point for nitrate synthesis—the plants use solar energy to build unsaturated carbon compounds, releasing hydrogen; the animals eat the plants and reduce those compounds again to the saturated form. There is even an equivalent of combustion. The reactions involve complex enzymes and . . . well, it's out of my line."

"Jovian biochemistry is pretty well understood, then."

"Oh, yes. Even in Totti's day, they had a highly developed biotic technology: Earth bacteria had already been synthesized and most gene structures pretty well mapped. The only reason it took so long to diagram Jovian life processes was the technical difficulty, high pressure and so on."

"When did you actually get a look at Jupiter's surface?"

"Gray managed that, about thirty years ago. Set a televisor ship down, a ship that lasted long enough to flash him quite a series of pictures. Since then, the technique has improved. We know that Jupiter is crawling with its own weird kind of life, probably more fertile than Earth. Extrapolating from the airborne microorganisms, our team made trial syntheses of metazoans and—"

Viken sighed. "Damn it, if only there were intelligent native life! Think what they could tell us, Cornelius, the data, the— Just think back how far we've gone since Lavoisier, with the low-pressure chemistry of Earth. Here's a chance to learn a high-pressure chemistry and physics at least as rich with possibilities!"

After a moment, Cornelius murmured slyly: "Are you certain there *aren't* any Jovians?"

"Oh, sure, there could be several billion of them," shrugged Viken. "Cities, empires, anything you like. Jupiter has the surface area of a hundred Earths, and we've only seen maybe a dozen small regions. But we do know there aren't any Jovians using radio. Considering their atmosphere, it's unlikely they ever would invent it for themselves—imagine how thick a vacuum tube has to be, how strong a pump you need! So it was finally decided we'd better make our own Jovians."

Cornelius followed him through the lab, into another room. This was less cluttered, it had a more finished appearance: the experimenter's haywire rig had yielded to the assured precision of an engineer.

Viken went over to one of the panels which lined the walls and looked at its gauges. "Beyond this lies another pseudo," he said. "Female, in this instance. She's at a pressure of two hundred atmospheres and a temperature of 194 Absolute. There's a . . . an umbilical arrangement, I guess you'd call it, to keep her alive. She was grown to adulthood in this, uh, fetal stage—we patterned our Jovians after the terrestrial mammal. She's never been conscious, she won't ever be till she's 'born.' We have a total of twenty males and sixty females waiting here. We can count on about half reaching the surface. More can be created as required.

"It isn't the pseudos that are so expensive, it's their transportation. So Joe is down there alone till we're sure that his kind *can* survive."

"I take it you experimented with lower forms first," said Cornelius.

"Of course. It took twenty years, even with forced-catalysis techniques, to work from an artificial airborne spore to Joe. We've used the psibeam to control everything from pseudoinsects on up. Interspecies control is possible, you know, if your puppet's nervous system is deliberately designed for it, and isn't given a chance to grow into a pattern different from the esman's."

"And Joe is the first specimen who's given trouble?"

"Yes."

"Scratch one hypothesis." Cornelius sat down on a workbench, dangling thick legs and running a hand through thin sandy hair. "I thought maybe some physical effect of Jupiter was responsible. Now it looks as if the difficulty is with Joe himself."

"We've all suspected that much," said Viken. He struck a cigarette and sucked in his cheeks around the smoke. His eyes were gloomy. "Hard to see how. The biotics engineers tell me *Pseudocentaurus sapiens* has been more carefully designed than any product of natural evolution."

"Even the brain?"

"Yes. It's patterned directly on the human, to make psibeam control possible, but there are improvements—greater stability."

"There are still the psychological aspects, though," said Cornelius. "In spite of all our amplifiers and other fancy gadgets, psi is essentially a branch of psychology, even today . . . or maybe it's the other way around.

Let's consider traumatic experiences. I take it the . . . the adult Jovian's fetus has a rough trip going down?"

"The ship does," said Viken. "Not the pseudo itself, which is wrapped up in fluid just like you were before birth."

"Nevertheless," said Cornelius, "the two hundred atmospheres pressure here is not the same as whatever unthinkable pressure exists down on Jupiter. Could the change be injurious?"

Viken gave him a look of respect. "Not likely," he answered. "I told you the J-ships are designed leaky. External pressure is transmitted to the, uh, uterine mechanism through a series of diaphragms, in a gradual fashion. It takes hours to make the descent, you realize."

"Well, what happens next?" went on Cornelius. "The ship lands, the uterine mechanism opens, the umbilical connection disengages, and Joe is, shall we say, born. But he has an adult brain. He is not protected by the only half-developed infant brain from the shock of sudden awareness."

"We thought of that," said Viken. "Anglesey was on the psibeam, in phase with Joe, when the ship left this moon. So it wasn't really Joe who emerged, who perceived. Joe has never been much more than a biological waldo. He can only suffer mental shock to the extent that Ed does, because it *is* Ed down there!"

"As you will," said Cornelius. "Still, you didn't plan for a race of puppets, did you?"

"Oh, heavens, no," said Viken. "Out of the question. Once we know Joe is well established, we'll import a few more esmen and get him some assistance in the form of other pseudos. Eventually females will be sent down, and uncontrolled males, to be educated by the puppets. A new generation will be born normally— Well, anyhow, the ultimate aim is a small civilization of Jovians. There will be hunters, miners, artisans, farmers, housewives, the works. They will support a few key members, a kind of priesthood. And that priesthood will be esp-controlled, as Joe is. It will exist solely to make instruments, take readings, perform experiments, and tell us what we want to know!"

Cornelius nodded. In a general way, this was the Jovian project as he had understood it. He could appreciate the importance of his own assignment.

Only, he still had no clue to the cause of that positive feedback in the K-tubes.

And what could he do about it?

His hands were still bruised. *Oh, God,* he thought with a groan, for the hundredth time, *does it affect me that much? While Joe was fighting down there, did I really hammer my fists on metal up here?*

His eyes smouldered across the room, to the bench where Cornelius worked. He didn't like Cornelius, fat cigar-sucking slob, interminably talking and talking. He had about given up trying to be civil to the Earthworm.

The psionicist laid down a screwdriver and flexed cramped fingers. *"Whuff!"* he smiled. "I'm going to take a break."

The half-assembled esprojector made a gaunt backdrop for his wide soft body, where it squatted toad-fashion on the bench. Anglesey detested the whole idea of anyone sharing this room, even for a few hours a day. Of late he had been demanding his meals brought here, left outside the door of his adjoining bedroom-bath. He had not gone beyond for quite some time now.

And why should I?

"Couldn't you hurry it up a little?" snapped Anglesey.

Cornelius flushed. "If you'd had an assembled spare machine, instead of loose parts—" he began. Shrugging, he took out a cigar stub and relit it carefully; his supply had to last a long time.

Anglesey wondered if those stinking clouds were blown from his mouth on malicious purpose. *I don't like you, Mr. Earthman Cornelius, and it is doubtless quite mutual.*

"There was no obvious need for one, until the other esmen arrive," said Anglesey in a sullen voice. "And the testing instruments report this one in perfectly good order."

"Nevertheless," said Cornelius, "at irregular intervals it goes into wild oscillations which burn out the K-tube. The problem is why. I'll have you try out this new machine as soon as it is ready, but, frankly, I don't believe the trouble lies in electronic failure at all—or even in unsuspected physical effects."

"Where, then?" Anglesey felt more at ease as the discussion grew purely technical.

"Well, look. What exactly is the K-tube? It's the heart of the esprojector. It amplifies your natural psionic pulses, uses them to modulate the carrier wave, and shoots the whole beam down at Joe. It also picks up Joe's resonating impulses and amplifies them for your benefit. Everything else is auxiliary to the K-tube."

"Spare me the lecture," snarled Anglesey.

"I was only rehearsing the obvious," said Cornelius, "because every now and then it is the obvious answer which is hardest to see. Maybe it isn't the K-tube which is misbehaving. Maybe it is you."

"What?" The white face gaped at him. A dawning rage crept red across its thin bones.

"Nothing personal intended," said Cornelius hastily. "But you know what a tricky beast the subconscious is. Suppose, just as a working hypothesis, that way down underneath you don't *want* to be on Jupiter. I imagine it is a rather terrifying environment. Or there may be some obscure Freudian element involved. Or, quite simply and naturally, your subconscious may fail to understand that Joe's death does not entail your own."

"Um-m-m—" *Mirabile dictu,* Anglesey remained calm. He rubbed his chin with one skeletal hand. "Can you be more explicit?"

"Only in a rough way," replied Cornelius. "Your conscious mind sends a motor impulse along the psibeam to Joe. Simultaneously, your subconscious mind, being scared of the whole business, emits the glandular-vascular-cardiac-visceral impulses associated with fear. These react on Joe, whose tension is transmitted back along the beam. Feeling Joe's somatic fear symptoms, your subconscious gets still more worried, thereby increasing the symptoms— Get it? It's exactly similar to ordinary neurasthenia, with this exception: that since there is a powerful amplier, the K-tube, involved, the oscillations can build up uncontrollably within a second or two. You should be thankful the tube does burn out —otherwise your brain might do so!"

For a moment Anglesey was quiet. Then he laughed. It was a hard, barbaric laughter. Cornelius started as it struck his eardrums.

"Nice idea," said the esman. "But I'm afraid it won't fit all the data. You see, I like it down there. I like being Joe."

He paused for a while, then continued in a dry impersonal tone: "Don't judge the environment from my notes. They're just idiotic things like estimates of wind velocity, temperature variations, mineral properties— insignificant. What I can't put in is how Jupiter looks through a Jovian's infrared-seeing eyes."

"Different, I should think," ventured Cornelius after a minute's clumsy silence.

"Yes and no. It's hard to put into language. Some of it I can't, because man hasn't got the concepts. But . . . oh, I can't describe it. Shakespeare himself couldn't. Just remember that everything about Jupiter which is cold and poisonous and gloomy to us is *right* for Joe."

Anglesey's tone grew remote, as if he spoke to himself:

"Imagine walking under a glowing violet sky, where great flashing clouds sweep the earth with shadow and rain strides beneath them. Imagine walking on the slopes of a mountain like polished metal, with a clean red flame exploding above you and thunder laughing in the ground. Imagine a cool wild stream, and low trees with dark coppery flowers, and a waterfall, methane-fall . . . whatever you like . . . leaping off a cliff, and the strong live wind shakes its mane full of rainbows! Imagine a whole forest, dark and breathing, and here and there you glimpse a pale-red wavering will-o'-the-wisp, which is the life radiation of some fleet shy animal, and . . . and—"

Anglesey croaked into silence. He stared down at his clenched fists, then he closed his eyes tight and tears ran out between the lids.

"Imagine being *strong!*"

Suddenly he snatched up the helmet, crammed it on his head, and twirled the control knobs. Joe had been sleeping, down in the night, but Joe was about to wake up and—roar under the four great moons till all the forest feared him?

Cornelius slipped quietly out of the room.

In the long brazen sunset light, beneath dusky cloud banks brooding storm, he strode up the hillslope with a sense of day's work done. Across his back, two woven baskets balanced each other, one laden with the pungent black fruit of the thorntree and one with cable-thick creepers to be used as rope. The axe on his shoulder caught the waning sunlight and tossed it blindingly back.

It had not been hard labor, but weariness dragged at his mind and he did not relish the household chores yet to be performed, cooking and cleaning and all the rest. Why couldn't they hurry up and get him some helpers?

His eyes sought the sky, resentfully. The moon Five was hidden—down here, at the bottom of the air ocean, you saw nothing but the sun and the four Galilean satellites. He wasn't even sure where Five was just now, in relation to himself . . . *wait a minute, it's sunset here, but if I went out to the viewdome I'd see Jupiter in the last quarter, or would I? Oh, hell, it only takes us half an Earth-day to swing around the planet anyhow—*

Joe shook his head. After all this time, it was still damnably hard, now and then, to keep his thoughts straight. *I, the essential I, am up in heaven, riding Jupiter V between coldstars. Remember that. Open your eyes, if you will, and see the dead control room superimposed on a living hillside.*

He didn't, though. Instead, he regarded the boulders strewn wind-blasted gray over the tough mossy vegetation of the slope. They were not much like Earth rocks, nor was the soil beneath his feet like terrestrial humus.

For a moment Anglesey speculated on the origin of the silicates, aluminates, and other stony compounds. Theoretically, all such materials should be inaccessibly locked in the Jovian core, down where the pressure got vast enough for atoms to buckle and collapse. Above the core should lie thousands of miles of allotropic ice, and then the metallic hydrogen layer. There should not be complex minerals this far up, but there were.

Well, possibly Jupiter had formed according to theory, but had thereafter sucked enough cosmic dust, meteors, gases, and vapors down its great throat of gravitation to form a crust several miles thick. Or more likely the theory was altogether wrong. What did they know, what *would* they know, the soft pale worms of Earth?

Anglesey stuck his—Joe's—fingers in his mouth and whistled. A baying sounded in the brush, and two midnight forms leaped toward him. He grinned and stroked their heads; training was progressing faster than he'd hoped with these pups of the black caterpillar beasts he had taken. They would make guardians for him, herders, servants.

On the crest of the hill, Joe was building himself a home. He had logged off an acre of ground and erected a stockade. Within the grounds there now stood a lean-to for himself and his stores, a methane well, and the beginnings of a large comfortable cabin.

But there was too much work for one being. Even with the half-intelligent caterpillars to help, and with cold storage for meat, most of his time would still go to hunting. The game wouldn't last forever, either; he had to start agriculture within the next year or so—Jupiter year, twelve Earth years, thought Anglesey. There was the cabin to finish and furnish; he wanted to put a waterwheel, no, methane wheel in the river to turn any of a dozen machines he had in mind, he wanted to experiment with alloyed ice and—

And, quite apart from his need of help, why should he remain alone, the single thinking creature on an entire planet? He was a male in this body, with male instincts—in the long run, his health was bound to suffer if he remained a hermit, and right now the whole project depended on Joe's health.

It wasn't right!

But I am not alone. There are fifty men on the satellite with me. I can talk to any of them, any time I wish. It's only that I seldom wish it, these days. I would rather be Joe.

Nevertheless . . . I, cripple, feel all the tiredness, anger, hurt, frustration, of that wonderful biological machine called Joe. The others don't understand. When the ammonia gale flays open his skin, it is I who bleed.

Joe lay down on the ground, sighing. Fangs flashed in the mouth of the black beast which humped over to lick his face. His belly growled with hunger, but he was too tired to fix a meal. Once he had the dogs trained—

Another pseudo would be so much more rewarding to educate.

He could almost see it, in the weary darkening of his brain. Down there, in the valley below the hill, fire and thunder as the ship came to rest. And the steel egg would crack open, the steel arms—already crumbling, puny work of worms!—lift out the shape within and lay it on the earth.

She would stir, shrieking in her first lungful of air,

looking about with blank mindless eyes. And Joe would come carry her home. And he would feed her, care for her, show her how to walk—it wouldn't take long, an adult body would learn those things very fast. In a few weeks she would even be talking, be an individual, a soul.

Did you ever think, Edward Anglesey, in the days when you also walked, that your wife would be a gray, four-legged monster?

Never mind that. The important thing was to get others of his kind down here, female *and* male. The station's niggling little plan would have him wait two more Earth-years, and then send him only another dummy like himself, a contemptible human mind looking through eyes which belonged rightfully to a Jovian. It was not to be tolerated!

If he weren't so tired—

Joe sat up. Sleep drained from him as the realization entered. *He* wasn't tired, not to speak of. Anglesey was. Anglesey, the human side of him, who for months had only slept in catnaps, whose rest had lately been interrupted by Cornelius—it was the human body which drooped, gave up, and sent wave after soft wave of sleep down the psibeam to Joe.

Somatic tension traveled skyward; Anglesey jerked awake.

He swore. As he sat there beneath the helmet, the vividness of Jupiter faded with his scattering concentration, as if it grew transparent; the steel prison which was his laboratory strengthened behind it. He was losing contact— Rapidly, with the skill of experience, he brought himself back into phase with the neutral currents of the other brain. He willed sleepiness on Joe, exactly as a man wills it on himself.

And, like any other insomniac, he failed. The Joe-body was too hungry. It got up and walked across the compound toward its shack.

The K-tube went wild and blew itself out.

The night before the ships left, Viken and Cornelius sat up late.

It was not truly a night, of course. In twelve hours the tiny moon was hurled clear around Jupiter, from darkness back to darkness, and there might well be a pallid little sun over its crags when the clocks said witches were abroad in Greenwich. But most of the personnel were asleep at this hour.

Viken scowled. "I don't like it," he said. "Too sudden a change of plans. Too big a gamble."

"You are only risking—how many?—three male and a dozen female pseudos," Cornelius replied.

"And fifteen J-ships. All we have. If Anglesey's notion doesn't work, it will be months, a year or more, till we can have others built and resume aerial survey."

"But if it does work," said Cornelius, "you won't need any J-ships, except to carry down more pseudos. You will be too busy evaluating data from the surface to piddle around in the upper atmosphere."

"Of course. But we never expected it so soon. We were going to bring more esmen out here, to operate some more pseudos—"

"But they aren't *needed,*" said Cornelius. He struck a cigar to life and took a long pull on it, while his mind sought carefully for words. "Not for a while, anyhow. Joe has reached a point where, given help, he can leap several thousand years of history—he may even have a radio of sorts operating in the fairly near future, which would eliminate the necessity of much of your esping. But without help, he'll just have to mark time. And it's stupid to make a highly trained human esman perform manual labor, which is all that the other pseudos are needed for at this moment. Once the Jovian settlement is well established, certainly, then you can send down more puppets."

"The question is, though," persisted Viken, "can Anglesey himself educate all those pseudos at once? They'll be helpless as infants for days. It will be weeks before they really start thinking and acting for themselves. Can Joe take care of them meanwhile?"

"He has food and fuel stored for months ahead," said Cornelius. "As for what Joe's capabilities are, well, hm-m-m . . . we just have to take Anglesey's judgment. He has the only inside information."

"And once those Jovians do become personalities," worried Viken, "are they necessarily going to string along with Joe? Don't forget, the pseudos are not carbon copies of each other. The uncertainty principle assures each one a unique set of genes. If there is only one human mind on Jupiter, among all those aliens—"

"One *human* mind?" It was barely audible. Viken opened his mouth inquiringly. The other man hurried on.

"Oh, I'm sure Anglesey can continue to dominate them," said Cornelius. "His own personality is rather—tremendous."

Viken looked startled. "You really think so?"

The psionicist nodded. "Yes. I've seen more of him in the past weeks than anyone else. And my profession naturally orients me more toward a man's psychology than his body or his habits. You see a waspish cripple. I see a mind which has reacted to its physical handicaps by developing such a hellish energy, such an inhuman power of concentration, that it almost frightens me. Give that mind a sound body for its use and nothing is impossible to it."

"You may be right, at that," murmured Viken after a pause. "Not that it matters. The decision is taken, the rockets go down tomorrow. I hope it all works out."

He waited for another while. The whirring of ventilators in his little room seemed unnaturally loud, the colors of a girlie picture on the wall shockingly garish. Then he said, slowly:

"You've been rather close-mouthed yourself, Jan. When do you expect to finish your own esprojector and start making the tests?"

Cornelius looked around. The door stood open to an empty hallway, but he reached out and closed it before he answered with a slight grin: "It's been ready for the past few days. But don't tell anyone."

"How's that?" Viken started. The movement, in low-gee, took him out of his chair and halfway across the table between the men. He shoved himself back and waited.

"I have been making meaningless tinkering motions," said Cornelius, "but what I waited for was a highly emotional moment, a time when I can be sure Anglesey's entire attention will be focused on Joe. This business tomorrow is exactly what I need."

"Why?"

"You see, I have pretty well convinced myself that the trouble in the machine is psychological, not physical. I think that for some reason, buried in his subconscious, Anglesey doesn't want to experience Jupiter. A conflict of that type might well set a psionic amplifier circuit oscillating."

"Hm-m-m." Viken rubbed his chin. "Could be. Lately Ed has been changing more and more. When he first came here, he was peppery enough, and he would at least play an occasional game of poker. Now he's pulled so far into his shell you can't even see him. I never thought of it before, but . . . yes, by God, Jupiter must be having some effect on him."

"Hm-m-m," nodded Cornelius. He did not elaborate: did not, for instance, mention that one altogether uncharacteristic episode when Anglesey had tried to describe what it was like to be a Jovian.

"Of course," said Viken thoughtfully, "the previous men were not affected especially. Nor was Ed at first, while he was still controlling lower-type pseudos. It's only since Joe went down to the surface that he's become so different."

"Yes, yes," said Cornelius hastily. "I've learned that much. But enough shop talk—"

"No. Wait a minute." Viken spoke in a low, hurried tone, looking past him. "For the first time, I'm starting to think clearly about this . . . never really stopped to analyze it before, just accepted a bad situation. There *is* something peculiar about Joe. It can't very well involve his physical structure, or the environment, because lower forms didn't give this trouble. Could it be the fact that—Joe is the first puppet in all history with a potentially human intelligence?"

"We speculate in a vacuum," said Cornelius. "Tomorrow, maybe, I can tell you. Now I know nothing."

Viken sat up straight. His pale eyes focused on the other man and stayed there, unblinking. "One minute," he said.

"Yes?" Cornelius shifted, half rising. "Quickly, please. It is past my bedtime."

"You know a good deal more than you've admitted," said Viken. "Don't you?"

"What makes you think that?"

"You aren't the most gifted liar in the universe. And then—you argued very strongly for Anglesey's scheme, this sending down the other pseudos. More strongly than a newcomer should."

"I told you, I want his attention focused elsewhere when—"

"Do you want it that badly?" snapped Viken.

Cornelius was still for a minute. Then he sighed and leaned back.

"All right," he said. "I shall have to trust your discretion. I wasn't sure, you see, how any of you old-time station personnel would react. So I didn't want to blabber out my speculations, which may be wrong. The confirmed facts, yes, I will tell them; but I don't wish to attack a man's religion with a mere theory."

Viken scowled. "What the devil do you mean?"

Cornelius puffed hard on his cigar; its tip waxed and waned like a miniature red demon star. "This Jupiter V is more than a research station," he said gently. "It is a way of life, is it not? No one would come here for even one hitch unless the work was important to him. Those who reenlist, they must find something in the work, something which Earth with all her riches cannot offer them. No?"

"Yes," answered Viken. It was almost a whisper. "I didn't think you would understand so well. But what of it?"

"Well, I don't want to tell you, unless I can prove it, that maybe this has all gone for nothing. Maybe you have wasted your lives and a lot of money and will have to pack up and go home."

Viken's long face did not flicker a muscle. It seemed to have congealed. But he said calmly enough: "Why?"

"Consider Joe," said Cornelius. "His brain has as much capacity as any adult human's. It has been recording every sense datum that came to it, from the moment of 'birth'—making a record in itself, in its own cells, not merely in Anglesey's physical memory bank up here. Also, you know, a thought is a sense datum too. And thoughts are not separated into neat little railway tracks; they form a continuous field. Every time Anglesey is in rapport with Joe, and thinks, the thought goes through Joe's synapses as well as his own—and every thought carries its own associations, and every associated memory is recorded. Like if Joe is building a hut, the shape of the logs might remind Anglesey of some geometric figure, which in turn would remind him of the Pythagorean theorem—"

"I get the idea," said Viken in a cautious way. "Given time, Joe's brain will have stored everything that ever was in Ed's."

"Correct. Now a functioning nervous system with an engrammatic pattern of experience—in this case, a *nonhuman* nervous system—isn't that a pretty good definition of a personality?"

"I suppose so—Good Lord!" Viken jumped. "You mean Joe is—taking over?"

"In a way. A subtle, automatic, unconscious way." Cornelius drew a deep breath and plunged into it. "The pseudojovian is so nearly perfect a life form: your biologists engineered into it all the experiences gained from nature's mistakes in designing *us*. At first, Joe was only a remote-controlled biological machine. Then Anglesey and Joe became two facets of a single personality. Then, oh, very slowly, the stronger, healthier body . . . more amplitude to its thoughts . . . do you see? Joe is becoming the dominant side. Like this business of sending down the other pseudos—Anglesey only thinks he has logical reasons for wanting it done. Actually, his 'reasons' are mere rationalizations for the instinctive desires of the Joe-facet.

"Anglesey's subconscious must comprehend the situation, in a dim reactive way; it must feel his human ego gradually being submerged by the steamroller force of *Joe's* instincts and *Joe's* wishes. It tries to defend its own identity, and is swatted down by the superior force of Joe's own nascent subconscious.

"I put it crudely," he finished in an apologetic tone, "but it will account for that oscillation in the K-tubes."

Viken nodded slowly, like an old man. "Yes, I see it," he answered. "The alien environment down there . . . the different brain structure . . . good God! Ed's being swallowed up in Joe! The puppet master is becoming the puppet!" He looked ill.

"Only speculation on my part," said Cornelius. All at once, he felt very tired. It was not pleasant to do this to Viken, whom he liked. "But you see the dilemma, no? If I am right, then any esman will gradually become a Jovian—a monster with two bodies, of which the human body is the unimportant auxiliary one. This means no esman will ever agree to control a pseudo—therefore the end of your project."

He stood up. "I'm sorry, Arne. You made me tell you what I think, and now you will lie awake worrying, and I am maybe quite wrong and you worry for nothing."

"It's all right," mumbled Viken. "Maybe you're not wrong."

"I don't know." Cornelius drifted toward the door. "I am going to try to find some answers tomorrow. Good night."

The moon-shaking thunder of the rockets, crash, crash, crash, leaping from their cradles, was long past. Now the fleet glided on metal wings, with straining secondary ramjets, through the rage of the Jovian sky.

As Cornelius opened the control-room door, he looked at his telltale board. Elsewhere a voice tolled the word to all the stations, *one ship wrecked, two ships wrecked,* but Anglesey would let no sound enter his presence when he wore the helmet. An obliging technician had haywired a panel of fifteen red and fifteen blue lights above Cornelius' esprojector, to keep him informed, too. Ostensibly, of course, they were only there for Anglesey's benefit, though the esman had insisted he wouldn't be looking at them.

Four of the red bulbs were dark and thus four blue ones would not shine for a safe landing. A whirlwind, a thunderbolt, a floating ice meteor, a flock of mantalike birds with flesh as dense and hard as iron—there could be a hundred things which had crumpled four ships and tossed them tattered across the poison forests.

Four ships, hell! Think of four living creatures, with an excellence of brain to rival your own, damned first to years in unconscious night and then, never awakening save for one uncomprehending instant, dashed in bloody splinters against an ice mountain. The wasteful callousness of it was a cold knot in Cornelius' belly. It had to be done, no doubt, if there was to be any thinking life on Jupiter at all; but then let it be done quickly and minimally, he thought, so the next generation could be begotten by love and not by machines!

He closed the door behind him and waited for a breathless moment. Anglesey was a wheelchair and a coppery curve of helmet, facing the opposite wall. No movement, no awareness whatsoever. Good!

It would be awkward, perhaps ruinous, if Anglesey learned of this most intimate peering. But he needn't, ever. He was blindfolded and ear-plugged by his own concentration.

Nevertheless, the psionicist moved his bulky form with care, across the room to the new esprojector. He did not much like his snooper's role; he would not have assumed it at all if he had seen any other hope. But neither did it make him feel especially guilty. If what he suspected was true, then Anglesey was all unawares being twisted into something not human; to spy on him might be to save him.

Gently, Cornelius activated the meters and started his tubes warming up. The oscilloscope built into Anglesey's machine gave him the other man's exact alpha rhythm, his basic biological clock. First you adjusted to that, then you discovered the subtler elements by feel, and when your set was fully in phase you could probe undetected and—

Find out what was wrong. Read Anglesey's tortured subconscious and see what there was on Jupiter that both drew and terrified him.

Five ships wrecked.

But it must be very nearly time for them to land. Maybe only five would be lost in all. Maybe ten would get through. Ten comrades for—Joe?

Cornelius sighed. He looked at the cripple, seated blind and deaf to the human world which had crippled him, and felt a pity and an anger. It wasn't fair, none of it was.

Not even to Joe. Joe wasn't any kind of soul-eating devil. He did not even realize, as yet, that he *was* Joe, that Anglesey was becoming a mere appendage. He hadn't asked to be created, and to withdraw his human counterpart from him would be very likely to destroy him.

Somehow, there were always penalties for everybody, when men exceeded the decent limits.

Cornelius swore at himself, voicelessly. Work to do. He sat down and fitted the helmet on his own head. The carrier wave made a faint pulse, inaudible, the trembling of neurones low in his awareness. You couldn't describe it.

Reaching up, he turned to Anglesey's alpha. His own had a somewhat lower frequency. It was necessary to carry the signals through a heterodyning process. Still no reception . . . well, of course, he had to find the exact wave form, timbre was as basic to thought as to music. He adjusted the dials, slowly, with enormous care.

Something flashed through his consciousness, a vision of clouds rolled in a violet-red sky, a wind that galloped across horizonless immensity—he lost it. His fingers shook as he turned back.

The psibeam between Joe and Anglesey broadened. It took Cornelius into the circuit. He looked through Joe's eyes, he stood on a hill and stared into the sky above the ice mountains, straining for sign of the first rocket; and simultaneously, he was still Jan Cornelius, blurrily seeing the meters, probing about for emotions, symbols, any key to the locked terror in Anglesey's soul.

The terror rose up and struck him in the face.

Psionic detection is not a matter of passive listening in. Much as a radio receiver is necessarily also a weak transmitter, the nervous system in resonance with a source of psionic-spectrum energy is itself emitting. Normally, of course, this effect is unimportant; but when you pass the impulses, either way, through a set of heterodyning and amplifying units, with a high negative feedback—

In the early days, psionic psychotherapy vitiated itself

because the amplified thoughts of one man, entering the brain of another, would combine with the latter's own neural cycles according to the ordinary vector laws. The result was that both men felt the new beat frequencies as a nightmarish fluttering of their very thoughts. An analyst, trained into self-control, could ignore it; his patient could not, and reacted violently.

But eventually the basic human wave-timbres were measured, and psionic therapy resumed. The modern esprojector analyzed an incoming signal and shifted its characteristics over to the "listener's" pattern. The *really* different pulses of the transmitting brain, those which could not possibly be mapped onto the pattern of the receiving neurones—as an exponential signal cannot very practicably be mapped onto a sinusoid—those were filtered out.

Thus compensated, the other thought could be apprehended as comfortably as one's own. If the patient were on a psibeam circuit, a skilled operator could tune in without the patient being necessarily aware of it. The operator could neither probe the other man's thoughts or implant thoughts of his own.

Cornelius' plan, an obvious one to any psionicist, had depended on this. He would receive from an unwitting Anglesey-Joe. If his theory were right, and the esman's personality was being distorted into that of a monster—his thinking would be too alien to come through the filters. Cornelius would receive spottily or not at all. If his theory was wrong, and Anglesey was still Anglesey, he would receive only a normal human stream-of-consciousness, and could probe for other trouble-making factors.

His brain roared!

What's happening to me?

For a moment, the interference which turned his thoughts to saw-toothed gibberish struck him down with panic. He gulped for breath, there in the Jovian wind, and his dreadful dogs sensed the alienness in him and whined.

Then, recognition, remembrance, and a blaze of anger so great that it left no room for fear. Joe filled his lungs and shouted it aloud, the hillside boomed with echoes:

"Get out of my mind!"

He felt Cornelius spiral down toward unconsciousness. The overwhelming force of his own mental blow had been too much. He laughed, it was more like a snarl, and eased the pressure.

Above him, between thunderous clouds, winked the first thin descending rocket flare.

Cornelius' mind groped back toward the light. It broke a watery surface, the man's mouth snapped after air, and his hands reached for the dials, to turn his machine off and escape.

"Not so fast, you." Grimly, Joe drove home a command that locked Cornelius' muscles rigid. "I want to know the meaning of this. Hold still and let me look!" He smashed home an impulse which could be rendered, perhaps, as an incandescent question mark. Remembrance exploded in shards through the psionicist's forebrain.

"So. That's all there is? You thought I was afraid to come down here and be Joe, and wanted to know why? But I *told* you I wasn't!"

I should have believed—whispered Cornelius.

"Well, get out of the circuit, then." Joe continued growling it vocally. "And don't ever come back in the control room, understand? K-tubes or no, I don't want to see you again. And I may be a cripple, but I can still take you apart cell by cell. Now—sign off—leave me alone. The first ship will be landing in minutes."

You a cripple . . . you, Joe-Anglesey?

"What?" The great gray being on the hill lifted his barbaric head as if to sudden trumpets. "What do you mean?"

Don't you understand? said the weak, dragging

thought. *You know how the esprojector works. You know I could have probed Anglesey's mind in Anglesey's brain without making enough interference to be noticed. And I could not have probed a wholly nonhuman mind at all, nor could it have been aware of me. The filters would not have passed such a signal. Yet you felt me in the first fractional second. It can only mean a human mind in a nonhuman brain.*

You are not the half-corpse on Jupiter V any longer, You're Joe—Joe-Anglesey.

"Well, I'll be damned," said Joe. "You're right."

He turned Anglesey off, kicked Cornelius out of his mind with a single brutal impulse, and ran down the hill to meet the spaceship.

Cornelius woke up minutes afterwards. His skull felt ready to split apart. He groped for the main switch before him, clashed it down, ripped the helmet off his head and threw it clanging on the floor. But it took a little while to gather the strength to do the same for Anglesey. The other man was not able to do anything for himself.

They sat outside sickbay and waited. It was a harshly lit barrenness of metal and plastic, smelling of antiseptics: down near the heart of the satellite, with miles of rock to hide the terrible face of Jupiter.

Only Viken and Cornelius were in that cramped little room. The rest of the station went about its business mechanically, filling in the time till it could learn what had happened. Beyond the door, three biotechnicians, who were also the station's medical staff, fought with death's angel for the thing which had been Edward Anglesey.

"Nine ships got down," said Viken dully. "Two males, seven females. It's enough to start a colony."

"It would be genetically desirable to have more," pointed out Cornelius. He kept his own voice low, in spite of its underlying cheerfulness. There was a certain awesome quality to all this.

"I still don't understand," said Viken.

"Oh, it's clear enough—now. I should have guessed it before, maybe. We had all the facts, it was only that we couldn't make the simple, obvious interpretation of them. No, we had to conjure up Frankenstein's monster."

"Well," Viken's words grated, "we have played Frankenstein, haven't we? Ed is dying in there."

"It depends on how you define death." Cornelius drew hard on his cigar, needing anything that might steady him. His tone grew purposely dry of emotion:

"Look here. Consider the data. Joe, now: a creature with a brain of human capacity, but without a mind—a perfect Lockean *tabula rasa,* for Anglesey's psibeam to write on. We deduced, correctly enough—if very belatedly—that when enough had been written, there would be a personality. But the question was: whose? Because, I suppose, of normal human fear of the unknown, we assumed that any personality in so alien a body had to be monstrous. Therefore it must be hostile to Anglesey, must be swamping him—"

The door opened. Both men jerked to their feet.

The chief surgeon shook his head. "No use. Typical deep-shock traumata, close to terminus now. If we had better facilities, maybe—"

"No," said Cornelius. "You cannot save a man who has decided not to live anymore."

"I know." The doctor removed his mask. "I need a cigarette. Who's got one?" His hands shook a little as he accepted it from Viken.

"But how could he—decide—anything?" choked the physicist. "He's been unconscious ever since Jan pulled him away from that . . . that thing."

"It was decided before then," said Cornelius. "As a matter of fact, that hulk in there on the operating table no longer has a mind. I know. I was there." He shuddered a little. A stiff shot of tranquilizer was all that held nightmare away from him. Later he would have to have that memory exorcised.

The doctor took a long drag of smoke, held it in his lungs a moment, and exhaled gustily. "I guess this winds up the project," he said. "We'll never get another esman."

"I'll say we won't." Viken's tone sounded rusty. "I'm going to smash that devil's engine myself."

"Hold on a minute," exclaimed Cornelius. "Don't you understand? This isn't the end. It's the beginning!"

"I'd better get back," said the doctor. He stubbed out his cigarette and went through the door. It closed behind him with a deathlike quietness.

"What do you mean?" Viken said it as if erecting a barrier.

"Won't you understand?" roared Cornelius. "Joe has all Anglesey's habits, thoughts, memories, prejudices, interests . . . oh, yes, the different body and the different environment, they do cause some changes—but no more than any man might undergo on Earth. If you were suddenly cured of a wasting disease, wouldn't you maybe get a little boisterous and rough? There is nothing abnormal in it. Nor is it abnormal to want to stay healthy—no? Do you see?"

Viken sat down. He spent a while without speaking.

Then, enormously slow and careful: "Do you mean Joe is Ed?"

"Or Ed is Joe. Whatever you like. He calls himself Joe now, I think—as a symbol of freedom—but he is still himself. What *is* the ego but continuity of existence?

"He himself did not fully understand this. He only knew—he told me, and I should have believed him—that on Jupiter he was strong and happy. Why did the K-tube oscillate? An hysterical symptom! Anglesey's subconscious was not afraid to stay on Jupiter—it was afraid to come back!

"And then, today, I listened in. By now, his whole

self was focused on Joe. That is, the primary source of libido was Joe's virile body, not Anglesey's sick one. This meant a different pattern of impulses—not too alien to pass the filters, but alien enough to set up interference. So he felt my presence. And he saw the truth, just as I did—

"Do you know the last emotion I felt, as Joe threw me out of his mind? Not anger anymore. He plays rough, him, but all he had room to feel was joy.

"I *knew* how strong a personality Anglesey has! Whatever made me think an overgrown child-brain like Joe's could override it? In there, the doctors—bah! They're trying to salvage a hulk which has been shed because it is useless!"

Cornelius stopped. His throat was quite raw from talking. He paced the floor, rolled cigar smoke around his mouth but did not draw it any farther in.

When a few minutes had passed, Viken said cautiously: "All right. You should know—as you said, you were there. But what do we do now? How do we get in touch with Ed? Will he even be interested in contacting us?"

"Oh, yes, of course," said Cornelius. "He is still himself, remember. Now that he has none of the cripple's frustrations, he should be more amiable. When the novelty of his new friends wears off, he will want someone who can talk to him as an equal."

"And precisely who will operate another pseudo?" asked Viken sarcastically. "I'm quite happy with this skinny frame of mine, thank you!"

"Was Anglesey the only hopeless cripple on Earth?" asked Cornelius quietly.

Viken gaped at him.

"And there are aging men, too," went on the psionicist, half to himself. "Someday, my friend, when you and I feel the years close in, and so much we would like to learn—maybe we, too, would enjoy an extra lifetime in a Jovian body." He nodded at his cigar. "A hard, lusty, stormy kind of life, granted—dangerous, brawling, violent—but life as no human, perhaps, has lived it since the days of Elizabeth the First. Oh, yes, there will be small trouble finding Jovians."

He turned his head as the surgeon came out again.

"Well?" croaked Viken.

The doctor sat down. "It's finished," he said.

They waited for a moment, awkwardly.

"Odd," said the doctor. He groped after a cigarette he didn't have. Silently, Viken offered him one. "Odd. I've seen these cases before. People who simply resign from life. This is the first one I ever saw that went out smiling—smiling all the time."

GOODBYE AMANDA JEAN

Wilma Shore

A vision of the days to come: compact, self-contained, offering the reader no explanations, no apologies, no comfort, and no mercy.

Jim Hailey had to look all through the house before he found his wife. She was soaking in the tub; her clothes lay strewn across the bathroom floor. "Say, Mona, what's all that meat on the front porch?" he said, frowning. "Looks like hell."

She burst into tears. "That's not meat, that's Amanda Jean."

"You must be kidding," exclaimed Jim. "Is this some damn fool joke?"

"Joke!" She started to laugh. Jim could see she was close to hysteria; he got her out of the tub and into bed and brought her a drink of brandy.

"Now, tell me all about it," he said calmly, although he was very upset himself. Amanda Jean was his favorite daughter.

She took a deep, shuddering breath. "We were walking from the bus stop, along Elm. I met her downtown and we took the bus home together. And this . . . big station wagon draws up alongside, this fellow . . . leans out with his . . . gun—"

"What kind of gun?"

"You know I don't know one from the other!"

"Long barrel or— Never mind. What happened then?"

"He missed. I gave her a push. We started running. She was out ahead, she's so fast. Was so fast. I was trying to . . . get in the way, you know?"

Jim touched her hand.

"I know."

"We got to the cedar hedge. So then I knew if we once got across the Hurst's lawn we could duck back of the big willow into the patio and be"—her mouth had to work to form the word—"safe. And I thought, Jim was right to put the willow there . . . ." His hand twitched on hers. "But as soon as we reached the lawn she . . . went down. I tripped on her and I . . . ."

Jim waited, stroking her arm. "There, there. You did everything you could." But his mind was not with her; his mind was out in the street, hearing the shot, seeing Amanda Jean fall, inventing a face for the man who shot her and trying to memorize the invented face, as though it were real; just to be doing something, anything.

"I crawled over, kind of laid across her. He said, 'Please look out.' I knew it was no use, but I just lay there, screaming, the way you do. So he pushed me aside . . ."

"You got off easy."

". . . and put another . . . shot in her neck."

"Not her head."

"Of course not! The head was what he *wanted!* I knew we should have cut her hair. I told you, remember? I said—"

"Go on, damn you!" he snarled.

She set up a wail.

"Oh, I'm sorry, Mona honey. Only when I feel so bad and then you say it's my fault—"

They clung to each other. She was shaking. "It was a rifle. I can see the long barrel . . . ."

"What did he look like? What kind of a looking fellow?"

"Why, do you know what he looks like? You know Lister Willings, from up the hill. That big house on Cerrito?"

"By sight. Not to speak to. Go on."

"Well, he carried her up on the porch and asked could I let him have a bucket of water and some newspaper. So I did and he cleaned it all up. Nice and neat, didn't you think?"

"Neat enough," he said. Her voice was fading and he needed a few more facts before she got to the end of her strength. "What did he take?"

"Well, the head, of course, and the patches. In this plastic carrying case. Then he asked did I want him to quarter the rest, and I . . . said yes. I didn't know *what* to say, and you weren't here . . . he would have carried them inside but I said no, I didn't want him in my house. So he took his case and his knives and left."

"And nobody came to give you a hand? None of the neighbors?"

"Louise Hurst came over, soon as he left. Then Mrs. Atterman. Helped me in, left a message for you at the office and all—but I sent them home, they have their dinner to fix. Jack Hurst'll be by when he sees your car. There's a new bottle of bourbon in the cupboard, underneath."

"Well, I'll be gone for a while." He found the sleeping pills and gave her two with a drink of water. "Just lie quiet and you'll drop off. I'll leave a note for the kids."

She brought his hand to her lips and lay back, eyes closed. He went downstairs and wrote the note, taping it to the refrigerator door so they would surely see it.

SOME BASTARD KILLED YOUR SISTER AMANDA JEAN. MAMA ASLEEP, DO NOT DISTURB. GET YOURSELVES DINNER. BACK LATER. PA.

He spread a plastic dropcloth on the back seat of his car, piled Amanda Jean's quarters on it, and drove down to the police station. But he could have saved himself the trouble. "Hell, Jim," said Captain Morck, "I feel really bad about this but you know it's the season. Here's a man got his permit and his license, she was fifteen years of age, not a darn thing in the world I can do."

"Shooting out of his station wagon?" cried Jim.

"Who says?"

"My wife was right there."

Dave Morck grabbed irritably at a fly. "It's up to you, Jim. You can bring a charge against him, get your wife up on the stand and put her through this awful experience all over again—and who's going to believe the girl's mother? And what's to stop him putting on a witness'll swear he was on foot?"

Jim knew Dave was talking sense but it made him wild. "Aren't you supposed to enforce the law? Didn't you take some kind of oath of office?"

"It's your wife," said Dave Morck. "You really want to put her through that, go ahead. And then what? Maybe he gets two years, out in ten months—that going to bring back your girl?"

"No." He slapped the desk, stood up slowly.

"Take it easy."

"Yeah." He walked out, making a brief gesture of greeting to Breierman and Foley. When he opened his car door he saw the flies on Amanda Jean and beat them off, swearing.

He drove up to the Willings place, through the gates and around to the front, or what he took to be the front, since it was where the driveway went. It was a real modern house. He walked up to the door and rang, looking the place over out of habit; sixty thousand in the house, ten for the lot, another ten for the tennis court and pool and some kind of barbecue out back—he could smell the charcoal.

The door opened. A heavy-set man in a flowered sport shirt said, "Yes?"

"Willings? I'm Jim Hailey, down on Juanita and Elm."

"Oh!" said Willings. "That was your daughter?" He stood back. "Come on in."

It was a good-sized room, fireplace, ceramic tile floor. "What do you drink?"

"Not now, thanks."

"Sit down anyhow." Willings indicated a big leather chair.

"Can't stay. I've got her quarters out in the car. How come you left them? I smelled barbecue just now—you're not vegetarian. Didn't think she'd eat good?"

"Oh, sure, but I hoped you could use them. My freezer's full, been pretty lucky this year. Say, actually, you like something succulent? Remember last fall, they opened up the preschoolers down in San Felipe? I've still got a few chops, little boy about three and a half, cuts like butter."

"I have everything I need," said Jim. "But I'd surely appreciate it if you could spare Amanda Jean's trophies."

Willings clucked, frowning. "No can do. They're at Hamilton's already. I'll have him ship them over to you when they're mounted. He's putting them on a slab of Honduras mahogany; you'll have something really nice." He put up one hand. "My pleasure, don't mention it."

"I wasn't about to, you dirty bastard. Sweet talking me, but I know you got her with a rolling shot. Real rodeo rifle, aren't you, Willings?"

Willings flushed. "I'm afraid you've been misinformed, Mr. Hailey. I wouldn't do a thing like that."

"But you would call my wife a liar," Jim said gently.

"Look here, Hailey—" began Willings. "I invited you into my home, offered you a drink—"

"And a pound of kindergarten cutlets and a piece of Honduras mahogany. You must figure I'm looking to be paid for my own daughter." Willings opened his mouth but Jim cut him off. "You might as well fix me that drink."

Willings turned to the bar. Jim looked around till he found the door to the kitchen. The wife was shredding cabbage. "Beg pardon, Ma'am. Could I trouble you to step in here?"

She put down her knife and came in, looking from him to Willings. Willings reached toward his gun rack but Jim got him first. He fell back across the bar with a crash of breaking glass and slid tinkling to the floor.

Jim lowered the wife—widow—gently into a chair. "You saw it, Ma'am. You saw it was a legal kill."

She nodded.

When he brought back the vacuum she was still nodding. He slapped her sharply to bring her out of it—but then he was sorry he did, because all the time he was scalping Willings she made a real nuisance of herself.

"I know how you feel, Ma'am," he said finally, "but I don't have all day. Got to get home, look after my kids." He got her back in the chair. "You ought to have somebody up here with you. You want me to call your people?"

He meant to do this right.

"No, I will," she said. He brought her the phone and she turned her head away and began talking in a low voice. When he was finished he went around and caught her eye, pointing to the quarters, but she shook her head, so he carried them out and dropped them in the back with Amanda Jean. He considered leaving his card in case she decided to sell—but then he figured to pass on the tip to Hank Schloss. He didn't want anything that would remind him of this day, not even a commission.

When he got home Mona was still asleep. The kids had fixed dinner and tidied up. They were good kids.

He called Billy away from TV to help with the wrapping and freezing but after a few minutes he let him go—the poor kid's eyes filled with tears every time he looked at his sister's slender quarters.

Then he had a sandwich and a glass of beer and went to bed, although he did not fall asleep for the longest time.

Next day he notified the school and the insurance company. Mona and the kids went through Amanda Jean's clothes and divided up her records and trinkets. It looked to Jim as if they were taking shifts crying—so soon as one dried up another started.

Then he thought he would just get past it, the way he did after Duane was shot—but maybe he was more attached to Amanda Jean than to Duane. Or maybe it was because he and Mona were older now, not likely to have any more kids. It was over and done with—her trophies were up over the mantel, Willings' scalp was cured and hung on the knotty pine scalp rack in the office; still he would be showing a property and his mind would go slipping away to the Willings' house, with the crash of glass, the smell of blood and whiskey, the feel of Willings' bald spot under his fingers during the scalping.

And still he kept seeing her out of the corner of his eye. But it was always one of the other girls.

He wasn't eating right or sleeping right. Mona kept after him but he didn't want to talk about it—it made him feel like a fool. Then one morning as he was leaving for the office she said, "Honey, I made a date for you to see Dr. Peabody."

He just stood and stared at her and she got flustered. "Well, not really a date. He said he'd be working on his sermon this afternoon if you wanted to drop by. But I can call and break it—"

He picked up his jacket. "Seems as if you did enough talking about me already. *I'll* call."

And he meant to. But as the morning wore on he got to wondering what Dr. Peabody would say when he heard the whole story—and after lunch Jim stopped by to tell it to him.

Dr. Peabody didn't say a thing, just took off his glasses, turned them around, and stared at them as if they were someone else's eyes. Jim sat forward. "Now, wasn't that wrong, Dr. Peabody? A person might close their eyes to the illegal shot, if it was a fellow needed food. But to drive off and leave her, all but the trophies—don't you say it was wrong?"

Dr. Peabody's uncovered eyes looked large and soft. "Of course there's a line between right and wrong. But it isn't straight and sharp, like a property line. It doesn't even stand still. It's more like the wet line that runs down the beach after a wave breaks. Ever watch? Then there's another wave and another wet line. Was it higher or lower this time? Is the tide coming in or going out?" Jim wasn't sure what Dr. Peabody was getting at, but he nodded politely. "Take your kill, Jim. Of Mr. Willings. Was that right?"

"It was a one hundred percent legal kill," said Jim. "Over and above that, it was to *uphold* the law. If more people would get out and do like I did, we could get the guns out of the cars and give our girls a sporting chance."

"I didn't ask if it was legal. I asked if it was right."

"It surely was!"

"Would you be here if you really believed that?" said Dr. Peabody quietly.

"What?" said Jim. He felt confused.

Dr. Peabody put his glasses on again—now his eyes were smaller, farther away.

"Jim. You killed in anger—did you not?"

"I never!" cried Jim. "I was cool as a butcher."

"Ah?" said Dr. Peabody. "Well, then, I must be mistaken. I suppose you've eaten him."

Jim looked at Dr. Peabody's chin. "I don't know. Maybe. Mona handles all that."

"Did you eat him, Jim?"

"No, sir," he muttered.

"Why not?"

Jim looked away, up one wall of Dr. Peabody's study and down the other.

"Why not, Jim?"

Jim looked down at his hands.

"Then, of course, you had no right to take his life. And you know it, don't you? In your heart. Don't you, Jim?"

All of a sudden he felt something snapping inside his chest, as if a great big rubber band had been holding him together. He walked to the door, tried to speak—and just went on out. He drove over to the far side of the golf course and sat in his car crying for about half an hour.

Then he went home and made himself a drink and began taking quarters out of the freezer.

"Call the gang," he told Mona. "Barbecue tomorrow."

Mona looked at him and kept her mouth shut. She was a really good wife.

Next morning early he started the fire and trimmed out the meat. Then he mixed up his own special sauce and began basting. He used a child's toy broom that he kept for barbecues. Once or twice he had a call from the office but mostly he just stood around painting on sauce and fussing with the fire.

That night Hank Schloss said it was the best he ever ate. "Only I wish I had a few days' notice, so's I could have worked up a real appetite! What came over you all of a sudden?"

"Why, Hank, you ought to know," said Jim. "There's three things a man don't like to hang around and wait for, once he gets the notion—and two of them's barbecue!" They all laughed.

But in fact he ate very little. And even so he was up most of the night, puking.

But next morning when he came downstairs he felt it was going to be all right. He stopped at the stove and laid his cheek against Mona's and she reached around and patted his shoulder with the oven mitt.

On his way to the office he stopped at the Peabody's and dropped off two fine rib roasts out of his freezer.

"Your very own girl!" exclaimed Mrs. Peabody. "I *am* touched! And what joy to have something *tender,* for a change!" She clapped her hand over her mouth. "Aren't I awful, talking like this? When people are so kind and generous about sharing with us? But you know, it generally turns out to be somebody's old aunt, for braising."

A MAN OF THE RENAISSANCE

Wyman Guin

There are few greater challenges for a writer than trying to tell a story whose protagonist is a man of genius. The superman theme carries with it a built-in drawback: How can a writer who is himself a mere fallible mortal succeed in imagining how a truly superior mind might function? It *has* been done, and more than once; Olaf Stapledon's *Odd John* is the prime example. Here we have another, a story handled with vigor and wit and gusto, the work of a man whose contributions to science fiction have, alas, been spaced excruciatingly widely over several decades. Connoisseurs of the mode please note that Guin chose to tell his superman story in the first person, no less—and, I think, brought the trick off.

I

Now that the revolution had succeeded the little Chacone and I were staying at the Stone Inn. As you might suspect from the name, there is not a piece of rock in the whole building. Nevertheless, it is the best address on my home island.

I sat at a window of my parlor and watched the

streetlamps gutter in oily smoke. The first gray of dawn pearled the mists between the lights. With day approaching, you could hear an occasional patter of feet on the worn, plank streets. The voices of our guards came more frequently from far and near.

"Halt, for inspection!"

I felt a sigh heave my chest. The rebel leader and I had not commanded our forces very brilliantly. There had been much more killing than I had anticipated. The defenders of the false king, together with our own dead, had been piled in the streets, and in the courtyard of the Tower, and up all the stairs of the Tower. Every burial pool on the island had been crowded with mourners for two days now.

From where I sat listening to the first stirring of the frightened city, I could see the dim lights in the shabby Tower of my home island. Our kings have never lived higher than six levels above the sea. Even the poor little island of Torne has a higher Tower.

Tonight, all of the rooms of our Tower were lighted as a protection for the young prince whom we had taken from his prison the night before last. We had him under the protection of the first overlord and those soldiers from the old army who had joined the revolution. The first overlord was now preparing the Tower for the ceremony at noon, today, in which the prince would be made king. Until that ceremony there was danger everywhere.

The people were happy about the death of the false king and about the placing of the young prince in the Tower. It was my own plans they were against. They wanted no part of my scheme to bind two other small, floating islands to our island and create one large, rich island. I had not lived on my home island since childhood and I was, to my rude people, a fancy foreigner with educated ideas.

Across the gray fog appeared the first ochre streams

of day. Sha'tule, our yellow sun, would rise shortly. About an hour later his bluish twin, Sha'charn, would come up. Then the fog would melt.

There was a gentle knock at the door between our apartments and the little Chacone entered. She was dressed in mourning for the "rebel dead."

Her black sheath did little to obscure her figure, and it set off her beautiful face dramatically. She was wearing a royal funeral tiara of the black diamonds that are mined by divers in the shallow Sea of Mourning. This was her right, since the beautiful women of Chacone are made true queens before they leave the island. From wherever in the world their masters may live, they participate by messenger in the highest affairs of Chacone. After all, the whole island is supported by these rare women.

She hesitated at the door to make sure she was not intruding. "I heard you moving about over an hour ago."

"I am just waiting for noon. Nothing is safe until noon."

Up the street I thought I glimpsed a furtive scuffle.

She was approaching me and I raised a hand. "Did you hear a cry?"

She stopped, but she did not glance out into the fog. "I heard nothing."

"I thought I heard a cry."

Now she came directly to me. She took my hands and raised them until I followed with my body to stand over her.

She said, "Darling, you are depressed about the killing. You have killed because you had to. Now, in a few hours, your people will have a good king."

"I killed because I want to bind three poor little islands into one rich, big island."

I spoke with conscious melodrama. "The men who

died will never share that wealth. The men who live do not want it."

I kissed her. "To put things clearly, the so-called 'false' king is 'false' only because he is dead. He got that way because he refused to sign the treaty I want with the islands of Torne and Parsos.

"He was a better administrator than this prince will be. Don't forget, I taught this prince while he attended the University of Hahn. I can tell you, he is something of a lout. But he will sign the treaty as I wish it, and so he is a 'true' king, in my estimation."

She put her golden arms about my shoulders and kissed my mouth. Since she had been trained from childhood in every nuance of love, and since she loved me deeply, it was a kind of kiss that would have made a common man throw sticks at his bride.

Her lips broke with a little laugh and she drew back. "Darling, I must be *seen* in my funeral finery. Won't you take me down to the dining room?"

Without offense, she had interjected a little lightheartedness. Since arriving on my island a few weeks ago the two of us had a joke about her.

In their natural habitat—the great cities on the rich islands of the world—the Chacone women display no vanity. For thousands of years the Chaconese have lived in ritual polyandry, breeding and perfecting these beautiful creatures for export. These women are so accomplished in manners and so talented in the arts that it usually does not occur to an ordinary woman to envy them. Still, there are always a few who do, and on many islands the native word for female vanity has been replaced by a phrase that means "trying to act like a Chacone."

While we had lived on the rich island of Hahn, she had been simply the most beautiful Chacone anyone had ever seen. Here on this naive island where none of the last three kings had been able to afford a Chacone, she was the most beautiful *human* anyone had ever seen. The adulation had shocked her at first. Then she had begun to revel in it because, once my people accept a stranger, it is all the way to the heart.

So we had this joke—that she was a Chacone trying to act like a vain wife. With her little parody, she had made me face the fact that my "guilt" about the killing was as unnecessary as her "vanity."

For the first time since the fighting had ceased, I began to get a grip on my depression.

I took her sweet face in my hands and kissed her again.

I debated about arming myself to go down to breakfast. Then I put on the Great Blade of Hahn and tucked my steel knife into my sash.

As I reached to open the door to the hallway there was a knock on it. I pressed her back and drew the knife and opened the door a crack. It was the big rebel leader.

We grasped forearms affectionately, and he bowed with respect to the Chacone.

As we went down the hall toward the stairs he fell into step beside me.

"There are things I do not like."

"For example?"

"The Tower is locked."

"The Tower is always locked on the day a king is made."

"Nevertheless, there are things I do not like. I am going to have a close look at everything."

Downstairs he bowed again to the Chacone. To me he said, "I will be back before Sha'charn rises."

He had succeeded in stirring some unease in me. When the Chacone and I entered the dining room, I let the attendant take my cloak and feathered hat, but I kept my Great Blade and my knife.

We were no more than seated at our table when I

caught evidence that I was right to be alert. A man at a table against the wall made a mistake.

He was having flashed gull eggs for breakfast. Instead of driving his sipping tube through the shell of the egg he was holding, he punched a delicate hole in it with his thumb nail.

He froze, and I swept my eyes to the face of the Chacone before he could inspect the dining room. The islands held by sea bandits have never adopted the sipping tube which is proper everywhere else.

I smiled at the Chacone and then made a disinterested survey of the room. He was looking directly at me. He had picked me as the only guest who might have noticed that a spy from the sea bandits had just broken an egg.

On any island where there is political strife, and even on islands where these clever men can smell it coming, there are spies for the sea bandits. When these spies report that an island is sufficiently divided and weakened, the bandits come in for brief, bloody raids.

I decided that as long as this man was worried about the manner in which he ate his eggs, we were safe from such a raid. Now that we knew him, he could be watched and it would be time enough to worry if he disappeared.

"Waiter."

He came around the table from where he had been watching the boys put saucers of fruit before us and fill our glasses with spiced rainwater.

"Yes, Master?"

"What is that shouting out in the street?"

"Both of the local printers have sheets out this morning that tell of the revolution. Shall I send one of the children?"

"Please do."

He beckoned an urchin of less than six years from the corner of the room and sent him for the papers.

"Is that all before I serve your first course, Master?"

"No. Look me in the eye."

This waiter had been very loyal to the revolution. He stood still and looked me in the eye.

"The man against that wall is a spy for the bandits."

"Ahhhh! Really?"

He was staring hard into my eyes trying to remember the guests in the direction I had glanced.

"Ahhhh! In the white blouse with lace?"

I had only to nod once.

"Really! I would never have guessed."

"Have him watched constantly."

"Of course."

"And waiter."

"Yes, Master?"

"Sha'tule is up. Many of the guests here, who are trying to stare at my lady are looking directly into the panes of this window. Why don't we draw the curtain for their benefit."

A smile passed his lips. "How gracious of you, Master."

She gasped, "Oh!," and with a little laugh she popped a berry into her mouth.

Just before the waiter drew the curtains, I saw dark shadows of soldiers race along the translucent panes on some emergency.

I grinned at her. "I must say, you are being *seen.*"

She dropped her delighted eyes in embarrassment. "Darling, please! It was only a silly joke."

The child returned with both papers. I looked into the pale, pinched face that you see so often in these children of my home island, and I overtipped him lavishly.

He hardly understood what I had given him. Instead of returning to his post in the corner of the room, he raced from the inn for home and mother.

The Chacone was shaking her head. "You shouldn't do that, darling. He may be accused of stealing."

I shook my head in turn. "I don't know why I do it to the little beggars."

Neither of us mentioned that I had a son of that age whom I had never seen. She simply reached out and covered the back of my hand with hers and asked, "May I have a paper, dear?"

One of the printers was still using wooden type, but the other had acquired the metal type that is now molded on the island of Hahn. I gave her the one printed with metal.

We had been served hot bitter-berry tea, and we both sipped while we read. Abruptly, she started exclaiming in whispers.

"Darling, it tells all about you here. It says that you are not *just* a Master of The Seven Arts, but the most learned and talented man in the world. It says that your books and scrolls are treasured by seven kings and countless lords. It says that your paintings in oil and your sculptures and your designs for the great Towers of the world are . . . ."

"Does it say anything about my flying machine?"

She glanced up and down the page. "No, I don't see anything about that."

"I didn't think you would. But if we had lost the revolution you would be reading a feature story about it."

"Did you have a flying machine?"

"No, I had a machine that didn't fly."

My paper, printed from the larger wooden type, was quite thick and I began hunting with excited annoyance for some mention of my great plan to bind together my home isle and the islands of Torne and Parsos. I could find no mention of it.

"Oh, darling, it tells about *me! Listen!* 'For his work in developing the steel of the Great Blade of Hahn, the Master was giving a beauteous Chacone by the king of

Hahn. It is said that the king paid for her the highest price ever paid to the Chaconese.'

"Oh, darling, listen to this!

" 'Our whole citizenry has been grateful these past weeks for her gracious—' "

"My dear. Calm yourself!"

" '—for her gracious presence . . . her wit . . . her taste and artistry . . . her . . . ' "

She was becoming quite breathless. She turned to me with the glazed stare of a completely ravished woman. "What was funny, darling?"

"I'll tell you what let's do. Give me that paper, now. Then, after breakfast, we'll go upstairs and snuggle into bed and read to each other about ourselves. Won't that be fun?"

She handed me the paper obediently. "Don't be silly."

While she sat in her daze, automatically rebathing in adulation, I searched the metal print for any mention of my plan to bind together the three little islands.

There was nothing.

Slowly, I lowered the paper to the table. It was an ominous sign. They were dead against it. In the moment of our triumph they did not dare mention it. But when the time came they would try to swing the popular dislike of my plan to influence the new king against it.

I heard my teeth gritting together and I found that I was trembling with anticipatory rage. I had not led hundreds to their deaths, killing other hundreds, only to let two smudge-fingered printers stand in my way.

I saw that the spy for the sea bandits was leaving. Then he hesitated, staring at the doorway.

II

The rebel leader was standing in the entrance. There was an air of urgency about him. The spy would have given anything if he had not already risen and headed for the entrance, but it was too late now, and he passed on out with only a glance at the rebel.

When the big man reached our table, I saw what the spy had seen. The blunt face was chalked with shock, the pupils dilated, the breathing shallow and fast.

I could feel the blood draining from my own face. My whole body was straining; first to swell into a giant of rage, then to shrivel to a beetle and scuttle for the wall.

He sat down, whispering hoarsely. "It is all lost. We have been tricked. The first overlord has locked the prince in the Tower dungeon. He commands the remnants of the old army against us. They have just taken the warehouse we were using as a garrison and killed over a hundred men."

I started to rise.

He grabbed my arm and pulled me down. "Listen to me. We are safe as long as we don't leave the hotel. Even if I'm captured I do not think the first overlord will have me killed. It is you and your plan he wants to stop. We must get you off the island."

He continued with heavy breathing, "Now, listen. The bamboo forests are still in fog. I am preparing a guarded way for us through the alleys to the edge of the city. I am also preparing a fast ship for you and your lady. If we are cut off from that, I am having a raft prepared for you."

I stared at him. "Rebel, we are surrounded by desert seas right now. I can't take a raft into those deserts."

"Master, I believe you can do anything. I only say that you cannot always do everything at once. If we are reduced to the raft, your lady will have to remain."

The little Chacone was clutching and unclutching my hand in hers. The dining room had electrified with terror and was emptying. We three had become a focal point where the sudden threat of death hummed in the ears like a stricken wasp.

The waiter hurried up to us. "Master, I have heard

about the treachery. But listen, there is more. The spy for the bandits has disappeared. In days, the sea about here will be swarming with them. If you were thinking of escaping with your lady . . . I beg you, don't."

She was shaking her heard piteously with tears glistening on her cheeks. "Please don't leave me. I do not fear any of these things. Please take me with you."

The rebel and I were staring at each other across the horrible thought of capture by sea bandits. I turned dazedly to the Chacone and shook my head.

She buried her face and wept.

The waiter declared, "Master, no harm will come to her. We will take good care of her." Then he excused himself and hurried away.

The rebel rose. "I will make one last check of the escape route while you say farewell to your lady." He left the dining room by way of the kitchens.

I stood up, and drew the Chacone up to me. Her lips moved warmly and her tears were hot on my face. Undoubtedly, for the last time, I was holding the world's most fabulous prize in my arms. Yet death, buzzing insistently in my ears, reminded me that I had been condemned, long ago, to love another.

The woman I loved was beautiful, but not this beautiful; talented, but not this talented; royal, but not this regal. She was the mother of my son, and perhaps I was condemned to love her simply because I could not have her.

I kissed the dear little Chacone over and over and promised her that I would return. Then I found that I was promising to return with soldiers and retake the Tower.

So there it was in the open . . . the killing had not been enough. It had only been in vain. Whether or not the sea bandits came I would come again, to kill again for my plan to bind together the three islands.

The rebel and I had no difficulty reaching the edge of the city. We were beckoned from point to point by our waiting comrades. Trouble began immediately when we entered the forests of bamboo.

A rebel came racing toward us from ochre banners of fog. "They have captured the boat and the three men guarding it. Take this side path to the raft. Hurry, they are right behind me."

He gestured wildly and fell at our feet with a sudden javelin in his back. We raced into the forest where the light of Sha'tule beat at the fog with a golden hammer.

Shrieks and moans from a thousand lost souls burst from the path ahead of us. I stopped dead in the path and the big rebel crashed into me.

We both simultaneously recognized the din as the pipes and strings of funeral music. The scale in which my people play their harsh instruments is fortunately unknown on other islands.

The rebel leader was pressing me forward. "Move in and mingle with the mourners. They will be hurrying the funeral to avoid the Sun Gods. They will not notice."

Masked by the racket and concentration of the ceremony, we went in among the mourners who encircled the pool. Smoking torches fluttered along the edge of the golden bowl of light about the pool . . . light that was now fretted with the blue of Sha'charn. A red-shrouded corpse was poised over the water on his bamboo slide. The burial stone to which his feet were bound was a rich one, fully a hand thick, and as big around as a man could encircle with his arms.

The wailing of the instruments ceased, and now the big rebel, his rocklike face unmoved, worked to still his deep breathing.

On all sides, presently, I could hear the soldiers moving quietly. They inspected the mourners from a pious distance and they passed right by us.

The Shaman mounted his stand at the head of the reclining corpse. After a long time in which little accidental sounds ceased, he started reading from his sacred scroll.

"All things that live on land, all the animals of the islands and the cities of men on the islands, float at the surface of the sea where there is storm and sinking and terror."

Suddenly the widow, who stood with her friends beside the Shaman's place, lifted her arms to the thinning fog and shrieked a curse. With a bound of my heart, I recognized that it was me at whom she hurled this hatred. The rebel turned to me, and he could not help grinning.

There was a little commotion near the widow and the rudely grinning rebel used the moment to whisper, "Master, they are praising you."

Now it made my throat ache to see this corpse. He had been Captain of the Guard at the Tower, and last to stand before the door to the apartments of the false king. I had had to run the brave man through.

The Shaman went on with his reading. "On the currents of the worldwide sea, our islands drift to the north and they drift to the south. They bring us to the depredations of the Ice Islanders. Our islands drift into the boiling waters of steam and pumicine and into the chill waters of ice and snow.

"All these terrors are controlled by the evil eyes of the stars which control all things at the surface of the sea."

This belief is the reason funerals are held at dawn or sunset. They want the dead to go to the sea floor without being seen by the evil stars or wrathful Sun Gods.

The Shaman continued. "But the eyes of the stars do not reach to the Floor of the Sea. Down there, where decay cannot occur, far from the storm and terror of living, there go all the dead . . . ."

Behind me a soldier coughed nervously, and from the

other side of the pool another also coughed. The rebel smiled sympathetically.

The Shaman had reached that part of sacred belief that is most distressing to a man of action, and presently I could hear the soldiers begin moving away. In the thinking of the pious, the Floor of the Sea is a great, calm plain on which, in static promenade, the buried dead stand about in the blue shrouds of women and the red shrouds of men, their feet bound to their burial stones, contemplating for eternity the aqueous silence.

Unable to bear such a prospect, the sailor has invented the lascivious Sea Women, and the soldier has named our twin suns Sha'tule and the Sha'charn . . . "commander of the dead that arise as mists" and "commander of the dead that arise as storms."

The drums about the burial pool began to murmur and the slide bearing the corpse was slowly tilted. I thought the brave captain would never let go of his slide. Then, as the drums reached a deafening roar, it was as though he remembered some gleeful prospect, so abruptly did he shoot into the black water.

My throat ached, but I found there were no words to say to him.

To make sure we would lose the soldiers, the rebel and I returned toward the city with the mourners. We left them where a narrow path headed back toward the island's edge. We raced down this, protected from any distant view by the thinning fog. The ground grew softer and now, only a few feet beneath us, was the sucking of the sea.

The rebel motioned to me and stopped. He studied things through the fog a bit and then whispered, "They are guarding the paths ahead. If we don't slip through them, run for the amphibial."

I whispered back, "If we are separated, tell our people I have gone to Thule for soldiers."

He stared at me in disbelief. "I thought the king of Thule had condemned you to the plank?"

"He will have forgiven me."

He continued to stare at me and shook his head. "Master, you have lost your mind to go back there."

Behind me a man shouted very loudly, "Aaaaeeee, here!"

III

He was hurling a bone-pointed javelin and it was sad for him that he missed my face. I drew the gleaming Blade of Hahn, the blade a stride long, a length unheard of in most of the world. I took two steps and ran him through.

The rebel was calling to me, "This way."

Soldiers seemed to rise out of the shallow ground, eager and yelling. I heard all about us as we ran that dry whisper of death—arrows clipping through the bashai leaves. We plunged into the rank growth of the amphibial where the thin ground waved under foot, where the thicket crawled with deadly snakes and toads.

While an island drifts through tropic waters it is bordered with this pumicine pack and its wildly growing plant life. No man would willingly venture there and the soldiers did not follow. They stood on the higher ground and waited.

When we started to move we waved the head-high, pulpy bush. A shower of arrows snickered through the leaves. There was laughter from the shore. They had themselves a real sport. If they didn't hit us, the snakes would.

I went ahead of the rebel with my Great Blade and in thirty steps I cut six filthy snakes. The soldiers showered arrows increasingly wide of us as the stir we caused drew out of their sight. Finally, we were free of the soldiers and there was only the great, hot hush of the amphibial.

The island had not passed through a storm in many months and so the amphibial was unusually solid. Even so, we frequently stepped through the treacherously waving earth and once the rebel went clear through till I grabbed the bushy hair of his head.

What a curse it is that this great military barrier around every island fails us when we need it most. As our islands drift north or south toward the Ice Islanders, the encircling amphibial shrivels. Creeping roots that have collected these great pumicine packs and rotting leaves in the long tropic heat now freeze. The snakes and poisonous toads retreat to the more solid land and burrow. The chill waves smash away all but a little rim of the once forbidding amphibial and when the Ice Islanders come in their fearsome, horned boats we must defend every pace of the frozen shore.

The rebel leader, an older man than I, floundered more and more frequently. We were desperate by the time we came upon a small boating channel.

The fishers maintain these channels with walls and bottom woven of bamboo. As an island heads for the tropics and an amphibial grows about it, the fishers add these cradles of bamboo making a channel to the sea for their craft.

We crawled onto the overhead cross members separating the bamboo walls of this channel. We lay in the hot sunlight unable to care what might happen.

At last I asked him, "Is the raft in this channel?"

He nodded without speaking to me.

It was mid-morning before we let ourselves down into the sea water and swam silently back to the land.

Two soldiers with bone-pointed javelins stood on the floating wharf watching the shore and whispering to each other. A raft had been upended on the wharf for repairs and the two stood with this between themselves and the shore. Not once as we approached did they worry about the surrounding amphibial.

I drew the rebel to me and whispered to him while our toes rested on the bamboo cross members at the bottom of the channel. With our heads barely above water we moved cautiously ahead.

When we reached the end of the wharf they were about ten paces away. I nodded to the rebel and he sank from sight.

I counted methodically to twenty. I drew my steel knife and threw it, a flash of light, between the ribs of the man on the left. His companion turned in astonishment. I grimaced and hissed a curse. He raised his javelin as, behind him, the rebel mounted the wharf.

I ducked and the javelin boiled into the water over my shoulders. I raised my head to see him kneeling with coy surprise before he rolled into the water. I mounted the wharf and retrieved my knife. We hurried to a fishing raft that was somewhat larger and more substantial than the others.

The rebel loosened the moorings. "You will have to do with what provisions are here," he whispered.

I turned to him in stunned disbelief. "Isn't it stocked? Are you trying to kill me? I have to cross a desert sea."

"Something has gone wrong. This isn't the raft we had prepared."

I opened the floor box of the raft and glimpsed gaffing rods and a coil of rope. I cast about the wharf frantically until I saw one of those huge baskets which fishermen sometimes tow behind them filled with live fish. I brought this and threw it onto the deck while the rebel was shoving past the end of the floating wharf. I leaped two paces to the deck and he handed me a paddle.

"I will help you paddle out to sea. If soldiers appear before we are out of sight I can duck back into the amphibial until dark."

Standing on opposite sides of the raft we paddled it back out the channel to the bobbing beds of free pumicine. I moored to the last bamboo stays of the channel and we rested.

He was a big man with a determined face and a blunt way. "I am not sure you will return. Your cause is not our cause."

"My cause includes your cause. We both want the young prince made king. Once he is king I will be able to take my business to him."

"You are sure he will sign the treaties you want with the islands of Torne and Parsos?"

"I know him. After all, I was his teacher when he was a boy. I taught him the first two of the Seven Arts."

"You think the kings of Torne and Parsos will sign?"

"They have already signed a proposal."

"What do *they* gain by this?"

I began to unroll the split bamboo sail. Since the wind was from the land the raft pulled at its mooring.

It made me angry to talk with him about this. Why could not the people of my homeland see that they would have no lasting prosperity until they federated with other freely floating islands?

The kings of Torne and Parsos were both convinced that my plan was feasible to bind together with great ropes these small islands so that eventually they would grow together in the tropic lushness. When next their lands drifted out of the north seas clean of amphibial, they planned to erect the great sails I had designed. They would try to maneuver their islands together and bind them. With three islands thus bound there would be so much less shore to defend and so many more to defend it the next time we drifted against the Ice Islanders. Such a man-joined island, ruled by these three peaceful kings, would be as wealthy and powerful as the great rock-latched islands of Thule and Hahn.

But the people of my homeland are stubborn and arrogant. The former king, who had obtained the Tower falsely, would never listen to me. So I had joined these rebels to place in the Tower the young prince to whom I could talk. One could not talk to these stubborn rebels about joining peaceful hands with a sister island. They were as independent as sea-going turtles.

This one shook his head profoundly. "You worry too much about the Ice Islanders. I wouldn't sleep on the same island with a Tornian. They are root grubbers."

I had the sail fully hoisted and the raft jerked at its mooring. He did not take the hint, so I went back and squatted near the rope to untie it.

I turned and snapped, "You, rebel, have not been taken from your home as a boy by the Ice Islanders. You have not spent two years as their slave. You are a small-island man and you think like a small . . ."

Suddenly, I saw on the sea, over his shoulder, what had happened to the raft that had been prepared for me. Four soldiers paddled it swiftly, silently toward us.

The rebel, as if answering my insult with an impudent gesture, thrust at me from his mouth the barbed head of an arrow.

I spun backward, drawing the Great Blade. I slashed the mooring, and the raft leaped into the pumicine beds. As a second arrow sang over the deck, I tore open the lid to the deck box and dived into this narrow confine. Two more arrows thudded into the deck and then no more. I peeked out and saw that the soldiers were struggling to mount their sail.

They would draw more water, and I was sure they could not overtake me. Nevertheless, I spent little ceremony in disposing of the dead rebel and assisting my flight by paddle. Soon they gave up the chase and headed back for the channel. I stopped paddling and let the sail bounce me over the pumicine.

Across our seas drift great reaches of this stone, some as large as a man's thumb tip, and most much smaller. If one cuts a piece of this stone on a lapidary's wheel he will find it filled with air spaces. If one digs anywhere on an island he will find, beneath the soil of rotted vegetation, a thick ground of pumicine tightly matted in wiry roots. On an old rock-latched island such as Thule, this base may be ten times as deep as a man stands.

IV

It is the belief of the pious that the islands were born in antiquity by fabled Sea Goddesses who sometimes cohabited with the Sun Gods. Thus, it is said that the beautiful isle of Ohme, which never leaves its narrowly circling current in the tropics, was begat by Sha'tule, commander of the mist. It is said that the Sea Goddess, Tora, in gratitude for this delightful gift, swore to retain the isle in her womb until it was the most beautiful in the world. She is said to have travailed for a thousand years to create Ohme, where the tiny red deer bound across emerald meadows and the balloon flowers loose themselves from their branches at night and copulate above the tree tops with little cries.

A man who notices what he sees instead of what he hears will not believe that Ohme, or any other island, was born in such a way.

In my lifetime our knowledge of the world has grown tremendously, and we are not so likely to believe that Sea Goddesses actually exist as we are to treasure them as myth.

I think this: The islands are being built each day. There are forces building them and forces tearing them apart. In many parts of the ocean, such as Chryo where stupendous rocks reach to the clouds, there are great boiling places out of which gouts of pumicine are coughed up from the water. In addition there are many places in the sea where cones of hot rock and fire rise high in the sky and two of these are near the rock-latched island of Hahn. From all these places comes stone filled with air spaces.

Where beds of such pumicine float in calm seas you

find them strewn with plant life, and if the time is long enough you can pick up clumps of floating stone tightly bound in wiry roots and already plastered on the underside with the bulbous red leaves of the bottom plant. Such a clump is a primitive little island which is being born only figuratively in the womb of a Sea Goddess. For the bottom plants suck up water and strain it of salt and deliver fresh water to the plants above. These in their turn are spread in the sunlight, which plants must have, and somehow they exchange sunlight with the bottom plants in the sea.

I think that shallow islands such as Chacone, where the soil is brackish and unfit for agriculture, will one day be deep islands like Thule. After a storm on any island, you find pumicine in the funeral pools which means it has been driven in under the island where it may be incorporated by the muscular bottom plants into a deeper ground.

At last I was free of the pumicine beds of my home isle. Now, about me, the green sea swelled like white-nippled breasts of the necrophilic seawomen. The raft slapped from wave to wave with a busy illusion of progress. I stepped forward of the sail and watched the horizon where a blue line lay. I decided that I had about two hours before I would be leaving the green sea.

I lashed the basket in the water at the rear of the raft, and used one of the gaffing hooks to land my food before I reached the desert. I was able to bring in six large blue stripes without harming them unduly and I dropped them into the basket. A seventh, I left on the deck for tonight's food.

I reached the endless blue of the desert. There would be no fishing here. The sparse plankton supported no life. Now my progress fretted me. The improbability of success began to depress me. The first overlord would probably assume the kingship tomorrow. Now was the time to overthrow him while the people were bitter that the young prince had not been placed.

Now was the time, and here I sat slapping from wave to wave. Worst of all had been the death of the rebel leader. Now the rebels would have to rise spontaneously when and if I reappeared.

Prospects were even gloomier ahead of me on Thule. I was going there to beg soldiers from a man who had last looked upon me in fabulous rage and had cried out in anguish, "Give him one hundred lashes. Nail him to a plank and put him adrift at sea."

I had been saved from that punishment. I had escaped to Parsos where the king had given me refuge against every threat and bribe from Thule. But I could not go to Parsos or Torne for help in this venture. If their soldiers came storming into my home isle killing lords and overlords—even putting the young prince in the Tower would not soothe the feelings of my people. After such a day there would never be a treaty such as I wanted.

The only source of soldiers close enough this year to be feasible was the rock-latched island of Thule near which our present currents were carrying us. The source was a good one. I was simply the worst possible ambassador.

I had heard that the rage of the king toward me had cooled. Definitely he had not torn down the Great Tower of Thule though at first he had threatened to do so.

How *could* he have done that? Of all my works, the Great Tower for the king of Thule is the crowning achievement. The huge platform on which it stands is built of hardwood raided from the Ice Islanders and is a hundred paces square. On the upper floors, I had directed a hundred lapidaries for two years to finish the mosaics of the outer walls. These are of ivory and pearl, wood and stone. They depict all the allegories of the Sea Deities and the highest levels depict the epics of the ancestors of the king of Thule.

The wood panels on the inner walls I had painted magically in oil so that the human form and all the animals and fishes of the world are seen in delightful poses and so real that the eye is bewitched.

This Tower rises fourteen levels over its massive columns, gleaming high above the lesser Towers of lords of Thule. Truly, the king of Thule is raised above the sea. How could he have brought himself to destroy such a work? And every day that he lived in those halls he looked upon the message of my hand. Surely he would have softened toward me.

That night I ate the raw fish and drank its water. I lay on my back watching the stars. I was steady on course. The Shamans say the stars are "evil eyes" that create all disaster. A man who thinks does not credit such talk. A man who sails (and whoever heard of a sailor Shaman?) knows the stars as friends.

There are many wonderful thoughts in the world today, new ideas that thrill you. One, that is most exciting to me, is the theory of the aged professor of astronomy at the University of Parsos. This theory is that the stars are really suns like Sha'tule and Sha'charn and that they are so small only because they are far from us. I like to think that there may be other worlds on which those suns shine.

I have tried to think of other worlds, for example, one where the sea would be almost dried up, perhaps by a closer sun. On such a world parts of the bottom of the sea might be exposed. Plants might grow on the exposed sea floor just as they do on pumicine. Animals would walk on solid rock. The Ice Islanders have great piles of rock which rise out of the ice and into the clouds and on which the hardwood grows. I mean . . . the whole world would be like that, and the islands would not move.

At night I tired of thinking of such different worlds and I wished that the little Chacone were with me.

When I awakened the suns lay hot on the horizon. I was startled. Hurriedly I checked the sea about me, and, as a good seaman should, I looked into the suns.

It is a good thing that I did. I recognized her at once. Practically all the ships sailed by sea bandits are built to a pattern. This ship came at me like a great, black bat skimming between the suns, and I had only moments to prepare. My heart fluttered wildly into my constricted throat.

I jerked open the deck box of the raft and brought out the gaffing poles. The advice of an old merchant seaman raced in my mind.

"I've boarded three of 'em and there's only one way to do it. They always approach you on their windward because that's high-boarding for them."

I wanted them to board me forward of my sail. Aft of the sail, I rammed the butts of the gaffing poles through the bamboo and braced them in the logs. Their vicious points were a formidable barrier to boarding there. I snatched the coil of rope out of the deck box and formed a noose as they bore down on me.

I counted nine men leaning over the rail and one at the rudder. Three of the men, hesitating before the ugly gaffing poles about me, leaped onto my forward deck.

I gave thanks to the rich ladies of Hahn. They are lavishly untrue to their husbands, and a student at that university is not worth his salt unless he can throw a noose to the second floor of a rich man's Tower. The bandit ship swept past, and I caught the rudder pommel neatly.

Desperation hoisted me to the railing, and one motion that drew and swung the Great Blade slashed the throat of the surprised helmsman.

The bandits came at me to take a live prize, but

when I opened the chest of a man from arm to arm they changed plan. The great Blade of Hahn is still as rare in the world as a king's Tower and greatly feared by fighting men. These five bandits now saw what I carried and they hurled club and javelin to kill. A javelin laid bare one of my ribs and a club momentarily stunned me and I fell heavily to my knees.

The voice of the old merchant man came back commandingly. "Board at the rudder and fight your way to the rear hatch." I followed the voice in a gleaming frenzy of the Great Blade. They would flay me a little at a time and salt my body if they took me.

I jumped down the stairs and slammed and bolted the door to the captain's cabin. Right behind me two of them hit it with terrifying fury. They would have it down in seconds, but if the old merchant man's advice held up they would be too late.

His voice lashed me to action. "Throw open the door to the forward compartment and jam it so you can see the forward hatch. Hurry back to the lee port in the captain's cabin and open it. Reach way up and you can cut loose the boom."

I watched through the door I had opened and when I saw light at the forward hatch I slashed the lashing of the boom with my knife. There was a sickening lurch through the ship and two men screamed. A leg that had started down the ladder in the forward hatch was whisked out again as if by the hand of a god. There followed two splashes in the sea.

The door to the captain's cabin was splintering, and I dashed forward. I went up the hatch ladder, blade first, and chopped off one of two bare feet that appeared before me on the deck. His unbalanced blow with a club smashed into the hatch and enough of my head to knock northern lights through my brain.

As I climbed groggily onto the deck I heard the two who had smashed open the captain's door yell disappointment and clamber back up the rear hatch for the deck.

The fellow who had lost a foot was trying to come at me with a knife. His head flew off with one swing of the Great Blade, and the two who had come up out of the rear hatch witnessed this. When I approached them they backed off respectfully. One of them dropped a stone ax to the deck. Presently he turned and dove into the sea.

The other man held a bone javelin hesitantly. I gestured over the side of the ship. He shook his head. I took a step toward him and he hurled the javelin. I chopped it out of the air. I raised the point of the Great Blade and I started backing him. When he reached the rail he just leaned away from the point until he fell overboard.

Then I understood why he had not done as had his companion. He could not swim. I had to listen to his screams while I brought the sail down to retrim the ship.

The three men who had boarded my raft had made some progress. The man who had jumped overboard and one of the men who had been knocked overboard by the boom were swimming for the raft.

The raft was still a hundred paces away when I began rehoisting the sail and felt the trim little bandit ship tighten like an airborne bird. I set my course for Thule and lashed the tiller.

By the time the raft was out of sight I had got rid of the bodies and swabbed the deck clean. Then I sat down near the tiller and carefully cleaned and polished my Great Blade.

What a marvel this metal was! Recently the Hahnese have been working the gray iron that flows from a fiery cone near their rock-latched island. I had learned to work it with charcoal to make blades such as these. It had been for this that the King of Hahn had given me the Chacone.

Unlike the killing in the revolution, I had no remorse

over the killing of the sea bandits. They are descendants of the Ice Islanders. For centuries their ancestors dominated our oceans; their raiding and slaughtering almost wiped civilization off most islands. Those dark centuries were ended only by the rise of the great navies of Thule and Hahn which have pushed the bandits back to a few poor islands from which they operate.

I was thinking these things as I finished cleaning the blade and I remembered that I had seen some writing on the table in the captain's cabin.

It is a seeming paradox that the bandits so love slaughter and torture that the most brutal man of another island shudders at the thought of them—and yet they are said to be constant poets. The long sagas of their history are marvels of myth and they are said to leave a scene of slaughter with every man vying to compose the best verse about it.

This captain had indeed been composing in a labored hand when I was sighted. His cup of morning tea had crashed to the floor when I later cut the broom. But the piece of parchment and his writing brush were where he had left them.

> "Up ecstatic towers we raced.
> With bone lance and flesh,
> Their women we pierced,
> Till thousands of doves
> Were cooing for death."

I reflected over the savage faces of the morning and decided that the man whose chest I had opened had been the captain. I tucked his lines under my sash.

V

As you approach Thule you understand that it takes a man two days to walk across this largest of all islands. It lies across the horizon like an endless, green cloud. The rocks to which it is latched do not rise out of the soil. But the gleaming Tower of the King of Thule, which is my design, can be seen from the sea.

Thule is the great stationary point of trade. All islands which are in currents that pass near her have cycles of industry and trade based on that fact. The approach near Thule is always festival time. When the currents bring an island into these waters, the stores of its products are traded for the exotic products from many islands. Even the Ice Islanders of the north sometimes appear in fearsome armadas to stand off Thule and conduct sullen trade.

I had not had Thule on the horizon more than a short time when the sails of a fighting ship came out in my direction. At this latitude there is little growth of amphibial and they keep a close watch on the sea. My ship, obviously a sea bandit, brought this fighter out under taut sail.

The fighter came about. The faces of the soldiers were many and they inspected every inch of my deck. I lowered sail rapidly and waited.

From about fifty paces the captain called to me, "Who are you?"

I cupped my hands and called back, "I am a Master of the Seven Arts. I call on the King of Thule."

The captain ordered his sail down and we drifted together in silent waiting. The grim soldiers did not speak with each other. They watched my deck. The soldiers of Thule are the finest in the world and their discipline is a thing to behold. The ship captains are always Lords of Thule.

"I'm alone," I shouted.

"How did you come by this ship?"

"I captured it."

"Alone?"

"If you retrace my course you will pick up five ugly sea bandits adrift on my raft. The other five I killed and I have brought their ship as a prize to the navy of Thule."

For the first time the soldiers looked at each other and there was laughter. I drew the Great Blade and flashed it between Sha' and Sha'. The laughter abruptly ceased. The Lords of Thule already carry such blades and these soldiers now believed me.

At five paces the captain ordered a line thrown to me, and I made it fast. I stepped to the deck of the fighter of Thule and prickles of fear were on my back. The captain studied my face, and he recognized me.

He exclaimed, "Master!"

I saw the many implications of this meeting storm across his rugged face.

A soldier whispered, "I'll swear on the Sea Floor, it is the builder of the Tower."

All motion about me ceased and there was silence in which no man heard more loudly than I that anguished cry, *Give him one hundred lashes. Nail him to a plank, and put him adrift at sea.*

The captain could only stare at me. I had painted for one of the inner walls of his own tower a scene that had since become famous. It depicts the legend of Namora. Startled from her bed of pearls, the chaste goddess fights off the advances of Ti, the sea serpent. With this painting I had at last achieved such depiction of the human body that all who saw it stood in awe. None of the paintings I had done on Parsos or Hahn equaled it. This captain had been proud of his association with me.

I saw on his face that the Lords of Thule would be dismayed at my return. In their eyes I had not done such a wrong. In the last great raid of the Ice Islanders my parents had been killed. All their servants, and I, their son, had been taken as slaves. It was not, to the Lords of Thule, a discredit to me that subsequently a false king had assumed the Tower of my home isle and had dissolved the lordship of my father.

If, then, I was a lord by desert, it was no great crime to have loved the youngest of the six daughters of their king. Unpolitic behavior, no doubt. But to be nailed to a plank! The thought is abhorrent even beyond its reality because of the belief that such cursed planks drift into the desert seas and remain afloat.

The Lord Captain who now stared into my face knew that my sentence was irrational. If the king had had a son, if one of his older daughters had had a son, I would today be married into the king's family. For in that circumstance a son of pure Thulian blood would not have been required of the youngest princess. In that circumstance my impropriety would have led, not to her ineligibility for royal marriage, but to our early marriage.

The captain took me aside. "Master, why have you brought this trial to me? I must take you to your death. Don't you wish to stand on the Sea Floor? Must you decay here at the surface?"

"You think he cannot forgive me?"

"He will go through with it because he commanded it. What in the name of Sha'charn has brought you here?"

"A false pretender holds the Tower of my home isle. I have come for soldiers to retake it."

"Why didn't you go to Parsos which is drifting close to you now?"

The sails of the fighter had been rehoisted and the light breeze heeled us away from the bandit ship which was returned with soldiers to pick up the raft-load of its former crewmen.

I explained to the captain why I could not use soldiers from Parsos.

The people of my homeland have an outlandish reputation for unpredictable and romantic action. The Lords of Thule and Hahn, the great powers that forced back the Ice Islanders, sometimes look down their noses at our violent political history. They call us "teri che" which is to say, "wild ones."

This captain now hurt my heart, as if he had slapped my face. He shook his head with a grim smile and said, "Teri che." Then, staring into my face uncomprehendingly, he went on, "You will not live to retake your Tower, let alone to carry out a scheme for binding islands together. You are going to be a dead patriot."

Then, without meaning to, he hurt me even more deeply. "Thule owes you better than a plank. I promise that after your death I will raise an invasion and straighten out your politics at home. I will place your *great* prince in his Tower."

With his contemptuous tone about our prince, which we agreed on, he expressed his evaluation of my plan to bind the islands, which he understood no better than my own people.

Neither by the rude nor by the sophisticated was my plan understood.

VI

Later, when we marched along a country road toward the city, with soldiers ahead and to the rear of us, I found there was one thing that rude people everywhere understood of me.

The news of my capture had run ahead. Tillers came down the neat rows of their fields to stand beside the road. They snickered and nudged each other and sometimes one could hear a suggestion that I must have a finer "tower" even than the king. The analogy had the inspired hurtfulness of the rude, and the hurt lay in the heart of the proud old man to whom I was being taken.

Twice soldiers had to dash to the side of the road and knock heads with their javelin butts. I began to understand why the King of Thule could not forgive me.

The flesh of my back crawled, and I perspired more than the day called for. The captain sometimes looked at me, but he said no more.

After the long walk through the country came the city. First, the two-level towers of the poor on their awkward stilts; then towers of more levels, and towers that reared gorgeous mosaics of ivory and wood and pearl, seven and nine levels into the blue and gold sunlight. These rich men were indeed raised resplendently above the monotony of the sea.

Here in these nacreous towers lived the charming people whose eyes I had dazzled with carvings and paintings, and whose minds I had thrilled with theories. Now they turned from me in grief. I felt at my back the north wind of fear.

Then came the great square of Thule which is actually paved from one end to the other with stone. All of this stone was raised two centuries ago from the great piles in the northern Ice Islands, and it is said that in the years of those raids a thousand Thulians died—and twice that many Ice Islanders.

Here in this great sunlit square they would nail me to the plank. As sharply and dryly as the breaking of small sticks would sound the stone mallet on the pegs. The sound of the mallet would spank along the decorated tower walls and die away, and they would lift the plank to carry it out to sea. The crowd in the square would melt away, fearful and brooding because another vengeful "shee-shoon," which is to say, condemned spirit, would be loose upon the sea.

So I would drift into deserts with the suns banging my eyes while my home isle drifted in poverty.

The work of my own hand was the final blow to my hopes. How awesome was this dwelling! At the far end of the square it soared fourteen levels into the sky. Its grounds were walled with stone to twice the height of a man. Inside there, in the spacious gardens, rose four more towers, and even these were nine levels high.

All this had been done to my design, and now I trembled before it.

They did not take me to him. Instead, he came to

me. He came in the night to the jail. I saw with pain that he was now an old man, as if something had broken in him and loosed the tensions of his haughty bearing. He stood before me and studied my fear.

He stood that way while they drew my hands up to the low ceiling in a noose and bound my feet to a shackle in the floor. Then he spoke and I learned that the voice was still his.

He asked softly, "How could you have done this to me? To me, who loved you and rewarded you and gloried in your work? How could you have taken from me my last hope?"

I could say nothing. Then, in the tiny, windowless jail, his terrible pride shrieked, "How could you have made a laughing stock of me?"

He tore the lash from the great brute beside him, and he smashed it into my face. Repeating over and over, "How could you have made a laughing stock of me?" he lashed my face and chest and groin, and I tasted what was to come.

As a boy I was tortured by the Ice Islanders. I do not bear torture well. I moaned when his weak flailing warned me of what the big jailer could do. When he had exhausted himself, he sat down on the damp floor and beat feebly with his fists.

The jailer took up the lash. He grinned pleasantly to me and asked politely, "How would you like it, Master? Slow, or fast?"

"No," I shouted. "No, Highest One, don't let him do this!"

But the poor old man was deaf to everything except his own misery and shame.

When I was again conscious, and the lights had stopped bursting in my eyes, the jailer was seated on a bench, resting. The fat of his chest heaved, and he ran a stubby hand across it to wipe away his sweat.

The king had risen from the floor. His silks were

dirty and disheveled. "How many have you given him?" he asked the jailer, hoarsely.

"Barely thirty, Highest One."

Through the swimming of the room, I saw the jailer rise and start toward me, and I screamed.

"Let him down. Be gentle with him."

I allowed myself to sink to the calm Sea Floor.

He had me taken to his own apartments, in the highest levels of the Tower. In silence, he came every day and washed my wounds and dressed them.

He came several times each day and repeated this care in silence so that I wept when I was alone for what I had done to him.

On the third day he spoke.

"The Lord Captain who took you has explained the reason you have come. It is good politics for the rock-latched islands like Thule and Hahn to strengthen the freely floating islands. You may have the soldiers. Whatever you need." With that he rose to leave.

Then at the door he turned, the whisper of his robes as loud as the shouting of a thousand soldiers.

"Be very clear about this. I do not waste a soldier for the sake of teri che. I believe your plan to bind those three little islands into one rich, strong island will work. By aiding that plan, I do one more little thing to keep back the Ice Islanders and keep down the sea bandits. It strengthens Thule."

His gray eyes lingered momentarily as he turned and left me.

Again and again, while the captain and I worked on the plans for storming my home isle, the king's words stung me. *"I do not waste a soldier for the sake of teri che."*

Again and again, this stinging drove my mind to the pool in the gardens of the Tower of my homeland. It is a hole into the sea for decorative purposes and salt lilies are grown there. On many islands there is such a pool in the gardens of the Tower.

I have often thought, "Behind all the guards at the walls of the Tower, there is a way in."

When the captain and I had completed our plans and had decided to embark in another four days, suddenly it came to me. "A craft can be built to go under the island and come up in the pool."

Such a surprise would save many soldiers of Thule, and many of my teri che.

In one moment things fell into place from countless observations and sources. How had I built and caulked the plumbing in the Great Tower of Thule? How does a fish roll in the water? How strong is the thickest of the round lenses of the glass of Hahn?

For two days, hardly taking time to eat or sleep, I stayed in my apartment drawing plans for such a craft. Once I went to the winery in the country and inspected two of the great hogsheads for storage which are large enough for a man to stand in.

The two giant hogsheads could be spliced together with more than enough strength and more room inside than would be needed by two men. This would be too buoyant, and so stone would have to line the bottom of the craft until it was almost ready to sink. Now, there would have to be a way to take on weight for sinking and get rid of it for coming back to the surface. So I would have a barrel braced on the floor midship and a pipe with a cock that would let water into it so that the craft would sink.

From the iron that flows near their island, the Hahnese have contrived a pump which a man may work by a handle and force water up a height. I would have to arrange one of these pumps so that water could be forced from the barrel back into the sea, and thus we would come again to the surface.

I saw that when the craft sank it would go on sinking, however slowly, unless a means other than emptying the barrel was used to stop this motion. So I would have structures along the sides like the fins of a fish that would maintain a level of descent as long as the craft was moving forward.

It was in moving the craft forward that I had trouble. There are no winds under the sea, and to paddle my hogsheads seemed to me out of the question. A boat can be moved forward by thrashing the rudder in a crude duplication of the fish tail. But I saw that no rudder I might design would move us from the edge of my home isle to the pool in the gardens of the Tower before the two or three occupants of the hogsheads fell from exhaustion.

I had to ask the captain for a delay in the embarkation. Naturally he was willing to wait for any plan that would spare his men. So I went back to my apartment and the problem of propulsion.

The more I thought about the clumsy action of a rudder, the more exasperated I became. There was something in this action that escaped me.

It was evening again, and I was utterly exhausted. I took a bottle of spirits from the cabinet and poured a drink. I sipped it while I stared at all the drawings I had made for propelling mechanisms. I poured another large drink and went to the windows.

I do not deny that in my goings and comings about the Tower I had never ceased to watch for the princess. I had not seen her and I did not see her now as my eyes searched the lawns and courts between the towers. But I longed deeply to see her, and suddenly I was drunk and very tired.

I awakened in the night with a headache. I rolled over in the luxurious bed and buried my face, and abruptly there was the idea for the propulsion.

The rudder need not move like the tail of a fish; it need not act like any living thing. It could be a spinning rudder of two blades tilted oppositely on their axis. This could be turned by a shaft extending into the craft. The shaft should have two cranks in it so that two men could turn at once.

Now, before noon, I finished all the drawings for my craft, and I sent a servant to the king. He invited me to lunch on his balcony, and there I showed him the drawings for this marvelous boat that would take men under the sea.

By the end of our lunch he had become as excited as I. Then suddenly we were both saddened that the old days were gone when we had planned together like this.

He said simply, "Have the Lord Captain procure craftsmen and proceed at once to build it."

I was dismissed. He shook his head to prevent me from speaking.

VII

We built the undersea craft on one of the navy wharfs. In barely seven days we were ready for a trial.

We let the boat into water. I had added a barrel to the top of the structure through which the occupants could enter and leave. In the front of this superstructure I had had them caulk a thick lens of the glass of Hahn so that I could look forward under water.

I had somehow miscalculated the buoyancy and we had to add some stone to the floor. Finally, when I and the soldier who would go with me were both aboard, little more than the superstructure remained above water.

The poor soldier was shaking with fright but determined to die for Thule. I climbed the rungs back up into the superstructure and told the Lord Captain to pole us away from the wharf.

A luxurious litter appeared and came toward us.

I knew at once that it was the king. He could not stay away from this trial. I waited, standing in a barrel in the sea. I hoped for some warning or some encouragement from him. He simply motioned the Lord Captain and soldiers to be at ease. Then he waved to me in silence and stood waiting.

We had placed one of the fighting ships of Thule at a good distance from shore. I took one last sighting on the fighter to make sure we were pointing toward it. Then, hurriedly, I closed and tightened the hatch in the top of the barrel and descended into the dark to hear the soldier's teeth chattering.

I said, "Soldier, are you standing by the crank?"

He gulped hard. "Yes, Master."

"Stay there. Start cranking when I tell you."

I fumbled in the dark and opened the cock of the barrel. Through the shallow, fast breathing of the soldier, I could hear water running into the barrel. Back at the window I caught a blurred glimpse of the fighter just before the sea lapped over the glass. Then I was looking at the cool, green of underwater and fishes turning past. My heart beat wildly. I let the light deepen a little and hurried back to close the cock, barking my shins on the bracings for the barrel.

"Now, soldier, start to crank!"

I joined my effort to his at my part of the shaft. I could hear his frightened breathing begin to even out with the labor over the cranks. I counted up to one hundred turns of the shaft while it became insufferably hot in the hogsheads.

"Keep cranking with all your might," I gasped and made my way up to the window.

The green light outside had deepened shockingly. For the first time I felt fear of the sea. I scrambled to the pump and worked it for fifteen back-breaking strokes. Then I turned the crank with the soldier for twenty-five turns, and I could restrain my anxiety no longer. I went to the window and wiped fog from the glass. The light was reassuringly brighter.

"Rest a while, soldier."

"What, Master?"

"Rest a while."

I kept wiping the fog from the window and watching the light brighten until I could see the swirling of the sea surface. Now we needed forward speed so the fins along the side would keep us from coming all the way to the surface.

"Let's start cranking again."

"Master, are we all right?"

"We're all right, soldier, as long as we crank."

I turned the crank another hundred times with the soldier and stumbled with exhaustion back to the window. The light was still all right. I looked hopefully ahead and to the sides, knowing we could not be near the fighter.

The soldier labored with great lung-bursting breaths. I told him to rest again, and I turned the crank alone for fifty times before I fell to the stones of the floor in a daze. The air was foul and hot and my lungs heaved desperately.

When I could speak, I commanded, "Turn the crank, soldier."

"Master, I'm dying."

"Soldier turn the crank or you *will* die."

At first with infinite weariness and then with dogged energy, I could hear him start turning the crank. I dragged myself up to the window. Just as I wiped away the fog, I saw something off to the left. Then it was no longer there. I fell back into the hogsheads yelling at the soldier. "Crank, man! Crank!"

I banged my head and ripped skin from my shins getting to the screws that controlled the rudder. I turned the rudder the wrong way. Then I turned it rightly. I made myself count slowly to twenty. Then I straightened the rudder.

When I again wiped the fog from the window, there

was the hull of the fighter, floating magically in a green-yellow sky.

"Soldier, we're there. Just a little more turning. Turn, soldier."

He turned and I turned with him. Then, gasping as if in death, I clambered back to the window and cried out.

"Stop, man. Crank the other way."

For a moment I had thought we might pass under the fighter and rip off the superstructure, but we stopped short of her.

The soldier had collapsed. I thought I would never finish pumping the water out of the barrel. For a time, after I was able to open the hatch, I stood and gulped at the air like a dying fish. Then I lifted the soldier and held him while he breathed it.

I climbed out the hatch and stood on the forward hogshead with water occasionally lapping my feet. We had come around the fighter and placed her between ourselves and the shore. All on her deck were at the other side watching for us toward the island. We drifted to a gentle bump against the ship. I reached up and caught the rail and pulled myself slowly to the deck.

I stood there for a moment looking at their backs, and then I said loudly, "Captain, we are here."

The King of Thule is a complex man. When the fighter, towing the undersea craft, brought us back, he stood before me for a time and simply nodded his head. Then, no longer able to restrain himself, he threw his arms about me and his old hands clapped my shoulders.

Still holding me he called to all about, "It is a holiday. The island must celebrate. There will be dancing and free wine."

As I walked back to the city beside his litter, I was not able to join in his enthusiasm. For I had not anticipated the agonies of the underwater trip. I knew that the distance out to the fighter had been little more than a third of the shortest distance from the shore of my home isle to the pool in its Tower gardens.

Suddenly I remembered the burial pools where we could surface for good air and rest in the protection of a tabooed place. Then I became as gay as the king was, and when I saw the many lords and ladies he invited to his apartments in my honor and the lavish banquet he served I knew that I had completely won his forgiveness. Somehow, having dissolved his shame by punishing me, his pride had risen again in the achievement of the day.

It was only natural that a gnawing hope rose in me. I watched every entering guest. I longed more than anything else in the world to see the princess, and I knew that it was impossible. He could not bring her here.

VIII

Two days later the undersea craft was ready on the deck of a cargo carrier, and the soldiers and ships were ready for the expedition to take the Tower of my homeland. I planned to take two soldiers to turn the crank. This would free me to handle the controls during the dangerous passage under the island and to keep careful eye on the beacons of daylight that would fall through the pools.

In the late afternoon, the king sent a servant for me. The man took me down smooth in one of the lifts I had designed for the Tower. Then he led me out to one of the spacious gardens where the king was waiting for me.

"First I must show you something over here in the garden house."

He led me to a small service house where the gardeners kept their tools. With poorly hidden excitement he pushed me through the entrance and closed the door behind me.

I was in blackness. Then I saw, glowing before me, a garden hoe and a fork. There was also a board with glowing letters. "Master, you are not the only inventor."

What an old fox this king was. The door opened and he was standing there as proud as Sha'charn.

"You know the glowing fish from the currents of Ohme?"

I nodded, smiling at his pleasure.

"I keep some of those fish in the pool over there. The light you saw in there is the stuff from their glowing stripes. It will last over a day, and you will have no trouble finding the controls of your craft."

Sha'tule, in sunset, and Sha'charn, yet a little higher, were splashing colors across a fluffy sky. The towers of the city were iridescent with fires. The king spoke as he suggested a stroll. He spoke softly, too softly, and he laid his hand affectionately on my arm.

"Would you go with me to have cakes and wine with the princess?"

The island rocked and I put out a hand.

I was dismayed at what was happening to me. I stammered, "No, Highest One. That would not be right. Do not stir this thing."

"I think so too, but I can deny her nothing. Also, I would give you an opportunity to ruin my last hope or to vindicate the faith I had in you."

This last, I did not really hear. I was too dazed. I walked the way he led me, and the island was rocked by a storm.

In a garden behind one of the lesser towers, we came to her. She sat at a table decorating a fabric. As we approached she dropped the needle and her hand trembled on the unfinished fabric.

I stared at her hand that was telling everything and then at her lovely face, and my chest ached. I bowed and it felt like I was being moved by strings. The king asked me to be seated and I stood unmindfully until he repeated his request. Then, after I was seated, I found that I was unable to speak.

She spoke, but her words meant nothing because her voice fluttered like a bird in a snare. "You have been traveling many years, Master."

"Pardon me, Princess?"

"I say . . . you have been away . . . a long time."

"Yes, I have been to many islands, Princess."

It seemed, after six years, that this was going to be all we had to say.

The king cleared his throat, and I was grateful for the compassion in his voice. "The Master has come for soldiers to retake the Tower of his homeland from a false pretender."

A nurse appeared at a nearby door, and I saw that she had with her the boy.

The nurse grasped frantically to return the lad to the rooms. He fled her like a deer, bounding over the pretty flowers, and threw himself into his mother's arms. She drew his head to her breast and kissed his forehead and admonished him.

The nurse hurried forward but the king waved her away. "Meet the child and me in a little while at the entrance to the Great Tower. I will go for a walk in the gardens with him."

Momentarily, I raised my eyes from the child to his mother's face, and found her staring at me with a great pride and warmth.

Now, suddenly, we had so much to say that we needed only our eyes to speak with.

The king rose and extended his hand to the child. "Come, my son, I will show you the luminous fish."

I stared at the boy and could not take my eyes from him. He was as favored as I had heard. He had his mother's famous looks. But I saw, too, the shock of hair that is my people's and the thin line of a mouth that is mine.

The king took the child's hand and repeated, "Come, my son." His message was not lost on me. For this *was* his son, the only heir he would ever have to the Tower of Thule.

When we were alone, I went and sat beside her. The light of Sha'charn was soft on her lovely head. I saw that she was now a woman, even as I was no longer a young man. I had forgotten the thick beat of my heart.

It was as though the years since our parting had stood for nothing. I felt my ambitions for my homeland melting away like a mist. What did I care to bind together three ridiculous little islands?

She assured me, between our kisses, that her father would make her Provincial Queen of the island of Lani and allow me to marry her as consort ruler if I but asked it. We both understood that this long separation would only deepen the delight of Lani. Our touch still had the magic of our first touch.

When I had, one last time, kissed her eyelids, her cheeks and her mouth, I left her and went to ask him for this simple happiness.

From behind a low cloud Sha'charn hurled a vast shaft of fire at the Great Tower of Thule. I was momentarily dazzled. I looked up the cascading mosaics of fire to where an old man waited in the pinnacle of flame.

Then I awakened and knew that Lani would never be.

When I was admitted to his apartments, he stood at a window looking out over the wealth of his city. He did not turn.

I waited in silence and presently he spoke. "Do not ask of me what she wishes. If you ask it I will allow it. I suffer with both of you. But do not ask it of me."

Her face, in its last look of love, appeared before me.

I heard his voice repeat, "Do not ask it of me."

I felt the huge wave of emotion on which she and I had risen begin to wash from me.

Then her face was gone and I was back in the reality of the king's room. From far below, the noisy happiness of the evening streets was a murmur of irony in this high place where the last light of Sha'charn lay across the rich carpet.

He turned to me and gestured as if he deprecated that of which he spoke. "It is not a law, but an expectation, that the King of Thule will be Thulian. The people often prefer to see laws broken, but they do not easily tolerate the disappointment of an expectation.

"I have not much longer to live. If I declare the princess to be Queen and Interim Ruler the people will in time forget you and there will be no more than ill mannered heckling when, eventually, the prince assumes the Tower. But if you marry her, if you remain about as a constant reminder . . ."

He spread his hands as a conclusion.

He turned again to the dying light from the window, and I knew that he saw a view to the sea that I had planned. "I have built Thule into the greatest power on the sea. I want my son to rule what I have built."

I went down to the streets. I understood that, all these years, I had existed on the hope that eventually he would let us live together. Now I found that I was going to have to live with the certainty that I would never again hold her.

I walked to the tower of the Lord Captain. While I awaited him, I looked for the last time upon my painting of Namora.

The captain came from his dining and looked at me questioningly.

"We leave tonight, Captain. It is the wish of the king."

We sailed with nine fighters. On the morning of the second day out, before Sha'tule had raised the first mists from the bobbing pumicine beds of my home isle, we lowered the underwater craft into the sea on a boom.

I remember the eerie light in the craft that came from the luminous stuff of the fishes, and I remember the soldiers cranking desperately in the stagnant air. I can still see the great balls of light from the burial pools where we surfaced and lay out on the hogsheads, gasping like monstrous fish.

Most clearly, I remember her face weeping in the dark of the sea.

I remember the garden pool of the Tower in my home isles from which I stared across the alabaster lilies and heard only her voice murmuring of Lani. The great sound of the soldiers of Thule storming through the streets of my homeland did not still her murmur, nor did the screams of the guards at the gates as we three came from behind and cut them down.

I suppose a quiet sea will always speak to me of Lani. In any case, I can recapture her face only as it drifts in the dark nether world.

There was a strange thing down there . . . little fish with rods straight up from their heads on which hung bell-like lanterns, brightly lighted. They came to the window and inspected me. Now they always invade her memory, like little clowns relieving tragedy.

IX

I had the prince made king that very noon. I was taking no more chances with the lords of my home island . . . and it is true, as has been claimed, that when we brought him from the prison to his Tower he stumbled over corpses. He *would* have to do *that!* . . . not once, but twice.

The officers of Thule laughed. It really looked like we were placing a dolt in the Tower to rule the teri che.

I gave him time to bathe and dine after the rudely rushed ceremony. Then I had myself brought to him in his shoddy administrative rooms. As the captain of a mercenary force asks his price for services rendered,

I put before our new king the treaty which had already been signed by the kings of Parsos and of Torne.

He hesitated fretfully. He asked many questions.

I had expected him, in gratitude to me, and out of respect for the two great men who had already signed the document, to grab a pen with haste.

Instead the lout kept bringing up matters of inconsequence. He interrupted my argument with asides to his new First Overlord.

This First Overlord was simply one of yesterday's rebels and behaved accordingly. His idea of polish was servility. Suddenly he glanced at me in fright.

Then, like a great bell, I reheard what this profound king had just asked yesterday's rebel.

He had asked, "Where is the Chacone they sent to me with food while I was in prison?"

He had asked this as though it had just now occurred to him.

Slowly I lowered the map which showed how Torne and Parsos could be most efficiently bound to our island.

The First Overlord was agitated. "She is here, Highest One. You asked that . . ."

"Never mind what I asked. Bring her."

Then he said to me apologetically, "Ah, Master, forgive these interruptions. So many things have come up. I know it is not important to you, but I have fallen in love. Desperately! It happens she is a Chacone, and I must determine to whom she belongs so that I may pay the man a fair price. My mind will be much more receptive to your theories when I have settled this affair of the heart."

I was suddenly suffering from a very bad chill. He took the map from my shaking hands and looked at it rather gaily and with new interest.

"Master, this is truly a moment in our history. To think that my signature will set this great plan in motion. You will be the hero of our people once they realize the greater prosperity and safety that will be theirs . . ."

The cringing First Overlord returned, and with him entered my little Chacone.

Like the broken barking of a north wind I tore at him. "Why you impudent little . . . you ungrateful . . . what do you know of love?"

He reddened and yammered, "You can't talk like that to me! I'm king now, not your pupil! Do you want to stand on a stone? What's this woman to you, anyway?"

"You know very well what she is to me. Do you think I'll bargain with you? No! I'll take her to Parsos and let you drift to Chryo."

He stormed out of the room. "You're under detention. Don't forget it. You're under detention." And then at the door, melodramatically, "Oh, that you should have blundered with her loveliness before I found her!"

I could have choked him through a thousand deaths. I went to the wall and beat my fist.

The little Chacone wept openly. She came and took my bruised hand and kissed it. She sobbed, "Oh, Master, my heart will break. I have known, Master. The way he looked at me from the jail, I knew this would happen. But my heart will break."

I caught the finality in her statement, and I took her shoulders and stared into her face. "What makes you think I would give you up?"

"You will have to. I heard them talking." She sobbed and indicated the First Overlord who still stood at the door. "You will not get the plan for the islands unless you do."

She knew me better than I knew myself. She knew I would go back to the table and stare at the map of three islands bound in one. She knew I would turn then to stare at her, because she did not wait for that. She left quietly with the First Overlord.

I was appalled at her certainty, and I knew that she was right. I knew it was a loathing that began to crawl in my belly like some hideous toad.

How could I be so dedicated to this plan of mine that I would destroy in this girl a delicate monolith of love? I was a crueler man than the sea bandit who had gloried that a thousand doves cooed for death. This dove would coo forever in some dark recess of her heart.

For it is true of the women of Chacone that they will kill themselves before they will let a man other than their owner come near them. But should that owner trade them to another they will remain as faithful to the new master, and will then savagely fight off the former owner. For this they are trained from childhood in some esoteric drilling of the spirit.

Thus I saw that I was going to shut myself from the heart of the Chacone, and my anger at the king dissolved in my loathing for myself. I went to him without the slightest accusation and got his signature on the treaty with Torne and Parsos.

I went down from the shabby Tower of my homeland and walked alone among my people which are called teri che. They love to drink and there are many taverns in the city. I went into one of these and ordered spirits. Then I also ordered one for the amiable sot who instantly joined me.

We drank in silence. I had nothing to say to any man. I stared without seeing across the talkative room and realized that a common man could come in here and brag with impunity that he had slept with the wives of ten lords. Then let him brag that he had slept with the Chacone of one lord, and he would be laughed out of the tavern.

The sot could stand the silence no longer. "Now, Master, you're done in, aren't you? Well, it's a fine thing you managed, getting the young prince to his Tower. Of course, this business of tying us up with

Parsos and Torne, I don't see. But I suppose the king will decide on that."

I stood up to go. He grabbed my sleeve. "Now, Master, don't take offense. You ought to get to know your homeland. You've been away too long doing fine things for other islands. You ought to build a new Tower for our . . ."

I crashed him over the table and into the wall.

For a moment the place went silent. The wine seller glanced from his counter and shook his head.

"Now, Master, it's a fine thing to get drunk and disorderly, but let's not tamper with life and limb."

I stalked out to the streets, and again I was alone among my people. I accepted their respectful nods and understood that I would always be separated from them by my heart that could love reason so deeply and reason away love so quickly.

They were right to fear my plan to bind the islands together. The threat of the Ice Islanders was too distant and the pinched faces of their children too close to weigh against the chilling logic of the step. For it was a plan born purely of reason. It threatened much of the spirit in them that was fashioned with such disorderly grandeur from pride and prejudice and the demands of provincialism.

The street-lighters had set the lamps guttering, and the fog moved in and turned to pearl between them. Somehow the fog brought restraint and order and a muffling of guilt. As I walked the lamps came from the fog in a regular cadence and the damp planks of the street became an orderly path through chaos.

My enormous crime against the Chacone settled into a knot of guilt that I was going to have to live with. It was a guilt fate had made necessary if I was to put through the plan . . . and only I could put it through.

I stopped involuntarily and declared to the fog, "I

am what I am!" Then, glancing about me, I walked on.

There was much to be set in motion so that the islands could be maneuvered together and bound. I would sail tomorrow for Parsos and get things started.

WALL OF CRYSTAL, EYE OF NIGHT

Algis Budrys

In style and decor this elegant tale of pursuit and bloodshed is very much an artifact of the late twentieth century. But the underlying armature is pure Jacobean drama. A seventeenth-century London theatergoer would have little difficulty attuning himself to the forces that drive this story; this hyperbolic fantasy reveals Budrys at last as the proper heir to Tourneur and Webster.

I

Soft as the voice of a mourning dove, the telephone sounded at Rufus Sollenar's desk. Sollenar himself was standing fifty paces away, his leonine head cocked, his hands flat in his hip pockets, watching the nighted world through the crystal wall that faced out over Manhattan Island. The window was so high that some of what he saw was dimmed by low cloud hovering over the rivers. Above him were stars; below him the city was traced out in light and brimming with light. A falling star—an interplanetary rocket—streaked down toward Long Island Facility like a scratch across the soot on the doors of Hell.

Sollenar's eyes took it in, but he was watching the total scene, not any particular part of it. His eyes were shining.

When he heard the telephone, he raised his left hand to his lips. "Yes?" The hand glittered with utilijem rings; the effect was that of an attempt at the sort of copper-binding that was once used to reinforce the ribbing of wooden warships.

His personal receptionist's voice moved from the air near his desk to the air near his ear. Seated at the monitor board in her office, wherever in this building her office was, the receptionist told him:

"Mr. Ermine says he has an appointment."

"No." Sollenar dropped his hand and returned to his panorama. When he had been twenty years younger—managing the modest optical factory that had provided the support of three generations of Sollenars—he had very much wanted to be able to stand in a place like this, and feel as he imagined men felt in such circumstances. But he felt unimaginable, now.

To be here was one thing. To have almost lost the right, and regained it at the last moment, was another. Now he knew that not only could he be here today but that tomorrow, and tomorrow, he could still be here. He had won. His gamble had given him EmpaVid—and EmpaVid would give him all.

The city was not merely a prize set down before his eyes. It was a dynamic system he had proved he could manipulate. He and the city were one. It buoyed and sustained him; it supported him, here in the air, with stars above and light-thickened mist below.

The telephone mourned: "Mr. Ermine states he has a firm appointment."

"I've never heard of him." And the left hand's utilijems fell from Sollenar's lips again. He enjoyed such toys. He raised his right hand, sheathed in insubstantial midnight-blue silk in which the silver threads of metallic wiring ran subtly toward the fingertips. He raised the hand, and touched two fingers together: music began to play behind and before him. He made contact between another combination of finger circuits, and a soft, feminine laugh came from the terrace at the other side of the room, where connecting doors had opened. He moved toward it. One layer of translucent drapery remained across the doorway, billowing lightly in the breeze from the terrace. Through it, he saw the taboret with its candle lit; the iced wine in the stand beside it; the two fragile chairs; Bess Allardyce, slender and regal, waiting in one of them—all these, through the misty curtain, like either the beginning or the end of a dream.

"Mr. Ermine reminds you the appointment was made for him at the Annual Business Dinner of the International Association of Broadcasters, in 1998."

Sollenar completed his latest step, then stopped. He frowned down at his left hand. "Is Mr. Ermine with the IAB's Special Public Relations Office?"

"Yes," the voice said after a pause.

The fingers of Sollenar's right hand shrank into a cone. The connecting door closed. The girl disappeared. The music stopped. "All right. You can tell Mr. Ermine to come up." Sollenar went to sit behind his desk.

The office door chimed. Sollenar crooked a finger of his left hand, and the door opened. With another gesture, he kindled the overhead lights near the door and sat in shadow as Mr. Ermine came in.

Ermine was dressed in rust-colored garments. His figure was spare, and his hands were empty. His face was round and soft, with long dark sideburns. His scalp was bald. He stood just inside Sollenar's office and said: "I would like some light to see you by, Mr. Sollenar."

Sollenar crooked his little finger.

The overhead lights came to soft light all over the office. The crystal wall became a mirror, with only the strongest city lights glimmering through it. "I only wanted to see you first," said Sollenar; "I thought perhaps we'd met before."

"No," Ermine said, walking across the office. "It's not likely you've ever seen me." He took a card case out of his pocket and showed Sollenar proper identification. "I'm not a very forward person."

"Please sit down," Sollenar said. "What may I do for you?"

"At the moment, Mr. Sollenar, I'm doing something for you."

Sollenar sat back in his chair. "Are you? Are you, now?" He frowned at Ermine. "When I became a party to the By-Laws passed at the '98 Dinner, I thought a Special Public Relations Office would make a valuable asset to the organization. Consequently, I voted for it, and for the powers it was given. But I never expected to have any personal dealings with it. I barely remembered you people had carte blanche with any IAB member."

"Well, of course, it's been a while since '98," Ermine said. "I imagine some legends have grown up around us. Industry gossip—that sort of thing."

"Yes."

"But we don't restrict ourselves to an enforcement function, Mr. Sollenar. You haven't broken any By-Laws, to our knowledge."

"Or mine. But nobody feels one hundred percent secure. Not under these circumstances." Nor did Sollenar yet relax his face into its magnificent smile. "I'm sure you've found that out."

"I have a somewhat less ambitious older brother who's with the Federal Bureau of Investigation. When I embarked on my own career, he told me I could expect everyone in the world to react like a criminal, yes," Ermine said, paying no attention to Sollenar's involuntary blink. "It's one of the complicating factors in a profession like my brother's, or mine. But I'm here to advise you, Mr. Sollenar. Only that."

"In what matter, Mr. Ermine?"

"Well, your corporation recently came into control of the patents for a new video system. I understand that this in effect makes your corporation the licensor for an extremely valuable sales and entertainment medium. Fantastically valuable."

"EmpaVid," Sollenar agreed. "Various subliminal stimuli are broadcast with and keyed to the overt subject matter. The home receiving unit contains feedback sensors which determine the viewer's reaction to these stimuli, and intensify some while playing down others in order to create complete emotional rapport between the viewer and the subject matter. EmpaVid, in other words, is a system for orchestrating the viewer's emotions. The home unit is self-contained, semiportable, and not significantly bulkier than the standard TV receiver. EmpaVid is compatible with standard TV receivers—except, of course, that the subject matter seems thin and vaguely unsatisfactory on a standard receiver. So the consumer shortly purchases an EV unit." It pleased Sollenar to spell out the nature of his prize.

"At a very reasonable price. Quite so, Mr. Sollenar. But you had several difficulties in finding potential licensees for this system, among the networks."

Sollenar's lips pinched out.

Mr. Ermine raised one finger. "First, there was the matter of acquiring the patents from the original inventor, who was also approached by Cortwright Burr."

"Yes, he was," Sollenar said in a completely new voice.

"Competition between Mr. Burr and yourself is long-standing and intense."

"Quite intense," Sollenar said, looking directly ahead of him at the one blank wall of the office. Burr's offices were several blocks downtown, in that direction.

"Well, I have no wish to enlarge on that point, Mr. Burr being an IAB member in standing as good as yours, Mr. Sollenar. There was, in any case, a further difficulty in licensing EV, due to the very heavy cost involved in equipping broadcasting stations and network relay equipment for this sort of transmission."

"Yes, there was."

"Ultimately, however, you succeeded. You pointed out, quite rightly, that if just one station made the change, and if just a few EV receivers were put into public places within the area served by that station, normal TV outlets could not possibly compete for advertising revenue."

"Yes."

"And so your last difficulties were resolved a few days ago, when your EmpaVid Unlimited—pardon me; when EmpaVid, a subsidiary of the Sollenar Corporation—became a major stockholder in the Transworld TV Network."

"I don't understand, Mr. Ermine," Sollenar said. "Why are you recounting this? Are you trying to demonstrate the power of your knowledge? All these transactions are already matters of record in the IAB confidential files, in accordance with the By-Laws."

Ermine held up another finger. "You're forgetting I'm only here to advise you. I have two things to say. They are:

"These transactions are on file with the IAB because they involve a great number of IAB members, and an increasingly large amount of capital. Also, Transworld's exclusivity, under the IAB By-Laws, will hold good only until thirty-three percent market saturation has been reached. If EV is as good as it looks, that will be quite soon. After that, under the By-Laws, Transworld will be restrained from making effective defenses against patent infringement by competitors. Then all of the IAB's membership and much of their capital will be involved with EV. Much of that capital is already in anticipatory motion. So a highly complex structure now ultimately depends on the integrity of the Sollenar

Corporation. If Sollenar stock falls in value, not just you but many IAB members will be greatly embarrassed. Which is another way of saying EV must succeed."

"I know all that! What of it? There's no risk. I've had every related patent on Earth checked. There will be no catastrophic obsolescence of the EV system."

Ermine said: "There are engineers on Mars. Martian engineers. They're a dying race, but no one knows what they can still do."

Sollenar raised his massive head.

Ermine said: "Late this evening, my office learned that Cortwright Burr has been in close consultation with the Martians for several weeks. They have made some sort of machine for him. He was on the flight that landed at the Facility a few moments ago."

Sollenar's fists clenched. The lights crashed off and on, and the room wailed. From the terrace came a startled cry, and a sound of smashed glass.

Mr. Ermine nodded, excused himself, and left.

—A few moments later, Mr. Ermine stepped out at the pedestrian level of the Sollenar Building. He strolled through the landscaped garden, and across the frothing brook toward the central walkway down the Avenue. He paused at a hedge to pluck a blossom and inhale its odor. He walked away, holding it in his naked fingers.

II

Drifting slowly on the thread of his spinneret, Rufus Sollenar came gliding down the wind above Cortwright Burr's building.

The building, like a spider, touched the ground at only the points of its legs. It held its wide, low bulk spread like a parasol over several downtown blocks. Sollenar, manipulating the helium-filled plastic drifter far above him, steered himself with jets of compressed gas from plastic bottles in the drifter's structure.

Only Sollenar himself, in all this system, was not effectively transparent to the municipal antiplane radar. And he himself was wrapped in long, fluttering streamers of dull black, metallic sheeting. To the eye, he was amorphous and nonreflective. To electronic sensors, he was a drift of static much like a sheet of foil picked by the wind from some careless trash heap. To all of the senses of all interested parties he was hardly there at all—and, thus, in an excellent position for murder.

He fluttered against Burr's window. There was the man, crouched over his desk. What was that in his hands—a pomander?

Sollenar clipped his harness to the edges of the cornice. Swayed out against it, his sponge-soled boots pressed to the glass, he touched his left hand to the window and described a circle. He pushed; there was a thud on the carpeting in Burr's office, and now there was no barrier to Sollenar. Doubling his knees against his chest, he catapulted forward, the riot pistol in his right hand. He stumbled and fell to his knees, but the gun was up.

Burr jolted up behind his desk. The little sphere of orange-gold metal, streaked with darker bronze, its surface vermicular with encrustations, was still in his hands. "Him!" Burr cried out as Sollenar fired.

Gasping, Sollenar watched the charge strike Burr. It threw his torso backward faster than his limbs and head could follow without dangling. The choked-down pistol was nearly silent. Burr crashed backward to end, transfixed, against the wall.

Pale and sick, Sollenar moved to take the golden ball. He wondered where Shakespeare could have seen an example such as this, to know an old man could have so much blood in him.

Burr held the prize out to him. Staring with eyes distended by hydrostatic pressure, his clothing raddled and his torso grinding its broken bones, Burr stalked away from the wall and moved as if to embrace Sollenar. It was queer, but he was not dead.

Shuddering, Sollenar fired again.

Again Burr was thrown back. The ball spun from his splayed fingers as he once more marked the wall with his body.

Pomander, orange, whatever—it looked valuable.

Sollenar ran after the rolling ball. And Burr moved to intercept him, nearly faceless, hunched under a great invisible weight that slowly yielded as his back groaned.

Sollenar took a single backward step.

Burr took a step toward him. The golden ball lay in a far corner. Sollenar raised the pistol despairingly and fired again. Burr tripped backward on tiptoe, his arms like windmills, and fell atop the prize.

Tears ran down Sollenar's cheeks. He pushed one foot forward . . . and Burr, in his corner, lifted his head and began to gather his body for the effort of rising.

Sollenar retreated to the window, the pistol sledging backward against his wrist and elbow as he fired the remaining shots in the magazine.

Panting, he climbed up into the window frame and clipped the harness to his body, craning to look over his shoulder . . . as Burr—shredded; leaking blood and worse than blood—advanced across the office.

He cast off his holds on the window frame and clumsily worked the drifter controls. Far above him, volatile ballast spilled out and dispersed in the air long before it touched ground. Sollenar rose, sobbing—

And Burr stood in the window, his shattered hands on the edges of the cut circle, raising his distended eyes steadily to watch Sollenar in flight across the enigmatic sky.

Where he landed, on the roof of a building in his possession, Sollenar had a disposal unit for his gun and his other trappings. He deferred for a time the question of why Burr had failed at once to die. Empty-handed, he returned uptown.

He entered his office, called and told his attorneys the exact times of departure and return, and knew the question of dealing with municipal authorities was thereby resolved. That was simple enough, with no witnesses to complicate the matter. He began to wish he hadn't been so irresolute as to leave Burr without the thing he was after. Surely, if the pistol hadn't killed the man—an old man, with thin limbs and spotted skin—he could have wrestled that thin-limbed, bloody old man aside—that spotted old man—and dragged himself and his prize back to the window, for all that the old man would have clung to him, and clutched at his legs, and fumbled for a handhold on his somber disguise of wrappings—that broken, immortal old man.

Sollenar raised his hand. The great window to the city grew opaque.

Bess Allardyce knocked softly on the door from the terrace. He would have thought she'd returned to her own apartments many hours ago. Tortuously pleased, he opened the door and smiled at her, feeling the dried tears crack on the skin of his cheeks.

He took her proffered hands. "You waited for me," he sighed. "A long time for anyone as beautiful as you to wait."

She smiled back at him. "Let's go out and look at the stars."

"Isn't it chilly?"

"I made spiced hot cider for us. We can sip it and think."

He let her draw him out onto the terrace. He leaned on the parapet, his arm around her pulsing waist, his cape drawn around both their shoulders.

"Bess, I won't ask if you'd stay with me no matter what the circumstances. But it might be a time will come when I couldn't bear to live in this city. What about that?"

"I don't know," she answered honestly.

And Cortwright Burr put his hand up over the edge of the parapet, between them.

Sollenar stared down at the straining knuckles, holding the entire weight of the man dangling against the sheer face of the building. There was a sliding, rustling noise, and the other hand came up, searched blindly for a hold and found it, hooked over the stone. The fingers tensed and rose, their tips flattening at the pressure as Burr tried to pull his head and shoulders up to the level of the parapet.

Bess breathed: "Oh, look at them! He must have torn them terribly climbing up!" Then she pulled away from Sollenar and stood staring at him, her hand to her mouth. "But he *couldn't* have climbed! We're so high!"

Sollenar beat at the hands with the heels of his palms, using the direct, trained blows he had learned at his athletic club.

Bone splintered against the stone. When the knuckles were broken the hands instantaneously disappeared, leaving only streaks behind them. Sollenar looked over the parapet. A bundle shrank from sight, silhouetted against the lights of the pedestrian level and the Avenue. It contracted to a pinpoint. Then, when it reached the brook and water flew in all directions, it disappeared in a final sunburst, endowed with glory by the many lights which found momentary reflection down there.

"Bess, leave me! Leave me, please!" Rufus Sollenar cried out.

III

Rufus Sollenar paced his office, his hands held safely still in front of him, their fingers spread and rigid.

The telephone sounded, and his secretary said to him: "Mr. Solenar, you are ten minutes from being late at the TTV Executives' Ball. This is a First Class obligation."

Sollenar laughed. "I thought it was, when I originally classified it."

"Are you now planning to renege, Mr. Sollenar?" the secretary inquired politely.

Certainly, Sollenar thought. He could as easily renege on the Ball as a king could on his coronation.

"Burr, you scum, what have you done to me?" he asked the air, and the telephone said: "Beg pardon?"

"Tell my valet," Sollenar said. "I'm going." He dismissed the phone. His hands cupped in front of his chest. A firm grip on emptiness might be stronger than any prize in a broken hand.

Carrying in his chest something he refused to admit was terror, Sollenar made ready for the Ball.

But only a few moments after the first dance set had ended, Malcolm Levier of the local TTV station executive staff looked over Sollenar's shoulder and remarked: "Oh, there's Cort Burr, dressed like a gallows bird."

Sollenar, glittering in the costume of the Medici, did not turn his head. "Is he? What would he want here?"

Levier's eyebrows arched. "He holds a little stock. He has entrée. But he's late." Levier's lips quirked. "It must have taken him some time to get that makeup on."

"Not in good taste, is it?"

"Look for yourself."

"Oh, I'll do better than that," Sollenar said. "I'll go and talk to him a while. Excuse me, Levier." And only then did he turn around, already started on his first pace toward the man.

But Cortwright Burr was only a pasteboard imitation of himself as Sollenar had come to know him. He stood to one side of the doorway, dressed in black and crimson robes, with black leather gauntlets on his hands, carrying a staff of weathered, natural wood. His face was shadowed by a sackcloth hood, the eyes well hidden. His face was powdered gray, and some blend of livid colors hollowed his cheeks. He stood motionless as Sollenar came up to him.

As he had crossed the floor, each step regular, the eyes of bystanders had followed Sollenar, until, anticipating his course, they found Burr waiting. The noise level of the Ball shrank perceptibly, for the lesser revelers who chanced to be present were sustaining it all alone. The people who really mattered here were silent and watchful.

The thought was that Burr, defeated in business, had come here in some insane reproach to his adversary, in this lugubrious, distasteful clothing. Why, he looked like a corpse. Or worse.

The question was, what would Sollenar say to him? The wish was that Burr would take himself away, back to his estates or to some other city. New York was no longer for Cortwright Burr. But what would Sollenar say to him now, to drive him back to where he hadn't the grace to go willingly?

"Cortwright," Sollenar said in a voice confined to the two of them. "So your Martian immortality works."

Burr said nothing.

"You got that in addition, didn't you? You knew how I'd react. You knew you'd need protection. Paid the Martians to make you physically invulnerable? It's a good system. Very impressive. Who would have thought the Martians knew so much? But who here is going to pay attention to you now? Get out of town, Cortwright. You're past your chance. You're dead as far as these people are concerned—all you have left is your skin."

Burr reached up and surreptitiously lifted a corner of his fleshed mask. And there he was, under it. The hood retreated an inch, and the light reached his eyes; and Sollenar had been wrong, Burr had less left than he thought.

"Oh, no, no, Cortwright," Sollenar said softly. "No, you're right—I can't stand up to that."

He turned and bowed to the assembled company. "Good night!" he cried, and walked out of the ballroom.

Someone followed him down the corridor to the elevators. Sollenar did not look behind him.

"I have another appointment with you now," Ermine said at his elbow.

They reached the pedestrian level. Sollenar said: "There's a cafe. We can talk there."

"Too public, Mr. Sollenar. Let's simply stroll and converse." Ermine lightly took his arm and guided him along the walkway. Sollenar noticed then that Ermine was costumed so cunningly that no one could have guessed the appearance of the man.

"Very well," Sollenar said.

"Of course."

They walked together, casually. Ermine said: "Burr's driving you to your death. Is it because you tried to kill him earlier? Did you get his Martian secret?"

Sollenar shook his head.

"You didn't get it." Ermine sighed. "That's unfortunate. I'll have to take steps."

"Under the By-Laws," Sollenar said, "I cry *laissez faire.*"

Ermine looked up, his eyes twinkling. *"Laissez faire?* Mr. Sollenar, do you have any idea how many of our members are involved in your fortunes? *They* will cry *laissez faire,* Mr. Sollenar, but clearly you persist in dragging them down with you. No, sir, Mr. Sollenar, my office now forwards an immediate recommendation to the Technical Advisory Committee of the IAB that Mr. Burr probably has a system superior to yours, and that stock in Sollenar, Incorporated, had best be disposed of."

"There's a bench," Sollenar said. "Let's sit down."

"As you wish." Ermine moved beside Sollenar to the bench, but remained standing.

"What is it, Mr. Sollenar?"

"I want your help. You advised me on what Burr had.

It's still in his office building, somewhere. You have resources. We can get it."

"*Laissez faire,* Mr. Sollenar. I visited you in an advisory capacity. I can do no more."

"For a partnership in my affairs could you do more?"

"Money?" Ermine tittered. "For me? Do you know the conditions of my employment?"

If he had thought, Sollenar would have remembered. He reached out tentatively. Ermine anticipated him.

Ermine bared his left arm and sank his teeth into it. He displayed the arm. There was no quiver of pain in voice or stance. "It's not a legend, Mr. Sollenar. It's quite true. We of our office must spend a year, after the nerve surgery, learning to walk without the feel of our feet, to handle objects without crushing them or letting them slip, or damaging ourselves. Our mundane pleasures are auditory, olfactory, and visual. Easily gratified at little expense. Our dreams are totally interior, Mr. Sollenar. The operation is irreversible. What would you buy for me with your money?"

"What would I buy for myself?" Sollenar's head sank down between his shoulders.

Ermine bent over him. "Your despair is your own, Mr. Sollenar. I have official business with you."

He lifted Sollenar's chin with a forefinger. "I judge physical interference to be unwarranted at this time. But matters must remain so that the IAB members involved with you can recover the value of their investments in EV. Is that perfectly clear, Mr. Sollenar? You are hereby enjoined under the By-Laws, as enforced by the Special Public Relations Office." He glanced at his watch. "Notice was served at 1:27 AM, City time."

"1:27," Sollenar said. "City time." He sprang to his feet and raced down a companionway to the taxi level.

Mr. Ermine watched him quizzically.

He opened his costume, took out his omnipresent medical kit, and sprayed coagulant over the wound in his forearm. Replacing the kit, he adjusted his clothing and strolled down the same companionway Sollenar had run. He raised an arm, and a taxi flittered down beside him. He showed the driver a card, and the cab lifted off with him, its lights glaring in a Priority pattern, far faster than Sollenar's ordinary legal limit allowed.

IV

Long Island Facility vaulted at the stars in great kangaroo leaps of arch and cantilever span, jeweled in glass and metal as if the entire port were a mechanism for navigating interplanetary space. Rufus Sollenar paced its esplanades, measuring his steps, holding his arms still, for the short time until he could board the Mars rocket.

Erect and majestic, he took a place in the lounge and carefully sipped liqueur, once the liner had boosted away from Earth and coupled in its Faraday main drives.

Mr. Ermine settled into the place beside him.

Sollenar looked over at him calmly. "I thought so."

Ermine nodded. "Of course you did. But I didn't almost miss you. I was here ahead of you. I have no objection to your going to Mars, Mr. Sollenar. *Laissez faire*. Provided I can go along."

"Well," Rufus Sollenar said. "Liqueur?" He gestured with his glass.

Ermine shook his head. "No, thank you," he said delicately.

Sollenar said: "Even your tongue?"

"Of course my tongue, Mr. Sollenar. I taste nothing, I touch nothing." Ermine smiled. "But I feel no pressure."

"All right, then," Rufus Sollenar said crisply. "We have several hours to landing time. You sit and dream your interior dreams, and I'll dream mine." He faced around in his chair and folded his arms across his chest.

"Mr. Sollenar," Ermine said gently.

"Yes?"

"I am once again with you by appointment as provided under the By-Laws."

"State your business, Mr. Ermine."

"You are not permitted to lie in an unknown grave, Mr. Sollenar. Insurance policies on your life have been taken out at a high premium rate. The IAB members concerned cannot wait the statutory seven years to have you declared dead. Do what you will, Mr. Sollenar, but I must take care I witness your death. From now on, I am with you wherever you go."

Sollenar smiled. "I don't intend to die. Why should I die, Mr. Ermine?"

"I have no idea, Mr. Sollenar. But I know Cortwright Burr's character. And isn't that he, seated there in the corner? The light is poor, but I think he's recognizable."

Across the lounge, Burr raised his head and looked into Sollenar's eyes. He raised a hand near his face, perhaps merely to signify greeting. Rufus Sollenar faced front.

"A worthy opponent, Mr. Sollenar," Ermine said. "A persevering, unforgiving, ingenious man. And yet—" Ermine seemed a little touched by bafflement. "And yet it seems to me, Mr. Sollenar, that he got you running rather easily. What *did* happen between you, after my advisory call?"

Sollenar turned a terrible smile on Ermine. "I shot him to pieces. If you'd peel his face, you'd see."

Ermine sighed. "Up to this moment, I had thought perhaps you might still salvage your affairs."

"Pity, Mr. Ermine? Pity for the insane?"

"Interest. I can take no part in your world. Be grateful, Mr. Sollenar. I am not the same gullible man I was when I signed my contract with IAB, so many years ago."

Sollenar laughed. Then he stole a glance at Burr's corner.

The ship came down at Abernathy Field, in Aresia, the Terrestrial city. Industrialized, prefabricated, jerry-built, and clamorous, the storm-proofed buildings huddled, but huddled proudly, at the desert's edge.

Low on the horizon was the Martian settlement—the buildings so skillfully blended with the landscape, so eroded, so much abandoned that the uninformed eye saw nothing. Sollenar had been to Mars—on a tour. He had seen the natives in their nameless dwelling place; arrogant, venomous, and weak. He had been told, by the paid guide, they trafficked with Earthmen as much as they cared to, and kept to their place on the rim of Earth's encroachment, observing.

"Tell me, Ermine," Sollenar said quietly as they walked across the terminal lobby. "You're to kill me, aren't you, if I try to go on without you?"

"A matter of procedure, Mr. Sollenar," Ermine said evenly. "We cannot risk the investment capital of so many IAB members."

Sollenar sighed. "If I were any other member, how I would commend you, Mr. Ermine! Can we hire a car for ourselves, then, somewhere nearby?"

"Going out to see the engineers?" Ermine asked. "Who would have thought they'd have something valuable for sale?"

"I want to show them something," Sollenar said.

"What thing, Mr. Sollenar?"

They turned the corner of a corridor, with branching hallways here and there, not all of them busy. "Come here," Sollenar said, nodding toward one of them.

They stopped out of sight of the lobby and the main corridor. "Come on," Sollenar said. "A little farther."

"No," Ermine said. "This is farther than I really wish. It's dark here."

"Wise too late, Mr. Ermine," Sollenar said, his arms flashing out.

One palm impacted against Ermine's solar plexus, and the other against the muscle at the side of his neck, but not hard enough to kill. Ermine collapsed, starved for oxygen, while Sollenar silently cursed having been cured of murder. Then Sollenar turned and ran.

Behind him Ermine's body struggled to draw breath by reflex alone.

Moving as fast as he dared, Sollenar walked back and reached the taxi lock, pulling a respirator from a wall rack as he went. He flagged a car and gave his destination, looking behind him. He had seen nothing of Cortwright Burr since setting foot on Mars. But he knew that, soon or late, Burr would find him.

A few moments later Ermine got to his feet. Sollenar's car was well away. Ermine shrugged and went to the local broadcasting station.

He commandeered a private desk, a firearm, and immediate time on the IAB interoffice circuit to Earth. When his call acknowledgement had come back to him from his office there, he reported:

"Sollenar is enroute to the Martian city. He wants a duplicate of Burr's device, of course, since he smashed the original when he killed Burr. I'll follow and make final disposition. The disorientation I reported previously is progressing rapidly. Almost all his responses now are inappropriate. On the flight out, he seemed to be staring at something in an empty seat. Quite often when spoken to he obviously hears something else entirely. I expect to catch one of the next few flights back."

There was no point in waiting for comment to wend its way back from Earth. Ermine left. He went to a cab rank and paid the exorbitant fee for transportation outside Aresian city limits.

Close at hand, the Martian city was like a welter of broken pots. Shards of wall and roof joined at savage angles and pointed to nothing. Underfoot, drifts of vitreous material, shaped to fit no sane configuration, and broken to fit such a mosaic as no church would contain, rocked and slid under Sollenar's hurrying feet.

What from Aresia had been a solid front of dun color was here a facade of red, green, and blue splashed about centuries ago and since then weathered only enough to show how bitter the colors had once been. The plum-colored sky stretched over all this like a frigid membrane, and the wind blew and blew.

Here and there, as he progressed, Sollenar saw Martian arms and heads protruding from the rubble. Sculptures.

He was moving toward the heart of the city, where some few unbroken structures persisted. At the top of a heap of shards he turned to look behind him. There was the dust-plume of his cab, returning to the city. He expected to walk back—perhaps to meet someone on the road, all alone on the Martian plain if only Ermine would forebear from interfering. Searching the flat, thin-aired landscape, he tried to pick out the plodding dot of Cortwright Burr. But not yet.

He turned and ran down the untrustworthy slope.

He reached the edge of the maintained area. Here the rubble was gone, the ancient walks swept, the statues kept upright on their pediments. But only broken walls suggested the fronts of the houses that had stood here. Knifing their sides up through the wind-rippled sand that only constant care kept off the street, the shadow-houses fenced his way and the sculptures were motionless as hope. Ahead of him, he saw the buildings of the engineers. There was no heap to climb and look to see if Ermine followed close behind.

Sucking his respirator, he reached the building of the Martian engineers.

A sounding strip ran down the doorjamb. He scratched his fingernails sharply along it, and the magnified vibration, ducted throughout the hollow walls, rattled his plea for entrance.

V

The door opened, and Martians stood looking. They were spindly limbed and slight, their faces framed by folds of leathery tissue. Their mouths were lipped with horn as hard as dentures, and pursed, forever ready to masticate. They were pleasant neither to look at nor, Sollenar knew, to deal with. But Cortwright Burr had done it. And Sollenar needed to do it.

"Does anyone here speak English?" he asked.

"I," said the central Martian, his mouth opening to the sound, closing to end the reply.

"I would like to deal with you."

"Whenever," the Martian said, and the group at the doorway parted deliberately to let Sollenar in.

Before the door closed behind him, Sollenar looked back. But the rubble of the abandoned sectors blocked his line of sight into the desert.

"What can you offer? And what do you want?" the Martian asked. Sollenar stood half-ringed by them, in a room whose corners he could not see in the uncertain light.

"I offer you Terrestrial currency."

The English-speaking Martian—the Martian who had admitted to speaking English—turned his head slightly and spoke to his fellows. There were clacking sounds as his lips met. The others reacted variously, one of them suddenly gesturing with what seemed a disgusted flip of his arm before he turned without further word and stalked away, his shoulders looking like the shawled back of a very old and very hungry woman.

"What did Burr give you?" Sollenar asked.

"Burr." The Martian cocked his head. His eyes were not multifaceted, but gave that impression.

"He was here and he dealt with you. Not long ago. On what basis?"

"Burr. Yes. Burr gave us currency. We will take currency from you. For the same thing we gave him?"

"For immortality, yes."

"Im— This is a new word."

"Is it? For the secret of not dying?"

"Not dying? You think we have not-dying for sale here?" The Martian spoke to the others again. Their lips clattered. Others left, like the first one had, moving with great precision and very slow step, and no remaining tolerance for Sollenar.

Sollenar cried out: "What did you sell him, then?"

The principal engineer said: "We made an entertainment device for him."

"A little thing. This size." Sollenar cupped his hands.

"You have seen it, then."

"Yes. And nothing more? That was all he bought here?"

"It was all we had to sell—or give. We don't yet know whether Earthmen will give us things in exchange for currency. We'll see, when we next need something from Aresia."

Sollenar demanded: "How did it work? This thing you sold him."

"Oh, it lets people tell stories to themselves."

Sollenar looked closely at the Martian. "What kind of stories?"

"Any kind," the Martian said blandly. "Burr told us what he wanted. He had drawings with him of an Earthman device that used pictures on a screen, and broadcast sounds, to carry the details of the story told to the auditor."

"He stole those patents! He couldn't have used them on Earth."

"And why should he? Our device needs to convey no precise details. Any mind can make its own. It only needs to be put into a situation, and from there it can do all the work. If an auditor wishes a story of contact with other sexes, for example, the projector simply makes it seem to him, the next time he is with the object of his desire, that he is getting positive feedback—that he is arousing a similar response in that object. Once that has been established for him, the auditor may then leave the machine, move about normally, conduct his life as usual—but always in accordance with the basic situation. It is, you see, in the end a means of introducing system into his view of reality. Of course, his society must understand that he is not in accord with reality, for some of what he does cannot seem rational from an outside view of him. So some care must be taken, but not much. If many such devices were to enter his society, soon the circumstances would become commonplace, and the society would surely readjust to allow for it," said the English-speaking Martian.

"The machine creates any desired situation in the auditor's mind?"

"Certainly. There are simple predisposing tapes that can be inserted as desired. Love, adventure, cerebration—it makes no difference."

Several of the bystanders clacked sounds out to each other. Sollenar looked at them narrowly. It was obvious there had to be more than one English-speaker among these people.

"And the device you gave Burr," he asked the engineer, neither calmly nor hopefully, "what sort of stories could its auditors tell themselves?"

The Martian cocked his head again. It gave him the look of an owl at a bedroom window. "Oh, there was one situation we were particularly instructed to include. Burr said he was thinking ahead to showing it to an acquaintance of his.

"It was a situation of adventure; of adventure with the fearful. And it was to end in loss and bitterness." The Martian looked even more closely at Sollenar. "Of course, the device does not specify details. No one but the auditor can know what fearful thing inhabits his story, or precisely how the end of it would come. You would, I believe, be Rufus Sollenar? Burr spoke of you and made the noise of laughing."

Sollenar opened his mouth. But there was nothing to say.

"You want such a device?" the Martian asked. "We've prepared several since Burr left. He spoke of machines that would manufacture them in astronomical numbers. We, of course, have done our best with our poor hands."

Sollenar said: "I would like to look out your door."

"Pleasure."

Sollenar opened the door slightly. Mr. Ermine stood in the cleared street, motionless as the shadow buildings behind him. He raised one hand in a gesture of unfelt greeting as he saw Sollenar, then put it back on the stock of his rifle. Sollenar closed the door and turned to the Martian. "How much currency do you want?"

"Oh, all you have with you. You people always have a good deal with you when you travel."

Sollenar plunged his hands into his pockets and pulled out his billfold, his change, his keys, his jeweled radio; whatever was there, he rummaged out onto the floor, listening to the sound of rolling coins.

"I wish I had more here," he laughed. "I wish I had the amount that man out there is going to recover when he shoots me."

The Martian engineer cocked his head. "But your dream is over, Mr. Sollenar," he clacked dryly. "Isn't it?"

"Quite so. But you to your purposes and I to mine. Now give me one of those projectors. And set it to predispose a situation I am about to specify to you. Take however long it needs. The audience is a patient one." He laughed, and tears gathered in his eyes.

Mr. Ermine waited, isolated from the cold, listening to hear whether the rifle stock was slipping out of his fingers. He had no desire to go into the Martian building after Sollenar and involve third parties. All he wanted was to put Sollenar's body under a dated marker, with as little trouble as possible.

Now and then he walked a few paces backward and forward, to keep from losing muscular control at his extremities because of low skin temperature. Sollenar must come out soon enough. He had no food supply with him, and though Ermine did not like the risk of engaging a man like Sollenar in a starvation contest, there was no doubt that a man with no taste for fuel could outlast one with the acquired reflexes of eating.

The door opened and Sollenar came out.

He was carrying something. Perhaps a weapon. Ermine let him come closer while he raised and carefully sighted his rifle. Sollenar might have some Martian weapon or he might not. Ermine did not particularly care. If Ermine died, he would hardly notice it—far less than he would notice a botched ending to a job of work already roiled by Sollenar's break away at the space field. If Ermine died, some other SPRO agent would be assigned almost immediately. No matter what happened, SPRO would stop Sollenar before he ever reached Abernathy Field.

So there was plenty of time to aim an unhurried, clean shot.

Sollenar was closer, now. He seemed to be in a very agitated frame of mind. He held out whatever he had in his hand.

It was another one of the Martian entertainment machines. Sollenar seemed to be offering it as a token to Ermine. Ermine smiled.

"What can you offer me, Mr. Sollenar?" he said, and shot.

The golden ball rolled away over the sand. "There, now," Ermine said. *"Now,* wouldn't you sooner be me than you? And where is the thing that made the difference between us?"

He shivered. He was chilly. Sand was blowing against

his tender face, which had been somewhat abraded during his long wait.

He stopped, transfixed.

He lifted his head.

Then, with a great swing of his arms, he sent the rifle whirling away. "The wind!" he sighed into the thin air. "I feel the wind." He leapt into the air, and sand flew away from his feet as he landed. He whispered to himself: "I feel the ground!"

He stared in tremblant joy at Sollenar's empty body. "What have you given me?" Full of his own rebirth, he swung his head up at the sky again, and cried in the direction of the sun: "Oh, you squeezing, nibbling people who made me incorruptible and thought that was the end of me!"

With love he buried Sollenar, and with reverence he put up the marker, but he had plans for what he might accomplish with the facts of this transaction, and the myriad others he was privy to.

A sharp bit of pottery had penetrated the sole of his shoe and gashed his foot, but he, not having seen it, hadn't felt it. Nor would he see it or feel it even when he changed his stockings; for he had not noticed the wound when it was made. It didn't matter. In a few days it would heal, though not as rapidly as if it had been properly attended to.

Vaguely, he heard the sound of Martians clacking behind their closed door as he hurried out of the city, full of revenge, and reverence for his savior.

FAITH OF OUR FATHERS

Philip K. Dick

The psychedelic revolution was no longer in the realm of science fiction even back in the dim, half-forgotten days of 1967 when this story first was published. At that distant point in time a good many people, including a few of your favorite science fiction writers, were already turning on and tuning in, if not necessarily dropping out. It would be an anachronistic error, then, to think that Phil Dick was crystal-balling the drug situation of the 1970s in this story; he was simply fastening on something that had begun to pervade the society of the time at which he was writing, and using it as his jumping-off point. What we have here, then, is not yet another dreary chunk of hallucinogenic propaganda; rather, it's a characteristically Dickian and characteristically brilliant exploration of the tricky nature of reality, which chooses to employ a couple of contemporary obsessions (drugs and Southeast Asia) as guiding metaphors for its theme.

On the streets of Hanoi he found himself facing a legless peddler who rode a little wooden cart and called shrilly to every passerby. Chien slowed, listened, but did not stop; business at the Ministry of Cultural Artifacts cropped into his mind and deflected his attention; it was as if he were alone, and none of those on bicycles and scooters and jet-powered motorcycles remained. And likewise it was as if the legless peddler did not exist.

"Comrade," the peddler called, however, and pursued him on his cart; a helium battery operated the drive and sent the cart scuttling expertly after Chien. "I possess a wide spectrum of time-tested herbal remedies complete with testimonials from thousands of loyal users; advise me of your malady and I can assist."

Chien, pausing, said, "Yes, but I have no malady." Except, he thought, for the chronic one of those employed by the Central Committee, that of career opportunism testing constantly the gates of each official position. Including mine.

"I can cure for example radiation sickness," the peddler chanted, still pursuing him. "Or expand, if necessary, the element of sexual prowess. I can reverse carcinomatous progressions, even the dreaded melanomae, what you would call black cancers." Lifting a tray of bottles, small aluminum cans, and assorted powders in plastic jars, the peddler sang, "If a rival persists in trying to usurp your gainful bureaucratic position, I can purvey an ointment which, appearing as a dermal balm, is in actuality a desperately effective toxin. And my prices, comrade, are low. And as a special favor to one so distinguished in bearing as yourself I will accept the postwar inflationary paper dollars reputedly of international exchange but in reality damn near no better than bathroom tissue."

"Go to hell," Chien said, and signaled a passing hovercar taxi; he was already three and one half minutes late for his first appointment of the day, and his various fat-assed superiors at the Ministry would be making quick mental notations—as would, to an even greater degree, his subordinates.

The peddler said quietly, "But, comrade; you *must* buy from me."

"Why?" Chien demanded. Indignation.

"Because, comrade, I am a war veteran. I fought in

the Colossal Final War of National Liberation with the People's Democratic United Front against the Imperialists; I lost my pedal extremities at the battle of San Francisco." His tone was triumphant, now, and sly. *"It is the law.* If you refuse to buy wares offered by a veteran you risk a fine and possible jail sentence—and in addition disgrace."

Wearily, Chien nodded the hovercab on. "Admittedly," he said. "Okay, I must buy from you." He glanced summarily over the meager display of herbal remedies, seeking one at random. "That," he decided, pointing to a paper-wrapped parcel in the rear row.

The peddler laughed. "That, comrade, is a spermatocide, bought by women who for political reasons cannot qualify for The Pill. It would be of shallow use to you, in fact none at all, since you are a gentleman."

"The law," Chien said bitingly, "does not require me to purchase anything useful from you; only that I purchase something. I'll take that." He reached into his padded coat for his billfold, huge with the postwar inflationary bills in which, four times a week, he as a government servant was paid.

"Tell me your problems," the peddler said.

Chien stared at him. Appalled by the invasion of privacy—and done by someone outside the government.

"All right, comrade," the peddler said, seeing his expression. "I will not probe; excuse me. But as a doctor—an herbal healer—it is fitting that I know as much as possible." He pondered, his gaunt features somber. "Do you watch television unusually much?" he asked abruptly.

Taken by surprise, Chien said, "Every evening. Except on Friday when I go to my club to practice the esoteric imported art from the defeated West of steer-roping." It was his only indulgence; other than that, he had totally devoted himself to Party activities.

The peddler reached, selected a gray paper packet. "Sixty trade dollars," he stated. "With a full guarantee;

if it does not do as promised, return the unused portion for a full and cheery refund."

"And what," Chien said cuttingly, "is it guaranteed to do?"

"It will rest eyes fatigued by the countenance of meaningless official monologues," the peddler said. "A soothing preparation; take it as soon as you find yourself exposed to the usual dry and lengthy sermons which—"

Chien paid the money, accepted the packet, and strode off. Balls, he said to himself. It's a racket, he decided, the ordinance setting up war vets as a privileged class. They prey off us—we, the younger ones—like raptors.

Forgotten, the gray packet remained deposited in his coat pocket, as he entered the imposing postwar Ministry of Cultural Artifacts building, and his own considerable stately office, to begin his workday.

A portly, middle-aged Caucasian male, wearing a brown Hong Kong silk suit, double-breasted with vest, waited in his office. With the unfamiliar Caucasian stood his own immediate superior, Ssu-Ma Tso-pin. Tso-pin introduced the two of them in Cantonese, a dialect which he used badly.

"Mr. Tung Chien, this is Mr. Darius Pethel. Mr. Pethel will be headmaster at the new ideological and cultural establishment of didactic character soon to open at San Fernando, California." He added, "Mr. Pethel has had a rich and full lifetime supporting the people's struggle to unseat imperialist-bloc countries via pedagogic media; therefore this high post."

They shook hands.

"Tea?" Chien asked the two of them; he pressed the switch of his infrared hibachi and in an instant the water in the highly ornamented ceramic pot—of Japanese origin—began to burble. As he seated himself at his desk he saw that trustworthy Miss Hsi had laid out the information poop-sheet (confidential) on Comrade

Pethel; he glanced over it, meanwhile pretending to be doing nothing in particular.

"The Absolute Benefactor of the People," Tso-pin said, "has personally met Mr. Pethel and trusts him. This is rare. The school in San Fernando will appear to teach run-of-the-mill Taoist philosophies but will, of course, in actuality maintain for us a channel of communication to the liberal and intellectual youth segment of western U.S. There are many of them still alive, from San Diego to Sacramento; we estimate at least ten thousand. The school will accept two thousand. Enrollment will be mandatory for those we select. Your relationship to Mr. Pethel's programing is grave. Ahem; your tea water is boiling."

"Thank you," Chien murmured, dropping in the bag of Lipton's tea.

Tso-pin continued, "Although Mr. Pethel will supervise the setting up of the courses of instruction presented by the school to its student body, all examination papers will oddly enough be relayed here to your office for your own expert, careful, ideological study. In other words, Mr. Chien, you will determine who among the two thousand students is reliable, which are truly responding to the programing and who is not."

"I will now pour my tea," Chien said, doing so ceremoniously.

"What we have to realize," Pethel rumbled in Cantonese even worse than that of Tso-pin, "is that, once having lost the global war to us, the American youth has developed a talent for dissembling." He spoke the last word in English; not understanding it, Chien turned inquiringly to his superior.

"Lying," Tso-pin explained.

Pethel said, "Mouthing the proper slogans for surface appearance, but on the inside believing them false. Test papers by this group will closely resemble those of genuine—"

"You mean that the test papers of *two thousand* students will be passing through my office?" Chien demanded. He could not believe it. "That's a full-time job in itself; I don't have time for anything remotely resembling that." He was appalled. "To give critical, official approval or denial of the astute variety which you're envisioning—" He gestured. "Screw that," he said, in English.

Blinking at the strong, Western vulgarity, Tso-pin said, "You have a staff. Plus also you can requisition several more from the pool; the Ministry's budget, augmented this year, will permit it. And remember: the Absolute Benefactor of the People has handpicked Mr. Pethel." His tone, now, had become ominous, but only subtly so. Just enough to penetrate Chien's hysteria, and to wither it into submission. At least temporarily. To underline his point, Tso-pin walked to the far end of the office; he stood before the full-length 3-D portrait of the Absolute Benefactor, and after an interval his proximity triggered the tape-transport mounted behind the portrait; the face of the Benefactor moved, and from it came a familiar homily, in more than familiar accents. "Fight for peace, my sons," it intoned gently, firmly.

"Ha," Chien said, still perturbed, but concealing it. Possibly one of the Ministry's computers could sort the examination papers; a yes-no-maybe structure could be employed, in conjunction with a preanalysis of the pattern of ideological correctness—and incorrectness. The matter could be made routine. Probably.

Darius Pethel said, "I have with me certain material which I would like you to scrutinize, Mr. Chien." He unzipped an unsightly, old-fashioned, plastic briefcase. "Two examination essays," he said as he passed the documents to Chien. "This will tell us if you're qualified." He then glanced at Tso-pin; their gazes met. "I understand," Pethel said, "that if you are successful in this venture you will be made vice-councilor of the Ministry, and His Greatness the Absolute Benefactor of the People will personally confer Kisterigian's medal on you." Both he and Tso-pin smiled in wary unison.

"The Kisterigian medal," Chien echoed; he accepted the examination papers, glanced over them in a show of leisurely indifference. But within him his heart vibrated in ill-concealed tension. "Why these two? By that I mean, what am I looking for, sir?"

"One of them," Pethel said, "is the work of a dedicated progressive, a loyal Party member of thoroughly researched conviction. The other is by a young *stilyagi* whom we suspect of holding petit bourgeois imperialist degenerate crypto-ideas. It is up to you, sir, to determine which is which."

Thanks a lot, Chien thought. But, nodding, he read the title of the top paper.

DOCTRINES OF THE ABSOLUTE BENEFACTOR ANTICIPATED IN THE POETRY OF BAHA AD-DIN ZUHAYR, OF THIRTEENTH-CENTURY ARABIA.

Glancing down the initial pages of the essay, Chien saw a quatrain familiar to him; it was called "Death" and he had known it most of his adult, educated life.

Once he will miss, twice he will miss,
He only chooses one of many hours;
For him nor deep nor hill there is,
But all's one level plain he hunts for flowers.

"Powerful," Chien said. "This poem."

"He makes use of the poem," Pethel said, observing Chien's lips moving as he reread the quatrain, "to indicate the age-old wisdom, displayed by the Absolute Benefactor in our current lives, that no individual is safe; everyone is mortal, and only the suprapersonal, historically essential cause survives. As it should be. Would you agree with him? With this student, I mean? Or—"

Pethel paused. "Is he in fact perhaps satirizing the Absolute Benefactor's promulgations?"

Cagily, Chien said, "Give me a chance to inspect the other paper."

"You need no further information; decide."

Haltingly, Chien said, "I—had never thought of this poem that way." He felt irritable. "Anyhow, it isn't by Baha ad-Din Zuhayr; it's part of the *Thousand and One Nights* anthology. It is, however, thirteenth century; I admit that." He quickly read over the text of the paper accompanying the poem. It appeared to be a routine, uninspired rehash of Party clichés, all of them familiar to him from birth. The blind, imperialist monster who mowed down and snuffed out (mixed metaphor) human aspiration, the calculations of the still extant anti-Party group in eastern United States . . . . He felt dully bored, and as uninspired as the student's paper. We must persevere, the paper declared. Wipe out the Pentagon remnants in the Catskills, subdue Tennessee and most especially the pocket of die-hard reaction in the red hills of Oklahoma. He sighed.

"I think," Tso-pin said, "we should allow Mr. Chien the opportunity of observing this difficult matter at his leisure." To Chien he said, "You have permission to take them home to your condominium, this evening, and adjudge them on your own time." He bowed, half mockingly, half solicitously. In any case, insult or not, he had gotten Chien off the hook, and for that Chien was grateful.

"You are most kind," he murmured, "to allow me to perform this new and highly stimulating labor on my own time. Mikoyan, were he alive today, would approve." You bastard, he said to himself. Meaning both his superior and the Caucasian Pethel. Handing me a hot potato like this, and on my own time. Obviously the CP USA is in trouble; its indoctrination academies aren't managing to do their job with the notoriously mulish, eccentric Yank youths. And you've passed that hot potato on and on until it reaches me.

Thanks for nothing, he thought acidly.

That evening in his small but well-appointed condominium apartment he read over the other of the two examination papers, this one by a Marion Culper, and discovered that it, too, dealt with poetry. Obviously this was speciously a poetry class, and he felt ill. It had always run against his grain, the use of poetry—of any art—for social purposes. Anyhow, comfortable in his special spine-straightening, simulated-leather easy chair, he lit a Cuesta Rey Number One English Market immense corona cigar and began to read.

The writer of the paper, Miss Culper, had selected as her text a portion of a poem of John Dryden, the seventeenth-century English poet, final lines from the well-known "A Song for St. Cecilia's Day."

> . . . So when the last and dreadful hour
> This crumbling pageant shall devour,
> The trumpet shall be heard on high,
> The dead shall live, the living die,
> And Music shall untune the sky.

Well, that's a hell of a thing, Chien thought to himself bitingly. Dryden, we're supposed to believe, anticipated the fall of capitalism? That's what he meant by the "crumbling pageant"? Christ. He leaned over to take hold of his cigar and found that it had gone out. Groping in his pockets for his Japanese-made lighter, he half rose to his feet. . . .

Tweeeeeee! the TV set at the far end of the living room said.

Aha, Chien said. We're about to be addressed by the Leader. By the Absolute Benefactor of the People, up there in Peking where he's lived for ninety years now;

or is it one hundred? Or, as we sometimes like to think of him, the Ass—

"May the ten thousand blossoms of abject self-assumed poverty flower in your spiritual courtyard," the TV announcer said. With a groan, Chien rose to his feet, bowed the mandatory bow of response; each TV set came equipped with monitoring devices to narrate to the Secpol, the Security Police, whether its owner was bowing and/or watching.

On the screen a clearly defined visage manifested itself, the wide, unlined, healthy features of the one-hundred-and-twenty-year-old leader of CP East, ruler of many—far too many, Chien reflected. Blah to you, he thought, and reseated himself in his simulated-leather easy chair, now facing the TV screen.

"My thoughts," the Absolute Benefactor said in his rich and slow tones, "are on you, my children. And especially on Mr. Tung Chien of Hanoi, who faces a difficult task ahead, a task to enrich the people of Democratic East, plus the American West Coast. We must think in unison about this noble, dedicated man and the chore which he faces, and I have chosen to take several moments of my time to honor him and encourage him. Are you listening, Mr. Chien?"

"Yes, Your Greatness," Chien said, and pondered to himself the odds against the Party Leader singling *him* out this particular evening. The odds caused him to feel uncomradely cynicism; it was unconvincing. Probably this transmission was being beamed to his apartment building alone—or at least this city. It might also be a lip-sync job, done at Hanoi TV, Incorporated. In any case he was required to listen and watch—and absorb. He did so, from a lifetime of practice. Outwardly he appeared to be rigidly attentive. Inwardly he was still mulling over the two test papers, wondering which was which; where did devout Party enthusiasm end and sardonic lampoonery begin? Hard to say . . . which of course explained why they had dumped the task in his lap.

Again he groped in his pockets for his lighter—and found the small gray envelope which the war-veteran peddler had sold him. Gawd, he thought, remembering what it had cost. Money down the drain and what did this herbal remedy do? Nothing. He turned the packet over and saw, on the back, small printed words. Well, he thought, and began to unfold the packet with care. The words had snared him—as of course they were meant to do.

> Failing as a Party member and human?
> Afraid of becoming obsolete and dis-
> carded on the ash heap of history by

He read rapidly through the text, ignoring its claims, seeking to find out what he had purchased.

Meanwhile the Absolute Benefactor droned on.

Snuff. The package contained snuff. Countless tiny black grains, like gunpowder, which sent up an interesting aromatic to tickle his nose. The title of the particular blend was Princes Special, he discovered. And very pleasing, he decided. At one time he had taken snuff—smoked tobacco for a time having been illegal for reasons of health—back during his student days at Peking U; it had been the fad, especially the amatory mixes prepared in Chungking, made from god knew what. Was this that? Almost any aromatic could be added to snuff, from essence of orange to pulverized babycrap . . . or so some seemed, especially an English mixture called High Dry Toast which had in itself more or less put an end to his yearning for nasal, inhaled tobacco.

On the TV screen the Absolute Benefactor rumbled monotonously on as Chien sniffed cautiously at the powder, read the claims—it cured everything from being late to work to falling in love with a woman of dubious political background. Interesting. But typical of claims—

His doorbell rang.

Rising, he walked to the door, opened it with full knowledge of what he would find. There, sure enough, stood Mou Kuei, the Building Warden, small and hard-eyed and alert to his task; he had his armband and metal helmet on, showing that he meant business. "Mr. Chien, comrade Party worker. I received a call from the television authority. You are failing to watch your screen and are instead fiddling with a packet of doubtful content." He produced a clipboard and ballpoint pen. "Two red marks, and hithertonow you are summarily ordered to repose yourself in a comfortable, stress-free posture before your screen and give the Leader your unexcelled attention. His words, this evening, are directed particularly to you, sir; to you."

"I doubt that," Chien heard himself say.

Blinking, Kuei said, "What do you mean?"

"The Leader rules eight billion comrades. He isn't going to single me out." He felt wrathful; the punctuality of the warden's reprimand irked him.

Kuei said, "But I distinctly heard with my own ears. You were mentioned."

Going over to the TV set, Chien turned the volume up. "But now he's talking about failures in People's India; that's of no relevance to me."

"Whatever the Leader expostulates is relevant." Mou Kuei scratched a mark on his clipboard sheet, bowed formally, turned away. "My call to come up here to confront you with your slackness originated at Central. Obviously they regard your attention as important; I must order you to set in motion your automatic transmission recording circuit and replay the earlier portions of the Leader's speech."

Chien farted. And shut the door.

Back to the TV set, he said to himself. Where our leisure hours are spent. And there lay the two student examination papers; he had that weighing him down, too. And all on my own time, he thought savagely. The hell with them. Up theirs. He strode to the TV set, started to shut it off; at once a red warning light winked on, informing him that he did not have permission to shut off the set—could not in fact end its tirade and image even if he unplugged it. Mandatory speeches, he thought, will kill us all, bury us; if I could be free of the noise of speeches, free of the din of the Party baying as it hounds mankind . . . .

There was no known ordinance, however, preventing him from taking snuff while he watched the Leader. So, opening the small gray packet, he shook out a mound of the black granules onto the back of his left hand. He then, professionally, raised his hand to his nostrils and deeply inhaled, drawing the snuff well up into his sinus cavities. Imagine the old superstition, he thought to himself. That the sinus cavities are connected to the brain, and hence an inhalation of snuff directly affects the cerebral cortex. He smiled, seated himself once more, fixed his gaze on the TV screen and the gesticulating individual known so utterly to them all.

The face dwindled away, disappeared. The sound ceased. He faced an emptiness, a vacuum. The screen, white and blank, confronted him and from the speaker a faint hiss sounded.

The frigging snuff, he said to himself. And inhaled greedily at the remainder of the powder on his hand, drawing it up avidly into his nose, his sinuses, and, or so it felt, into his brain; he plunged into the snuff, absorbing it elatedly.

The screen remained blank and then, by degrees, an image once more formed and established itself. It was not the Leader. Not the Absolute Benefactor of the People; in point of fact not a human figure at all.

He faced a dead mechanical construct, made of solid-state circuits, of swiveling pseudopodia, lenses, and a squawk-box. And the box began, in a droning din, to harangue him.

Staring fixedly, he thought, *What is this?* Reality? Hallucination, he thought. The peddler came across some of the psychedelic drugs used during the War of Liberation—he's selling the stuff and I've taken some, taken a whole lot!

Making his way unsteadily to the vidphone he dialed the Secpol station nearest his building. "I wish to report a pusher of hallucinogenic drugs," he said into the receiver.

"Your name, sir, and conapt location?" Efficient, brisk, and impersonal bureaucrat of the police.

He gave them the information, then haltingly made it back to his simulated-leather easy chair, once again to witness the apparition on the TV screen. This is lethal, he said to himself. It must be some preparation developed in Washington, D.C., or London—stronger and stranger than the LSD-25 which they dumped so effectively into our reservoirs. And I thought it was going to relieve me of the burden of the Leader's speeches . . . this is far worse, this electronic, sputtering, swiveling, metal and plastic monstrosity yammering away—this is terrifying.

To have to face *this* the remainder of my life—

It took ten minutes for the Secpol two-man team to come rapping at his door. And by then, in a deteriorating set of stages, the familiar image of the Leader had seeped back into focus on the screen, had supplanted the horrible artificial construct which waved its 'podia and squalled on and on. He let the two cops in shakily, led them to the table on which he had left the remains of the snuff in its packet.

"Psychedelic toxin," he said thickly. "Of short duration. Absorbed into the blood stream directly, through nasal capillaries. I'll give you details as to where I got it, from whom, all that." He took a deep shaky breath; the presence of the police was comforting.

Ballpoint pens ready, the two officers waited. And all the time, in the background, the Leader rattled out his endless speech. As he had done a thousand evenings before in the life of Tung Chien. But, he thought, it'll never be the same again, at least not for me. Not after inhaling that near-toxic snuff.

He wondered, Is that what they intended?

It seemed odd to him, thinking of a *they*. Peculiar—but somehow correct. For an instant he hesitated, not giving out the details, not telling the police enough to find the man. A peddler, he started to say. I don't know where; can't remember. But he did; he remembered the exact street intersection. So, with unexplainable reluctance, he told them.

"Thank you, Comrade Chien." The boss of the team of police carefully gathered up the remaining snuff—most of it remained—and placed it in his uniform—smart, sharp uniform—pocket. "We'll have it analyzed at the first available moment," the cop said, "and inform you immediately in case counter medical measures are indicated for you. Some of the old wartime psychedelics were eventually fatal, as you have no doubt read."

"I've read," he agreed. That had been specifically what he had been thinking.

"Good luck and thanks for notifying us," both cops said, and departed. The affair, for all their efficiency, did not seem to shake them; obviously such a complaint was routine.

The lab report came swiftly—surprisingly so, in view of the vast state bureaucracy. It reached him by vidphone before the Leader had finished his TV speech.

"It's not a hallucinogen," the Secpol lab technician informed him.

"No?" he said, puzzled and, strangely, not relieved. Not at all.

"On the contrary. It's a phenothiazine, which as you doubtless know is antihallucinogenic. A strong dose per gram of admixture, but harmless. Might lower your blood pressure or make you sleepy. Probably stolen from a wartime cache of medical supplies. Left by the retreating barbarians. I wouldn't worry."

Pondering, Chien hung up the vidphone in slow motion. And then walked to the window of his conapt—the window with the fine view of other Hanoi high-rise conapts—to think.

The doorbell rang. Feeling as if he were in a trance, he crossed the carpeted living room to answer it.

The girl standing there, in a tan raincoat with a babushka over her dark, shiny, and very long hair, said in a timid little voice, "Um, Comrade Chien? Tung Chien? Of the Ministry of—"

He led her in, reflexively, and shut the door after her. "You've been monitoring my vidphone," he told her; it was a shot in darkness, but something in him, an unvoiced certitude, told him that she had.

"Did—they take the rest of the snuff?" She glanced about. "Oh, I hope not; it's so hard to get these days."

"Snuff," he said, "is easy to get. Phenothiazine isn't. Is that what you mean?"

The girl raised her head, studied him with large, moon-darkened eyes. "Yes. Mr. Chien—" She hesitated, obviously as uncertain as the Secpol cops had been assured. "Tell me what you saw; it's of great importance for us to be certain."

"I had a choice?" he said acutely.

"Y-yes, very much so. That's what confuses us; that's what is not as we planned. We don't understand; it fits nobody's theory." Her eyes even darker and deeper, she said, "Was it the aquatic horror shape? The thing with slime and teeth, the extraterrestrial life form? Please tell me; we have to know." She breathed irregularly, with effort, the tan raincoat rising and falling; he found himself watching its rhythm.

"A machine," he said

"Oh!" She ducked her head, nodding vigorously.

"Yes, I understand; a mechanical organism in no way resembling a human. Not a simulacrum, something constructed to resemble a man."

He said, "This did not look like a man." He added to himself, And it failed—did not try—to talk like a man.

"You understand that it was not an hallucination."

"I've been officially told that what I took was a phenothiazine. That's all I know." He said as little as possible; he did not want to talk but to hear. Hear what the girl had to say.

"Well, Mr. Chien—" She took a deep, unstable breath. "If it was not an hallucination, then what was it? What does that leave? What is called 'extraconsciousness'—could that be it?"

He did not answer; turning his back, he leisurely picked up the two student test papers, glanced over them, ignoring her. Waiting for her next attempt.

At his shoulder, she appeared, smelling of spring rain, smelling of sweetness and agitation, beautiful in the way she smelled, and looked, and, he thought, speaks. So different from the harsh plateau speech patterns we hear on the TV—have heard since I was a baby.

"Some of them," she said huskily, "who take the stelazine—it was stelazine you got, Mr. Chien—see one apparition, some another. But distinct categories have emerged; there is not an infinite variety. Some see what you saw; we call it the Clanker. Some the aquatic horror; that's the Gulper. And then there's the Bird, and the Climbing Tube, and—" She broke off. "But other reactions tell you very little. Tell *us* very little." She hesitated, then plunged on. "Now that this has happened to you, Mr. Chien, we would like you to join our gathering. Join your particular group, those who see what you see. Group Red. We want to know what it *really* is, and—" She gestured with tapered, wax-smooth fingers. "It can't be *all* those manifestations." Her tone was poignant, naïvely so. He felt his caution relax—a trifle.

He said, "What do you see? You in particular?"

"I'm a part of Group Yellow. I see—a storm. A whining, vicious whirlwind. That roots everything up, crushes condominium apartments built to last a century." She smiled wanly. "The Crusher. Twelve groups in all, Mr. Chien. Twelve absolutely different experiences, all from the same phenothiazines, all of the Leader as he speaks over TV. As *it* speaks, rather." She smiled up at him, lashes long—probably protracted artificially—and gaze engaging, even trusting. As if she thought he knew something or could do something.

"I should make a citizen's arrest of you," he said presently.

"There is no law, not about this. We studied Soviet juridical writings before we—found people to distribute the stelazine. We don't have much of it; we have to be very careful whom we give it to. It seemed to us that you constituted a likely choice . . . a well-known, postwar, dedicated young career man on his way up." From his fingers she took the examination papers. "They're having you pol-read?" she asked.

" 'Pol-read'?" He did not know the term.

"Study something said or written to see if it fits the Party's current world view. You in the hierarchy merely call it 'read,' don't you?" Again she smiled. "When you rise one step higher, up with Mr. Tso-pin, you will know that expression." She added somberly, "And with Mr. Pethel. He's very far up. Mr. Chien, there is no ideological school in San Fernando; these are forged exam papers, designed to read back to them a thorough analysis of *your* political ideology. And have you been able to distinguish which paper is orthodox and which is heretical?" Her voice was pixie-like, taunting with amused malice. "Choose the wrong one and your budding career stops dead, cold, in its tracks. Choose the proper one—"

"Do you know which is which?" he demanded.

"Yes." She nodded soberly. "We have listening devices in Mr. Tso-pin's inner offices; we monitored his conversation with Mr. Pethel—who is not Mr. Pethel but the Higher Secpol Inspector Judd Craine. You have possibly heard mention of him; he acted as chief assistant to Judge Vorlawsky at the '98 war crimes trial in Zurich."

With difficulty he said, "I—see." Well, that explained that.

The girl said, "My name is Tanya Lee."

He said nothing; he merely nodded, too stunned for any cerebration.

"Technically, I am a minor clerk," Miss Lee said, "a your Ministry. You have never run into me, however, that I can at least recall. We try to hold posts wherever we can. As far up as possible. My own boss—"

"Should you be telling me this?" He gestured at the TV set, which remained on. "Aren't they picking this up?"

Tanya Lee said, 'We introduced a noise factor in the reception of both vid and aud material from this apartment building; it will take them almost an hour to locate the sheathing. So we have"—she examined the tiny wristwatch on her slender wrist—"fifteen more minutes. And still be safe."

"Tell me," he said, "which paper is orthodox."

"Is that what you care about? Really?"

"What," he said, "should I care about?"

"Don't you see, Mr. Chien? You've learned something. The Leader is not the Leader; he is something else, but we can't tell what. Not yet. Mr. Chien, with all due respect, have you ever had your drinking water analyzed? I know it sounds paranoiac, but have you?"

"No," he said "Of course not." Knowing what she was going to say.

Miss Lee said briskly, "Our tests show that it's saturated with hallucinogens. It is, has been, will continue to be. Not the ones used during the war; not the disorienting ones, but a synthetic quasi-ergot derivative called Datrox-3. You drink it here in the building from the time you get up; you drink it in restaurants and other apartments that you visit. You drink it at the Ministry; it's all piped from a central, common source." Her tone was bleak and ferocious. "We solved that problem; we knew, as soon as we discovered it, that any good phenothiazine would counter it. What we did not know, of course, was this—a *variety* of authentic experiences; that makes no sense, rationally. It's the hallucination which should differ from person to person, and the reality experience which should be ubiquitous—it's all turned around. We can't even construct an ad hoc theory which accounts for that, and god knows we've tried. Twelve mutually exclusive hallucinations—that would be easily understood. But not one hallucination and twelve realities." She ceased talking, then, and studied the two test papers, her forehead wrinkling. "The one with the Arabic poem is orthodox," she stated. "If you tell them that they'll trust you and give you a higher post. You'll be another notch up in the hierarchy of Party officialdom." Smiling—her teeth were perfect and lovely—she finished, "Look what you received back for your investment this morning. Your career is underwritten for a time. And by us."

He said, "I don't believe you." Instinctively, his caution operated within him, always, the caution of a lifetime lived among the hatchet men of the Hanoi branch of the CP East. They knew an infinitude of ways by which to ax a rival out of contention—some of which he himself had employed; some of which he had seen done to himself and to others. This could be a novel way, one unfamiliar to him. It could always be.

"Tonight," Miss Lee said, "in the speech the Leader singled you out. Didn't this strike you as strange? You, of all people? A minor officeholder in a meager ministry—"

"Admitted," he said. "It struck me that way; yes."

"That was legitimate. His Greatness is grooming an elite cadre of younger men, postwar men, he hopes will infuse new life into the hidebound, moribund hierarchy of old fogies and Party hacks. His Greatness singled you out for the same reason that we singled you out; if pursued properly, your career could lead you all the way to the top. At least for a time . . . as we know. That's how it goes."

He thought, So virtually everyone has faith in me. Except myself; and certainly not after this, the experience with the antihallucinatory snuff. It had shaken years of confidence, and no doubt rightly so. However, he was beginning to regain his poise; he felt it seeping back, a little at first, then with a rush.

Going to the vidphone, he lifted the receiver and began, for the second time that night, to dial the number of the Hanoi Security Police.

"Turning me in," Miss Lee said, "would be the second most regressive decision you could make. I'll tell them that you brought me here to bribe me; you thought, because of my job at the Ministry, I would know which examination paper to select."

He said, "And what would be my first most regressive decision?"

"Not taking a further dose of phenothiazine," Miss Lee said evenly.

Hanging up the phone, Tung Chien thought to himself, I don't understand what's happening to me. Two forces, the Party and His Greatness on one hand—this girl with her alleged group on the other. One wants me to rise as far as possible in the Party hierarchy; the other —*What did Tanya Lee want?* Underneath the words, inside the membrane of an almost trivial contempt for the Party, the Leader, the ethical standards of the People's Democratic United Front—what was she after in regard to him?

He said curiously, "Are you anti-Party?"

"No."

"But—" He gestured. "That's all there is; Party and anti-Party. You must be Party, then." Bewildered, he stared at her; with composure she returned the stare. "You have an organization," he said, "and you meet. What do you intend to destroy? The regular function of government? Are you like the treasonable college students of the United States during the Vietnam War who stopped troop trains, demonstrated—"

Wearily Miss Lee said, "It wasn't like that. But forget it; that's not the issue. What we want to know is this: who or what is leading us? We must penetrate far enough to enlist someone, some rising young Party theoretician, who could conceivably be invited to a tête-à-tête with the Leader—you see?" Her voice lifted; she consulted her watch, obviously anxious to get away: the fifteen minutes were almost up. "Very few persons actually see the Leader, as you know. I mean really see him."

"Seclusion," he said. "Due to his advanced age."

"We have hope," Miss Lee said, "that if you pass the phony test which they have arranged for you—and with my help you have—you will be invited to one of the stag parties which the Leader has from time to time, which of course the 'papes don't report. Now do you see?" Her voice rose shrilly, in a frenzy of despair. "Then we would know; if you could go in there under the influence of the antihallucinogenic drug, could see him face to face as he actually is—"

Thinking aloud, he said, "And end my career of public service. If not my life."

"You owe us something," Tanya Lee snapped, her cheeks white. "If I hadn't told you which exam paper to choose you would have picked the wrong one and your dedicated public service career would be over anyhow; you would have failed—failed at a test you didn't even realize you were taking!"

He said mildly, "I had a fifty-fifty chance."

"No." She shook her head fiercely. "The heretical one is faked up with a lot of Party jargon; they deliberately constructed the two texts to trap you. They *wanted* you to fail!"

Once more he examined the two papers, feeling confused. Was she right? Possibly. Probably. It rang true, knowing the Party functionaries as he did, and Tso-pin, his superior, in particular. He felt weary then. Defeated. After a time he said to the girl, "What you're trying to get out of me is a quid pro quo. You did something for me—you got, or claim you got—the answer to this Party inquiry. But you've already done your part. What's to keep me from tossing you out of here on your head? I don't have to do a goddam thing." He heard his voice, toneless, sounding the poverty of empathic emotionality so usual in Party circles.

Miss Lee said, "There will be other tests, as you continue to ascend. And we will monitor for you with them too." She was calm, at ease; obviously she had foreseen his reaction.

"How long do I have to think it over?" he said.

"I'm leaving now. We're in no rush; you're not about to receive an invitation to the Leader's Yellow River villa in the next week or even month." Going to the door, opening it, she paused. "As you're given covert rating tests we'll be in contact, supplying the answers—so you'll see one or more of us on those occasions. Probably it won't be me; it'll be that disabled war veteran who'll sell you the correct response sheets as you leave the Ministry building." She smiled a brief, snuffed-out-candle smile. "But one of these days, no doubt unexpectedly, you'll get an ornate, official, very formal invitation to the villa, and when you go you'll be heavily sedated with stelazine . . . possibly our last dose of our dwindling supply. Good night." The door shut after her; she had gone.

My god, he thought. They can blackmail me. For what I've done. And she didn't even bother to mention it; in view of what they're involved with it was not worth mentioning.

But blackmail for what? He had already told the Secpol squad that he had been given a drug which had proved to be a phenothiazine. *Then they know,* he realized. They'll watch me; they're alert. Technically, I haven't broken a law, but—they'll be watching, all right.

However, they always watched anyhow. He relaxed slightly, thinking that. He had, over the years, become virtually accustomed to it, as had everyone.

I will see the Absolute Benefactor of the People as he is, he said to himself. Which possibly no one else has done. What will it be? Which of the subclasses of non-hallucination? Classes which I do not even know about . . . a view which may totally overthrow me. How am I going to be able to get through the evening, to keep my poise, if it's like the shape I saw on the TV screen? The Crusher, the Clanker, the Bird, the Climbing Tube, the Gulper—or worse.

He wondered what some of the other views consisted of . . . and then gave up that line of speculation; it was unprofitable. And too anxiety-inducing.

The next morning Mr. Tso-pin and Mr. Darius Pethel met him in his office, both of them calm but expectant. Wordlessly, he handed them one of the two "exam papers." The orthodox one, with its short and heart-smothering Arabian poem.

"This one," Chien said tightly, "is the product of a dedicated Party member or candidate for membership. The other—" He slapped the remaining sheets. "Reactionary garbage." He felt anger. "In spite of a superficial—"

"All right, Mr. Chien," Pethel said, nodding. "We don't have to explore each and every ramification; your analysis is correct. You heard the mention regarding you in the Leader's speech last night on TV?"

"I certainly did," Chien said.

"So you have undoubtedly inferred," Pethel said, "that there is a good deal involved in what we are attempting here. The Leader has his eye on you; that's clear. As a matter of fact, he has communicated to myself regarding you." He opened his bulging briefcase and rummaged. "Lost the goddam thing. Anyhow—" He glanced at Tso-pin, who nodded slightly. "His Greatness would like to have you appear for dinner at the Yangtze River Ranch next Thursday night. Mrs. Fletcher in particular appreciates—"

Chien said, " 'Mrs. Fletcher'? Who is 'Mrs. Fletcher'?"

After a pause Tso-pin said dryly, "The Absolute Benefactor's wife. His name—which you of course had never heard—is Thomas Fletcher."

"He's a Caucasian," Pethel explained. "Originally from the New Zealand Communist Party; he participated in the difficult take-over there. This news is not in the strict sense secret, but on the other hand it hasn't been noised about." He hesitated, toying with his watch-chain. "Probably it would be better if you forgot about that. Of course, as soon as you meet him, see him face to face, you'll realize that, realize that he's a Cauc. As I am. As many of us are."

"Race," Tso-pin pointed out, "has nothing to do with loyalty to the Leader and the Party. As witness Mr. Pethel, here."

But His Greatness, Chien thought, jolted. He did not appear, on the TV screen, to be occidental. "On TV—" he began.

"The image," Tso-pin interrupted, "is subjected to a variegated assortment of skillful refinements. For ideological purposes. Most persons holding higher offices are aware of this." He eyed Chien with hard criticism.

So everyone agrees, Chien thought. What we see every night is not real. The question is, How unreal? Partially? Or—completely?

"I will be prepared," he said tautly. And he thought, There has been a slipup. They weren't prepared for me—the people that Tanya Lee represents—to gain entry so soon. Where's the antihallucinogen? Can they get it to me or not? Probably not on such short notice.

He felt, strangely, relief. He would be going into the presence of His Greatness in a position to see him as a human being, see him as he—and everybody else—saw him on TV. It would be a most stimulating and cheerful dinner party, with some of the most influential Party members in Asia. I think we can do without the phenothiazines, he said to himself. And his sense of relief grew.

"Here it is, finally," Pethel said suddenly, producing a white envelope from his briefcase. "Your card of admission. You will be flown by Sino-rocket to the Leader's villa Thursday morning; there the protocol officer will brief you on your expected behavior. It will be formal dress, white tie and tails, but the atmosphere will be cordial. There are always a great number of toasts." He added, "I have attended two such stag get-togethers. Mr. Tso-pin"—he smiled creakily—"has not been honored in such a fashion. But as they say, all things come to him who waits. Ben Franklin said that."

Tso-pin said, "It has come for Mr. Chien rather prematurely, I would say." He shrugged philosophically. "But my opinion has never at any time been asked."

"One thing," Pethel said to Chien. "It is possible that when you see His Greatness in person you will be in some regards disappointed. Be alert that you do not let this make itself apparent, if you should so feel. We have, always, tended—been trained—to regard him as more than a man. But at table he is"—he gestured—"a forked radish. In certain respects like ourselves. He may for instance indulge in moderately human oral-aggressive and -passive activity; he possibly may tell an off-color joke or drink too much. . . . To be candid, no one ever knows in advance how these things will work out, but they do generally hold forth until late the following morning. So it would be wise to accept the dosage of amphetamines which the protocol officer will offer you."

"Oh?" Chien said. This was news to him, and interesting.

"For stamina. And to balance the liquor. His Greatness has amazing staying power; he often is still on his feet and raring to go after everyone else has collapsed."

"A remarkable man," Tso-pin chimed in. "I think his—indulgences only show that he is a fine fellow. And fully in the round; he is like the ideal Renaissance man; as, for example, Lorenzo de' Medici."

"That does come to mind," Pethel said; he studied Chien with such intensity that some of last night's chill returned. Am I being led into one trap after another? Chien wondered. That girl—was she in fact an agent of the Secpol probing me, trying to ferret out a disloyal, anti-Party streak in me?

I think, he decided, I will make sure that the legless peddler of herbal remedies does not snare me when I leave work; I'll take a totally different route back to my conapt.

He was successful. That day he avoided the peddler and the same the next, and so on until Thursday.

On Thursday morning the peddler scooted from beneath a parked truck and blocked his way, confronting him.

"My medication?" the peddler demanded. "It helped? I know it did; the formula goes back to the Sung Dynasty—I can tell it did. Right?"

Chien said, "Let me go."

"Would you be kind enough to answer?" The tone was not the expected, customary whining of a street peddler operating in a marginal fashion, and that tone came across to Chien; he heard loud and clear . . . as the Imperialist puppet troops of long ago phrased it.

"I know what you gave me," Chien said. "And I don't want any more. If I change my mind I can pick it up at a pharmacy. Thanks." He started on, but the cart, with the legless occupant, pursued him.

"Miss Lee was talking to me," the peddler said loudly.

"Hmmm," Chien said, and automatically increased his pace; he spotted a hovercab and began signaling for it.

"It's tonight you're going to the stag dinner at the Yangtze River villa," the peddler said, panting for breath in his effort to keep up. "Take the medication—now!" He held out a flat packet, imploringly. "Please, Party Member Chien; for your own sake, for all of us. So we can tell what it is we're up against. Good lord, it may be nonterran; that's our most basic fear. Don't you understand, Chien? What's your goddam career compared with that? If we can't find out—"

The cab bumped to a halt on the pavement; its door slid open. Chien started to board it.

The packet sailed past him, landed on the entrance sill of the cab, then slid into the gutter, damp from earlier rain.

"Please," the peddler said. "And it won't cost you anything; today it's free. Just take it, use it before the stag dinner. And don't use the amphetamines; they're a thalamic stimulant, contraindicated whenever an adrenal suppressant such as a phenothiazine is—"

The door of the cab closed after Chien. He seated himself.

"Where to, comrade?" the robot drive-mechanism inquired.

He gave the ident tag number of his conapt.

"That half-wit of a peddler managed to infiltrate his seedy wares into my clean interior," the cab said. "Notice; it reposes by your foot."

He saw the packet—no more than an ordinary-looking envelope. I guess, he thought, this is how drugs come to you; all of a sudden they're lying there. For a moment he sat, and then he picked it up.

As before, there was a written enclosure above and beyond the medication, but this time, he saw, it was handwritten. A feminine script: from Miss Lee:

We were surprised at the suddenness. But thank heaven we were ready. Where were you Tuesday and Wednesday? Anyhow, here it is, and good luck. I will approach you later in the week; I don't want you to try to find me.

He ignited the note, burned it up in the cab's disposal ashtray.

And kept the dark granules.

All this time, he thought. Hallucinogens in our water supply. Year after year. Decades. And not in wartime but in peacetime. And not to the enemy camp but here in our own. The evil bastards, he said to himself. Maybe I ought to take this; maybe I ought to find out what he or it is and let Tanya's group know.

I will, he decided. And—he was curious.

A bad emotion, he knew. Curiosity was, especially in Party activities, often a terminal state careerwise.

A state which, at the moment, gripped him thoroughly. He wondered if it would last through the evening, if, when it came right down to it, he would actually take the inhalant.

Time would tell. Tell that and everything else. We are blooming flowers, he thought, on the plain, which he picks. As the Arabic poem had put it. He tried to remember the rest of the poem but could not.

That probably was just as well.

The villa protocol officer, a Japanese named Kimo Okubara, tall and husky, obviously a quondam wrestler, surveyed him with innate hostility, even after he presented his engraved invitation and had successfully managed to prove his identity.

"Surprise you bother to come," Okubara muttered. "Why not stay home and watch on TV? Nobody miss you. We got along fine without up to right now."

Chien said tightly, "I've already watched on TV."

And anyhow the stag dinners were rarely televised; they were too bawdy.

Okubara's crew double-checked him for weapons, including the possibility of an anal suppository, and then gave him his clothes back. They did not find the phenothiazine, however. Because he had already taken it. The effects of such a drug, he knew, lasted approximately four hours; that would be more than enough. And, as Tanya had said, it was a major dose; he felt sluggish and inept and dizzy, and his tongue moved in spasms of pseudo Parkinsonism—an unpleasant side effect which he had failed to anticipate.

A girl, nude from the waist up, with long eoppery hair down her shoulders and back, walked by. Interesting.

Coming the other way, a girl nude from the bottom up made her appearance. Interesting, too. Both girls looked vacant and bored, and totally self-possessed.

"You go in like that too," Okubara informed Chien.

Startled, Chien said, "I understood white tie and tails."

"Joke," Okubara said. "At your expense. Only girls wear nude; you even get so you enjoy, unless you homosexual."

Well, Chien thought, I guess I had better like it. He wandered on with the other guests—they, like him, wore white tie and tails or, if women, floor-length gowns—and felt ill at ease, despite the tranquilizing effect of the stelazine. Why am I here? he asked himself. The ambiguity of his situation did not escape him. He was here to advance his career in the Party apparatus, to obtain the intimate and personal nod of approval from His Greatness . . . and in addition he was here to decipher His Greatness as a fraud; he did not know what variety of fraud, but there it was: fraud against the Party, against all the peace-loving democratic peoples of Terra. Ironic, he thought. And continued to mingle.

A girl with small, bright, illuminated breasts approached him for a match; he absent-mindedly got out his lighter. "What makes your breasts glow?" he asked her. "Radioactive injections?"

She shrugged, said nothing, passed on, leaving him alone. Evidently he had responded in the incorrect way.

Maybe it's a wartime mutation, he pondered.

"Drink, sir." A servant graciously held out a tray; he accepted a martini—which was the current fad among the higher Party classes in People's China—and sipped the ice-cold dry flavor. Good English gin, he said to himself. Or possibly the original Holland compound; juniper or whatever they added. Not bad. He strolled on, feeling better; in actuality he found the atmosphere here a pleasant one. The people here were self-assured; they had been successful and now they could relax. It evidently was a myth that proximity to His Greatness produced neurotic anxiety: he saw no evidence here, at least, and felt little himself.

A heavy-set elderly man, bald, halted him by the simple means of holding his drink glass against Chien's chest. "That frably little one who asked you for a match," the elderly man said, and sniggered. "The quig with the Christmas-tree breasts—that was a boy, in drag." He giggled. "You have to be cautious around here."

"Where, if anywhere," Chien said, "do I find authentic women? In the white ties and tails?"

"Darn near," the elderly man said, and departed with a throng of hyperactive guests, leaving Chien alone with his martini.

A handsome, tall woman, well dressed, standing near Chien, suddenly put her hand on his arm; he felt her fingers tense and she said, "Here he comes. His Greatness. This is the first time for me; I'm a little scared. Does my hair look all right?"

"Fine," Chien said reflexively, and followed her gaze,

seeking a glimpse—his first—of the Absolute Benefactor.

What crossed the room toward the table in the center was not a man.

And it was not, Chien realized, a mechanical construct either; it was not what he had seen on TV. That evidently was simply a device for speechmaking, as Mussolini had once used an artificial arm to salute long and tedious processions.

God, he thought, and felt ill. Was this what Tanya Lee had called the "aquatic horror" shape? It had no shape. Nor pseudopodia, either flesh or metal. It was, in a sense, not there at all; when he managed to look directly at it, the shape vanished; he saw through it, saw the people on the far side—but not it. Yet if he turned his head, caught it out of a sidelong glance, he could determine its boundaries.

It was terrible; it blasted him with its awfulness. As it moved it drained the life from each person in turn; it ate the people who had assembled, passed on, ate again, ate more with an endless appetite. It hated; he felt its hate. It loathed; he felt its loathing for everyone present—in fact he shared its loathing. All at once he and everyone else in the big villa were each a twisted slug, and over the fallen slug carcasses the creature savored, lingered, but all the time coming directly toward him—or was that an illusion? If this is an hallucination, Chien thought, it is the worst I have ever had; if it is not, then it is evil reality; it's an evil thing that kills and injures. He saw the trail of stepped-on, mashed men and women remnants behind it; he saw them trying to reassemble, to operate their crippled bodies; he heard them attempting speech.

I know who you are, Tung Chien thought to himself. You, the supreme head of the world-wide Party structure. You, who destroy whatever living object you touch; I see that Arabic poem, the searching for the flowers of life to eat them—I see you astride the plain which to you is Earth, plain without hills, without valleys. You go anywhere, appear any time, devour anything; you engineer life and then guzzle it, and you enjoy that.

He thought, You are God.

"Mr. Chien," the voice said, but it came from inside his head, not from the mouthless spirit that fashioned itself directly before him. "It is good to meet you again. You know nothing. Go away. I have no interest in you. Why should I care about slime? Slime; I am mired in it, I must excrete it, and I choose to. I could break you; I can break even myself. Sharp stones are under me; I spread sharp pointed things upon the mire. I make the hiding places, the deep places, boil like a pot; to me the sea is like a pot of ointment. The flakes of my flesh are joined to everything. You are me. I am you. It makes no difference, just as it makes no difference whether the creature with ignited breasts is a girl or boy; you could learn to enjoy either." It laughed.

He could not believe it was speaking to him; he could not imagine—it was too terrible—that it had picked him out.

"I have picked everybody out," it said. "No one is too small; each falls and dies and I am there to watch. I don't need to do anything but watch; it is automatic; it was arranged that way." And then it ceased talking to him; it disjoined itself. But he still saw it; he felt its manifold presence. It was a globe which hung in the room, with fifty thousand eyes, with a million eyes—billions: an eye for each living thing as it waited for each thing to fall, and then stepped on the living things as it lay in a broken state. Because of this it had created the things, and he knew; he understood. What had seemed in the Arabic poem to be death was not death but god; or rather God was death, it was one force, one hunter, one cannibal thing, and it missed again and again but, having all eternity, it could afford to miss.

Both poems, he realized; the Dryden one too. The crumbling; that is our world and you are doing it. Warping it to come out that way; bending us.

But at least, he thought, I still have my dignity. With dignity he set down his drink glass, turned, walked toward the doors of the room. He passed through the doors. He walked down a long carpeted hall. A villa servant dressed in purple opened a door for him; he found himself standing out in the night darkness, on a veranda, alone.

Not alone.

It had followed after him. Or it had already been here before him; yes, it had been expecting. It was not really through with him.

"Here I go," he said, and made a dive for the railing; it was six stories down, and there below gleamed the river and death, real death, not what the Arabic poem had seen.

As he tumbled over, it put an extension of itself on his shoulder.

"Why?" he said. But, in fact, he paused. Wondering. Not understanding, not at all.

"Don't fall on my account," it said. He could not see it because it had moved behind him. But the piece of it on his shoulder—it had begun to look like a human hand.

And then it laughed.

"What's funny?" he demanded, as he teetered on the railing, held back by its pseudo-hand.

"You're doing my task for me," it said. "You aren't waiting; don't you have time to wait? I'll select you out from among the others; you don't need to speed the process up."

"What if I do?" he said. "Out of revulsion for you?"

It laughed. And didn't answer.

"You won't even say," he said.

Again no answer. He started to slide back, onto the

veranda. And at once the pressure of its pseudo-hand lifted.

"You founded the Party?" he asked.

"I founded everything. I founded the anti-Party and the Party that isn't a Party, and those who are for it and those who are against, those that you call Yankee Imperialists, those in the camp of reaction, and so on endlessly. I founded it all. As if they were blades of grass."

"And you're here to enjoy it?" he said.

"What I want," it said, "is for you to see me, as I am, as you have seen me, and then trust me."

"What?" he said, quavering. "Trust you to what?"

It said, "Do you believe in me?"

"Yes," he said. "I can see you."

"Then go back to your job at the Ministry. Tell Tanya Lee that you saw an overworked, overweight, elderly man who drinks too much and likes to pinch girls' rear ends."

"Oh, Christ," he said.

"As you live on, unable to stop, I will torment you," it said. "I will deprive you, item by item, of everything you possess or want. And then when you are crushed to death I will unfold a mystery."

"What's the mystery?"

"The dead shall live, the living die. I kill what lives; I save what has died. And I will tell you this: *There are things worse than I.* But you won't meet them because by then I will have killed you. Now walk back into the dining room and prepare for dinner. Don't question what I'm doing; I did it long before there was a Tung Chien and I will do it long after."

He hit it as hard as he could.

And experienced violent pain in his head.

And darkness, with the sense of falling.

After that, darkness again. He thought, I will get you. I will see that you die too. That you suffer; you're going to suffer, just like us, exactly in every way we do. I'll nail you; I swear to god I'll nail you up somewhere. And it will hurt. As much as I hurt now.

He shut his eyes.

Roughly, he was shaken. And heard Mr. Kimo Okubara's voice. "Get to your feet, common drunk. Come on!"

Without opening his eyes he said, "Get me a cab."

"Cab already waiting. You go home. Disgrace. Make a violent scene out of yourself."

Getting shakily to his feet, he opened his eyes, examined himself. Our Leader whom we follow, he thought, is the One True God. And the enemy whom we fight and have fought is God too. They are right; he is everywhere. But I didn't understand what that meant. Staring at the protocol officer, he thought, You are God too. So there is no getting away, probably not even by jumping. As I started, instinctively, to do. He shuddered.

"Mix drinks with drugs," Okubara said witheringly. "Ruin career. I see it happen many times. Get lost."

Unsteadily, he walked toward the great central door of the Yangtze River villa; two servants, dressed like medieval knights, with crested plumes, ceremoniously opened the door for him and one of them said, "Good night, sir."

"Up yours," Chien said, and passed out into the night.

At a quarter to three in the morning, as he sat sleepless in the living room of his conapt, smoking one Cuesta Rey Astoria after another, a knock sounded at the door.

When he opened it he found himself facing Tanya Lee in her trenchcoat, her face pinched with cold. Her eyes blazed, questioningly.

"Don't look at me like that," he said roughly. His cigar had gone out; he relit it. "I've been looked at enough," he said.

"You saw it," she said.

He nodded.

She seated herself on the arm of the couch and after a time she said, "Want to tell me about it?"

"Go as far from here as possible," he said. "Go a long way." And then he remembered; no way was long enough. He remembered reading that too. "Forget it," he said; rising to his feet, he walked clumsily into the kitchen to start up the coffee.

Following after him, Tanya said, "Was—it that bad?"

"We can't win," he said. "You can't win; I don't mean me. I'm not in this; I just want to do my job at the Ministry and forget it. Forget the whole damned thing."

"Is it nonterrestrial?"

"Yes." He nodded.

"Is it hostile to us?"

"Yes," he said. "No. Both. Mostly hostile."

"Then we have to—"

"Go home," he said, "and go to bed." He looked her over carefully; he had sat a long time and he had done a great deal of thinking. About a lot of things. "Are you married?" he said.

"No. Not now. I used to be."

He said, "Stay with me tonight. The rest of tonight, anyhow. Until the sun comes up." He added, "The night part is awful."

"I'll stay," Tanya said, unbuckling the belt of her raincoat, "but I have to have some answers."

"What did Dryden mean," Chien said, "about music untuning the sky? I don't get that. What does music do to the sky?"

"All the celestial order of the universe ends," she said as she hung her raincoat up in the closet of the bedroom; under it she wore an orange striped sweater and stretchpants.

He said, "And that's bad."

Pausing, she reflected. "I don't know. I guess so."

"It's a lot of power," he said, "to assign to music."

"Well, you know that old Pythagorean business about

the 'music of the spheres.' " Matter-of-factly she seated herself on the bed and removed her slipperlike shoes.

"Do you believe in that?" he said. "Or do you believe in God?"

" 'God'!" She laughed. "That went out with the donkey steam engine. What are you talking about? God, or god?" She came over close beside him, peering into his face.

"Don't look at me so closely," he said, sharply drawing back. "I don't ever want to be looked at again." He moved away, irritably.

"I think," Tanya said, "that if there is a God He has very little interest in human affairs. That's my theory, anyhow. I mean, He doesn't seem to care if evil triumphs or people and animals get hurt and die. I frankly don't see Him anywhere around. And the Party has always denied any form of—"

"Did you ever see Him?" he asked. "When you were a child?"

"Oh, sure, as a child. But I also believed—"

"Did it ever occur to you," Chien said, "that good and evil are names for the same thing? That God could be both good and evil at the same time?"

"I'll fix you a drink," Tanya said, and padded barefoot into the kitchen.

Chien said, "The Crusher. The Clanker. The Gulper and the Bird and the Climbing Tube—plus other names, forms, I don't know. I had an hallucination. At the stag dinner. A big one. A terrible one."

"But the stelazine—"

"It brought on a worse one," he said.

"Is there any way," Tanya said somberly, "that we can fight this thing you saw? This apparition you call an hallucination but which very obviously was not?"

He said, "Believe in it."

"What will that do?"

"Nothing," he said wearily. "Nothing at all. I'm tired; I don't want a drink—let's just go to bed."

"Okay." She padded back into the bedroom, began pulling her striped sweater over her head. "We'll discuss it more thoroughly later."

"An hallucination," Chien said, "is merciful. I wish I had it; I want mine back. I want to be before your peddler got to me with that phenothiazine."

"Just come to bed. It'll be toasty. All warm and nice."

He removed his tie, his shirt—and saw, on his right shoulder, the mark, the stigma, which it had left when it stopped him from jumping. Livid marks which looked as if they would never go away. He put his pajama top on, then; it hid the marks.

"Anyhow," Tanya said as he got into the bed beside her, "your career is immeasurably advanced. Aren't you glad about that?"

"Sure," he said, nodding sightlessly in the darkness. "Very glad."

"Come over against me," Tanya said, putting her arms around him. "And forget everything else. At least for now."

He tugged her against him, then, doing what she asked and what he wanted to do. She was neat; she was swiftly active; she was successful and she did her part. They did not bother to speak until at last she said, "Oh!" And then she relaxed.

"I wish," he said, "that we could go on forever."

"We did," Tanya said. "It's outside of time; it's boundless, like an ocean. It's the way we were in Cambrian times, before we migrated up onto the land; it's the ancient primary waters. This is the only time we get to go back, when this is done. That's why it means so much. And in those days we weren't separate; it was like a big jelly, like those blobs that float up on the beach."

"Float up," he said, "and are left there to die."

"Could you get me a towel?" Tanya asked. "Or a washcloth? I need it."

He padded into the bathroom for a towel. There—he was naked, now—he once more saw his shoulder, saw where it had seized hold of him and held on, dragged him back, possibly to toy with him a little more.

The marks, unaccountably, were bleeding.

He sponged the blood away. More oozed forth at once and, seeing that, he wondered how much time he had left. Probably only hours.

Returning to bed, he said, "Could you continue?"

"Sure. If you have any energy left; it's up to you." She lay gazing up at him unwinkingly, barely visible in the dim nocturnal light.

"I have," he said. And hugged her to him.

THAT SHARE OF GLORY

C. M. Kornbluth

John W. Campbell, whose editorship of the magazine variously known as *Astounding* and *Analog* has spanned all of recorded human history, must have been poring over Machiavelli when other little boys were reading about Robin Hood. Certainly Campbell has published an extraordinary number of science-fiction stories devoted to the working-out of Machiavellian propositions, and any writer who can dream up a newer and cleverer Bureau of Slick Tricks finds a ready market for his wares in Campbell's magazine. The late Cyril Kornbluth appeared infrequently in *Astounding,* but each of his stories there was a notable one—as, for example, the one that follows, which handles the Campbell-Machiavelli plot formula in a particularly agreeable and convincing manner.

Young Alen, one of a thousand in the huge refectory, ate absent-mindedly as the reader droned into the perfect silence of the hall. Today's lesson happened to be a word list of the Thetis VIII planet's sea-going folk.

"*Tlon*—a ship," droned the reader.

"*Rtlo*—some ships, number unknown.

"*Long*—some ships, number known, always modified by cardinal.

"Ongr—a ship in a collection of ships, always modified by ordinal.

"Ngrt—the first ship in a collection of ships; an exception to *ongr."*

A lay brother tiptoed to Alen's side. "The Rector summons you," he whispered.

Alen had no time for panic, though that was the usual reaction to a summons from the Rector to a novice. He slipped from the refectory, stepped onto the northbound corridor, and stepped off at his cell, a minute later and a quarter mile farther on. Hastily, but meticulously, he changed from his drab habit to the heraldic robes in the cubicle with its simple stool, washstand, desk, and paperweight or two. Alen, a level-headed young fellow, was not aware that he had broken any section of the Order's complicated Rule, but he was aware that he could have done so without knowing it. It might, he thought, be the last time he would see the cell.

He cast a glance which he hoped would not be the final one over it; a glance which lingered a little fondly on the reel rack where were stowed: "Nicholson on Martian Verbs," "The New Oxford Venusian Dictionary," the ponderous six-reeler "Deutche-Ganymediche Konversasionslexikon" published long ago and far away in Leipzig. The later works were there, too: "The Tongues of the Galaxy—An Essay in Classification," "A Concise Grammar of Cephean," "The Self-Pronouncing Vegan II Dictionary"—scores of them, and, of course, the worn reel of old Machiavelli's "The Prince."

Enough of that! Alen combed out his small, neat beard and stepped onto the southbound corridor. He transferred to an eastbound at the next intersection and minutes later was before the Rector's lay secretary.

"You'd better review your Lyran irregulars," said the secretary disrespectfully. "There's a trader in there who's looking for a cheap herald on a swindling trip to Lyra VI." Thus unceremoniously did Alen learn that he was not to be ejected from the Order but that he was to be elevated to Journeyman. But as a Herald should, he betrayed no sign of his immense relief. He did, however, take the secretary's advice and sensibly reviewed his Lyran.

While he was in the midst of a declension which applied only to inanimate objects, the voice of the Rector —and what a mellow voice it was!—floated through the secretary's intercom.

"Admit the novice, Alen," said the Master Herald.

A final settling of his robes and the youth walked into the Rector's huge office, with the seal of the Order blazing in diamonds above his desk. There was a stranger present; presumably the trader—a black-bearded fellow whose rugged frame didn't carry his Vegan cloak with ease.

Said the Rector: "Novice, this is to be the crown of your toil if you are acceptable to—?" He courteously turned to the trader, who shrugged irritably.

"It's all one to me," growled the blackbeard. "Somebody cheap, somebody who knows the cant of the thievish Lyran gem peddlers, above all, somebody *at once.* Overhead is devouring my flesh day by day as the ship waits at the field. And when we are spaceborne, my imbecile crew will doubtless waste liter after priceless liter of my fuel. And when we land the swindling Lyrans will without doubt make my ruin complete by tricking me even out of the minute profit I hope to realize. Good Master Herald, let me have the infant cheap and I'll bid you good day."

The Rector's shaggy eyebrows drew down in a frown. "Trader," he said sonorously, "our mission of galactic utilitarian culture is not concerned with your margin of profit. I ask you to test this youth and, if you find him able, to take him as your Herald on your voyage. He will serve you well, for he has been taught that commerce and words, its medium, are the unifying bonds which will one day unite the cosmos into a single humankind. Do not conceive that the College and Order of Heralds is a mere aid to you in your commercial adventure."

"Very well," growled the trader. He addressed Alen in broken Lyran: "Boy, how you make up Vegan stones of three fires so Lyran women like, come buy, buy again?"

Alen smoothly replied: "The Vegan triple-fire gem finds most favor on Lyra and especially among its women when set in a wide glass anklet if large, and when arranged in the Lyran 'lucky five' pattern in a glass thumb-ring if small." He was glad, very glad, he had come across—and as a matter of course memorized, in the relentless fashion of the Order—a novel which touched briefly on the Lyran jewel trade.

The trader glowered and switched to Cephean—apparently his native tongue. "That was well-enough said, Herald. Now tell me whether you've got guts to man a squirt in case we're intercepted by the thieving so-called Customs collectors of Eyolf's Realm between here and Lyra?"

Alen knew the Rector's eyes were on him. "The noble mission of our Order," he said, "forbids me to use any weapon but the truth in furthering cosmic utilitarian civilization. No, master trader, I shall not man one of your weapons."

The trader shrugged. "So I must take what I get. Good Master Herald, make me a price."

The Rector said casually: "I regard this chiefly as a training mission for our novice; the fee will be nominal. Let us say twenty-five percent of your net as of blastoff from Lyra, to be audited by Journeyman-Herald Alen."

The trader's howl of rage echoed in the dome of the huge room. "It's not fair!" he roared. "Who but you thievish villains with your Order and your catch-'em-young and your years of training can learn the tongues of the galaxy? What chance has a decent merchant busy with profit and loss got to learn the cant of every race between Sirius and the Coalsack? It's not fair! It's not fair and I'll say so until my dying breath!"

"Die outside if you find our terms unacceptable," said the Rector. "The Order does not haggle."

"Well I know it," sighed the trader brokenly. "I should have stuck to my own system and my good father's pump-flange factory. But no! I had to pick up a bargain in gems on Vega! Enough of this—bring me your contract and I'll sign it."

The Rector's shaggy eyebrows went up. "There is no contract," he said. "A mutual trust between Herald and trader is the cornerstone upon which cosmoswide amity and understanding will be built."

"At twenty-five percent for an unlicked pup," muttered blackbeard to himself in Cephean.

None of his instructors had played Polonius as Alen, with the seal of the Journeyman-Herald on his brow, packed for blastoff and vacated his cell. He supposed they knew that twenty years of training either had done their work or had not.

The trader taking Alen to the field where his ship waited was less wise. "The secret of successful negotiation," he weightily told his Herald, "is to yield willingly. This may strike you as a paradox, but it is the veritable key to my success in maintaining the profits of my good father's pump-flange trade. The secret is to yield with rueful admiration of your opponent—but *only in unimportant details*. Put up a little battle about delivery date or about terms of credit and then let him have his way. But you never give way a hair's breadth on your asking price unless—"

Alen let him drivel on as they drove through the outer works of the College. He was glad the car was open. For the first time he was being accorded the doffed hat that is the due of Heralds from their inferiors in the Order, and the grave nod of salutation from equals. Five-year-old postulants seeing his brow-seal tugged off their headgear with comical celerity; fellow novices, equals a few hours before, uncovered as though he were the Rector himself.

The ceremonial began to reach the trader. When, with a final salutation, a lay warder let them through the great gate of the curtain wall, he said with some irritation: "They appear to hold you in high regard, boy."

"I am better addressed as 'Herald,' " said Alen composedly.

"A plague descend on the College and Order! Do you think I don't know my manners? Of course, I call a Herald 'Herald,' but we're going to be cooped up together and you'll be working for me. What'll happen to ship's discipline if I have to kowtow to you?"

"There will be no problem," said Alen.

Blackbeard grunted and trod fiercely on the accelerator.

"That's my ship," he said at length. "*Starsong.* Vegan registry—it may help passing through Eyolf's Realm, though it cost me overmuch in bribes. A crew of eight, lazy, good-for-nothing wastrels—agh! Can I believe my eyes?" The car jammed to a halt before the looming ship and blackbeard was up the ladder and through the port in a second. Settling his robes, Alen followed.

He found the trader fiercely denouncing his chief engineer for using space drive to heat the ship; he had seen the faint haze of a minimum exhaust from the stern tubes.

"For that, dolt," screamed blackbeard, "we have a thing known as electricity. Have you by chance ever heard of it? Are you aware that a chief engineer's responsibility is the efficient and *economical* operation of his ship's drive mechanism?"

The chief, a cowed-looking Cephean, saw Alen with relief and swept off his battered cap. The Herald nodded gravely and the trader broke off in irritation. "We need none of that bowing and scraping for the rest of the voyage," he declared.

"Of course not, sir," said the chief. "O'course not. I was just welcoming the Herald aboard. Welcome aboard, Herald. I'm Chief Elwon, Herald. And I'm glad to have a Herald with us." A covert glance at the trader. "*I've* voyaged with Heralds and without, and I don't mind saying I feel safer indeed with you aboard."

"May I be taken to my quarters?" asked Alen.

"Your—?" began the trader, stupefied.

The chief broke in: "I'll fix you a cabin, Herald. We've got some bulkheads I can rig aft for a snug little space, not roomy, but the best a little ship like this can afford."

The trader collapsed into a bucket seat as the chief bustled aft and Alen followed.

"Herald," the chief said with some embarrassment after he had collared two crewmen and set them to work, "you'll have to excuse our good master trader. He's new to the interstar lanes and he doesn't exactly know the jets yet. Between us we'll get him squared away."

Alen inspected the cubicle run up for him—a satisfactory enclosure affording him the decent privacy he rated. He dismissed the chief and the crewmen with a nod and settled himself on the cot.

Beneath the iron composure in which he had been trained, he felt scared and alone. Not even old Machiavelli seemed to offer comfort or counsel: "There is nothing more difficult to take in hand, more perilous to conduct, or more uncertain in its success, than to take the lead in the introduction of a new order of things," said Chapter Six.

But what said Chapter Twenty-Six? "Where the willingness is great, the difficulties cannot be great."

Starsong was not a happy ship. Blackbeard's nagging stinginess hung over the crew like a thundercloud, but Alen professed not to notice. He walked regularly fore and aft for two hours a day greeting the crew members in their various native tongues and then wrapping himself in the reserve the Order demanded—though he longed to salute them man-to-man, eat with them, gossip about their native planets, the past misdeeds that had brought them to their berths aboard the miserly *Starsong,* their hopes for the future. The Rule of the College and Order of Heralds decreed otherwise. He accepted the uncoverings of the crew with a nod and tried to be pleased because they stood in growing awe of him that ranged from Chief Elwon's lively appreciation of a Herald's skill to Wiper Jukkl's superstitious reverence. Jukkl was a low-browed specimen from a planet of the decadent Sirius system. He outdid the normal slovenliness of an all-male crew on a freighter—a slovenliness in which Alen could not share. Many of his waking hours were spent in his locked cubicle burnishing his metal and cleaning and pressing his robes. A Herald was never supposed to suggest by his appearance that he shared moral frailties.

Blackbeard himself yielded a little, to the point of touching his cap sullenly. This probably was not so much awe at Alen's studied manner as respect for the incisive, lightning-fast job of auditing the Herald did on the books of the trading venture—absurdly complicated books with scores of accounts to record a simple matter of buying gems cheap on Vega and chartering a ship in the hope of selling them dearly on Lyra. The complicated books and overlapping accounts did tell the story, but they made it very easy for an auditor to erroneously read a number of costs as far higher than they actually were. Alen did not fall into the trap.

On the fifth day after blastoff, Chief Elwon rapped, respectfully but urgently, on the door of Alen's cubicle.

"If you please, Herald," he urged, "could you come to the bridge?"

Alen's heart bounded in his chest, but he gravely said: "My meditation must not be interrupted. I shall join you on the bridge in ten minutes." And for ten minutes he methodically polished a murky link in the massive gold chain that fastened his boat-cloak—the "meditation." He donned the cloak before stepping out; the summons sounded like a full-dress affair in the offing.

The trader was stamping and fuming. Chief Elwon was riffling through his spec book unhappily. Astrogator Hufner was at the plot computer running up trajectories and knocking them down again. A quick glance showed Alen that they were all high-speed trajectories in the "evasive action" class.

"Herald," said the trader grimly, "we have broken somebody's detector bubble." He jerked his thumb at a red-lit signal. "I expect we'll be overhauled shortly. Are you ready to earn your twenty-five percent of the net?"

Alen overlooked the crudity. "Are you rigged for color video, merchant?" he asked.

"We are."

"Then I am ready to do what I can for my client."

He took the communicator's seat, stealing a glance in the still-blank screen. The reflection of his face was reassuring, though he wished he had thought to comb his small beard.

Another light flashed on, and Hufner quit the operator to study the detector board. "Big, powerful, and getting closer," he said tersely. "Scanning for us with directionals now. Putting out plenty of energy—"

The loudspeaker of the ship-to-ship audio came to life.

"What ship are you?" it demanded in Vegan. "We are a Customs cruiser of the Realm of Eyolf. What ship are you?"

"Have the crew man the squirts," said the trader softly to the chief.

Elwon looked at Alen, who shook his head. "Sorry, sir," said the engineer apologetically. "The Herald—"

"We are the freighter *Starsong,* Vegan registry," said Alen into the audio mike as the trader choked. "We are carrying Vegan gems to Lyra."

"They're on us," said the astrogator despairingly, reading his instruments. The ship-to-ship video flashed on, showing an arrogant, square-jawed face topped by a battered naval cap.

"Lyra indeed! We have plans of our own for Lyra. You will heave to—" began the officer in the screen, before he noted Alen. "My pardon, Herald," he said sardonically. "Herald, will you please request the ship's master to heave to for boarding and search? We wish to assess and collect Customs duties. You are aware, of course, that your vessel is passing through the Realm."

The man's accented Vegan reeked of Algol IV. Alen switched to that obscure language to say: "We were not aware of that. Are you aware that there is a reciprocal trade treaty in effect between the Vegan system and the Realm which specifies that freight in Vegan bottoms is dutiable only when consigned to ports in the Realm?"

"You speak Algolian, do you? You Heralds have not been underrated, but don't plan to lie your way out of this. Yes, I am aware of some such agreement as you mentioned. We shall board you, as I said, and assess and collect duty in kind. If, regrettably, there has been any mistake you are, of course, free to apply to the Realm for reimbursement. Now, heave to!"

"I have no intentions of lying. I speak the solemn truth when I say that we shall fight to the last man any attempt of yours to board and loot us."

Alen's mind was racing furiously through the catalog of planetary folkways the Rule had decreed that he master. Algol IV—some ancestor worship; veneration of mother; hand-to-hand combat with knives; complimentary greeting, "May you never strike down a weaker foe"; folk-hero Gaarek unjustly accused of slaying a cripple and exiled but it was an enemy's plot—

A disconcerted shadow was crossing the face of the

officer as Alen improvised: "You will, of course, kill us all. But before this happens I shall have messaged back to the College and Order of Heralds the facts in the case, with a particular request that your family be informed. Your name, I think, will be remembered as long as Gaarek's—though not in the same way, of course; the Algolian whose hundred-man battle cruiser wiped out a virtually unarmed freighter with a crew of eight."

The officer's face was dark with rage. "You devil!" he snarled. "Leave my family out of this! I'll come aboard and fight you man-to-man if you have the stomach for it!"

Alen shook his head regretfully. "The Rule of my Order forbids recourse to violence," he said. "Our only permissible weapon is the truth."

"We're coming aboard," said the officer grimly. "I'll order my men not to harm your people. We'll just be collecting customs. If your people shoot first, my men will be under orders to do nothing more than disable them."

Alen smiled and uttered a sentence or two in Algolian.

The officer's jaw dropped and he croaked, after a pause: "I'll cut you to ribbons. You can't say that about my mother, you—" and he spewed back some of the words Alen had spoken.

"Calm yourself," said the Herald gravely. "I apologize for my disgusting and unheraldic remarks. But I wished to prove a point. You would have killed me if you could; I touched off a reaction which had been planted in you by your culture. I will be able to do the same with the men of yours who come aboard. For every race of man there is the intolerable insult that must be avenged in blood.

"Send your men aboard under orders not to kill if you wish; I shall goad them into a killing rage. We shall be massacred, yours will be the blame, and you will be disgraced and disowned by your entire planet." Alen hoped desperately that the naval crews of the Realm were, as reputed, a barbarous and undisciplined lot—

Evidently they were, and the proud Algolian dared not risk it. In his native language he spat again: "You devil!" and switched back into Vegan. "Freighter *Starsong,*" he said bleakly, "I find that my space fix was in error and that you are not in Realm territory. You may proceed."

The astrogator said from the detector board, incredulously: "He's disengaging. He's off us. He's accelerating, Herald, *what* did you say to him?"

But the reaction from blackbeard was more gratifying. Speechless, the trader took off his cap. Alen acknowledged the salute with a grave nod before he started back to his cubicle. It was just as well, he reflected, that the trader didn't know his life and his ship had been unconditionally pledged in a finish fight against a hundred-man battle cruiser.

Lyra's principal spaceport was pocked and broken, but they made a fair-enough landing. Alen, in full heraldic robes, descended from *Starsong* to greet a handful of port officials.

"Any metals aboard?" demanded one of them.

"None for sale," said the Herald.

"We have Vegan gems, chiefly triple-fire." He knew that the dull little planet was short of metals and, having made a virtue of necessity, was somehow prejudiced against their import.

"Have your crew transfer the cargo to the Customs shed," said the port official studying *Starsong*'s papers. "And all of you wait there."

All of them—except Alen—lugged numbered sacks and boxes of gems to the low brick building designated. The trader was allowed to pocket a handful for samples before the shed was sealed—a complicated business. A brick was mortared over the simple ironwood latch that closed the ironwood door, a pat of clay was slapped over the brick and the port seal stamped in it. A mechanic with what looked like a pottery blowtorch fed by powdered coal played a flame on the clay seal until it glowed orange-red and that was that.

"Herald," said the port official, "tell the merchant to sign here and make his fingerprints."

Alen studied the document; it was a simple identification form. Blackbeard signed with the reed pen provided and fingerprinted the document. After two weeks in space he scarcely needed to ink his fingers first.

"Now tell him that we'll release the gems on his written fingerprinted order to whatever Lyran citizens he sells to. And explain that this roundabout system is necessary to avoid metal smuggling. Please remove *all* metal from your clothes and stow it on your ship. Then we will seal that, too, and put it under guard until you are ready to take off. We regret that we will have to search you before we turn you loose, but we can't afford to have our economy disrupted by irresponsible introduction of metals." Alen had not realized it was that bad.

After the thorough search that extended to the confiscation of forgotten watches and pins, the port officials changed a sheaf of the trader's uranium-backed Vegan currency into Lyran legal tender based on man-hours. Blackbeard made a partial payment to the crew, told them to have a good liberty and check in at the port at sunset tomorrow for probable take-off.

Alen and the trader were driven to town in an unlikely vehicle whose power plant was a pottery turbine. The driver, when they were safely out on the open road, furtively asked whether they had any metal they wanted to discard.

The trader asked sharply in his broken Lyran: "What you do you get metal? Where sell, how use?"

The driver, following a universal tendency, raised his voice and lapsed into broken Lyran himself to tell the strangers: "Black market science men pay much, much for little bit metal. Study, use, build. Politicians make law no metal, what I care politicians? But you no tell, gentlemen?"

"We won't tell," said Alen. "But we have no metal for you."

The driver shrugged.

"Herald," said the trader, "what do you make of it?"

"I didn't know it was a political issue. We concern ourselves with the basic patterns of a people's behavior, not the day-to-day expressions of the patterns. The planet's got no heavy metals, which means there were no metals available to the primitive Lyrans. The lighter metals don't occur in native form or in easily split compounds. They proceeded along the ceramic line instead of the metallic line and appear to have done quite well for themselves up to a point. No electricity, of course, no aviation, and no space flight."

"And," said the trader, "naturally the people who make these buggies and that blowtorch we saw are scared witless that metals will be imported and put them out of business. So naturally they have laws passed prohibiting it."

"Naturally," said the Herald, looking sharply at the trader. But blackbeard was back in character a moment later. "An outrage," he growled. "Trying to tell a man what he can and can't import when he sees a decent chance to make a bit of profit."

The driver dropped them at a boardinghouse. It was half-timbered construction, which appeared to be swankier than the more common brick. The floors were plate glass, roughened for traction. Alen got them a double room with a view.

"What's that thing?" demanded the trader, inspecting the view.

The thing was a structure looming above the slate and tile roofs of the town—a round brick tower for its first twenty-five meters and then wood for another fifteen. As they studied it, it pricked up a pair of ears at the top and began to flop them wildly.

"Semaphore," said Alen.

A minute later blackbeard piteously demanded from the bathroom: *"How* do you make water come out of the tap? I touched it all over but nothing happened."

"You have to turn it," said Alen, demonstrating. "And that thing—you pull it sharply down, hold it, and then release."

"Barbarous," muttered the trader. "Barbarous."

An elderly maid came in to show them how to string their hammocks and ask if they happened to have a bit of metal to give her for a souvenir. They sent her away and, rather than face the public dining room, made a meal from their own stores and turned in for the night.

It's going well, thought Alen drowsily: going very well indeed.

He awoke abruptly, but made no move. It was dark in the double room, and there were stealthy, furtive little noises nearby. A hundred thoughts flashed through his head of Lyran treachery and double-dealing. He lifted his eyelids a trifle and saw a figure silhouetted against the faint light of the big window. If a burglar, he was a clumsy one.

There was a stirring from the other hammock, the trader's. With a subdued roar that sounded like "Thieving villains!" blackbeard launched himself from the hammock at the intruder. But his feet tangled in the hammock cords and he belly-flopped on the floor.

The burglar, if it was one, didn't dash smoothly and efficiently for the door. He straightened himself against the window and said resignedly: "You need not fear. I will make no resistance."

Alen rolled from the hammock and helped the trader to his feet. "He said he doesn't want to fight," he told the trader.

Blackbeard seized the intruder and shook him like a rat. "So the rogue is a coward too!" he boomed. "Give us a light, Herald."

Alen uncovered the slow-match, blew it to a flame, squeakily pumped up a pressure torch until a jet of pulverized coal sprayed from its nozzle, and ignited it. A dozen strokes more and there was enough heat feeding back from the jet to maintain the pressure cycle.

Through all of this the trader was demanding in his broken Lyran: "What make here, thief? What reason thief us room?"

The Herald brought the hissing pressure lamp to the window. The intruder's face was not the unhealthy, neurotic face of a criminal. Its thin lines told of discipline and thought.

"What did you want here?" asked Alen.

"Metal," said the intruder simply. "I thought you might have a bit of iron."

It was the first time a specific metal had been named by any Lyran. He used, of course, the Vegan word for iron.

"You are particular," remarked the Herald, "Why iron?"

"I have heard that it possesses certain properties—perhaps you can tell me before you turn me over to the police. Is it true, as we hear, that a mass of iron whose crystals have been aligned by a sharp blow will strongly attract another piece of iron with a force related to the distance between them?"

"It is true," said the Herald, studying the man's face. It was lit with excitement. Deliberately Alen added: "This alignment is more easily and uniformly effected by placing the mass of iron in an electric field—that is, a space surrounding the passage of an electron stream through a conductor." Many of the words he used had to be Vegan; there were no Lyran words for "electric," "electron," or "conductor."

The intruder's face fell. "I have tried to master the

concept you refer to," he admitted. "But it is beyond me. I have questioned other interstar voyagers and they have touched on it, but I cannot grasp it— But thank you, sir; you have been very courteous. I will trouble you no further while you summon the watch."

"You give up too easily," said Alen. "For a scientist, much too easily. If we turn you over to the watch, there will be hearings and testimony and whatnot. Our time is limited here on your planet; I doubt that we can spare any for your legal processes."

The trader let go of the intruder's shoulder and grumbled: "Why you no ask we have iron, I tell you no. Search, search, take all metal away. We no police you. I sorry hurted you arms. Here for you." Blackbeard brought out a palmful of his sample gems and picked out a large triple-fire stone. "You not be angry me," he said, putting it in the Lyran's hand.

"I can't—" said the scientist.

Blackbeard closed his fingers over the stone and growled: "I give, you take. Maybe buy iron with, eh?"

"That's so," said the Lyran. "Thank you both, gentlemen. Thank you—"

"You go," said the trader. "You go, we sleep again."

The scientist bowed with dignity and left their room.

"Gods of space," swore the trader. "To think that Jukkl, the *Starsong*'s wiper, knows more about electricity and magnetism than a brainy fellow like that."

"And they are the key to physics," mused Alen. "A scientist here is dead-ended forever, because their materials are all insulators! Glass, clay, glaze, wood."

"Funny, all right," yawned blackbeard. "Did you see me collar him once I got on my feet? Sharp, eh? Good night, Herald." He gruntingly hauled himself into the hammock again, leaving Alen to turn off the hissing light and cover the slow-match with its perforated lid.

They had roast fowl of some sort or other for breakfast in the public dining room. Alen was required by his

Rule to refuse the red wine that went with it. The trader gulped it approvingly. "A sensible, though backward people," he said. "And now if you'll inquire of the management where the thievish jewel-buyers congregate, we can get on with our business and perhaps be off by dawn tomorrow."

"So quickly?" asked Alen, almost forgetting himself enough to show surprise.

"My charter on *Starsong,* good Herald—thirty days to go, but what might not go wrong in space? And then there would be penalties to mulct me of whatever minute profit I may realize."

Alen learned that Gromeg's Tavern was the gem mart and they took another of the turbine-engined cabs through the brick-paved streets.

Gromeg's was a dismal, small-windowed brick barn with heavy-set men lounging about, an open kitchen at one end and tables at the other. A score of smaller, sharp-faced men were at the tables sipping wine and chatting.

"I am Journeyman-Herald Alen," announced Alen clearly, "with Vegan gems to dispose of."

There was a silence of elaborate unconcern, and then one of the dealers spat and grunted: "Vegan gems. A drug on the market. Take them away, Herald."

"Come, master trader," said Alen in the Lyran tongue. "The gem dealers of Lyra do not want your wares." He started for the door.

One of the dealers called languidly: "Well, wait a moment. I have nothing better to do; since you've come all this way I'll have a look at your stuff."

"You honor us," said Alen. He and blackbeard sat at the man's table. The trader took out a palmful of samples, counted them meaningfully, and laid them on the boards.

"Well," said the gem dealer, "I don't know whether to be amused or insulted. I am Garthkint, the gem dealer —not a retailer of *beads*. However, I have no hard feelings. A drink for your frowning friend, Herald? I know you gentry don't indulge." The drink was already on the table, brought by one of the hulking guards.

Alen passed Garthkint's own mug of wine to the trader, explaining politely: "In my master trader's native Cepheus it is considered honorable for the guest to sip the drink his host laid down and none other. A charming custom, is it not?"

"Charming, though unsanitary," muttered the gem dealer—and he did not touch the drink he had ordered for blackbeard.

"I can't understand a word either of you is saying—too flowery. Was this little rat trying to drug me?" demanded the trader in Cephean.

"No," said Alen. "Just trying to get you drunk." To Garthkint in Lyran, he explained, "The good trader was saying that he wishes to leave at once. I was agreeing with him."

"Well," said Garthkint, "perhaps I can take a couple of your gauds. For some youngster who wishes a cheap ring."

"He's getting to it," Alen told the trader.

"High time," grunted blackbeard.

"The trader asks me to inform you," said Alen, switching back to Lyran, "that he is unable to sell in lots smaller than five hundred gems."

"A compact language, Cephean," said Garthkint, narrowing his eyes.

"Is it not?" Alen blandly agreed.

The gem dealer's forefinger rolled an especially fine three-fire stone from the little pool of gems on the table. "I suppose," he said grudgingly, "that this is what I must call the best of the lot. What, I am curious to know, is the price you would set for five hundred equal in quality and size to this poor thing?"

"This," said Alen, "is the good trader's first venture to your delightful planet. He wishes to be remembered and welcomed all of the many times he anticipates returning. Because of this he has set an absurdly low price, counting good will as more important than a prosperous voyage. Two thousand Lyran credits."

"Absurd," snorted Garthkint. "I cannot do business with you. Either you are insanely rapacious or you have been pitifully misguided as to the value of your wares. I am well-known for my charity; I will assume that the latter is the case. I trust you will not be too downcast when I tell you that five hundred of these muddy, undersized, out-of-round objects are worth no more than two hundred credits."

"If you are serious," said Alen with marked amazement, "we would not dream of imposing on you. At the figure you mention, we might as well not sell at all but return with our wares to Cepheus and give these gems to children in the streets for marbles. Good gem trader, excuse us for taking up so much of your time and many thanks for your warm hospitality in the matter of the wine." He switched to Cephean and said: "We're dickering now. Two thousand and two hundred. Get up; we're going to start to walk out."

"What if he lets us go?" grumbled blackbeard, but he did heave himself to his feet and turn to the door as Alen rose.

"My trader echoes my regrets," the Herald said in Lyran. "Farewell."

"Well, stay a moment," said Garthkint. "I am well-known for my soft heart toward strangers. A charitable man might go as high as five hundred and absorb the inevitable loss. If you should return some day with a passable lot of *real* gems, it would be worth my while for you to remember who treated you with such benevolence and give me fair choice."

"Noble Lyran," said Alen, apparently almost overcome. "I shall not easily forget your combination of acumen and charity. It is a lesson to traders. It is a lesson to me. I shall *not* insist on two thousand. I shall cut the throat of my trader's venture by reducing his price to eighteen hundred credits, though I wonder how I shall dare tell him of it."

"What's going on now?" demanded blackbeard.

"Five hundred and eighteen hundred," said Alen. "We can sit down again."

"Up, down—up, down," muttered the trader.

They sat, and Alen said in Lyran: "My trader unexpectedly endorses the reduction. He says, 'Better to lose some than all'—an old proverb in the Cephean tongue. And he forbids any further reduction."

"Come, now," wheedled the gem dealer. "Let us be men of the world about this. One must give a little and take a little. Everybody knows he can't have his own way forever. I shall offer a good, round eight hundred credits and we'll close on it, eh? Pilquis, fetch us a pen and ink!" One of the burly guards was right there with an inkpot and a reed pen. Garthkint had a Customs form out of his tunic and was busily filling it in to specify the size, number and fire of gems to be released to him.

"What's it now?" asked blackbeard.

"Eight hundred."

"Take it!"

"Garthkint," said Alen regretfully, "you heard the firmness and decision in my trader's voice? What can I do? I am only speaking for him. He is a hard man but perhaps I can talk him around later. I offer you the gems at a ruinous fifteen hundred credits."

"Split the difference," said Garthkint resignedly.

"Done at eleven-fifty," said Alen.

That blackbeard understood. "Well done!" he boomed at Alen and took a swig at Garthkint's winecup. "Have him fill in 'Sack eighteen' on his paper. It's five hundred of that grade."

The gem dealer counted out twenty-three fifty-credit notes and blackbeard signed and fingerprinted the release.

"Now," said Garthkint, "you will please remain here

while I take a trip to the spaceport for my property." Three or four of the guards were suddenly quite close.

"You will find," said Alen dryly, "that our standard of commercial morality is no lower than yours."

The dealer smiled politely and left.

"Who will be the next?" asked Alen of the room at large.

"I'll look at your gems," said another dealer, sitting at the table.

With the ice-breaking done, the transactions went quicker. Alen had disposed of a dozen lots by the time their first buyer returned.

"It's all right," he said. "We've been tricked before, but your gems are as represented. I congratulate you, Herald, on driving a hard, fair bargain."

"That means," said Alen regretfully, "that I should have asked for more." The guards were once more lounging in corners and no longer seemed so menacing.

They had a midday meal and continued to dispose of their wares. At sunset Alen held a final auction to clean up the odd lots that remained over and was urged to stay to dinner.

The trader, counting a huge wad of the Lyran man-power-based notes, shook his head. "We should be off before dawn, Herald," he told Alen. "Time is money, time is money."

"They are very insistent."

"And I am very stubborn. Thank them and let us be on our way before anything else is done to increase my overhead."

Something did turn up—a city watchman with a bloody nose and split lip.

He demanded of the Herald: "Are you responsible for the Cephean maniac known as Elwon?"

Garthkint glided up to mutter in Alen's ear: "Beware how you answer!"

Alen needed no warning. His grounding included

Lyran legal concepts—and on the backward little planet touched with many relics of feudalism "responsible" covered much territory.

"What has Chief Elwon done?" he parried.

"As you see," the watchman glumly replied, pointing to his wounds. "And the same to three others before we got him out of the wrecked wineshop and into the castle. Are you responsible for him?"

"Let me speak with my trader for a moment. Will you have some wine meantime?" He signaled and one of the guards brought a mug.

"Don't mind if I do. I can use it," sighed the watchman.

"We are in trouble," said Alen to blackbeard. "Chief Elwon is in the 'castle'—prison—for drunk and disorderly conduct. You as his master are considered responsible for his conduct under Lyran law. You must pay his fines or serve his penalties. Or you can 'disown' him, which is considered dishonorable but sometimes necessary. For paying his fine or serving his time you have a prior lien on his services, without pay—but of course that's unenforceable off Lyra."

Blackbeard was sweating a little. "Find out from the policeman how long all this is likely to take. I don't want to leave Elwon here and I do want us to get off as soon as possible. Keep him occupied, now, while I go about some business."

The trader retreated to a corner of the darkening barnlike tavern, beckoning Garthkint and a guard with him as Alen returned to the watchman.

"Good keeper of the peace," he said, "will you have another?"

He would.

"My trader wishes to know what penalties are likely to be levied against the unfortunate Chief Elwon."

"Going to leave him in the lurch, eh?" asked the watchman a little belligerently. "A fine master you have!"

One of the dealers at the table indignantly corroborated him. "If you foreigners aren't prepared to live up to your obligations, why did you come here in the first place? What happens to business if a master can send his man to steal and cheat and then say: 'Don't blame *me*—it was *his* doing!"

Alen patiently explained: "On other planets, good Lyrans, the tie of master and man is not so strong that a man would obey if he were ordered to go and steal or cheat."

They shook their heads and muttered. It was unheard-of.

"Good watchman," pressed the Herald, "my trader does not *want* to disown Chief Elwon. Can you tell me what recompense would be necessary—and how long it would take to manage the business?"

The watchman started on a third cup which Alen unostentatiously signaled for. "It's hard to say," he told the Herald weightily. "For my damages, I would demand a hundred credits at least. The three other members of the watch battered by your lunatic could ask no less. The wineshop suffered easily five hundred credits' damage. The owner of it was beaten, but that doesn't matter, of course."

"No imprisonment?"

"Oh, a flogging, of course"—Alen started before he recalled that the "flogging" was a few half-hearted symbolic strokes on the covered shoulders with a light cane—"but no imprisonment. His Honor, Judge Krarl, does not sit on the night bench. Judge Krarl is a new-fangled reformer, stranger. He professes to believe that mulcting is unjust—that it makes it easy for the rich to commit crime and go scot-free."

"But doesn't it?" asked Alen, drawn off-course in spite of himself. There was pitying laughter around him.

"Look you," a dealer explained kindly. "The good watchman suffers battery, the mad Cephean or his master is mulcted for damages, the watchman is repaid for his injuries. What kind of justice is it to the watchman if the mad Cephean is locked away in a cell unfined?"

The watchman nodded approvingly. "Well-said," he told the dealer. "Luckily we have on the night bench a justice of the old school, His Honor, Judge Treel. Stern, but fair. You should hear him! 'Fifty credits! A hundred credits and the lash! Robbed a ship, eh? Two thousand credits!' " He returned to his own voice and said with awe: "For a murder, he never assesses less than *ten thousand credits!*"

And if the murderer couldn't pay, Alen knew, he became a "public charge," "responsible to the state"—that is, a slave. If he could pay, of course, he was turned loose.

"And His Honor, Judge Treel," he pressed, "is sitting tonight? Can we possibly appear before him, pay the fines, and be off?"

"To be sure, stranger. I'd be a fool if I waited until morning, wouldn't I?" The wine had loosened his tongue a little too far and he evidently realized it. "Enough of this," he said. "Does your master honorably accept responsibility for the Cephean? If so, come along with me, the two of you, and we'll get this over with."

"Thanks, good watchman. We are coming."

He went to blackbeard, now alone in his corner, and said: "It's all right. We can pay off—about a thousand credits—and be on our way."

The trader muttered darkly: "Lyran jurisdiction or not, it's coming out of Elwon's pay. The bloody fool!"

They rattled through the darkening streets of the town in one of the turbine-powered wagons, the watchman sitting up front with the driver and the trader and the Herald behind.

"Something's burning," said Alen to the trader, sniffing the air.

"This stinking buggy—" began blackbeard. "Oops,"

he said, interrupting himself and slapping at his cloak.

"Let me, trader," said Alen. He turned back the cloak, licked his thumb, and rubbed out a crawling ring of sparks spreading across a few centimeters of the cloak's silk lining. And he looked fixedly at what had started the little fire. It was an improperly covered slow-match protruding from a holstered device that was unquestionably a hand weapon.

"I bought it from one of their guards while you were parleying with the policeman," explained blackbeard embarrassedly. "I had a time making him understand. That Garthkint fellow helped." He fiddled with the perforated cover of the slow-match, screwing it on more firmly.

"A pitiful excuse for a weapon," he went on, carefully arranging his cloak over it. "The trigger isn't a trigger and the thumb-safety isn't a safety. You pump the trigger a few times to build up pressure, and a little air squirts out to blow the match to life. Then you uncover the match and pull back the cocking-piece. This levers a dart into the barrel. *Then* you push the thumb-safety which puffs coaldust into the firing chamber and also swivels down the slow-match onto a touch-hole. *Poof,* and away goes the dart if you didn't forget any of the steps or do them in the wrong order. Luckily, I also got a knife."

He patted the nape of his neck and said, "That's where they carry 'em here. A little sheath between the shoulder blades—wonderful for a fast draw-and-throw, though it exposes you a little more than I like when you reach. The knife's black glass. Splendid edge and good balance.

"And the thieving Lyrans knew they had me where it hurt. Seven thousand, five hundred credits for the knife and gun—if you can call it that—and the holsters. By rights I should dock Elwon for them, the bloody fool. Still, it's better to buy his way out and leave no hard feelings behind us, eh, Herald?"

"Incomparably better," said Alen. "And I am amazed that you even entertained the idea of an armed jail delivery. What if Chief Elwon had to serve a few days in a prison? Would that be worse than forever barring yourself from the planet and blackening the names of all traders with Lyra? Trader, do not hope to put down the credits that your weapons cost you as a legitimate expense of the voyage. I will not allow it when I audit your books. It was a piece of folly on which you spent personal funds, as far as the College and Order of Heralds is concerned."

"Look here," protested blackbeard. "You're supposed to be spreading utilitarian civilization, aren't you. What's utilitarian about leaving one of my crewmen here?"

Alen ignored the childish argument and wrapped himself in angry silence. As to civilization, he wondered darkly whether such a trading voyage and his part in it was relevant at all. Were the slanders true? Was the College and Order simply a collection of dupes headed by cynical oldsters greedy for luxury and power?

Such thoughts hadn't crossed his mind in a long time. He'd been too busy to entertain them, cramming his head with languages, folkways, mores, customs, underlying patterns of culture, of hundreds of galactic peoples—and for what? So that this fellow could make a profit and the College and Order take a quarter of that profit. If civilization was to come to Lyra, it would have to come in the form of metal. If the Lyrans didn't want metal, *make* them take it.

What did Machiavelli say? "The chief foundations of all states are good laws and good arms; and as there cannot be good laws where the state is not well-armed, it follows that where they are well-armed, they have good laws." It was odd that the teachers had slurred over such a seminal idea, emphasizing instead the spiritual integrity of the weaponless College and Order—or was it?

The disenchantment he felt creeping over him was terrifying.

"The castle," said the watchman over his shoulder, and their wagon stopped with a rattle before a large but unimpressive brick structure of five stories.

"You wait," the trader told the driver after they got out. He handed him two of his fifty-credit bills. "You wait, you get many, many more money. You understand, wait?"

"I wait plenty much," shouted the driver delightedly. "I wait all night, all day. You wonderful master. You great, great master, I wait—"

"All right," growled the trader, shutting him off. "You wait."

The watchman took them through an entrance hall lit by hissing pressure lamps and casually guarded by a few liveried men with truncheons. He threw open the door of a medium-sized, well-lit room with a score of people in it, looked in, and uttered a despairing groan.

A personage on a chair that looked like a throne said sharply, "Are those the star-travelers? Well, don't just stand there. Bring them in!"

"Yes, your honor, Judge Krarl," said the watchman unhappily.

"It's the wrong judge!" Alen hissed at the trader. "This one gives out jail sentences!"

"Do what you can," said blackbeard grimly.

The watchman guided them to the personage in the chair and indicated a couple of low stools, bowed to the chair, and retired to stand at the back of the room.

"Your honor," said Alen, "I am Journeyman-Herald Alen, Herald for the trading voyage—"

"Speak when you're spoken to," said the judge sharply. "Sir, with the usual insolence of wealth you have chosen to keep us waiting. I do not take this personally; it might have happened to Judge Treel, who—to your evident dismay—I am replacing because of a sudden illness, or to any other member of the bench. But as an insult to our justice, we cannot overlook it. Sir, consider your reprimanded. Take your seats. Watchman, bring in the Cephean."

"Sit down," Alen murmured to the trader. "This is going to be bad."

A watchman brought in Chief Elwon, bleary-eyed, tousled, and sporting a few bruises. He gave Alen and the trader a shamefaced grin as his guard sat him on a stool beside them. The trader glared back.

Judge Krarl mumbled perfunctorily: "Letbattlebejoin-edamongtheseveralpartiesinthisdisputeletnomanquestion ourimpartialawardingofthevictoryspeaknowifyouyieldin-steadtoourjudgment. *Well?* Speak up, you watchmen!"

The watchman who had brought the Herald and the trader started and said from the back of the room: "I yieldinsteadtoyourhonorsjudgment."

Three other watchmen and a battered citizen, the wineshop keeper, mumbled in turn: "Iyieldinsteadtoyour honorsjudgment."

"Herald, speak for the accused," snapped the judge.

Well, thought Alen, I can try. "Your honor," he said, "Chief Elwon's master does not yield to your honor's judgment. He is ready to battle the other parties in the dispute or their masters."

"What insolence is this?" screamed the judge, leaping from his throne. "The barbarous customs of other worlds do not prevail in this court! Who spoke of battle—?" He shut his mouth with a snap, evidently abruptly realizing that *he* had spoken of battle in an archaic phrase that harked back to the origins of justice on the planet. The judge sat down again and told Alen, more calmly: "You have mistaken a mere formality. The offer was not made in earnest." Obviously, he didn't like the sound of that himself, but he proceeded, "Now say 'I yieldinsteadtoyourhonorsjudgment,' and we can get on with it. For your information, trial by combat has not been practiced for many generations on our enlightened planet."

Alen said politely: "Your honor, I am a stranger to many of the ways of Lyra, but our excellent College and Order of Heralds instructed me well in the underlying principles of your law. I recall that one of your most revered legal maxims declares: 'The highest crime against man is murder; the highest crime against man's society is breach of promise.' "

Purpling, the judge snarled: "Are you presuming to bandy law with me, you slippery-tongued foreigner? Are you presuming to accuse me of the high crime of breaking my promise? For your information, a promise consists of an offer to do, or refrain from doing, a thing in return for a consideration. There must be the five elements of promiser, promisee, offer, substance, and consideration."

"If you will forgive a foreigner," said Alen, suddenly feeling the ground again under his feet, "I maintain that you offered the parties in the dispute your services in awarding the victory."

"An empty argument," snorted the judge. "Just as an offer with substance from somebody to nobody for a consideration is no promise, or an offer without substance from somebody to somebody for a consideration is no promise, so my offer was no promise, for there was no consideration involved."

"Your honor, must the consideration be from the promisee to the promiser?"

"Of course not. A third party may provide the consideration."

"Then I respectfully maintain that your offer was a promise, since a third party, the government, provided you with the considerations of salary and position in return for you offering your services to the disputants."

"Watchmen, clear the room of disinterested persons," said the judge hoarsely. While it was being done, Alen swiftly filled in the trader and Chief Elwon. Blackbeard grinned at the mention of a five-against-one battle royal, and the engineer looked alarmed.

When the doors closed leaving the nine of them in privacy, the judge said bitterly: "Herald, where did you learn such devilish tricks?"

Alen told him: "My College and Order instructed me well. A similar situation existed on a planet called England during an age known as the Victorious. Trial by combat had long been obsolete, there as here, but had never been declared so—there as here. A litigant won a hopeless lawsuit by publishing a challenge to his opponent and appearing at the appointed place in full armor. His opponent ignored the challenge and so lost the suit by default. The English dictator, one Disraeli, hastily summoned his parliament to abolish trial by combat."

"And so," mused the judge, "I find myself accused in my own chamber of high crime if I do not permit you five to slash away at each other and decide who won."

The wineshop keeper began to blubber that he was a peaceable man and didn't intend to be carved up by that blackbearded, bloodthirsty star-traveler. All he wanted was his money.

"Silence!" snapped the judge. "Of course there will be no combat. Will you, shopkeeper, and you, watchmen, withdraw if you receive satisfactory financial settlements?"

They would.

"Herald, you may dicker with them."

The four watchmen stood fast by their demand for a hundred credits apiece, and got it. The terrified shopkeeper regained his balance and demanded a thousand. Alen explained that his blackbearded master from a rude and impetuous world might be unable to restrain his rage when he, Alen, interpreted the demand and, ignoring the consequences, might beat him, the shopkeeper, to a pulp. The asking price plunged to a reasonable five hundred, which was paid over. The shopkeeper got the judge's permission to leave and backed out, bowing.

"You see, trader," Alen told blackbeard, "that it was needless to buy weapons when the spoken word—"

"And now," said the judge with a sneer, "we are easily out of *that* dilemma. Watchmen, arrest the three star-travelers and take them to the cages."

"Your honor!" cried Alen, outraged.

"Money won't get you out of *this* one. I charge you with treason."

"The charge is obsolete—" began the Herald hotly, but he broke off as he realized the vindictive strategy.

"Yes, it is. And one of its obsolete provisions is that treason charges must be tried by the parliament at a regular session, which isn't due for two hundred days. You'll be freed and I may be reprimanded, but by my head, for two hundred days you'll regret that you made a fool of *me*. Take them away."

"A trumped-up charge against us. Prison for two hundred days," said Alen swiftly to the trader as the watchmen closed in.

"Why buy weapons?" mocked the blackbeard, showing his teeth. His left arm whipped up and down, there was a black streak through the air—and the judge was pinned to his throne with a black glass knife through his throat and the sneer of triumph still on his lips.

The trader, before the knife struck, had the clumsy pistol out, with the cover off the glowing match and the cocking piece back. He must have pumped and cocked it under his cloak, thought Alen numbly as he told the watchmen, without prompting: "Get back against the wall and turn around." They did. They wanted to live, and the grinning blackbeard who had made meat of the judge with a flick of the arm was a terrifying figure.

"Well done, Alen," said the trader. "Take their clubs, Elwon. Two for you, two for the Herald. Alen, don't argue! I had to kill the judge before he raised an alarm

—nothing but death will silence his breed. You may have to kill too before we're out of this. Take the clubs." He passed the clumsy pistol to Chief Elwon and said: "Keep it on their backs. The thing that looks like a thumb-safety is a trigger. Put a dart through the first one who tries to make a break. Alen, tell the fellow on the end to turn around and come to me slowly."

Alen did. Blackbeard swiftly stripped him, tore and knotted his clothes into ropes, and bound and gagged him. The others got the same treatment in less than ten minutes.

The trader holstered the gun and rolled the watchmen out of the line of sight from the door of the chamber. He recovered his knife and wiped it on the judge's shirt. Alen had to help him prop the body behind the throne's high back.

"Hide those clubs," blackbeard said. "Straight faces. Here we go."

They went out, single file, opening the door only enough to pass. Alen, last in line, told one of the liveried guards nearby: "His honor, Judge Krarl, does not wish to be disturbed."

"That's news?" asked the tipstaff sardonically. He put his hand on the Herald's arm. "Only yesterday he gimme a blast when I brought him a mug of water he asked me for himself. An outrageous interruption, he called me, and he asked for the water himself. What do you think of that?"

"Terrible," said Alen hastily. He broke away and caught up with the trader and the engineer at the entrance hall. Idlers and loungers were staring at them as they headed for the waiting wagon.

"I wait!" the driver told them loudly. "I wait long, much. You pay more, more?"

"We pay more," said the trader. "You start."

The driver brought out a smoldering piece of punk, lit a pressure torch, lifted the barn-door section of the wagon's floor to expose the pottery turbine, and preheated it with the torch. He pumped squeakily for minutes, spinning a flywheel with his other hand, before the rotor began to turn on its own. Down went the hatch, up onto the seats went the passengers.

"The spaceport," said Alen. With a slate-pencil screech the driver engaged his planetary gear and they were off.

Through it all, blackbeard had ignored frantic muttered questions from Chief Elwon, who had wanted nothing to do with murder, especially of a judge. "You sit up there," growled the trader, "and every so often you look around and see if we're being followed. Don't alarm the driver. And if we get to the spaceport and blast off without any trouble, keep your story to yourself." He settled down in the back seat with Alen and maintained a gloomy silence. The young Herald was too much in awe of this stranger, so suddenly competent in assorted forms of violence, to question him.

They did get to the spaceport without trouble, and found the crew in the Customs shed, emptied of the gems by dealers with releases. They had built a fire for warmth.

"We wish to leave immediately," said the trader to the port officer. "Can you change my Lyran currency?"

The officers began to sputter apologetically that it was late and the vault was sealed for the night—

"That's all right. We'll change it on Vega. It'll get back to you. Call off your guards and unseal our ship."

They followed the port officer to *Starsong*'s dim bulk out on the field. The officer cracked the seal on her with his club in the light of a flaring pressure lamp held by one of the guards.

Alen was sweating hard through it all. As they started across the field he had seen what looked like two closely spaced green stars low on the horizon toward town suddenly each jerk up and toward each other in minute arcs. The semaphore!

The signal officer in the port administration building would be watching too—but nobody on the field, preoccupied with the routine of departure, seemed to have noticed.

The lights flipped this way and that. Alen didn't know the code and bitterly regretted the lack. After some twenty signals the lights flipped to the "rest" position again as the port officer was droning out a set of take-off regulations: bearing, height above settled areas, permissible atomic fuels while in atmosphere—Alen saw somebody start across the field toward them from the administration building. The guards were leaning on their long, competent-looking weapons.

Alen inconspicuously detached himself from the group around *Starsong* and headed across the dark field to meet the approaching figure. Nearing it, he called out a low greeting in Lyran, using the noncom-to-officer military form.

"Sergeant," said the signal officer quietly, "go and draw off the men a few meters from the star-travelers. Tell them the ship mustn't leave, that they're to cover the foreigners and shoot if—"

Alen stood dazedly over the limp body of the signal officer. And then he quickly hid the bludgeon again and strolled back to the ship, wondering whether he'd cracked the Lyran's skull.

The port was open by then and the crew filing in. He was last. "Close it fast," he told the trader. "I had to—"

"I saw you," grunted blackbeard. "A semaphore message?" He was working as he spoke, and the metal port closed.

"Astrogator and engineer, take over," he told them.

"All hands to their bunks," ordered Astrogator Hufner. "Blast-off immediate."

Alen took to his cubicle and strapped himself in. Blast-off deafened him, rattled his bones, and made him thoroughly sick as usual. After what seemed like several wretched hours, they were definitely spaceborne under smooth acceleration, and his nausea subsided.

Blackbeard knocked, came in, and unbuckled him.

"Ready to audit the books of the voyage?" asked the trader.

"No," said Alen feebly.

"It can wait," said the trader. "The books are the least important part, anyway. We have headed off a frightful war."

"War? We have?"

"War between Eyolf's Realm and Vega. It is the common gossip of chancellories and trade missions that both governments have cast longing eyes on Lyra, that they have plans to penetrate its economy by supplying metals to the planet without metals—by force, if need be. Alen, we have removed the pretext by which Eyolf's Realm and Vega would have attempted to snap up Lyra and inevitably have come into conflict. Lyra is getting its metal now, and without imperialist entanglements."

"I saw none," the Herald said blankly.

"You wondered why I was in such haste to get off Lyra, and why I wouldn't leave Elwon there. It is because our Vegan gems were most unusual gems. I am not a technical man, but I understand they are actual gems which were treated to produce a certain effect at just about this time."

Blackbeard glanced at his wrist chronometer and said dreamily: "Lyra is getting metal. Wherever there is one of our gems, pottery is decomposing into its constituent aluminum, silicon, and oxygen. Fluxes and glazes are decomposing into calcium, zinc, barium, potassium, chromium, *and iron*. Buildings are crumbling, pants are dropping as ceramic beltbuckles disintegrate—"

"It means chaos!" protested Alen.

"It means civilization and peace. An ugly clash was

in the making." Blackbeard paused and added deliberately: "Where neither their property nor their honor is touched, most men live content."

" 'The Prince,' Chapter 19. You are—"

"There was another important purpose to the voyage," said the trader, grinning. "You will be interested in this." He handed Alen a document which, unfolded, had the seal of the College and Order at its head.

Alen read in a daze: "Examiner 19 to the Rector—final clearance of Novice—"

He lingered pridefully over the paragraph that described how he had "with coolness and great resource" foxed the battle cruiser of the Realm, "adapting himself readily in a delicate situation requiring not only physical courage but swift recall, evaluation, and application of a minor planetary culture."

Not so pridefully he read: "—inclined toward pomposity of manner somewhat ludicrous in one of his years, though not unsuccessful in dominating the crew by his bearing—"

And: "—highly profitable disposal of our gems; a feat of no mean importance since the College and Order must, after all, maintain itself."

And: "—cleared the final and crucial hurdle with some mental turmoil if I am any judge, but did clear it. After some twenty years of indoctrination in unrealistic nonviolence, the youth was confronted with a situation where nothing but violence would serve, correctly evaluated this, and applied violence in the form of a truncheon to the head of a Lyran signal officer, thereby demonstrating an ability to learn and common sense as precious as it is rare."

And, finally, simply: "Recommended for training."

"Training?" gasped Alen. "You mean there's more?"

"Not for most, boy. Not for most. The bulk of us are what we seem to be: oily, gun-shy, indispensable adjuncts to trade who feather our nest with percentages. We need those percentages and we need gun-shy Heralds."

Alen recited slowly: "Among other evils which being unarmed brings you, it causes you to be despised."

"Chapter 14," said blackbeard mechanically. "We leave such clues lying by their bedsides for twenty years, and they never notice them. For the few of us who do—more training."

"Will I learn to throw a knife like you?" asked Alen, repelled and fascinated at once by the idea.

"On your own time, if you wish. Mostly it's ethics and morals so you'll be able to weigh the values of such things as knife-throwing."

"Ethics! Morals!"

"We started as missionaries, you know."

"Everybody knows that. But the Great Utilitarian Reform—"

"Some of us," said blackbeard dryly, "think it was neither great, nor utilitarian, nor a reform."

It was a staggering idea. "But we're spreading utilitarian civilization!" protested Alen. "Or if we're not, what's the sense of it all?"

Blackbeard told him: "We have our different motives. One is a sincere utilitarian; another is a gambler—happy when he's in danger and his pulses are pounding. Another is proud and likes to trick people. More than a few conceive themselves as servants of mankind. I'll let you rest for a bit now." He rose.

"But you?" asked Alen hesitantly.

"Me? You will find me in Chapter Twenty-Six," grinned blackbeard. "And perhaps you'll find someone else." He closed the door behind him.

Alen ran through the chapter in his mind, puzzled, until—that was it.

It had a strange and inevitable familiarity to it as if he had always known that he would be saying it aloud, welcomingly, in this cramped cubicle aboard a battered starship:

"God is not willing to do everything, and thus take away our free will and that share of glory which belongs to us."

THE MEN RETURN

Jack Vance

And what if cause were sundered from effect? And what if reason itself perished? In one of his least-known stories, Jack Vance, the celebrated author of such science-fiction classics as *To Live Forever* and *The Dragon Masters*, offers us a dizzying peek into nightmare.

The Relict came furtively down the crag, a shambling gaunt creature with tortured eyes. He moved in a series of quick dashes using panels of dark air for concealment, running behind each passing shadow, at times crawling on all fours, head low to the ground. Arriving at the final low outcrop of rock, he halted, peered across the plain.

Far away rose low hills, blurring into the sky, which was mottled and sallow like poor milk-glass. The intervening plain spread like rotten velvet, black-green and wrinkled, streaked with ocher and rust. A fountain of liquid rock jetted high in the air, branched out into black coral. In the middle distance a family of gray objects evolved with a sense of purposeful destiny: spheres melted into pyramids, became domes, tufts of white spires, sky-piercing poles; then, as a final *tour de force,* tesseracts.

The Relict cared nothing for this; he needed food:

out on the plain were plants. They would suffice in lieu of anything better. They grew in the ground, or sometimes on a floating lump of water, or to a core of hard black gas. There were dank black flaps of leaf, clumps of haggard thorn, pale green bulbs, stalks with leaves and contorted flowers. There were no definite growths or species, and the Relict had no means of knowing if the leaves and tendrils he had eaten yesterday would poison him today.

He tested the surface of the plain with his foot. The glassy surface (though it likewise seemed a construction of red and gray-green pyramids) accepted his weight, then suddenly sucked at his leg. In a frenzy he tore himself free, jumped back, squatted on the temporarily solid rock.

Hunger rasped at his stomach. He must eat. He contemplated the plain. Not too far away a pair of Organisms played—sliding, diving, dancing, striking flamboyant poses. Should they approach he would try to kill one of them. They resembled men, and so should make a good meal.

He waited. A long time? A short time? It might have been either; duration had neither quantitative nor qualitative reality. The sun had vanished, there was no standard cycle or recurrence. Time was a word blank of meaning.

Matters had not always been so. The Relict retained a few tattered recollections of the old days, before system and logic had been rendered obsolete. Man had dominated Earth by virtue of a single assumption: that an effect could be traced to a cause, itself the effect of a previous cause.

Manipulation of this basic law yielded rich results; there seemed no need for any other tool or instrumentality. Man congratulated himself on his generalized structure. He could live on desert, on plain or ice, in forest or in city; Nature had not shaped him to a special environment.

He was unaware of his vulnerability. Logic was the special environment; the brain was the special tool.

Then came the terrible hour when Earth swam into a pocket of noncausality, and all the ordered tensions of cause-effect dissolved. The special tool was useless; it had no purchase on reality. From the two billions of men, only a few survived—the mad. They were now the Organisms, lords of the era, their discords so exactly equivalent to the vagaries of the land as to constitute a peculiar wild wisdom. Or perhaps the disorganized matter of the world, loose from the old organization, was peculiarly sensitive to psychokinesis.

A handful of others, the Relicts, managed to exist, but only through a delicate set of circumstances. They were the ones most strongly charged with the old causal dynamic. It persisted sufficiently to control the metabolism of their bodies, but could extend no further. They were fast, fast dying, for sanity provided no leverage against the environment. Sometimes their own minds sputtered and jangled, and they would go raving and leaping out across the plain.

The Organisms observed with neither surprise nor curiosity; how could surprise exist? The mad Relict might pause by an Organism, and try to duplicate the creature's existence. The Organism ate a mouthful of plant; so did the Relict. The Organism rubbed his feet with crushed water; so did the Relict. Then presently the Relict would die of poison or rent bowels or skin lesions, while the Organism relaxed in the dank black grass. Or the Organism might seek to eat the Relict; and the Relict would run off in terror, unable to abide any part of the world—running, bounding, breasting the thick air; eyes wide, mouth open, calling and gasping until finally he foundered in a pool of black iron or blundered into a vacuum pocket, to bat around like a fly in a bottle.

The Relicts now numbered very few. Finn, he who crouched on the rock overlooking the plain, lived with four others. Two of these were old men and soon would die. Finn likewise would die unless he found food.

Out on the plain one of the Organisms, Alpha, sat down, caught a handful of air, a globe of blue liquid, a rock, kneaded them together, pulled the mixture like taffy, gave it a great heave. It uncoiled from his hand like rope. The Relict crouched low. No telling what deviltry would occur to the creature. He and all the rest of them—unpredictable! The Relict valued their flesh to eat; but they also would eat him if opportunity offered. In the competition he was at a great disadvantage. Their random acts baffled him. Seeking to escape, he ran, and then the terror began. The direction he set his face was seldom the direction the varying frictions of the ground let him move. Behind was the Organism, as random and uncommitted as the environment. The double set of vagaries sometimes compounded, sometimes canceled each other. In the latter case the Organism might catch him. . . . It was inexplicable. But then, what was not? The word "explanation" had no meaning.

They were moving toward him. Had they seen him? He flattened himself against the sullen yellow rock.

The Organisms paused not far away. He could hear their sounds, and crouched, sick from conflicting pangs of hunger and fear.

Alpha sank to his knees, lay flat on his back, arms and legs flung out at random, addressing the sky in a series of musical cries, sibilants, guttural groans. It was a personal language he had only now improvised, but Beta understood him well.

"A vision," cried Alpha. "I see past the sky. I see knots, spinning circles. They tighten into hard points; they will never come undone."

Beta perched on a pyramid, glanced over his shoulder at the mottled sky.

"An intuition," chanted Alpha, "a picture out of the other time. It is hard, merciless, inflexible."

Beta poised on the pyramid, dove through the glassy surface, swam under Alpha, emerged, lay flat beside him.

"Observe the Relict on the hillside. In his blood is the whole of the old race—the narrow men with minds like cracks. He has exuded the intuition. Clumsy thing—a blunderer," said Alpha.

"They are all dead, all of them," cried Beta. "Although three or four remain." (When *past, present,* and *future* are no more than ideas left over from another era, like boats on a dry lake—then the completion of a process can never be defined.)

Alpha said, "This is the vision. I see the Relicts swarming the Earth; then whisking off to nowhere, like gnats in the wind. That is behind us."

The Organisms lay quiet, considering the vision.

A rock, or perhaps a meteor, fell from the sky, struck into the surface of the pond. It left a circular hole which slowly closed. From another part of the pool a gout of fluid splashed into the air, floated away.

Alpha spoke: "Again—the intuition comes strong! There will be lights in the sky."

The fever died in him. He hooked a finger into the air, hoisted himself to his feet.

Beta lay quiet. Slugs, ants, flies, beetles were crawling on him, boring, breeding. Alpha knew that Beta could rise, shake off the insects, stride off. But Beta seemed to prefer passivity. That was well enough. He could produce another Beta should he choose, or a dozen of him. Sometimes the world swarmed with Organisms, all sorts, all colors, tall as steeples, short and squat as flowerpots. Sometimes they hid quietly in deep caves, and sometimes the tentative substance of Earth would shift, and perhaps one, or perhaps thirty, would be shut in the subterranean cocoon, and all would sit gravely waiting, until such time as the ground would open and they could peer blinking and pallid out into the light.

"I feel a lack," said Alpha. "I will eat the Relict." He set forth, and sheer chance brought him near to the ledge of yellow rock. Finn the Relict sprang to his feet in panic.

Alpha tried to communicate, so that Finn might pause while Alpha ate. But Finn had no grasp for the many-valued overtones of Alpha's voice. He seized a rock, hurled it at Alpha. The rock puffed into a cloud of dust, blew back into the Relict's face.

Alpha moved closer, extended his long arms. The Relict kicked. His feet went out from under him, he slid out on the plain. Alpha ambled complacently behind him. Finn began to crawl away. Alpha moved off to the right—one direction was as good as another. He collided with Beta, and began to eat Beta instead of the Relict. The Relict hesitated; then approached, and, joining Alpha, pushed chunks of pink flesh into his mouth.

Alpha said to the Relict, "I was about to communicate an intuition to him whom we dine upon. I will speak to you."

Finn could not understand Alpha's personal language. He ate as rapidly as possible.

Alpha spoke on. "There will be lights in the sky. The great lights."

Finn rose to his feet and, warily watching Alpha, seized Beta's legs, began to pull him toward the hill. Alpha watched with quizzical unconcern.

It was hard work for the spindly Relict. Sometimes Beta floated; sometimes he wafted off on the air; sometimes he adhered to the terrain. At last he sank into a knob of granite which froze around him. Finn tried to jerk Beta loose, pry him up with a stick, without success.

He ran back and forth in an agony of indecision. Beta began to collapse, wither, like a jellyfish on hot sand. The Relict abandoned the hulk. Too late, too late! Food going to waste! The world was a hideous place of frustration!

Temporarily his belly was full. He started back up the crag, and presently found the camp, where the four other Relicts waited—two ancient males, two females. The females, Gisa and Reak, like Finn, had been out foraging. Gisa had brought in a slab of lichen, Reak a bit of nameless carrion.

The old men, Boad and Tagart, sat quietly waiting either for food or for death.

The women greeted Finn sullenly. "Where is the food you went forth to find?"

"I had a whole carcass," said Finn. "I could not carry it."

Boad had slyly stolen the slab of lichen and was cramming it into his mouth. It had come alive; it quivered and exuded a red ichor which was poison, and the old man died.

"Now there is food," said Finn. "Let us eat."

But the poison created a putrescence; the body seethed with blue foam, flowed away of its own energy.

The women turned to look at the other old man, who said in a quavering voice, "Eat me if you must—but why not choose Reak, who is younger than I?"

Reak, the younger of the women, gnawing on the bit of carrion, made no reply.

Finn said hollowly, "Why do we worry ourselves? Food is ever more difficult, and we are the last of all men."

"No, no," spoke Reak, "not the last. We saw others on the green mound."

"That is long ago," said Gisa. "Now they are surely dead."

"Perhaps they have found a source of food," suggested Reak.

Finn rose to his feet, looked across the plain. "Who knows? Perhaps there is a more pleasant land beyond the horizon."

"There is nothing anywhere but waste and evil creatures," snapped Gisa.

"What could be worse than here?" Finn argued.

No one could find grounds for disagreement.

"Here is what I propose," said Finn. "Notice this tall peak. Notice the layers of hard air. They bump into the peak; they bounce off; they float in and out and disappear past the edge of sight. Let us all climb this peak, and when a sufficiently large bank of air passes, we will throw ourselves on top, and allow it to carry us to the beautiful regions which may exist just out of sight."

There was an argument. The old man Tagart protested his feebleness; the women derided the possibility of the bountiful regions Finn envisioned, but presently, grumbling and arguing, they began to clamber up the pinnacle.

It took a long time; the obsidian was soft as jelly; Tagart several times professed himself at the limit of his endurance. But still they climbed, and at last reached the pinnacle. There was barely room to stand. They could see in all directions, far out over the landscape, till vision was lost in the watery gray.

The women bickered and pointed in various directions; but there was small sign of happier territory. In one direction blue-green hills shivered like bladders full of oil. In another direction lay a streak of black—a gorge or a lake of clay. In another direction were blue-green hills—the same they had seen in the first direction; somehow there had been a shift. Below was the plain, gleaming like an iridescent beetle, here and there pocked with black velvet spots, overgrown with questionable vegetation.

They saw Organisms, a dozen shapes loitering by ponds, munching vegetable pods or small rocks or insects. There came Alpha. He moved slowly, still awed by his vision, ignoring the other Organisms. Their play went on, but presently they stood quiet, sharing the oppression.

On the obsidian peak, Finn caught hold of a passing

filament of air, drew it in. "Now—all on, and we sail away to the Land of Plenty."

"No," protested Gisa, "there is no room, and who knows if it will fly in the right direction?"

"Where is the right direction?" asked Finn. "Does anyone know?"

No one knew, but the women still refused to climb aboard the filament. Finn turned to Tagart. "Here, old one, show these women how it is; climb on!"

"No, no," he cried. "I fear the air; this is not for me."

"Climb on, old man, then we follow."

Wheezing and fearful, clenching his hands deep into the spongy mass, Tagart put himself out on the air, spindly shanks hanging over into nothing. "Now," spoke Finn, "who next?"

The women still refused. "You go then, yourself," cried Gisa.

"And leave you, my last guarantee against hunger?' Aboard now!"

"No, the air is too small; let the old one go and we will follow on a larger."

"Very well." Finn released his grip. The air floated off over the plain, Tagart straddling and clutching for dear life.

They watched him curiously. "Observe," said Finn, "how fast and easily moves the air. Above the Organisms, over all the slime and uncertainty."

But the air itself was uncertain, and the old man's raft dissolved. Clutching at the department wisps, Tagart sought to hold his cushion together. It fled from under him, and he fell.

On the peak the three watched the spindly shape flap and twist on its way to earth far below.

"Now," Reak exclaimed vexatiously, "we even have no more meat."

"None," said Gisa, "except the visionary Finn himself."

They surveyed Finn. Together they would more than outmatch him.

"Careful," cried Finn. "I am the last of the Men. You are my women, subject to my orders."

They ignored him, muttering to each other, looking at him from the side of their faces. "Careful!" cried Finn. "I will throw you both from this peak."

"That is what we plan for you," said Gisa.

They advanced with sinister caution.

"Stop! I am the last man!"

"We are better off without you."

"One moment! Look at the Organisms!"

The women looked. The Organisms stood in a knot, staring at the sky.

"Look at the sky!"

The women looked; the frosted glass was cracking, breaking, curling aside.

"The blue! The blue sky of old times!"

A terribly bright light burnt down, seared their eyes. The rays warmed their naked backs.

"The sun," they said in awed voices. "The sun has come back to Earth."

The shrouded sky was gone; the sun rode proud and bright in a sea of blue. The ground below churned, cracked, heaved, solidified. They felt the obsidian harden under their feet; its color shifted to glossy black. The Earth, the sun, the galaxy, had departed the region of freedom; the other time with its restrictions and logic was once more with them.

"This is Old Earth," cried Finn. "We are Men of Old Earth! The land is once again ours!"

"And what of the Organisms?"

"If this is the Earth of old, then let the Organisms beware!"

The Organisms stood on a low rise of ground beside a runnel of water that was rapidly becoming a river flowing out onto the plain.

Alpha cried, "Here is my intuition! It is exactly as I knew. The freedom is gone; the tightness, the constriction are back!"

"How will we defeat it?" asked another Organism.

"Easily," said a third. "Each must fight a part of the battle. I plan to hurl myself at the sun, and blot it from existence." And he crouched, threw himself into the air. He fell on his back and broke his neck.

"The fault," said Alpha, "is in the air; because the air surrounds all things."

Six Organisms ran off in search of air and, stumbling into the river, drowned.

"In any event," said Alpha, "I am hungry." He looked around for suitable food. He seized an insect which stung him. He dropped it. "My hunger remains."

He spied Finn and the two women descending from the crag. "I will eat one of the Relicts," he said. "Come, let us all eat."

Three of them started off—as usual in random directions. By chance Alpha came face to face with Finn. He prepared to eat, but Finn picked up a rock. The rock remained a rock, hard, sharp, heavy. Finn swung it down, taking joy in the inertia. Alpha died with a crushed skull. One of the other Organisms attempted to step across a crevass twenty feet wide and so disappeared; the other sat down, swallowed rocks to assuage his hunger, and presently went into convulsions.

Finn pointed here and there around the fresh new land. "In that quarter, the new city, like that of the legends. Over here the farms, the cattle."

"We have none of these," protested Gisa.

"No," said Finn. "Not now. But once more the sun rises and sets; once more rock has weight and air has none. Once more water falls as rain and flows to the sea." He stepped forward over the fallen Organism. "Let us make plans."

THE VOICES OF TIME

J. G. Ballard

Conventional science fiction is much concerned with plot: Who did what to whom, and why, and how it can be undone. Even at the beginning of his stormy career, Britian's J. G. Ballard had other matters on his mind. Plot-oriented narrative makes sense only when the word itself makes some sense; but in a dislocated cosmos, ticking toward its ultimate entropic disintegration, the linear development of plot can come to seem a pointless endeavor. In recent years Ballard has abandoned even the semblance of conventional form and tells his "stories" now in a strange and eerie fashion of his own devising. This one, dating from 1960, employs the superficial mannerisms of the orthodox narrative, but in its dreamlike progression of events it foreshadows the evolving Ballard of a decade later.

I

Later Powers often thought of Whitby, and the strange grooves the biologist had cut, apparently at random, all over the floor of the empty swimming pool. An inch deep and twenty feet long, interlocking to form an elaborate ideogram like a Chinese character, they had taken him all summer to complete, and he had obviously thought about little else, working away tirelessly through the long desert afternoons. Powers had watched him from his office window at the far end of the Neurology wing, carefully marking out his pegs and string, carrying away the cement chips in a small canvas bucket. After Whitby's suicide no one had bothered about the grooves, but Powers often borrowed the supervisor's key and let himself into the disused pool, and would look down at the labyrinth of moldering gulleys, half-filled with water leaking in from the chlorinator, an enigma now past any solution.

Initially, however, Powers was too preoccupied with completing his work at the Clinic and planning his own final withdrawal. After the first frantic weeks of panic he had managed to accept an uneasy compromise that allowed him to view his predicament with the detached fatalism he had previously reserved for his patients. Fortunately he was moving down the physical and mental gradients simultaneously—lethargy and inertia blunted his anxieties, a slackening metabolism made it necessary to concentrate to produce a connected thought-train. In fact, the lengthening intervals of dreamless sleep were almost restful. He found himself beginning to look forward to them, made no effort to wake earlier than was essential.

At first he had kept an alarm clock by his bed, tried to compress as much activity as he could into the narrowing hours of consciousness, sorting out his library, driving over to Whitby's laboratory every morning to examine the latest batch of X-ray plates, every minute and hour rationed like the last drops of water in a canteen.

Anderson, fortunately, had unwittingly made him realize the pointlessness of this course.

After Powers had resigned from the Clinic he still

continued to drive in once a week for his checkup, now little more than a formality. On what turned out to be the last occasion Anderson had perfunctorily taken his blood count, noting Powers' slacker facial muscles, fading pupil reflexes, the unshaven cheeks.

He smiled sympathetically at Powers across the desk, wondering what to say to him. Once he had put on a show of encouragement with the more intelligent patients, even tried to provide some sort of explanation. But Powers was too difficult to reach—neurosurgeon extraordinary, a man always out on the periphery, only at ease working with unfamiliar materials. To himself he thought: *I'm sorry, Robert. What can I say—"Even the sun is growing cooler—?"* He watched Powers drum his fingers restlessly on the enamel desk top, his eyes glancing at the spinal level charts hung around the office. Despite his unkempt appearance—he had been wearing the same unironed shirt and dirty white plimsoles a week ago—Powers looked composed and self-possessed, like a Conrad beachcomber more or less reconciled to his own weaknesses.

"What are you doing with yourself, Robert?" he asked. "Are you still going over to Whitby's lab?"

"As much as I can. It takes me half an hour to cross the lake, and I keep on sleeping through the alarm clock. I may leave my place and move in there permanently."

Anderson frowned. "Is there much point? As far as I could make out Whitby's work was pretty speculative—" He broke off, realizing the implied criticism of Powers' own disastrous work at the Clinic, but Powers seemed to ignore this, was examining the pattern of shadows on the ceiling. "Anyway, wouldn't it be better to stay where you are, among your own things, read through Toynbee and Spengler again?"

Powers laughed shortly. "That's the last thing I want to do. I want to *forget* Toynbee and Spengler, not try to remember them. In fact, Paul, I'd like to forget everything. I don't know whether I've got enough time, though. How much can you forget in three months?"

"Everything, I suppose, if you want to. But don't try to race the clock."

Powers nodded quietly, repeating this last remark to himself. Racing the clock was exactly what he had been doing. As he stood up and said goodbye to Anderson he suddenly decided to throw away his alarm clock, escape from his futile obsession with time. To remind himself he unfastened his wristwatch and scrambled the setting, then slipped it into his pocket. Making his way out to the car park he reflected on the freedom this simple act gave him. He would explore the lateral by-ways now, the side doors, as it were, in the corridors of time. Three months could be an eternity.

He picked his car out of the line and strolled over to it, shielding his eyes from the heavy sunlight beating down across the parabolic sweep of the lecture theater roof. He was about to climb in when he saw that someone had traced with a finger across the dust caked over the windshield:

96,688,365,498,721

Looking over his shoulder, he recognized the white Packard parked next to him, peered inside, and saw a lean-faced young man with blonde sun-bleached hair and a high cerebrotonic forehead watching him behind dark glasses. Sitting beside him at the wheel was a raven-haired girl whom he had often seen around the psychology department. She had intelligent but somehow rather oblique eyes, and Powers remembered that the younger doctors called her "the girl from Mars."

"Hello, Kaldren," Powers said to the young man. "Still following me around?"

Kaldren nodded. "Most of the time, Doctor." He sized Powers up shrewdly. "We haven't seen very much of you recently, as a matter of fact. Anderson said you'd resigned, and we noticed your laboratory was closed."

Powers shrugged. "I felt I needed a rest. As you'll understand, there's a good deal that needs rethinking."

Kaldren frowned half-mockingly. "Sorry to hear that, Doctor. But don't let these temporary setbacks depress you." He noticed the girl watching Powers with interest. "Coma's a fan of yours. I gave her your papers from *American Journal of Psychiatry*, and she's read through the whole file."

The girl smiled pleasantly at Powers, for a moment dispelling the hostility between the two men. When Powers nodded to her she leaned across Kaldren and said: "Actually I've just finished Noguchi's autobiography—the great Japanese doctor who discovered the spirochete. Somehow you remind me of him—there's so much of yourself in all the patients you worked on."

Powers smiled wanly at her, then his eyes turned and locked involuntarily on Kaldren's. They stared at each other somberly for a moment, and a small tic in Kaldren's right cheek began to flicker irritatingly. He flexed his facial muscles, after a few seconds mastered it with an effort, obviously annoyed that Powers should have witnessed this brief embarrassment.

"How did the clinic go today?" Powers asked. "Have you had any more . . . headaches?"

Kaldren's mouth snapped shut, he looked suddenly irritable. "Whose care am I in, doctor? Yours or Anderson's? Is that the sort of question you should be asking now?"

Powers gestured deprecatingly. "Perhaps not." He cleared his throat; the heat was ebbing the blood from his head and he felt tired and eager to get away from them. He turned toward his car, then realized that Kaldren would probably follow, either try to crowd him into the ditch or block the road and make Powers sit in his dust all the way back to the lake. Kaldren was capable of any madness.

"Well, I've got to go and collect something," he said, adding in a firmer voice: "Get in touch with me, though, if you can't reach Anderson."

He waved and walked off behind the line of cars. Reflected in the windows he could see Kaldren looking back and watching him closely.

He entered the Neurology wing, paused thankfully in the cool foyer, nodding to the two nurses and the armed guard at the reception desk. For some reason the terminals sleeping in the adjacent dormitory block attracted hordes of would-be sightseers, most of them cranks with some magical antinarcoma remedy, or merely the idly curious, but a good number of quite normal people, many of whom had traveled thousands of miles, impelled towards the Clinic by some strange instinct, like animals migrating to a pre-view of their racial graveyards.

He walked along the corridor to the supervisor's office overlooking the recreation deck, borrow the key, and made his way out through the tennis courts and calisthenics rigs to the enclosed swimming pool at the far end. It had been disused for months, and only Powers' visits kept the lock free. Stepping through, he closed it behind him and walked past the peeling wooden stands to the deep end.

Putting a foot up on the diving board, he looked down at Whitby's ideogram. Damp leaves and bits of paper obscured it, but the outlines were just distinguishable. It covered almost the entire floor of the pool and at first glance appeared to represent a huge solar disc, with four radiating diamond-shaped arms, a crude Jungian mandala.

Wondering what had prompted Whitby to carve the device before his death, Powers noticed something moving through the debris in the center of the disc. A black, horny-shelled animal about a foot long was nosing about in the slush, heaving itself on tired legs. Its shell was articulated, and vaguely resembled an armadillo's. Reaching the edge of the disc, it stopped and hesitated, then slowly backed away into the center again, apparently unwilling or unable to cross the narrow groove.

Powers looked around, then stepped into one of the changing stalls and pulled a small wooden clothes locker off its rusty wall bracket. Carrying it under one arm, he climbed down the chromium ladder into the pool and walked carefully across the slithery floor toward the animal. As he approached it sidled away from him, but he trapped it easily, using the lid to lever it into the box.

The animal was heavy, at least the weight of a brick. Powers tapped its massive olive-black carapace with his knuckle, noting the triangular warty head jutting out below its rim like a turtle's, the thickened pads beneath the first digits of the pentadactyl forelimbs.

He watched the three-lidded eyes blinking at him anxiously from the bottom of the box.

"Expecting some really hot weather?" he murmured. "That lead umbrella you're carrying around should keep you cool."

He closed the lid, climbed out of the pool, and made his way back to the supervisor's office, then carried the box out to his car.

> ". . . Kaldren continues to reproach me [*Powers wrote in his diary*]. For some reason he seems unwilling to accept his isolation, is elaborating a series of private rituals to replace the missing hours of sleep. Perhaps I should tell him of my own approaching zero, but he'd probably regard this as the final unbearable insult, that I should have in excess what he so desperately yearns for. God knows what might happen. Fortunately the nightmarish visions appear to have receded for the time being . . ."

Pushing the diary away, Powers leaned forward across the desk and stared out through the window at the white floor of the lake bed stretching toward the hills along the horizon. Three miles away, on the far shore, he could see the circular bowl of the radio-telescope revolving slowly in the clear afternoon air, as Kaldren tirelessly trapped the sky, sluicing in millions of cubic parsecs of sterile ether, like the nomads who trapped the sea along the shores of the Persian Gulf.

Behind him the airconditioner murmured quietly, cooling the pale blue walls half-hidden in the dim light. Outside the air was bright and oppressive, the heat waves rippling up from the clumps of gold-tinted cacti below the Clinic blurring the sharp terraces of the twenty-story Neurology block. There, in the silent dormitories behind the sealed shutters, the terminals slept their long dreamless sleep. There were now over five hundred of them in the Clinic, the vanguard of a vast somnambulist army massing for its last march. Only five years had elapsed since the first narcoma syndrome had been recognized, but already huge government hospitals in the east were being readied for intakes in the thousands, as more and more cases came to light.

Powers felt suddenly tired, and glanced at his wrist, wondering how long he had to eight o'clock, his bed-time for the next week or so. Already he missed the dusk, soon would wake to his last dawn.

His watch was in his hip pocket. He remembered his decision not to use his timepieces, and sat back and stared at the bookshelves beside the desk. There were rows of green-covered AEC publications he had removed from Whitby's library, papers in which the biologist described his work out in the Pacific after the H-tests. Many of them Powers knew almost by heart, read a hundred times in an effort to grasp Whitby's last conclusions. Toynbee would certainly be easier to forget.

His eyes dimmed momentarily, as the tall black wall in the rear of his mind cast its great shadow over his brain. He reached for the diary thinking of the girl in Kaldren's car—Coma he had called her, another of his insane jokes—and her reference to Noguchi. Actually the comparison should have been made with Whitby, not himself; the monsters in the lab were nothing more than fragmented mirrors of Whitby's mind, like the grotesque radio-shielded frog he had found that morning in the swimming pool.

Thinking of the girl Coma, and the heartening smile she had given him, he wrote:

> Woke 6:33 am. Last session with Anderson. He made it plain he's seen enough of me, and from now on I'm better alone. To sleep 8:00? (These countdowns terrify me.)

He paused, then added:

> *Goodbye, Eniwetok.*

II

He saw the girl again the next day at Whitby's laboratory. He had driven over after breakfast with the new specimen, eager to get it into a vivarium before it died. The only previous armored mutant he had come across had nearly broken his neck. Speeding along the lake road a month or so earlier he had struck it with the offside front wheel, expecting the small creature to flatten instantly. Instead its hard lead-packed shell had remained rigid, even though the organism within it had been pulped, had flung the car heavily into the ditch. He had gone back for the shell, later weighed it at the laboratory, found it contained over 600 grams of lead.

Quite a number of plants and animals were building up heavy metals as radiological shields. In the hills behind the beach house a couple of old-time propectors were renovating the derelict gold-panning equipment abandoned over eighty years ago. They had noticed the bright yellow tints of the cacti, run an analysis, and found that the plants were assimilating gold in extractable quantities, although the soil concentrations were unworkable. Oak Ridge was at last paying a dividend!!

Waking that morning just after 6:45—ten minutes later than the previous day (he had switched on the radio, heard one of the regular morning programs as he climbed out of bed)—he had eaten a light unwanted breakfast, then spent an hour packing away some of the books in his library, crating them up and taping on address labels to his brother.

He reached Whitby's laboratory half an hour later. This was housed in a 100-foot wide geodesic dome built beside his chalet on the west shore of the lake about a mile from Kaldren's summer house. The chalet had been closed after Whitby's suicide, and many of the experimental plants and animals had died before Powers had managed to receive permission to use the laboratory.

As he turned into the driveway he saw the girl standing on the apex of the yellow-ribbed dome, her slim figure silhouetted against the sky. She waved to him, then began to step down across the glass polyhedrons and jumped nimbly into the driveway beside the car.

"Hello," she said, giving him a welcoming smile. "I came over to see your zoo. Kaldren said you wouldn't let me in if he came so I made him stay behind."

She waited for Powers to say something while he searched for his keys, then volunteered: "If you like, I can wash your shirt."

Powers grinned at her, peered down ruefully at his dust-stained sleeves. "Not a bad idea. I thought I was beginning to look a little uncared-for." He unlocked the door, took Coma's arm. "I don't know why Kaldren told you that—he's welcome here any time he likes."

"What have you got in there?" Coma asked, pointing at the wooden box he was carrying as they walked between the gear-laden benches.

"A distant cousin of ours I found. Interesting little chap. I'll introduce you in a moment."

Sliding partitions divided the dome into four chambers. Two of them were storerooms, filled with spare tanks, apparatus, cartons of animal food, and test rigs. They crossed the third section, almost filled by a powerful X-ray projector, a giant 250-mega-amp G.E. Maxitron, angled onto a revolving table, concrete shielding blocks lying around ready for use like huge building bricks.

The fourth chamber contained Powers' zoo, the vivaria jammed together along the benches and in the sinks, big colored cardboard charts and memos pinned onto the draft hoods above them, a tangle of rubber tubing and power leads trailing across the floor. As they walked past the lines of tanks dim forms shifted behind the frosted glass, and at the far end of the aisle there was a sudden scurrying in a large-scale cage by Powers' desk.

Putting the box down on his chair, he picked a packet of peanuts off the desk and went over to the cage. A small black-haired chimpanzee wearing a dented jet pilot's helmet swarmed deftly up the bars to him, chirped happily, and then jumped down to a miniature control panel against the rear wall of the cage. Rapidly it flicked a series of buttons and toggles, and a succession of colored lights lit up like a juke box and jangled out a two-second blast of music.

"Good boy," Powers said encouragingly, patting the chimp's back and shoveling the peanuts into its hands.

"You're getting much too clever for that one, aren't you?"

The chimp tossed the peanuts into the back of its throat with the smooth easy motions of a conjuror, jabbering at Powers in a singsong voice.

Coma laughed and took some of the nuts from Powers. "He's sweet. I think he's talking to you."

Powers nodded. "Quite right, he is. Actually he's got a two-hundred-word vocabulary, but his voice box scrambles it all up." He opened a small refrigerator by the desk, took out half a packet of sliced bread, and passed a couple of pieces to the chimp. It picked an electric toaster off the floor and placed it in the middle of a low wobbling table in the center of the cage, whipped the pieces into the slots. Powers pressed a tab on the switchboard beside the cage and the toaster began to crackle softly.

"He's one of the brightest we've had here, about as intelligent as a five-year-old child, though much more self-sufficient in a lot of ways." The two pieces of toast jumped out of their slots and the chimp caught them neatly, nonchalantly patting its helmet each time, then ambled off into a small ramshackle kennel and relaxed back with one arm out of a window, sliding the toast into its mouth.

"He built that house himself," Powers went on, switching off the toaster. "Not a bad effort, really." He pointed to a yellow polythene bucket by the front door of the kennel, from which a battered-looking geranium protruded. "Tends that plant, cleans up the cage, pours out an endless stream of wisecracks. Pleasant fellow all round."

Coma was smiling broadly to herself. "Why the space helmet, though?"

Powers hesitated. "Oh, it—er—it's for his own protection. Sometimes he gets rather bad headaches. His predecessors all—" He broke off and turned away. "Let's have a look at some of the other inmates."

He moved down the line of tanks, beckoning Coma with him. "We'll start at the beginning." He lifted the glass lid off one of the tanks, and Coma peered down into a shallow bath of water, where a small round organism with slender tendrils was nestling in a rockery of shells and pebbles.

"Sea anemone. Or was. Simple coelenterate with an open-ended body cavity." He pointed down to a thickened ridge of tissue around the base. "It's sealed up the cavity, converted the channel into a rudimentary notochord. Later the tendrils will knot themselves into a ganglion, but already they're sensitive to color. Look." He borrowed the violet handkerchief in Coma's breast pocket and spread it across the tank. The tendrils flexed and stiffened, began to weave slowly, as if they were trying to focus.

"The strange thing is that they're completely insensitive to white light. Normally the tendrils register shifting pressure gradients, like the tympanic diaphragms in your ears. Now it's almost as if they can *hear* primary colors, suggests it's readapting itself for a non-aquatic existence in a static world of violent color contrasts."

Coma shook her head, puzzled. "Why, though?"

"Hold on a moment. Let me put you in the picture first." They moved along the bench to a series of drum-shaped cages made of wire mosquito netting. Above the first was a large white cardboard screen bearing a blown-up microphoto of a tall pagodalike chain, topped by the legend: *"Drosophila: 15 roentgens/min."*

Powers tapped a small perspex window in the drum. "Fruitfly. Its huge chromosomes make it a useful test vehicle." He bent down, pointed to a gray V-shaped honeycomb suspended from the roof. A few flies emerged from entrances, moving about busily. "Usually it's solitary, a nomadic scavenger. Now it forms itself into well-knit social groups, has begun to secrete a thin sweet lymph something like honey."

"What's this?" Coma asked, touching the screen.

"Diagram of a key gene in the operation." He traced a spray of arrows leading from a link in the chain. The arrows were labeled: *"Lymph gland"* and subdivided *"sphincter muscles, epithelium, templates."*

"It's rather like the perforated sheet music of a player piano," Powers commented, "or a computer punch tape. Knock out one link with an X-ray beam, lose a characteristic, change the score."

Coma was peering through the window of the next cage and pulling an unpleasant face. Over her shoulder Powers saw she was watching an enormous spiderlike insect, as big as a hand, its dark hairy legs as thick as fingers. The compound eyes had been built up so that they resembled giant rubies.

"He looks unfriendly," she said. "What's that sort of rope ladder he's spinning?" As she moved a finger to her mouth the spider came to life, retreated into the cage, and began spewing out a complex skein of interlinked gray thread which it slung in long loops from the roof of the cage.

"A web," Powers told her. "Except that it consists of nervous tissue. The ladders form an external neural plexus, an inflatable brain as it were, that he can pump up to whatever size the situation calls for. A sensible arrangement, really; far better than our own."

Coma backed away. "Gruesome. I wouldn't like to go into his parlor."

"Oh, he's not as frightening as he looks. Those huge eyes staring at you are blind. Or, rather, their optical sensitivity has shifted down the band; the retinas will only register gamma radiation. Your wristwatch has luminous hands. When you moved it across the window he started thinking. World War IV should really bring him into his element."

They strolled back to Powers' desk. He put a coffee pan over a bunsen and pushed a chair across to Coma. Then he opened the box, lifted out the armored frog, and put it down on a sheet of blotting paper.

"Recognize him? Your old childhood friend, the common frog. He's built himself quite a solid little air raid shelter." He carried the animal across to a sink, turned on the tap, and let the water play softly over its shell. Wiping his hands on his shirt, he came back to the desk.

Coma brushed her long hair off her forehead, watched him curiously.

"Well, what's the secret?"

Powers lit a cigarette. "There's no secret. Teratologists have been breeding monsters for years. Have you ever heard of the 'silent pair'?"

She shook her head.

Powers stared moodily at the cigarette for a moment, riding the kick the first one of the day always gave him. "The so-called 'silent pair' is one of modern genetics' oldest problems, the apparently baffling mystery of the two inactive genes which occur in a small percentage of all living organisms, and appear to have no intelligible role in their structure or development. For a long while now biologists have been trying to activate them, but the difficulty is partly in identifying the silent genes in the fertilized germ cells of parents known to contain them, and partly in focusing a narrow enough X-ray beam which will do no damage to the remainder of the chromosome. However, after about ten years' work Dr. Whitby successfully developed a whole-body irradiation technique based on his observation of radiobiological damage at Eniwetok."

Powers paused for a moment. "He had noticed that there appeared to be more biological damage after the tests—that is, a greater transport of energy—than could be accounted for by direct radiation. What was happening was that the protein lattices in the genes were building up energy in the way that any vibrating membrane accumulates energy when it resonates—you remember the analogy of the bridge collapsing under the soldiers marching in step—and it occurred to him that if he could first identify the critical resonance frequency of the lattices in any particular silent gene he could then radiate the entire living organism, and not simply its germ cells, with a low field that would act selectively on the silent gene and cause no damage to the remainder of the chromosomes, whose lattices would resonate critically only at other specific frequencies."

Powers gestured around the laboratory with his cigarette. "You see some of the fruits of this 'resonance transfer' technique around you."

Coma nodded: "They've had their silent genes activated?"

"Yes, all of them. These are only a few of the thousands of specimens who have passed through here, and, as you've seen, the results are pretty dramatic."

He reached up and pulled across a section of the sun curtain. They were sitting just under the lip of the dome, and the mounting sunlight had begun to irritate him.

In the comparative darkness Coma noticed a stroboscope winking slowly in one of the tanks at the end of the bench behind her. She stood up and went over to it, examining a tall sunflower with a thickened stem and greatly enlarged receptacle. Packed around the flower, so that only its head protruded, was a chimney of gray-white stones, neatly cemented together and labeled: *"Cretaceous Chalk: 60,000,000 years."*

Beside it on the bench were three other chimneys, these labeled: *"Devonian Sandstone: 290,000,000 years", "Asphalt: 20 years", "Polyvinylchloride: 6 months."*

"Can you see those moist white discs on the sepals?" Powers pointed out. "In some way they regulate the plant's metabolism. It literally *sees* time. The older the surrounding environment, the more sluggish its metabolism. With the asphalt chimney it will complete its annual cycle in a week, with the PVC one in a couple of hours."

"Sees time," Coma repeated, wonderingly. She looked up at Powers, chewing her lower lip reflectively. "It's fantastic. Are these the creatures of the future, doctor?"

"I don't know," Powers admitted. "But if they are their world must be a monstrous, surrealist one."

He went back to the desk, pulled two cups from a drawer, and poured out the coffee, switching off the bunsen. "Some people have speculated that organisms possessing the silent pair of genes are the forerunners of a massive move up the evolutionary slope, that the silent genes are a sort of code, a divine message that we inferior organisms are carrying for our more highly developed descendants. It may well be true—perhaps we've broken the code too soon."

"Why do you say that?"

"Well, as Whitby's death indicates, the experiments in this laboratory have all come to a rather unhappy conclusion. Without exception the organisms we've irradiated have entered a final phase of totally disorganized growth, producing dozens of specialized sensory organs whose function we can't even guess. The results are catastrophic—the anemone will literally explode, the Drosophila cannibalize themselves, and so on. Whether the future implicit in these plants and animals is ever intended to take place, or whether we're merely extrapolating—I don't know. Sometimes I think, though, that the new sensory organs developed are parodies of their real intentions. The specimens you've seen today are all in an early stage of their secondary growth cycles. Later on they begin to look distinctly bizarre."

Coma nodded. "A zoo isn't complete without its keeper," she commented. "What about Man?"

Powers shrugged. "About one in every 100,000—the usual average—contains the silent pair. You might have them—or I. No one has volunteered yet to undergo whole-body irradiation. Apart from the fact that it would be classified as suicide, if the experiments here are any guide the experience would be savage and violent."

He sipped at the thin coffee, feeling tired and somehow bored. Recapitulating the laboratory's work had exhausted him.

The girl leaned forward. "You look awfully pale," she said solicitously. "Don't you sleep well?"

Powers managed a brief smile. "Too well," he admitted. "It's no longer a problem with me."

"I wish I could say that about Kaldren. I don't think he sleeps anywhere near enough. I hear him pacing around all night." She added, "Still, I suppose it's better than being a terminal. Tell me, Doctor, wouldn't it be worth trying this radiation technique on the sleepers at the Clinic? It might wake them up before the end. A few of them must possess the silent genes."

"They *all* do," Powers told her. "The two phenomena are very closely linked, as a matter of fact." He stopped, fatigue dulling his brain, and wondered whether to ask the girl to leave. Then he climbed off the desk and reached behind it, picked up a tape recorder.

Switching it on, he zeroed the tape and adjusted the speaker volume.

"Whitby and I often talked this over. Toward the end I took it all down. He was a great biologist, so let's hear it in his own words. It's absolutely the heart of the matter."

He flipped the table on, adding, "I've played it over to myself a thousand times, so I'm afraid the quality is poor."

An older man's voice, sharp and slightly irritable,

sounded out above a low buzz of distortion, but Coma could hear it clearly.

> *(Whitby)* . . . for heaven's sake, Robert, look at those FAO statistics. Despite an annual increase of five percent in acreage sown over the past fifteen years, world wheat crops have continued to decline by a factor of about two percent. The same story repeats itself ad nauseam. Cereals and root crops, dairy yields, ruminant fertility—are all down. Couple these with a mass of parallel symptoms, anything you care to pick from altered migratory routes to longer hibernation periods, and the overall pattern is incontrovertible.

> *(Powers)* Population figures for Europe and North America show no decline, though.

> *(Whitby)* Of course not, as I keep pointing out. It will take a century for such a fractional drop in fertility to have any effect in areas where extensive birth control provides an artificial reservoir. One must look at the countries of the Far East, and particularly at those where infant mortality has remained at a steady level. The population of Sumatra, for example, has declined by over fifteen percent in the last twenty years. A fabulous decline! Do you realize that only two or three decades ago the Neo-Malthusians were talking about a 'world population explosion'? In fact, it's an implosion. Another factor is—

Here the tape had been cut and edited, and Whitby's voice, less querulous this time, picked up again.

> . . . just as a matter of interest, tell me something: How long do you sleep each night?

(Powers) I don't know exactly; about eight hours, I suppose.

(Whitby) The proverbial eight hours. Ask anyone and they say automatically, 'eight hours.' As a matter of fact you sleep about ten and a half hours, like the majority of people. I've timed you on a number of occasions. I myself sleep eleven. Yet thirty years ago people did indeed sleep eight hours, and a century before that they slept six or seven. In Vasari's *Lives* one reads of Michelangelo sleeping for only four or five hours, painting all day at the age of eighty, and then working through the night over his anatomy table with a candle strapped to his forehead. Now he's regarded as a prodigy, but it was unremarkable then. How do you think the ancients, from Plato to Shakespeare, Aristotle to Aquinas, were able to cram so much work into their lives? Simply because they had an extra six or seven hours every day. Of course, a second disadvantage under which we labor is a lowered basal metabolic rate—another factor no one will explain.

(Powers) I suppose you could take the view that the lengthened sleep interval is a compensation device, a sort of mass neurotic attempt to escape from the terrifying pressures of urban life in the late twentieth century.

(Whitby) You could, but you'd be wrong. It's simply a matter of biochemistry. The ribonucleic acid templates which unravel the protein chains in all living organisms are wearing out, the dies enscribing the protoplasmic signature have become blunted. After all, they've been running now for over a thousand million years. It's time to retool. Just as an individual organism's life span is finite,

or the life of a yeast colony or a given species, so the life of an entire biological kingdom is of fixed duration. It's always been assumed that the evolutionary slope reaches forever upward, but in fact the peak has already been reached, and the pathway now leads downward to the common biological grave. It's a despairing and at present unacceptable vision of the future, but it's the only one. Five thousand centuries from now our descendants, instead of being multibrained starmen, will probably be naked prognathous idiots with hair on their foreheads, grunting their way through the remains of this Clinic like Neolithic men caught in a macabre inversion of time. Believe me, I pity them, as I pity myself. My total failure, my absolute lack of any moral or biological right to existence, is implicit in every cell of my body . . .

The tape ended; the spool ran free and stopped. Powers closed the machine, then massaged his face. Coma sat quietly, watching him and listening to the chimp playing with a box of puzzle dice.

"As far as Whitby could tell," Powers said, "the silent genes represent a last desperate effort of the biological kingdom to keep its head above the rising waters. Its total life period is determined by the amount of radiation emitted by the sun, and once this reaches a certain point the sure-death line has been passed and extinction is inevitable. To compensate for this, alarms have been built in which alter the form of the organism and adapt it to living in a hotter radiological climate. Soft-skinned organisms develop hard shells; these contain heavy metals as radiation screens. New organs of perception are developed too. According to Whitby, though, it's all wasted effort in the long run—but sometimes I wonder."

He smiled at Coma and shrugged. "Well, let's talk about something else. How long have you known Kaldren?"

"About three weeks. Feels like ten thousand years."

"How do you find him now? We've been rather out of touch lately."

Coma grinned. "I don't seem to see very much of him either. He makes me sleep all the time. Kaldren has many strange talents, but he lives just for himself. You mean a lot to him, Doctor. In fact, you're my one serious rival."

"I thought he couldn't stand the sight of me."

"Oh, that's just a sort of surface symptom. He really thinks of you continuously. That's why we spend all our time following you around." She eyed Powers shrewdly. "I think he feels guilty about something."

"Guilty?" Powers exclaimed. "*He* does? I thought I was supposed to be the guilty one."

"Why?" she pressed. She hesitated, then said, "You carried out some experimental surgical technique on him, didn't you?"

"Yes," Powers admitted. "It wasn't altogether a success, like so much of what I seem to be involved with. If Kaldren feels guilty, I suppose it's because he feels he must take some of the responsibility."

He looked down at the girl, her intelligent eyes watching him closely. "For one or two reasons it may be necessary for you to know. You said Kaldren paced around all night and didn't get enough sleep. Actually he doesn't get any sleep at all."

The girl nodded. "You . . ." She made a snapping gesture with her fingers.

". . . narcotomized him," Powers completed. "Surgically speaking, it was a great success; one might well share a Nobel for it. Normally the hypothalamus regulates the period of sleep, raising the threshold of consciousness in order to relax the venous capillaries in the brain and drain them of accumulating toxins. However, by sealing off some of the control loops the subject is unable to receive the sleep cue, and the capillaries drain while he remains conscious. All he feels is a temporary lethargy, but this passes within three or four hours. Physically speaking, Kaldren has had another twenty years added to his life. But the psyche seems to need sleep for its own private reasons, and consequently Kaldren has periodic storms that tear him apart. The whole thing was a tragic blunder."

Coma frowned pensively. "I guessed as much. Your papers in the neurosurgery journals referred to the patient as K. A touch of pure Kafka that came all too true."

"I may leave here for good, Coma," Powers said. "Make sure that Kaldren goes to his clinics. Some of the deep scar tissue will need to be cleaned away."

"I'll try. Sometimes I feel I'm just another of his insane terminal documents."

"What are those?"

"Haven't you heard? Kaldren's collection of final statements about *Homo sapiens*. The complete works of Freud, Beethoven's deaf quartets, transcripts of the Nuremburg trials, an automatic novel, and so on." She broke off. "What's that you're drawing?"

"Where?"

She pointed to the desk blotter, and Powers looked down and realized he had been unconsciously sketching an elaborate doodle, Whitby's four-armed sun. "It's nothing," he said. Somehow, though, it had a strangely compelling force.

Coma stood up to leave. "You must come and see us, Doctor. Kaldren has so much he wants to show you. He's just got hold of an old copy of the last signals sent back by the Mercury Seven twenty years ago when they reached the moon, and can't think about anything else. You remember the strange messages they recorded before they died, full of poetic ramblings about the white gardens. Now that I think about it they behaved rather like the plants in your zoo here."

She put her hands in her pockets, then pulled something out. "By the way, Kaldren asked me to give you this."

It was an old index card from the observatory library. In the center had been typed the number:

96,688,365,498,720

"It's going to take a long time to reach zero at this rate," Powers remarked dryly. "I'll have quite a collection when we're finished."

After she had left he chucked the card into the waste bin and sat down at the desk, staring for an hour at the ideogram on the blotter.

Halfway back to his beach house the lake road forked to the left through a narrow saddle that ran between the hills to an abandoned Air Force weapons range on one of the remoter salt lakes. At the nearer end were a number of small bunkers and camera towers, one or two metal shacks, and a low-roofed storage hangar. The white hills encircled the whole area, shutting it off from the world outside, and Powers liked to wander on foot down the gunnery aisles that had been marked down the two-mile length of the lake toward the concrete sight-screens at the far end. The abstract patterns made him feel like an ant on a bone-white chessboard, the rectangular screens at one end and the towers and bunkers at the other like opposing pieces.

His session with Coma had made Powers feel suddenly dissatisfied with the way he was spending his last months. *Goodbye, Eniwetok,* he had written, but in fact systematically forgetting everything was exactly the same as remembering it, a cataloguing in reverse, sorting out all the books in the mental library and putting them back in their right places upside down.

Powers climbed one of the camera towers, leaned on the rail, and looked out along the aisles toward the sight-screens. Ricocheting shells and rockets had chipped away large pieces of the circular concrete bands that ringed the target bulls, but the outlines of the huge 100-yard-wide discs, alternately painted blue and red, were still visible.

For half an hour he stared quietly at them, formless ideas shifting through his mind. Then without thinking, he abruptly left the rail and climbed down the companionway. The storage hangar was fifty yards away. He walked quickly across to it, stepped into the cool shadows, and peered around the rusting electric trolleys and empty flare drums. At the far end, behind a pile of lumber and bales of wire, were a stack of unopened cement bags, a mound of dirty sand, and an old mixer.

Half an hour later he had backed the Buick into the hangar and hooked the cement mixer, charged with sand, cement, and water scavenged from the drums lying around outside, onto the rear bumper, then loaded a dozen more bags into the car's trunk and rear seat. Finally he selected a few straight lengths of timber, jammed them through the window, and set off across the lake toward the central target bull.

For the next two hours he worked away steadily in the center of the great blue disc, mixing up the cement by hand, carrying it across to the crude wooden forms he had lashed together from the timber, smoothing it down so that it formed a six-inch-high wall around the perimeter of the bull. He worked without pause, stirring the cement with a tire lever, scooping it out with a hubcap prized off one of the wheels.

By the time he finished and drove off, leaving his equipment where it stood, he had completed a thirty-foot long section of wall.

IV

JUNE 7: Conscious, for the first time, of the brevity of each day. As long as I was awake for over twelve hours I still orientated my time around the meridian; morning and afternoon set their old rhythms. Now, with just over eleven hours of consciousness left, they form a continuous interval, like a length of tape measure. I can see exactly how much is left on the spool and can do little to affect the rate at which it unwinds. Spend the time slowly packing away the library; the crates are too heavy to move and lie where they are filled.

Cell count down to 400,000.

Woke 8:10. To sleep 7:15. (Appear to have lost my watch without realizing it; had to drive into town to buy another.)

JUNE 14: 9½ hours. Time races, flashing past like an expressway. However, the last week of a holiday always goes faster than the first. At the present rate there should be about four to five weeks left. This morning I tried to visualize what the last week or so—the final, 3, 2, 1, out—would be like, had a sudden chilling attack of pure fear, unlike anything I've ever felt before. Took me half an hour to steady myself enough for an intravenous.

Kaldren pursues me like my luminescent shadow, chalked up on the gateway '96,688,365,498,702.' Should confuse the mail man.

Woke 9:05. To sleep 6:36.

JUNE 19: 8¾ hours. Anderson rang up this morning. I nearly put the phone down on him, but managed to go through the pretence of making the final arrangements. He congratulated me on my stoicism, even used the word 'heroic.' Don't feel it. Despair erodes everything—courage, hope, self-discipline, all the better qualities. It's so damned difficult to sustain that impersonal attitude of passive acceptance implicit in the scientific tradition. I try to think of Galileo before the Inquisition, Freud surmounting the endless pain of his jaw cancer surgery.

Met Kaldren downtown, had a long discussion about the Mercury Seven. He's convinced that they refused to leave the moon deliberately, after the 'reception party' waiting for them had put them in the cosmic picture. They were told by the mysterious emissaries from Orion that the exploration of deep space was pointless, that they were too late as the life of the universe is now virtually over!!! According to K. there are Air Force generals who take this nonsense seriously, but I suspect it's simply an obscure attempt on K.'s part to console me.

Must have the phone disconnected. Some contractor keeps calling me up about payment for fifty bags of cement he claims I collected ten days ago. Says he helped me load them onto a truck himself. I did drive Whitby's pickup into town but only to get some lead screening. What does he think I'd do with all that cement? Just the sort of irritating thing you don't expect to hang over your final exit. (Moral: don't try too hard to forget Eniwetok.)

Woke 9:40. To sleep 4:15.

JUNE 25: 7½ hours. Kaldren was snooping around the lab again today. Phoned me there; when I answered a recorded voice he'd rigged up rambled out a long string of numbers, like an insane super-Tim. These practical jokes of his get rather wearing. Fairly soon I'll have to go over and come to terms with him, much as I hate the prospect. Anyway, Miss Mars is a pleasure to look at.

One meal is enough now, topped up with a glucose shot. Sleep is still "black," completely unrefreshing. Last night I took a 16-mm film of the first three hours, screened it this morning at the lab. The first true horror movie; I looked like a half-animated corpse.

Woke 10:25. To sleep 3:45.

JULY 3: 5¾ hours. Little done today. Deepening lethargy; dragged myself over to the lab, nearly left the road twice. Concentrated enough to feed the zoo and get the log up to date. Read through the operating manuals Whitby left for the last time, decided on a delivery rate of 40 roentgens/min., target distance of 350 cm. Everything is ready now.

Woke 11:05. To sleep 3:15.

Powers stretched, shifted his head slowly across the pillow, focusing on the shadows cast onto the ceiling by the blind. Then he looked down at his feet, saw Kaldren sitting on the end of the bed, watching him quietly.

"Hello, Doctor," he said, putting out his cigarette. "Late night? You look tired."

Powers heaved himself onto one elbow, glanced at his watch. It was just after eleven. For a moment his brain blurred, and he swung his legs around and sat on the edge of the bed, elbows on his knees, massaging some life into his face.

He noticed that the room was full of smoke. "What are you doing here?" he asked Kaldren.

"I came over to invite you to lunch." He indicated the bedside phone. "Your line was dead so I drove round. Hope you don't mind me climbing in. Rang the bell for about half an hour. I'm surprised you didn't hear it."

Powers nodded, then stood up and tried to smooth the creases out of his cotton slacks. He had gone to sleep without changing for over a week, and they were damp and stale.

As he started for the bathroom door Kaldren pointed

to the camera tripod on the other side of the bed. "What's this? Going into the blue movie business, Doctor?"

Powers surveyed him dimly for a moment, glanced at the tripod without replying, and then noticed his open diary on the bedside table. Wondering whether Kaldren had read the last entries, he went back and picked it up, then stepped into the bathroom and closed the door behind him.

From the mirror cabinet he took out a syringe and an ampoule, after the shot leaned against the door waiting for the stimulant to pick up.

Kaldren was in the lounge when he returned to him, reading the labels on the crates lying about in the center of the floor.

"O.K., then," Powers told him, "I'll join you for lunch." He examined Kaldren carefully. He looked more subdued than usual; there was an air almost of deference about him.

"Good," Kaldren said. "By the way, are you leaving?"

"Does it matter?" Powers asked curtly. "I thought you were in Anderson's care?"

Kaldren shrugged. "Please yourself. Come round at about twelve," he suggested, adding pointedly, "That'll give you time to clean up and change. What's that all over your shirt? Looks like lime."

Powers peered down, brushed at the white streaks. After Kaldren had left he threw the clothes away, took a shower, and unpacked a clean suit from one of the trunks.

Until this liaison with Coma, Kaldren lived alone in the old abstract summer house on the north shore of the lake. This was a seven-story folly originally built by an eccentric millionaire mathematician in the form of a spiraling concrete ribbon that wound around itself like an insane serpent, serving walls, floors, and ceilings. Only Kaldren had solved the building, a geometric model of $\sqrt{-1}$, and consequently he had been able to take it off the agents' hands at a comparatively low rent. In the evenings Powers had often watched him from the laboratory, striding restlessly from one level to the next, swinging through the labyrinth of inclines and terraces to the rooftop, where his lean angular figure stood out like a gallows against the sky, his lonely eyes sifting out radio lanes for the next day's trapping.

Powers noticed him there when he drove up at noon, poised on a ledge 150 feet above, head raised theatrically to the sky.

"Kaldren!" he shouted up suddenly into the silent air, half-hoping he might be jolted into losing his footing.

Kaldren broke out of his reverie and glanced down into the court. Grinning obliquely, he waved his right arm in a slow semicircle.

"Come up," he called, then turned back to the sky.

Powers leaned against the car. Once, a few months previously, he had accepted the same invitation, stepped through the entrance, and within three minutes lost himself helplessly in a second-floor cul de sac. Kaldren had taken half an hour to find him.

Powers waited while Kaldren swung down from his eyrie, vaulting through the wells and stairways, then rode up in the elevator with him to the penthouse suite.

They carried their cocktails through into a wide glass-roofed studio, the huge white ribbon of concrete uncoiling around them like toothpaste squeezed from an enormous tube. On the staged levels running parallel and across them rested pieces of gray abstract furniture, giant photographs on angled screens, carefully labeled exhibits laid out on low tables, all dominated by twenty-foot-high black letters on the rear wall which spelt out the single vast word:

YOU

Kaldren pointed to it. "What you might call the supraliminal approach." He gestured Powers in conspiratorially, finishing his drink in a gulp. "This is *my* laboratory, Doctor," he said with a note of pride. "Much more significant than yours, believe me."

Powers smiled wryly to himself and examined the first exhibit, an old ECG tape traversed by a series of faded inky wriggles. It was labeled, *"Einstein, A.; Alpha Waves, 1922."*

He followed Kaldren around, sipping slowly at his drink, enjoying the brief feeling of alertness the amphetamine provided. Within two hours it would fade, leave his brain feeling like a block of blotting paper.

Kaldren chattered away, explaining the significance of the so-called Terminal Documents. "They're end-prints, Powers, final statements, the products of total fragmentation. When I've got enough together I'll build a new world for myself out of them." He picked a thick paperbound volume off one of the tables, riffled through its pages. "Association tests of the Nuremburg Twelve. I have to include these . . ."

Powers strolled on absently without listening. Over in the corner were what appeared to be three ticker-tape machines, lengths of tape hanging from their mouths. He wondered whether Kaldren was misguided enough to be playing the stock market, which had been declining slowly for twenty years.

"Powers," he heard Kaldren say. "I was telling you about the Mercury Seven." He pointed to a collection of typewritten sheets tacked to a screen. "These are transcripts of their final signals radioed back from the recording monitors."

Powers examined the sheets cursorily, read a line at random.

". . . Blue . . . People . . . Recycle . . . Orion . . . Telemeters . . ."

Powers nodded noncommittally. "Interesting. What are the ticker tapes for over there?"

Kaldren grinned. "I've been waiting for months for you to ask me that. Have a look."

Powers went over and picked up one of the tapes. The machine was labeled, *"Auriga 225-G. Interval: 69 hours."*

The tape read:

96,688,365,498,695
96,688,365,498,694
96,688,365,498,693
96,688,365,498,692

Powers dropped the tape. "Looks rather familiar. What does the sequence represent?"

Kaldren shrugged. "No one knows."

"What do you mean? It must replicate something."

"Yes, it does. A diminishing mathematical progression. A countdown, if you like."

Powers picked up the tape on the right, tabbed, *"Aries 44R951. Interval: 49 days."*

Here the sequence ran:

876,567,988,347,779,877,654,434
876,567,988,347,779,877,654,433
876,567,988,347,779,877,654,432

Powers looked round. "How long does it take each signal to come through?"

"Only a few seconds. They're tremendously compressed laterally, of course. A computer at the observatory breaks them down. They were first picked up at Jodrell Bank about twenty years ago. Nobody bothers to listen to them now."

Powers turned to the last tape.

6,554
6,553
6,552
6,551

"Nearing the end of its run," he commented. He glanced at the label on the hood, which read: *"Unidentified radio source, Canes Venatici. Interval: 97 weeks."*

He showed the tape to Kaldren. "Soon be over."

Kaldren shook his head. He lifted a heavy directory-sized volume off a table, cradled it in his hands. His face had suddenly become somber and haunted. "I doubt it," he said. "Those are only the last four digits. The whole number contains over 50 million."

He handed the volume to Powers, who turned to the title page. *"Master Sequence of Serial Signal received by Jodrell Bank Radio-Observatory, University of Manchester, England, 0012:59 hours, 21-5-72. Source: NGC 9743, Canes Venatici."* He thumbed the thick stack of closely printed pages, millions of numerals, as Kaldren had said, running up and down across a thousand consecutive pages.

Powers shook his head, picked up the tape again, and stared at it thoughtfully.

"The computer only breaks down the last four digits," Kaldren explained. "The whole series comes over in each 15-second-long package, but it took IBM more than two years to unscramble one of them."

"Amazing," Powers commented. "But what is it?"

"A countdown, as you can see. NGC 9743, somewhere in Canes Venatici. The big spirals there are breaking up, and they're saying goodbye. God knows who they think we are but they're letting us know all the same, beaming it out on the hydrogen line for everyone in the universe to hear." He paused. "Some people have put other interpretations on them, but there's one piece of evidence that rules out everything else."

"Which is?"

Kaldren pointed to the last tape from Canes Venatici. "Simply that it's been estimated that by the time this series reaches zero the universe will have just ended."

Powers fingered the tape reflectively. "Thoughtful of them to let us know what the real time is," he remarked.

"I agree, it is," Kaldren said quietly. "Applying the inverse square law that signal source is broadcasting at a strength of about three million megawatts raised to the hundredth power. About the size of the entire Local Group. Thoughtful is the word."

Suddenly he gripped Powers' arm, held it tightly, and peered into his eyes closely, his throat working with emotion.

"You're not alone, Powers, don't think you are. These are the voices of time, and they're all saying goodbye to you. Think of yourself in a wider context. Every particle in your body, every grain of sand, every galaxy carries the same signature. As you've just said, you know what the time is now, so what does the rest matter? There's no need to go on looking at the clock."

Powers took his hand, squeezed it firmly. "Thanks, Kaldren. I'm glad you understand." He walked over to the window, looked down across the white lake. The tension between himself and Kaldren had dissipated; he felt that all his obligations to him had at last been met. Now he wanted to leave as quickly as possible, forget him as he had forgotten the faces of the countless other patients whose exposed brains had passed between his fingers.

He went back to the ticker machines, tore the tapes from their slots, and stuffed them into his pockets. "I'll take these along to remind myself. Say goodbye to Coma for me, will you."

He moved toward the door, when he reached it looked back to see Kaldren standing in the shadow of the three giant letters on the far wall, his eyes staring listlessly at his feet.

As Powers drove away he noticed that Kaldren had gone up onto the roof, watched him in the driving mirror waving slowly until the car disappeared around a bend.

V

The outer circle was now almost complete. A narrow segment, an arc about ten feet long, was missing, but otherwise the low perimeter wall ran continuously six inches off the concrete floor around the outer lane of the target bull, enclosing the huge rebus within it. Three concentric circles, the largest a hundred yards in diameter, separated from each other by ten-foot intervals, formed the rim of the device, divided into four segments by the arms of an enormous cross radiating from its center, where a small round platform had been built a foot above the ground.

Powers worked swiftly, pouring sand and cement into the mixer, tipping in water until a rough paste formed, then carried it across to the wooden forms and tamped the mixture down into the narrow channel.

Within ten minutes he had finished, quickly dismantled the forms before the cement had set, and slung the timbers into the back seat of the car. Dusting his hands on his trousers, he went over to the mixer and pushed it fifty yards away into the long shadow of the surrounding hills.

Without pausing to survey the gigantic cipher on which he had labored patiently for so many afternoons, he climbed into the car and drove off on a wake of bone-white dust, splitting the pools of indigo shadow.

He reached the laboratory at three o'clock, jumped from the car as it lurched back on its brakes. Inside the entrance he first switched on the lights, then hurried round, pulling the sun curtains down and shackling them to the floor slots, effectively turning the dome into a steel tent.

In their tanks behind him the plants and animals stirred quietly, responding to the sudden flood of cold fluorescent light. Only the chimpanzee ignored him.

It sat on the floor of its cage, neurotically jamming the puzzle dice into the polythene bucket, exploding in bursts of sudden rage when the pieces refused to fit.

Powers went over to it, noticing the shattered glass fiber reinforcing panels bursting from the dented helmet. Already the chimp's face and forehead were bleeding from self-inflicted blows. Powers picked up the remains of the geranium that had been hurled through the bars, attracted the chimp's attention with it, then tossed a black pellet he had taken from a capsule in the desk drawer. The chimp caught it with a quick flick of the wrist, for a few seconds juggled the pellet with a couple of dice as it concentrated on the puzzle, then pulled it out of the air and swallowed it in a gulp.

Without waiting, Powers slipped off his jacket and stepped toward the X-ray theater. He pulled back the high sliding doors to reveal the long glassy metallic snout of the Maxitron, then started to stack the lead screening shields against the rear wall.

A few minutes later the generator hummed into life.

The anemone stirred. Basking in the warm subliminal sea of radiation rising around it, prompted by countless pelagic memories, it reached tentatively across the tank, groping blindly toward the dim uterine sun. Its tendrils flexed, the thousands of dormant neural cells in their tips regrouping and multiplying, each harnessing the unlocked energies of its nucleus. Chains forged themselves, lattices tiered upward into multifaceted lenses, focused slowly on the vivid spectral outlines of the sounds dancing like phosphorescent waves around the darkened chamber of the dome.

Gradually an image formed, revealing an enormous black fountain that poured an endless stream of brilliant light over the circle of benches and tanks. Beside it a figure moved, adjusting the flow through its mouth. As it stepped across the floor its feet threw off vivid bursts of color, its hands racing along the benches conjured up a dazzling chiaroscura, balls of blue and violet light that exploded fleetingly in the darkness like miniature star-shells.

Photons murmured. Steadily, as it watched the glimmering screen of sounds around it, the anemone continued to expand. Its ganglia linked, heeding a new source of stimuli from the delicate diaphragms in the crown of its notochord. The silent outlines of the laboratory began to echo softly; waves of muted sound fell from the arc lights and echoed off the benches and furniture below. Etched in sound, their angular forms resonated with sharp persistent overtones. The plastic-ribbed chairs were a buzz of staccato discords, the square-sided desk a continuous double-featured tone.

Ignoring these sounds once they had been perceived, the anemone turned to the ceiling, which reverberated like a shield in the sounds pouring steadily from the fluorescent tubes. Streaming through a narrow skylight, its voice clear and strong, interweaved by numberless overtones, the sun sang . . .

It was a few minutes before dawn when Powers left the laboratory and stepped into his car. Behind him the great dome lay silent in the darkness, the thin shadows of the white moonlit hills falling across its surface. Powers free-wheeled the car down the long curving drive to the lake road below, listening to the tires cutting across the blue gravel, then let out the clutch and accelerated the engine.

As he drove along, the limestone hills half hidden in the darkness on his left, he gradually became aware that, although no longer looking at the hills, he was still in some oblique way conscious of their forms and outlines in the back of his mind. The sensation was undefined but none the less certain, a strange almost visual impression that emanated most strongly from the deep clefts and ravines dividing one cliff face from the next. For a few minutes Powers let it play upon him, without trying to identify it, a dozen strange images moving across his brain.

The road swung up around a group of chalets built onto the lake shore, taking the car right under the lee of the hills, and Powers suddenly felt the massive weight of the escarpment rising up into the dark sky like a cliff of luminous chalk, and realized the identity of the impression now registering powerfully within his mind. Not only could he see the escarpment, but he was aware of its enormous age, felt distinctly the countless millions of years since it had first reared out of the magma of the earth's crust. The ragged crests three hundred feet above him, the dark gulleys and fissures, the smooth boulders by the roadside at the foot of the cliff, all carried a distinct image of themselves across to him, a thousand voices that together told of the total time that had elapsed in the life of the escarpment, a psychic picture as defined and clear as the visual image brought to him by his eyes.

Involuntarily, Powers had slowed the car, and turning his eyes away from the hill face he felt a second wave of time sweep across the first. The image was broader but of shorter perspectives, radiating from the wide disc of the salt lake, breaking over the ancient limestone cliffs like shallow rollers dashing against a towering headland.

Closing his eyes, Powers lay back and steered the car along the interval between the two time fronts, feeling the images deepen and strengthen within his mind. The vast age of the landscape, the inaudible chorus of voices resonating from the lake and from the white hills, seemed to carry him back through time, down endless corridors to the first thresholds of the world.

He turned the car off the road along the track leading toward the target range. On either side of the culvert the cliff faces boomed and echoed with vast impenetrable time fields, like enormous opposed magnets. As he finally emerged between them onto the flat surface of the lake it seemed to Powers that he could feel the separate identity of each sand grain and salt crystal calling to him from the surrounding ring of hills.

He parked the car beside the mandala and walked slowly toward the outer concrete rim curving away into the shadows. Above him he could hear the stars, a million cosmic voices that crowded the sky from one horizon to the next, a true canopy of time. Like jostling radio beacons, their long aisles interlocking at countless angles, they plunged into the sky from the narrowest recesses of space. He saw the dim red disc of Sirius, heard its ancient voice, untold millions of years old, dwarfed by the huge spiral nebulae in Andromeda, a gigantic carousel of vanished universes, their voices almost as old as the cosmos itself. To Powers the sky seemed an endless babel, the time-song of a thousand galaxies overlaying each other in his mind. As he moved slowly toward the center of the mandala he craned up at the glittering traverse of the Milky Way, searching the confusion of clamoring nebulae and constellations.

Stepping into the inner circle of the mandala, a few yards from the platform at its center, he realized that the tumult was beginning to fade, and that a single stronger voice had emerged and was dominating the others. He climbed onto the platform, raised his eyes to the darkened sky, moving through the constellations to the island galaxies beyond them, hearing the thin archaic voices reaching to him across the millennia. In his pockets he felt the paper tapes, and turned to find the distant diadem of Canes Venatici, heard its great voice mounting in his mind.

Like an endless river, so broad that its banks were below the horizons, it flowed steadily toward him, a vast course of time that spread outwards to fill the sky and the universe, enveloping everything within them. Moving slowly, the forward direction of its majestic current almost imperceptible, Powers knew that its source was the source of the cosmos itself. As it passed him, he felt its massive magnetic pull, let himself be drawn into it, borne gently on its powerful back. Quietly it carried him away, and he rotated slowly, facing the direction of the tide. Around him the outlines of the hills and the lake had faded, but the image of the mandala, like a cosmic clock, remained fixed before his eyes, illuminating the broad surface of the stream. Watching it constantly, he felt his body gradually dissolving, its physical dimensions melting into the vast continuum of the current, which bore him out into the center of the great channel sweeping him onward, beyond hope now but at rest, down the broadening reaches of the river of eternity.

As the shadows faded, retreating into the hill slopes, Kaldren stepped out of his car, walked hesitantly toward the concrete rim of the outer circle. Fifty yards away, at the center, Coma knelt beside Powers' body, her small hands pressed to his dead face. A gust of wind stirred the sand, dislodging a strip of tape that drifted toward Kaldren's feet. He bent down and picked it up, then rolled it carefully in his hands and slipped it into his pocket. The dawn air was cold, and he turned up the collar of his jacket, watching Coma impassively.

"It's six o'clock," he told her after a few minutes. "I'll go and get the police. You stay with him." He paused and then added, "Don't let them break the clock."

Coma turned and looked at him. "Aren't you coming back?"

"I don't know." Nodding to her, Kaldren swung on his heel and went over to the car.

He reached the lake road, five minutes later parked the car in the drive outside Whitby's laboratory.

The dome was in darkness, all its windows shuttered, but the generator still hummed in the X-ray theater. Kaldren stepped through the entrance and switched on the lights. In the theater he touched the grilles of the generator, felt the warm cylinder of the beryllium end-window. The circular target table was revolving slowly, its setting at 1 r.p.m., a steel restraining chair shackled to it hastily. Grouped in a semicircle a few feet away were most of the tanks and cages, piled on top of each other haphazardly. In one of them an enormous squidlike plant had almost managed to climb from its vivarium. Its long translucent tendrils clung to the edges of the tank, but its body had burst into a jellified pool of globular mucilage. In another an enormous spider had trapped itself in its own web, hung helplessly in the center of a huge three-dimensional maze of phosphorescing thread, twitching spasmodically.

All the experimental plants and animals had died. The chimp lay on its back among the remains of the hutch, the helmet forward over its eyes. Kaldren watched it for a moment, then sat down on the desk and picked up the phone.

While he dialed the number he noticed a film reel lying on the blotter. For a moment he stared at the label, then slid the reel into his pocket beside the tape.

After he had spoken to the police he turned off the lights and went out to the car, drove off slowly down the drive.

When he reached the summer house the early sunlight was breaking across the ribbonlike balconies and terraces. He took the lift to the penthouse, made his way through into the museum. One by one he opened the shutters and let the sunlight play over the exhibits. Then he pulled a chair over to a side window, sat back, and stared up at the light pouring through into the room.

Two or three hours later he heard Coma outside, calling up to him. After half an hour she went away, but a little later a second voice appeared and shouted up at Kaldren. He left his chair and closed all the shutters overlooking the front courtyard, and eventually he was left undisturbed.

Kaldren returned to his seat and lay back quietly, his eyes gazing across the lines of exhibits. Half-asleep, periodically he leaned up and adjusted the flow of light through the shutter, thinking to himself, as he would do through the coming months, of Powers and his strange mandala, and of the seven and their journey to the white gardens of the moon, and the blue people who had come from Orion and spoken in poetry to them of ancient beautiful worlds beneath golden suns in the island galaxies, vanished forever now in the myriad deaths of the cosmos.

THE BURNING OF THE BRAIN

Cordwainer Smith

Herewith a small segment of the late Cordwainer Smith's dazzling, many-paneled history of the future: a tragic vignette of the interstellar epoch, when Go-Captains drive the great starships across the boundless emptinesses of the Up-and-Out.

I.
DOLORES OH

I tell you, it is sad, it is more than sad, it is fearful—for it is a dreadful thing to go into the Up-and-Out, to fly without flying, to move between the stars as a moth may drift among the leaves on a summer night.

Of all the men who took the great ships into planoform none was braver, none stronger, than Captain Magno Taliano.

Scanners had been gone for centuries and the jonasoidal effect had become so simple, so manageable, that the traversing of light-years was no more difficult to most of the passengers of the great ships than to go from one room to the other.

Passengers moved easily.

Not the crew.

Least of all the captain.

The captain of a jonasoidal ship which had embarked on an interstellar journey was a man subject to rare and overwhelming strains. The art of getting past all the complications of space was far more like the piloting of turbulent waters in ancient days than like the smooth seas which legendary men once traversed with sails alone.

Go-Captain on the *Wu-Feinstein,* finest ship of its class, was Magno Taliano.

Of him it was said, "He could sail through hell with the muscles of his left eye alone. He could plow space with his living brain if the instruments failed . . ."

Wife to the Go-Captain was Dolores Oh. The name was Japonical, from some nation of the ancient days. Dolores Oh had been once beautiful, so beautiful that she took men's breath away, made wise men into fools, made young men into nightmares of lust and yearning. Wherever she went men had quarreled and fought over her.

But Dolores Oh was proud beyond all common limits of pride. She refused to go through the ordinary rejuvenescence. A terrible yearning a hundred or so years back must have come over her. Perhaps she said to herself, before that hope and terror which a mirror in a quiet room becomes to anyone:

"Surely I am me. There must be a *me* more than the beauty of my face; there must be a something other than the delicacy of skin and the accidental lines of my jaw and my cheekbone.

"What have men loved if it wasn't me? Can I ever find out who I am or what I am if I don't let beauty perish and live on in whatever flesh age gives me?"

She had met the Go-Captain and had married him in a romance that left forty planets talking and half the ship lines stunned.

Magno Taliano was at the very beginning of his genius. Space, we can tell you, is rough—rough like the wildest of storm-driven waters, filled with perils which only the most sensitive, the quickest, the most daring of men can surmount.

Best of them all, class for class, age for age, out of class, beating the best of his seniors, was Magno Taliano.

For him to marry the most beautiful beauty of forty worlds was a wedding like Heloise and Abelard's or like the unforgettable romance of Helen America and Mr. Grey-no-more.

The ships of the Go-Captain Magno Taliano became more beautiful year by year, century by century.

As ships became better he always obtained the best. He maintained his lead over the other Go-Captains so overwhelmingly that it was unthinkable for the finest ship of mankind to sail out amid the roughness and uncertainties of two-dimensional space without himself at the helm.

Stop-Captains were proud to sail space beside him. (Though the Stop-Captains had nothing more to do than to check the maintenance of the ship, its loading and unloading when it was in normal space, they were still more than ordinary men in their own kind of world, a world far below the more majestic and adventurous universe of the Go-Captains.)

Magno Taliano had a niece who in the modern style used a place instead of a name: she was called "Dita from the Great South House."

When Dita came aboard the *Wu-Feinstein* she had heard much of Dolores Oh, her aunt by marriage who had once captivated the men in many worlds. Dita was wholly unprepared for what she found.

Dolores greeted her civilly enough, but the civility was a sucking pump of hideous anxiety, the friendliness was the driest of mockeries, the greeting itself an attack.

What's the matter with the woman? thought Dita.

As if to answer her thought, Dolores said aloud and in words: "It's nice to meet a woman who's not trying to take Taliano from me. I love him. Can you believe that? Can you?"

"Of course," said Dita. She looked at the ruined face of Dolores Oh, at the dreaming terror in Dolores' eyes, and she realized that Dolores had passed all limits of nightmare and had become a veritable demon of regret, a possessive ghost who sucked the vitality from her husband, who dreaded companionship, hated friendship, rejected even the most casual of acquaintances, because she feared forever and without limit that there was really nothing to herself, and feared that without Magno Taliano she would be more lost than the blackest of whirlpools in the nothing between the stars.

Magno Taliano came in.

He saw his wife and niece together.

He must have been used to Dolores Oh. In Dita's eyes Dolores was more frightening than a mud-caked reptile raising its wounded and venomous head with blind hunger and blind rage. To Magno Taliano the ghastly woman who stood like a witch beside him was somehow the beautiful girl he had wooed and had married one hundred sixty-four years before.

He kissed the withered cheek, he stroked the dried and stringy hair, he looked into the greedy terror-haunted eyes as though they were the eyes of a child he loved. He said, lightly and gently, "Be good to Dita, my dear."

He went on through the lobby of the ship to the inner sanctum of the planoforming room.

The Stop-Captain waited for him. Outside on the world of Sherman the scented breezes of that pleasant planet blew in through the open windows of the ship.

Wu-Feinstein, finest ship of its class, had no need for metal walls. It was built to resemble an ancient, prehistoric estate named Mount Vernon, and when it sailed between the stars it was encased in its own rigid and self-renewing field of force.

The passengers went through a few pleasant hours of

strolling on the grass, enjoying the spacious rooms, chatting beneath a marvelous simulacrum of an atmosphere-filled sky.

Only in the planoforming room did the Go-Captain know what happened. The Go-Captain, his pinlighters sitting beside him, took the ship from one compression to another, leaping hotly and frantically through space, sometimes one light-year, sometimes a hundred light-years, jump, jump, jump, jump until the ship, the light touches of the captain's mind guiding it, passed the perils of millions upon millions of worlds, came out at its appointed destination, and settled as lightly as one feather resting upon others, settled into an embroidered and decorated countryside where the passengers could move as easily away from their journey as if they had done nothing more than to pass an afternoon in a pleasant old house by the side of a river.

II.
THE LOST LOCKSHEET

Magno Taliano nodded to his pinlighters. The Stop-Captain bowed obsequiously from the doorway of the planoforming room. Taliano looked at him sternly, but with robust friendliness. With formal and austere courtesy he asked, "Sir and colleague, is everything ready for the jonasoidal effect?"

The Stop-Captain bowed even more formally. "Truly ready, sir and master."

"The locksheets in place?"

"Truly in place, sir and master."

"The passengers secure?"

"The passengers are secure, numbered, happy, and ready, sir and master."

Then came the last and most serious of questions. "Are my pinlighters warmed with their pin-sets and ready for combat?"

"Read for combat, sir and master." With these words

the Stop-Captain withdrew. Magno Taliano smiled to his pinlighters. Through the minds of all of them there passed the same thought.

How could a man that pleasant stay married all those years to a hag like Dolores Oh? How could that witch, that horror, have ever been a beauty? How could that beast have ever been a woman, particularly the divine and glamorous Dolores Oh whose image we still see in four-di every now and then?

Yet pleasant he was, though long he may have been married to Dolores Oh. Her loneliness and greed might suck at him like a nightmare, but his strength was more than enough strength for two.

Was he not the captain of the greatest ship to sail between the stars?

Even as the pinlighters smiled their greetings back to him, his right hand depressed the golden ceremonial lever of the ship. This instrument alone was mechanical. All other controls in the ship had long since been formed telepathically or electronically.

Within the planoforming room the black skies became visible and the tissue of space shot up around them like boiling water at the base of a waterfall. Outside that one room the passengers still walked sedately on scented lawns.

From the wall facing him, as he sat rigid in his Go-Captain's chair, Magno Taliano sensed the forming of a pattern which in three or four hundred milliseconds would tell him where he was and would give him the next clue as to how to move.

He moved the ship with the impulses of his own brain, to which the wall was a superlative complement.

The wall was a living brickwork of locksheets, laminated charts, one hundred thousand charts to the inch, the wall preselected and preassembled for all imaginable contingencies of the journey which, each time afresh, took the ship across half-unknown immensities of time and space. The ship leapt, as it had before.

The new star focused.

Magno Taliano waited for the wall to show him where he was, expecting (in partnership with the wall) to flick the ship back into the pattern of stellar space, moving it by immense skips from source to destination.

This time nothing happened.

Nothing?

For the first time in a hundred years his mind knew panic.

It couldn't be nothing. Not *nothing*. Something had to focus. The locksheets always focused.

His mind reached into the locksheets and he realized with a devastation beyond all limits of ordinary human grief that they were lost as no ship had ever been lost before. By some error never before committed in the history of mankind, the entire wall was made of duplicates of the same locksheet.

Worst of all, the Emergency Return sheet was lost. They were amid stars none of them had ever seen before, perhaps as little as five hundred million miles, perhaps as far as forty parsecs.

And the locksheet was lost.

And they would die.

As the ship's power failed coldness and blackness and death would crush in on them in a few hours at the most. That then would be all, all of the *Wu-Feinstein,* all of Dolores Oh.

III.
THE SECRET OF THE OLD DARK BRAIN

Outside of the planoforming room of the *Wu-Feinstein* the passengers had no reason to understand that they were marooned in the nothing-at-all.

Dolores Oh rocked back and forth in an ancient rocking chair. Her haggard face looked without pleasure at the imaginary river that ran past the edge of the lawn. Dita from the Great South House sat on a hassock by her aunt's knees.

Dolores was talking about a trip she had made when she was young and vibrant with beauty, a beauty which brought trouble and hate wherever it went.

". . . so the guardsman killed the captain and then came to my cabin and said to me, 'You've got to marry me now. I've given up everything for your sake,' and I said to him, 'I never said that I loved you. It was sweet of you to get into a fight, and in a way I suppose it is a compliment to my beauty, but it doesn't mean that I belong to you the rest of my life. What do you think I am, anyhow?' "

Dolores Oh sighed a dry, ugly sigh, like the crackling of subzero winds through frozen twigs. "So you see, Dita, being beautiful the way you are is no answer to anything. A woman has got to be herself before she finds out what she is. I know that my lord and husband, the Go-Captain, loves me because my beauty is gone, and with my beauty gone there is nothing but *me* to love, is there?"

An odd figure came out on the verandah. It was a pinlighter in full fighting costume. Pinlighters were never supposed to leave the planoforming room, and it was most extraordinary for one of them to appear among the passengers.

He bowed to the two ladies and said with the utmost courtesy:

"Ladies, will you please come into the planoforming room? We have need that you should see the Go-Captain now."

Dolores' hand leapt to her mouth. Her gesture of grief was as automatic as the striking of a snake. Dita sensed that her aunt had been waiting a hundred years and more for disaster, that her aunt had craved ruin for her husband the way that some people crave love and others crave death.

Dita said nothing. Neither did Dolores, apparently at second thought, utter a word.

They followed the pinlighter silently into the planoforming room.

The heavy door closed behind them.

Magno Taliano was still rigid in his Captain's chair.

He spoke very slowly, his voice sounding like a record played too slowly on an ancient parlophone.

"We are lost in space, my dear," said the frigid, ghostly voice of the Captain, still in his Go-Captain's trance. *"We are lost in space and I thought that perhaps if your mind aided mine we might think of a way back."*

Dita started to speak.

A pinlighter told her: "Go ahead and speak, my dear. Do you have any suggestion?"

"Why don't we just go back? It would be humiliating, wouldn't it? Still it would be better than dying. Let's use the Emergency Return Locksheet and go on right back. The world will forgive Magno Taliano for a single failure after thousands of brilliant and successful trips."

The pinlighter, a pleasant enough young man, was as friendly and calm as a doctor informing someone of a death or of a mutilation. "The impossible has happened, Dita from the Great South House. All the locksheets are wrong. They are all the same one. And not one of them is good for emergency return."

With that the two women knew where they were. They knew that space would tear into them like threads being pulled out of a fiber so that they would either die bit by bit as the hours passed and as the material of their bodies faded away a few molecules here and a few there. Or, alternatively, they could die all at once in a flash if the Go-Captain chose to kill himself and the ship rather than to wait for a slow death. Or, if they believed in religion, they could pray.

The pinlighter said to the rigid Go-Captain, "We think we see a familiar pattern at the edge of your own brain. May we look in?"

Taliano nodded very slowly, very gravely.

The pinlighter stood still.

The two women watched. Nothing visible happened, but they knew that beyond the limits of vision and yet before their eyes a great drama was being played out. The minds of the pinlighters probed deep into the mind of the frozen Go-Captain, searching amid the synapses for the secret of the faintest clue to their possible rescue.

Minutes passed. They seemed like hours.

At last the pinlighter spoke. "We can see into your midbrain, Captain. At the edge of your paleocortex there is a star pattern which resembles the upper left rear of our present location."

The pinlighter laughed nervously. "We want to know can you fly the ship home on your brain?"

Magno Taliano looked with deep tragic eyes at the inquirer. His slow voice came out at them once again since he dared not leave the half-trance which held the entire ship in stasis. *"Do you mean can I fly the ship on a brain alone? It would burn out my brain and the ship would be lost anyhow . . . ."*

"But we're lost, lost, lost," screamed Dolores Oh. Her face was alive with hideous hope, with a hunger for ruin, with a greedy welcome of disaster. She screamed at her husband, "Wake up, my darling, and let us die together. At least we can belong to each other that much, that long, forever!"

"Why die?" said the pinlighter softly. "You tell him, Dita."

Said Dita, "Why not try, sir and uncle?"

Slowly Magno Taliano turned his face toward his niece. Again his hollow voice sounded. *"If I do this I shall be a fool or a child or a dead man but I will do it for you."*

Dita had studied the work of the Go-Captains and she knew well enough that if the paleocortex was lost the personality became intellectually sane, but emotionally crazed. With the most ancient part of the brain gone the fundamental controls of hostility, hunger, and sex disappeared. The most ferocious of animals and the most brilliant of men were reduced to a common level—a level of infantile friendliness in which lust and playfulness and gentle, unappeasable hunger became the eternity of their days.

Magno Taliano did not wait.

He reached out a slow hand and squeezed the hand of Dolores Oh. *"As I die you shall at last be sure I love you."*

Once again the women saw nothing. They realized they had been called in simply to give Magno Taliano a last glimpse of his own life.

A quiet pinlighter thrust a beam-electrode so that it reached square into the paleocortex of Captain Magno Taliano.

The planoforming room came to life. Strange heavens swirled about them like milk being churned in a bowl.

Dita realized that her partial capacity of telepathy was functioning even without the aid of a machine. With her mind she could feel the dead wall of the locksheets. She was aware of the rocking of the *Wu-Feinstein* as it leapt from space to space, as uncertain as a man crossing a river by leaping from one ice-covered rock to the other.

In a strange way she even knew that the paleocortical part of her uncle's brain was burning out at last and forever, that the star patterns which had been frozen in the locksheets lived on in the infinitely complex pattern of his own memories, and that with the help of his own telepathic pinlighters he was burning out his brain cell by cell in order for them to find a way to the ship's destination. This indeed was his last trip.

Dolores Oh watched her husband with a hungry greed surpassing all expression.

Little by little his face became relaxed and stupid.

Dita could see the midbrain being burned blank, as the ship's controls with the help of the pinlighters searched through the most magnificent intellect of its time for a last course into harbor.

Suddenly Dolores Oh was on her knees, sobbing by the hand of her husband.

A pinlighter took Dita by the arm.

"We have reached destination," he said.

"And my uncle?"

The pinlighter looked at her strangely.

She realized he was speaking to her without moving his lips—speaking mind-to-mind with pure telepathy.

"Can't you see it?"

She shook her head dazedly.

The pinlighter thought his emphatic statement at her once again.

"As your uncle burned out his brain, you picked up his skills. Can't you sense it? You are a Go-Captain yourself and one of the greatest of us."

"And he?"

The pinlighter thought a merciful comment at her.

Magno Taliano had risen from his chair and was being led from the room by his wife and consort, Dolores Oh. He had the amiable smile of an idiot, and his face for the first time in more than a hundred years trembled with shy and silly love.

THE SHAKER REVIVAL

Gerald Jonas

We know all about The Kids—the Consciousness III generation, to make use of a phrase that passed from perception to cliché in record time. What happens next, though—as today's freaks become tomorrow's bourgeoisie? Gerald Jonas, a staff writer for *The New Yorker* and a longtime science-fictionist, provides some diverting extrapolation here.

TO: Arthur Stock, Executive Editor, *Ideas Illustrated,* New York City, 14632008447

FROM: Raymond Senter, c/o Hudson Junction Rotel, Hudson Junction, N. Y. 28997601910

ENCLOSED: Tentative Lead for *"The Shaker Revival."* Pix, tapes upcoming.

JERUSALEM WEST, N. Y., Thursday, June 28, 1995—The work of Salvation goes forward in this green and pleasant Hudson Valley hamlet to the high-pitched accompaniment of turbo-car exhausts and the amplified beat of the "world's loudest jag-rock band." Where worm-eaten apples fell untended in abandoned orchards less than a decade ago a new religious sect has burst into full bloom. In their fantastic four-year history the so-called New Shakers—or United Society of Believers (Revived), to give them their official title—have provoked the hottest controversy in Christendom since

Martin Luther nailed his ninety-five theses to the door of All Saints Church in Wittenberg, Germany, on October 31, 1517. Boasting a membership of more than a hundred thousand today, the New Shakers have been processing applications at the rate of nine hundred a week. Although a handful of these "recruits" are in their early and middle twenties—and last month a New Jersey man was accepted into the Shaker Family at Wildwood at the ripe old age of thirty-two—the average New Shaker has not yet reached his eighteenth birthday.

Richard F, one of the members of the "First Octave" who have been honored with "uncontaminated" Shaker surnames, explains it this way: "We've got nothing against feebies. They have a piece of the Gift inside just like anyone else. But it's hard for them to travel with the Family. Jag-rock hurts their ears, and they can't sync with thc Four Noes, no matter how hard they try. So we say to them, 'Forget it, star. Your wheels are not our wheels. But we're all going somewhere, right? See you at the other end.' "

It is hardly surprising that so many "feebies"—people over thirty—have trouble with the basic Believers' Creed: "No hate, No war, No money, No sex." Evidently, in this final decade of the twentieth century, sainthood is only possible for the very young.

The "Roundhouse" at Jerusalem West is, in one sense, the Vatican of the nationwide movement. But in many ways it is typical of the New Shaker communities springing up from La Jolla, California, to Seal Harbor, Maine. At last count there were sixty-one separate "tribes," some containing as many as fifteen "families" of a hundred and twenty-eight members each. Each Shaker family is housed in an army-surplus pliodesic dome—covering some ten thousand square feet of bare but vinyl-hardened earth—which serves as bedroom, living room, workshop and holy tabernacle, all in one. There is a much smaller satellite dome forty feet from the main building which might be called the Outhouse, but isn't—the New Shakers themselves refer to it as Sin City. In keeping with their general attitude toward the bodily functions, Sin City is the only place in the Jerusalem West compound that is off-limits to visitors.

As difficult as it may be for most North Americans to accept, today's typical Shaker recruit comes from a background of unquestioned abundance and respectability. There is no taint of the Ghetto and no evidence of serious behavioral problems. In fact, Preliminary School records show that these young people often excelled in polymorphous play and responded quite normally to the usual spectrum of chemical and electrical euphorics. As underteens, their proficiency in programed dating was consistently rated "superior" and they were often cited as leaders in organizing multiple-outlet experiences. Later, in Modular School, they scored in the fiftieth percentile or better on Brand-Differentiation tests. In short, according to all the available figures, they would have had no trouble gaining admission to the college of their choice or obtaining a commission in the Consumer Corps or qualifying for a Federal Travel Grant. Yet for some reason, on the very brink of maturity, they turned their backs on all the benefits their parents and grandparents fought so hard for in the Cultural Revolution—and plunged instead into a life of regimented sense-denial.

On a typical summer's afternoon at Jerusalem West, with the sun filtering through the translucent dome and bathing the entire area in a soft golden glow, the Roundhouse resembles nothing so much as a giant, queenless beehive. In the gleaming chrome-and-copper kitchen blenders whirr and huge pots bubble as a squad of white-smocked Food Deacons prepares the copious vegetable stew that forms the staple of the Shaker diet. In the sound-proofed garage sector the Shop Deacons are busily transforming another hopeless-looking junk-heap into the economical, turbine-powered "hotrod"—one already known to connoisseurs in this country and abroad as the Shakerbike—and the eight Administrative Deacons and their assistants are directing family business from a small fiber-walled cubicle known simply as The Office. And the sixteen-piece band is cutting a new liturgical tape for the Evening Service—a tape that may possibly end up as number one on the federal pop charts like the recent Shaker hit, *This Freeway's Plenty Wide Enough.* No matter where one turns beneath the big dome, one finds young people humming, tapping their feet, breaking into snatches of song and generally living up to the New Shaker motto: "Work is Play." One of their most popular songs—a characteristic coupling of Old Shaker words to a modern jag-rock background—concludes with this no-nonsense summation of the Shaker life-style:

It's the Gift to be simple,
The Gift to be free,
The Gift to come down
Where the Gift ought to be.

MORE TO COME

XEROGRAM: June 28 (11:15 P.M.)
TO: The Dean, Skinner Free Institute, Ronkonkoma, New Jersey 72441333965
FROM: Raymond Senter, c/o Hudson Junction Rotel, Hudson Junction, N. Y. 28997601910

Friend:

My son Bruce Senter, age 14, was enrolled in your institute for a six-week seminar in Applied Physiology beginning May 10. According to the transcript received by his Modular School (NYC118A), he successfully completed his course of studies on June 21. Mrs. Senter and I have had no word from him since. He had earlier talked with his Advisor about pursuing a Field-research project in Intensive Orgasm. I would appreciate any further information you can give me as to his post-seminar whereabouts. Thank you.

TO: Stock, Ex-Ed, *I.I.*
FROM: Senter
ENCLOSED: Background tape. Interview with Harry G (born "Guardino"), member of First Octave. Edited Transcript, June 29.

Q: Suppose we begin by talking a little about your position here as one of the—well, what shall I say? Founding Fathers of the Shaker Revival?
A: First you better take a deep breath, star. That's all out of sync. There's no Founding Fathers here. Or Founding Mothers or any of that jag. There's only one Father and one Mother and they're everywhere and nowhere, understand?
Q: What I meant was—as a member of the First Octave you have certain duties and responsibilities—
A: Like I said, star, everyone's equal here.
Q: I was under the impression that your rules stress obedience to a hierarchy?
A: Oh, there has to be order, sure, but it's nothing personal. If you can punch a computer—you sync with the Office Deacons. If you make it with wheels—you're in the Shop crew. Me—I fold my bed in the morning, push a juice-horn in the band and talk to reporters when they ask for me. That doesn't make me Pope.
Q: What about the honorary nomenclature?
A: What's that?
Q: The initials. Instead of last names.
A: Oh, yeah. They were given to us as a sign. You want to know what of?
Q: Please.

A: As a sign that no one's stuck with his birth kit. Sure, you may start with a Chevvie Six chassis and I have to go with a Toyota. That's the luck of the DNA. But we all need a spark of the chamber to get it moving. That's the Gift. And if I burn clean and keep in tune I may leave you flat in my tracks. Right?

Q: What about the Ghetto?

A: Even the Blacks have a piece of the Gift. What they do with it is their trip.

Q: There's been a lot of controversy lately about whether your movement is really Christian—in a religious sense. Would you care to comment on that?

A: You mean like "Jesus Christ, the Son of God?" Sure, we believe that. And we believe in Harry G, the Son of God and Richard F, the Son of God and—what's your name, star?—Raymond Senter, the Son of God. That's the gift. That's what it's all about. Jesus found the Gift inside. So did Buddha, Mother Ann, even Malcolm X—we don't worry too much about who said what first. First you find the Gift—then you live it. The Freeway's plenty wide enough.

Q: Then why all the emphasis on your Believers' Creed, and the Articles of Faith, and your clothes?

A: Look, star, every machine's got a set of specs. You travel with us, you learn our set. We keep the chrome shiny, the chambers clean. And we don't like accidents.

Q: Your prohibitions against money and sex—

A: "Prohibitions" is a feebie word. We're free from money and sex. The Four Noes are like a Declaration of Independence. See, everybody's really born free—but you have to know it. So we don't rob cradles. We say, let them grow up, learn what it's all about—the pill, the puffer, the feel-o-mat—all the perms and combos. Then, when they're fifteen or sixteen, if they still crave those chains, okay. If not, they know where to find us.

Q: What about the people who sign up and then change their minds?

A: We have no chains—if that's what you mean.

Q: You don't do anything to try to keep them?

A: Once you've really found the Gift inside there's no such thing as "changing your mind."

Q: What's your attitude toward the Old Shakers? They died out, didn't they, for lack of recruits?

A: Everything is born and dies and gets reborn again.

Q: Harry, what would happen if this time the whole world became Shakers?

A: Don't worry, star. You won't be around to see it.

MORE TO COME

XEROGRAM: June 29 (10:43 P.M.)
TO: Connie Fine, Director, Camp Encounter, Wentworth, Maine, 47119650023
FROM: Raymond Senter, Hudson Junction Rotel, Hudson Junction, N. Y., 28997601910

Connie:

Has Bruce arrived yet? Arlene and I have lost contact with him in the last week, and it occurred to me that he may have biked up to camp early and simply forgotten to buzz us—he was so charged up about being a full counselor-leader of his own T-group this season. Anyway, would you please buzz me soonest at the above zip? You know how mothers tend to overload the worry-circuits until they know for sure that their little wriggler is safely plugged in somewhere. Joy to you and yours, Ray.

TO: Stock, Ex-Ed., *I.I.*
FROM: Senter
ENCLOSED: Fact sheet on Old Shakers

FOUNDRESS—Mother Ann Lee, b. Feb. 29, 1736, Manchester, England.

ANTECEDENTS—Early Puritan "seekers" (Quakers), French "Prophets" (Camisards).

ORIGIN—Following an unhappy marriage—four children, all dead in infancy—Mother Ann begins to preach that "concupiscence" is the root of all evil. Persecutions and imprisonment.

1774—Mother Ann and seven early disciples sail to America aboard the ship *Mariah*. Group settles near Albany. Public preaching against concupiscence. More persecutions. More converts. Ecstatic, convulsive worship. Mother Ann's "miracles."

1784—Mother Ann dies.

1787—Mother Ann's successors, Father Joseph and Mother Lucy, organize followers into monastic communities and "separate" themselves from sinful world.

1787–1794—Expansion of sect through New York State and New England.

1806–1826—Expansion of sect across Western frontier—Ohio, Kentucky, Indiana.

1837–1845—Mass outbreak of spiritualism. Blessings, songs, spirit-drawings and business advice transmitted by deceased leaders through living "instruments."

1850's—Highpoint of Society. Six thousand members, 18 communities, fifty-eight "Families."

Total recorded membership—from late 18th century to late 20th century—approximately seventeen thousand.

Old Shakers noted for—mail-order seed business, handicrafts (brooms, baskets and boxes), furniture-manufacture.

Credited with invention of—common clothes pin, cut nails, circular saw, turbine waterwheel, steam-driven washing machine.

Worship—Emphasis on communal singing and dancing. Early "convulsive" phase gives way in nineteenth century to highly organized performances and processions—ring dances, square order shuffles.

Beliefs—Celibacy, Duality of Deity (Father and Mother God), Equality of the Sexes, Equality in Labor, Equality in Property. Society to be perpetuated by "admission of serious-minded persons and adoption of children."

Motto—"Hands to work and Hearts to God."

MORE TO COME

XEROGRAM: June 30 (8:15 A.M.)
TO: Mrs. Rosemary Collins, 133 Escorial Drive, Baywater, Florida, 92635776901
FROM: Raymond Senter, Hudson Junction Rotel, Hudson Junction, N. Y. 28997601910

Dear Rosie:

Has that little wriggler of ours been down your way lately? Bruce is off again on an unannounced sidetrip, and it struck me that he might have hopped down south to visit his favorite aunt. Not to mention his favorite cousin! How is that suntanned teaser of yours? Still taking after you in the S-L-N department? Give her a big kiss for me—you know where! And if Bruce does show up please buzz me right away at the above zip. Much Brotherly Love, Ray.

TO: Stock, Ex-Ed., *I.I.*
FROM: Senter
ENCLOSED: Caption tape for film segment on Worship Service.

JERUSALEM WEST, Saturday, June 30—I'm standing at the entrance to the inner sanctum of the huge Roundhouse here, the so-called Meeting Center, which is used only for important ceremonial functions—like the Saturday Night Dance scheduled to begin in exactly five minutes. In the Holy Corridor to my right the entire congregation has already assembled in two rows, one for boys and one for girls, side by side but not touching. During the week the Meeting Center is separated from the work and living areas by curved translucent partitions which fit together to make a little dome-within-a-dome. But when the sun begins to set on Saturday night the partitions are removed to reveal a circular dance floor, which is in fact the hub of the building. From this slightly raised platform of gleaming fibercast, I can look down each radial corridor—past the rows of neatly folded beds in the dormitories, past the shrouded machines in the repair shops, past the partly finished Shakerbikes in the garage, past the scrubbed formica tables in the kitchen—to the dim horizon line where the dome comes to rest on the sacred soil of Jerusalem West.

All artificial lights have been extinguished for the Sabbath celebration. The only illumination comes from the last rays of the sun, a dying torch that seems to have set the dome material itself ablaze. It's a little like standing inside the fiery furnace of Nebuchadnezzar with a hundred and twenty-eight unworried prophets of the Lord. The silence is virtually complete—not a cough, not the faintest rustle of fabric is heard. Even the air vents have been turned off—at least for the moment. I become aware of the harsh sound of my own respiration.

At precisely eight o'clock the two lines of worshippers begin to move forward out of the Holy Corridor. They circle the dance floor, the boys moving to the right, the girls to the left. Actually, it's difficult to tell them apart. The Shakers use no body ornaments at all—no paints, no wigs, no gems, no bugs, no dildoes, no flashers. All wear their hair cropped short, as if sheared with the aid of an overturned bowl. And all are dressed in some variation of Shaker gear—a loosely fitting, long-sleeved, buttonless and collarless shirt slit open at the neck for two inches and hanging free at the waist over a pair of baggy trousers pulled tight around each ankle by a hidden elastic band.

The garments look vaguely North African. They are made of soft dynaleen and they come in a variety of pastel shades. One girl may be wearing a pale pink top and a light blue bottom. The boy standing opposite her may have on the same colors, reversed. Others in the procession have chosen combinations of lilac and peach, ivory and lemon or turquoise and butternut. The range of hues seems endless but the intensity never varies, so that the entire spectacle presents a living demonstration of one of the basic Articles of Faith of the Shaker Revival—Diversity in Uniformity.

Now the procession has ended. The worshipers have formed two matching arcs, sixty-four boys on one side, sixty-four girls on the other, each standing precisely an arm's length from each neighbor. All are barefoot. All are wearing the same expression—a smile so modest as to be virtually undetectable if it were not mirrored and remirrored a hundred and twenty-eight times around the circumference of the ritual circle. The color of the dome has begun to change to a darker, angrier crimson. Whether the natural twilight's being artificially augmented—either from inside or outside the building—is impossible to tell. All eyes are turned upward to a focus about twenty-five feet above the center of the floor, where an eight-sided loudspeaker hangs by a chrome-plated cable from the midpoint of the dome. The air begins to fill with a pervasive vibration like the rumble of a distant monocar racing toward you in the night. And then the music explodes into the supercharged air. Instantly the floor is alive with jerking, writhing bodies—it's as if each chord were an electrical impulse applied directly to the nerve ends of the dancers —and the music is unbelievably loud.

The dome must act as an enormous soundbox. I can feel the vibrations in my feet and my teeth are chattering with the beat—but as wild as the dancing is, the circle is still intact. Each Shaker is "shaking" in his own place. Some are uttering incomprehensible cries, the holy gibberish that the Shakers call their Gift of Tongues—ecstatic prophesies symbolizing the Wordless Word of the Deity. One young girl with a gaunt but beautiful face is howling like a coyote. Another is grunting like a pig. A third is alternately spitting into the air and slapping her own cheeks viciously with both hands.

Across the floor a tall skinny boy has shaken loose from the rim of the circle. Pirouetting at high speed, his head thrown straight back so that his eyes are fixed on the crimson membrane of the dome, he seems to be propelling himself in an erratic path toward the center of the floor. And now the dome is changing color again, clotting to a deeper purple—like the color of a late evening sky but flecked with scarlet stars that seem to be darting about with a life of their own, colliding, coalescing, reforming.

A moment of relative calm has descended on the dancers. They are standing with their hands at their sides—only their heads are moving, lolling first to one side, then the other, in keeping with the new, subdued rhythm of the music. The tall boy in the center has begun to spin around and around in place, picking up speed with each rotation—now he's whirling like a top, his head still bent back, his eyes staring sightlessly. His right arm shoots out from the shoulder, the elbow locked, the fingers stiff, the palm flat—this is what the Shakers call the Arrow Sign, a manifestation of the Gift of Prophecy, directly inspired by the Dual Deity, Father Power and Mother Wisdom. The tall boy is the "instrument" and he is about to receive a message from on high.

His head tilts forward. His rotation slows. He comes to a halt with his right arm pointing at a short red-haired girl. The girl begins to shake all over as if struck by a high fever. The music rises to an ear-shattering crescendo and ends in mid-note.

"Everyone's a mirror," the tall boy shouts. "Clean, clean, clean—oh, let it shine! My dirt's not my own but it stains the earth. And the earth's not my own—the Mother and Father are light above light but the light can't shine alone. Only a mirror can shine, shine, shine. Let the mirror be mine, be mine, be mine!"

The red-haired girl is shaking so hard her limbs are flailing like whips. Her mouth has fallen open and she begins to moan, barely audibly at first. What she utters might be a single-syllable word like "clean" or "mine" or "shine" repeatedly, so rapidly that the consonants break down and the vowels flow into one unending stream of sound. But it keeps getting louder and louder and still louder, like the wail of an air-raid siren, until all resemblance to speech disappears and it seems impossible that such a sound can come from a human throat. You can almost hear the blood vessels straining, bursting.

Then the loudspeaker cuts in again in mid-note with the loudest, wildest jag-rock riff I have ever heard, only it's no longer something you can hear—it's inside you or you're inside it. And the dome has burst into blooms of color! A stroboscopic fireworks display that obliterates all outlines and shatters perspective and you can't tell whether the dancers are moving very, very slowly or very, very fast. The movement is so perfectly synchronized with the sound and the sound with the color that there seems to be no fixed reference point anywhere.

All you can say is: "There is color, there is sound, there is movement—"

This is the Gift of Seizure, which the New Shakers prize so highly—and whether it is genuinely mystical, as they claim, or autohypnotic or drug-induced, as some critics maintain, or a combination of all of these or something else entirely, it is an undeniably real—and profoundly disturbing—experience.

XEROGRAM: July 1 (7:27 A.M.)
TO: Frederick Rickover, Eastern Supervisor, Feel-O-Mat Corp., Baltimore, Maryland, 6503477502
FROM: Raymond Senter, Hudson Junction Rotel, Hudson Junction, N. Y., 28997601910

(*WARNING: PERSONALIZED ENVELOPE: CONTENTS WILL POWDER IF OPENED IMPROPERLY*)

Fred:

I'm afraid it's back-scratching time again. I need a code-check on DNA No. 75/62/HR/tl/4-9-06^{5}. I'm interested in whether the codee has plugged into a feel-o-mat anywhere in the Federation during the past two weeks. This one's a family matter, not business, so buzz me only at the above zip. I won't forget it. Gratefully, Ray.

TO: Stock. Ex-Ed., *I.I.*
FROM: Senter
ENCLOSED: Three tapes. New Shaker "testimonies." Edited transcripts, July 1.

TAPE I (Shaker name, "Farmer Brown"). What kind of mike is this? No kidding. I didn't know they made a re-amper this small. Chinese? Oh. Right. Well, let's see—I was born April 17, 1974, in Ellsworth, Saskatchewan. My breath-father's a foreman at a big refinery there. My breath-mother was a consumer-housewife. She's gone over now. It's kind of hard to remember details. When I was real little, I think I saw the feds scratch a Bomb-thrower on the steps of City Hall. But maybe that was only something I saw on 2-D. School was—you know, the usual. Oh, once a bunch of us kids got hold of some fresh spores from the refinery—I guess we stole them somehow. Anyway, there was still a lot of open land around and we planted them and raised our own crop of puffers. I didn't come down for a week. That was my farming experience. *(Laughter)* I applied for a bummer-grant on my fifteenth birthday, got a two-year contract and took off the next day for the sun. Let's see—Minneapolis, Kansas City, Mexico—what a jolt! There weren't so many feel-o-mats in the small towns down there and I was into all the hard stuff you could get in those days—speed, yellow, rock-juice, little-annie—I guess the only thing I never tried for a jolt was the Process and there were times when I was just about ready.

When the grant ran out, I just kept bumming on my own. At first you think it's going to be real easy. Half the people you know are still on contract and they share it around. Then your old friends start running out faster than you make new ones and there's a whole new generation on the road. And you start feeling more and more like a feebie and acting like one. I was lucky because I met this sweet little dove in Nashville—she had a master's in Audio-Visual but she was psycho for bummers, especially flat ones.

Anyway, she comes back to her coop one day with a new tape and puts it on and says, "This'll go right through you. It's a wild new group called the Shakers."

She didn't know two bobby's worth about the Shakers and I didn't either—the first Shaker tapes were just hitting the market about then. Well, I can tell you, that jagged sound gave me a jolt. I mean, it was bigger than yellow, bigger than juice, only it let you down on your feet instead of your back. I had this feeling I had to hear more. I got all the tapes that were out but they weren't enough. So I took off one night for Wildwood and before I knew it I was in a Prep Meeting and I was home free—you know, I've always kind of hoped that little dove makes it on her own—Oh, yeah, the band.

Well, I'm one of the Band Deacons, which is what's called a Sacrificial Gift because it means handling the accounts—and that's too close to the jacks and bobbys for comfort. But someone has to do it. You can't stay alive in an impure world without getting a little stained and if outsiders want to lay the Kennedys on us for bikes and tapes, that's a necessary evil. But we don't like to spread the risk in the Family. So the Deacons sign the checks and deal with the agents and the stain's on us alone. And everyone prays a little harder to square it with the Father and Mother.

TAPE II (Shaker name, "Mariah Moses"). I was born in Darien, Connecticut. I'm an Aquarius with Leo rising. Do you want my breath-name? I don't mind—it's Cathy Ginsberg. My breath-parents are both full-time consumers. I didn't have a very interesting childhood, I guess. I went to Mid-Darien Modular School. I was a pretty good student—my best subject was World Culture. I consummated on my third date, which was about average, I've been told, for my class. Do you really want all this background stuff? I guess the biggest thing that happened to the old me was when I won a second prize in the Maxwell Puffer Civic Essay contest when I was fourteen. The subject was *The Joys of Spectatorism* and the prize was a Programed Weekend in Hawaii for two. I don't remember who I went with. But Hawaii was really nice. All those brown-skinned boys—we went to a big luaü on Saturday night. That's a native-style orgy. They taught me things we never even learned in school.

I remember thinking, *Oh, star, this is the living end!*

But when it was all over I had another thought. If this was the living end—what came next? I don't know if it was the roast pig or what but I didn't feel so good for a few days. The night we got back home—Herbie! That was the name of my date, Herbie Alcott—he had short curly hair all over his back—anyway, the night I got home my breath-parents picked me up at the airport and on the way back to Darien they started asking me what I wanted to do with my life. They were trying to be so helpful, you know. I mean, you could see they would have been disappointed if I got involved in production of some kind but they weren't about to say that in so many words. They just asked me if I had decided how I wanted to plug into the Big Board. It was up to me to choose between college or the Consumer Corps or a Travel Grant—they even asked me if Herbie and I were getting serious and if we wanted to have a baby—because the waiting-list at the Marriage Bureau was already six-months long and getting longer. The trouble was I was still thinking about the luau and the roast pig and I felt all—burned out. Like a piece of charcoal that still looks solid but is really just white ash—and if you touch it it crumbles and blows away. So I said I'd think about it but what I was really thinking was *I'm not signing up for any more orgies just yet.*

And a few days later the miracle happened. A girl in our glass was reported missing and a friend of mine heard someone say that she'd become a Shaker.

I said, "What's that?"

My friend said, "It's a religion that believes in No hate, No war, No money, No sex."

And I felt this thrill go right through me. And even though I didn't know what it meant at the time, that was the moment I discovered my Gift. It was such a warm feeling, like something soft and quiet curled up inside you, waiting. And the day I turned fifteen I hiked up to Jerusalem and I never went home. That was eleven months ago . . . oh, you can't describe what happens at Preparative Meeting. It's what happens inside you that counts. Like now, when I think of all my old friends from Darien, I say a little prayer.

Father Power, Mother Wisdom, touch their Gifts, set them free . . . .

TAPE III (Shaker name, "Earnest Truth"). I'm aware that I'm something of a rarity here. I assume that's why you asked me for a testimony. But I don't want you categorizing me as a Shaker intellectual or a Shaker theologian or anything like that. I serve as Legal Deacon because that's my Gift. But I'm also a member of the vacuum detail in Corridor Three and that's my Gift too. I'd be just as good a Shaker if I only cleaned the floor and nothing else. Is that clear? Good. Well then, as briefly as possible (READS FROM PREPARED TEXT): I'm twenty-four years old, from Berkeley, California. Breath-parents were on the faculty at the University; killed in an air crash when I was ten. I was raised by the state. Pacific Highlands Modular School: First honors. Consumer Corps: Media-aide First-class. Entered the University at seventeen. Pre-law. Graduated *magna cum* in nineteen-ninety. Completed four-year Law School in three years. In my final year I became interested in the literature of religion—or, to be more precise, the literature of mysticism—possibly as a counterpoise to the increasing intensity of my formal studies. Purely as an intellectual diversion I began to read St. John of the Cross, George Fox, the Vedas, Tao, Zen, the Kabbala, the Sufis. But when I came across the early Shakers I was struck at once with the daring and clarity of this purely American variant. All mystics seek spiritual union with the Void, the Nameless, the Formless, the Ineffable. But the little band of Shaker pilgrims, confronted with a vast and apparently unbounded wilderness, took a marvelous quantum leap of faith and decided that the union had already been accomplished. The wilderness was the Void. For those who had eyes to see—this was God's Kingdom. And by practicing a total communism, a total abnegation, a total dedication, they made the wilderness flower for two hundred years. Then, unable to adjust to the methodologies of the Industrial Revolution, they quietly faded away; it was as if their gentle spirit had found a final resting place in the design of their utterly simple and utterly beautiful wooden furniture—each piece of which has since become a collector's item. When I began reading about the Old Shakers I had of course heard about the New Shakers—but I assumed that they were just another crackpot fundamentalist sect like the Holy Rollers or the Snake Handlers, an attempt to keep alive the pieties of a simpler day in the present age of abundance. But eventually my curiosity—or so I called it at the time—led me to investigate a Preparative Meeting that had been established in the Big Sur near Jefferstown. And I found my Gift. The experience varies from individual to individual. For me it was the revelation that the complex machine we refer to as the Abundant Society is the real anachronism. All the euphorics we feed ourselves cannot change the fact that the machinery of abundance has long since reached its limit as a vital force and is now choking on its own waste products—Pollution, Overpopulation, Dehumanization. Far from being a breakthrough, the so-called Cultural Revolution was merely the last gasp of the old order trying to maintain itself by programing man's most private senses into the machine. And the childish Bomb-throwers were nothing but retarded romantics, an anachronism within an anachronism. At this juncture in history, only the Shaker Revival offers a true alternative—in the utterly simple, and therefore utterly profound, Four Noes. The secular world usually praises us for our rejection of Hate and War and mocks us for our rejection of Money and Sex. But the Four Noes constitute a beautifully balanced ethical equation, in which each term is a function of the other three. There are no easy Utopias. Non-Shakers often ask: What would happen if everyone became a Shaker? Wouldn't that be the end of the human race? My personal answer is this: Society is suffering from the sickness unto death—a plague called despair. Shakerism is the only cure. As long as the plague rages more and more people will find the strength to take the medicine required, no matter how bitter it may seem. Perhaps at some future date, the very spread of Shakerism will restore Society to health, so that the need for Shakerism will again slacken. Perhaps the cycle will be repeated. Perhaps not. It is impossible to know what the Father and Mother have planned for their children. Only one thing is certain. The last of the Old Shaker prophetesses wrote in 1956: "The flame may flicker but the spark can never be allowed to die out until the salvation of the world is accomplished."

I don't think you'll find the flame flickering here.

MORE TO COME

XEROGRAM: July 1 (11:30 P.M.)
TO: Stock, Ex-Ed., *I.I.*
FROM: Raymond Senter, c/o Hudson Junction Rotel
(*WARNING: PERSONALIZED ENVELOPE: CONTENTS WILL POWDER IF OPENED IMPROPERLY*)

Art:

Cooperation unlimited here—until I mention "Preparative Meeting." Then they all get tongue-tied. Too holy for impure ears. No one will even say where or when. Working hypothesis: It's a compulsory withdrawal session. Recruits obviously must kick all worldly habits before taking final vows. Big question: How do they do it? Conscious or unconscious? Cold-turkey, hypno-suggestion, or re-conditioning? Legal or illegal? Even Control would like to know. I'm tapping the Reception Deacon tomorrow. If you approve, I'll start putting the pressure on. The groundwork's done. We may get a story yet. Ray.

XEROGRAM: July 2 (2:15 A.M.)
TO: Joseph Harger, Coordinator, N.Y. State Consumer Control, Albany, N.Y. 31118002311
FROM: Raymond Senter, c/o Hudson Junction Rotel, Hudson Junction, N.Y. 28997601910
(*WARNING: PERSONALIZED ENVELOPE: CONTENTS WILL POWDER IF OPENED IMPROPERLY*)

Joe:

I appreciate your taking a personal interest in this matter. My wife obviously gave the wrong impression to the controller she contacted. She tends to get hysterical. Despite what she may have said I assure you my son's attitude toward the Ghetto was a perfectly healthy blend of scorn and pity. Bruce went with me once to see the Harlem Wall—must have been six or seven—and Coordinator Bill Quaite let him sit in the Scanner's chair for a few minutes. He heard a muzzein call from the top of one of those rickety towers. He saw the wild rats prowling in the stench and garbage. He also watched naked children fighting with wooden knives over a piece of colored glass. I am told there are young people today stupid enough to think that sneaking over the Wall is an adventure and that the process is reversible—but my son is definitely not one of them. And he is certainly not a bomb-thrower. I know that you have always shared my publication's view that a selective exposure to the harsher realities makes for better consumers. (I'm thinking of that little snafu in data-traffic in the Albany Grid last summer.) I hope you'll see your way clear to trusting me again. I repeat: there's not the slightest indication that my son was going over to the Blacks. In fact, I have good reason to believe that he will turn up quite soon, with all discrepancies accounted for. But I need a little time. A Missing Persons Bulletin would only make things harder at the moment. I realize it was my wife who initiated the complaint. But I'd greatly appreciate it if she got misfiled for forty-eight hours. I'll handle any static on this side. Discreetly, Ray.

TO: Stock, Ex-Ed., *I.I.*
FROM: Senter
ENCLOSED: Background tape; interview with Antonia Cross, age 19, Reception Deacon, Jerusalem West Edited Transcript, July 2.

Q: (I waited silently for her to take the lead.)
A: Before we begin, I think we better get a few things straight. It'll save time and grief in the long run. First of all, despite what your magazine and others may have said in the past, we never proselytize. Never. So please don't use that word. We just try to live our Gift—and if other people are drawn to us, that's the work of the Father and Mother, not us. We don't have to preach. When someone's sitting in filth up to his neck he doesn't need a preacher to tell him he smells. All he needs to hear is that there's a cleaner place somewhere. Second, we don't prevent anyone from leaving, despite all rumors to the contrary. We've had exactly three apostates in the last four years. They found out their wheels were not our wheels and they left.

Q: Give me their names.

A: There's no law that says we have to disclose the names of backsliders. Find them yourself. That shouldn't be too hard, now that they're plugged back in to the Big Board.

Q: You overestimate the power of the press.

A: False modesty is not considered a virtue among Shakers.

Q: You mentioned three backsliders. How many applicants are turned away before taking final vows?

A: The exact percentage is immaterial. Some applicants are more serious than others. There is no great mystery about our reception procedure. You've heard the expression, "Weekend Shakers." Anybody can buy the gear and dance and sing and stay pure for a couple of days. It's even considered a "jolt," I'm told. We make sure that those who come to us know the difference between a weekend and a life-time. We explain the Gift, the Creed, the Articles of Faith. Then we ask them why they've come to us. We press them pretty hard. In the end, if they're still serious, they are sent to Preparative Meeting for a while until a Family is ready to accept them.

Q: How long is a while?

A: Preparative Meeting can take days or weeks. Or longer.

Q: Are they considered full-fledged Shakers during that time?

A: The moment of Induction is a spiritual, not a temporal, phenomenon.

Q: But you notify the authorities only after a recruit is accepted in a Family?

A: We comply with all the requirements of the Full Disclosure Law.

Q: What if the recruit is underage and lies about it? Do you run a routine DNA check?

A: We obey the law.

Q: But a recruit at a Prep Meeting isn't a Shaker and

so you don't have to report his presence. Is that right?

A: We've had exactly nine complaints filed against us in four years. Not one has stuck.

Q: Then you do delay acceptance until you can trace a recruit's identity?

A: I didn't say that. We believe in each person's right to redefine his set, no matter what the Big Board may say about him. But such administrative details tend to work themselves out.

Q: How? I don't understand.

A: The ways of the Father and Mother sometimes passeth understanding.

Q: You say you don't proselytize, but isn't that what your tapes are—a form of preaching? Don't most of your recruits come to you because of the tapes? And don't most of them have to be brought down from whatever they're hooked on before you'll even let them in?

A: The world—your world—is filth. From top to bottom. We try to stay as far away as we can. But we have to eat. So we sell you our tapes and our Shakerbikes. There's a calculated risk of contamination. But it works the other way too. Filth can be contaminated by purity. That's known as Salvation. It's like a tug of war. We'll see who takes the greatest risk.

Q: That's what I'm here for—to see at first hand. Where is the Jerusalem West Preparative Meeting held?

A: Preparative Meetings are private. For the protection of all concerned.

Q: Don't you mean secret? Isn't there something going on at these meetings that you don't want the public to know?

A: If the public is ignorant of the life of the spirit, that is hardly our fault.

Q: Some people believe that your recruits are "prepared" with drugs or electro-conditioning.

A: Some people think that Shaker stew is full of saltpeter. Are you going to print that, too?

Q: You have been accused of brain-tampering. That's a serious charge. And unless I get a hell of a lot more cooperation from you than I've been getting I will have to assume that you have something serious to hide.

A: No one ever said you'd be free to see everything. You'll just have to accept our—guidance—in matters concerning religious propriety.

Q: Let me give you a little guidance, Miss Cross. You people already have so many enemies in that filthy world you despise that one unfriendly story from *I.I.* might just tip the scales.

A: The power of the press? We'll take our chances.

Q: What will you do if the police crack down?

A: We're not afraid to die. And the Control authorities have found that it's more trouble than it's worth to put us in jail. We seem to upset the other inmates.

Q: Miss Cross—

A: We use no titles here. My name is Antonia.

Q: You're obviously an intelligent, dedicated young woman. I would rather work with you than against you. Why don't we try to find some middle ground? As a journalist my primary concern is human nature —what happens to a young recruit in the process of becoming a full-fledged Shaker. You won't let me into a Prep Meeting to see for myself. All right, you have your reasons, and I respect them. But I ask you to respect mine. If I can look through your Reception files—just the last two or three weeks will do—I should be able to get some idea of what kind of raw material you draw on. You can remove the names, of course.

A: Perhaps we can provide a statistical breakdown for you.

Q: I don't want statistics. I want to look at their pictures, listen to their voices—you say you press them pretty hard in the first interview. That's what I need: their response under pressure, the difference between those who stick it through and those who don't.

A: How do we know you're not looking for something of a personal nature—to embarrass us?

Q: For God's sakes, I'm one of the best-known tapemen in the Federation. Why not just give me the benefit of the doubt?

A: You invoke a Deity that means nothing to you.

Q: I'm sorry.

A: The only thing I can do is transmit your request to the Octave itself. Any decision on such a matter would have to come from a Full Business Meeting.

Q: How long will it take?

A: The Octave is meeting tomorrow, before Evening Service.

Q: All right. I can wait till then. I suppose I should apologize again for losing my temper. I'm afraid it's an occupational hazard.

A: We all have our Gift.

MORE TO COME

TO: Stock, Ex-Ed., *I.I.*
FROM: Senter
ENCLOSED: First add on Shaker Revival; July 3.

It is unclear whether the eight teenagers—six boys and two girls—who banded together one fateful evening in the spring of 1991 to form a jag-rock combo called The Shakers had any idea of the religious implications of the name. According to one early account in *Riff* magazine, the original eight were thinking only of a classic rock-and-roll number of the nineteen-fifties,

Shake, Rattle, and Roll (a title not without sexual as well as musicological overtones). On the other hand, there is evidence that Harry G was interested in astrology, palmistry, scientology and other forms of modern occultism even before he left home at the age of fifteen. (Harry G was born Harry Guardino, on December 18, 1974, in Schoodic, Maine, the son of a third-generation lobster fisherman.) Like many members of his generation he applied for a Federal Travel Grant on graduation from Modular School and received a standard two-year contract. But unlike most of his fellow-bummers, Harry did not immediately take off on an all-expenses-paid tour of the seamier side of life in the North American Federation. Instead, he hitched a ride to New York City, where he established a little basement coop on the lower west side that soon became a favorite way-station for other, more restless bummers passing through the city. No reliable account of this period is available. The rumors that he dabbled in a local Bomb-throwers cell appear to be unfounded. But it is known that sometime during the spring of 1991 a group of bummers nearing the end of their grants gathered in Harry G's coop to discuss the future. By coincidence or design the eight young people who came together that night from the far corners of the Federation all played some instrument and shared a passion for jag-rock. And as they talked and argued among themselves about the best way possible to "plug into the Big Board," it slowly began to dawn on them that perhaps their destinies were linked —or, as Harry G himself has put it, "We felt we could make beautiful music together. Time has made us one."

Building a reputation in the jag-rock market has never been easy—not even with divine intervention. For the next two months, The Shakers scrambled for work, playing a succession of one-night stands in consumers' centers, schools, fraternal lodges—wherever someone wanted live entertainment and was willing to put the group up. The Shakers traveled in a second-hand Chevrolet van which was kept running only by the heroic efforts of the group's electric-oud player, Richard Fitzgerald (who later—as Richard F—helped to design the improved version of the turbo-adapter which forms the basis of today's Shakerbike).

On the night of June the first the group arrived in Hancock, Massachusetts, where they were scheduled to play the next evening at the graduation dance of the Grady L. Parker Modular School. They had not worked for three days and their finances had reached a most precarious stage—they were now sharing only four bummer-grants between them, the other four contracts having expired in the previous weeks. From the very beginning of their relationship the eight had gone everywhere and done everything as a group—they even insisted on sleeping together in one room on the theory that the "bad vibrations" set up by an overnight absence from each other might adversely affect their music. As it turned out, there was no room large enough at the local Holiday Inn, so, after some lengthy negotiations, the Modular School principal arranged for them to camp out on the grounds of the local Shaker Museum, a painstaking restoration of an early New England Shaker community dating back to 1790. Amused but not unduly impressed by the coincidence in names, the eight Shakers bedded down for the night within sight of the Museum's most famous structure, the Round Stone Barn erected by the original Shakers in 1826. Exactly what happened between midnight and dawn on that fog-shrouded New England meadow may never be known—the validation of mystical experience being by its very nature a somewhat inexact science. According to Shaker testimony, however, the spirit of Mother Ann, sainted foundress of the original sect, touched the Gifts of the eight where they lay and in a vision of the future—which Amelia D later said was "as clear and bright as a holograph"—revealed why they had been chosen: The time had come for a mass revival of Shaker beliefs and practices. The eight teenagers awoke at the same instant, compared visions, found them to be identical and wept together for joy. They spent the rest of the day praying for guidance and making plans. Their first decision was to play as scheduled at the Grady L. Parker graduation dance.

"We decided to go on doing just what we had been doing—only more so," Amelia D later explained. "Also, I guess, we needed the jacks."

Whatever the reason, the group apparently played as never before. Their music opened up doors to whole new ways of hearing and feeling—or so it seemed to the excited crowd of seniors who thronged around the bandstand when the first set was over. Without any premeditation, or so he later claimed, Harry Guardino stood up and announced the new Shaker dispensation, including the Believers' Creed (the Four Noes) and a somewhat truncated version of the Articles of Faith of the United Society of Believers (Revived): "All things must be kept decent and in good order," "Diversity in Uniformity," and "Work is Play." According to the Hancock newspaper, seventeen members of the senior class left town that morning with the Shakers—in three cars "borrowed" from parents and later returned. Drawn by a Gift of Travel, the little band of pilgrims made their way to the quiet corner of New York State now known as Jerusalem West, bought some land—with funds obtained from anonymous benefactors—and settled down to their strange experiment in monastic and ascetic communism.

The actual historical connections between Old Shakers and New Shakers remains a matter of conjecture. It is not clear, for instance, whether Harry G and his associates had a chance to consult the documentary material on display at the Hancock Museum. There is no doubt that the First Article of Faith of the Shaker Revival is a word-for-word copy of the first part of an early Shaker motto. But it has been given a subtly different meaning in present-day usage. And while many of the New Shaker doctrines and practices can be traced to the general tenor of traditional Shakerism, the adaptations are often quite free and sometimes wildly capricious. All in all, the Shaker Revival seems to be very much a product of our own time. Some prominent evolutionists even see it as part of a natural process of weeding out those individuals incapable of becoming fully consuming members of the Abundant Society. They argue that Shakerism is a definite improvement, in this respect, over the youthful cult of Bomb-throwers which had to be suppressed in the early days of the Federation.

But there are other observers who see a more ominous trend at work. They point especially to the serious legal questions raised by the Shakers' efforts at large-scale proselytization. The twenty-seventh Amendment to the Federal Constitution guarantees the right of each white citizen over the age of fifteen to the free and unrestricted enjoyment of his own senses, provided that such enjoyment does not interfere with the range or intensity of any other citizen's sensual enjoyment. Presumably this protection also extends to the right of any white citizen to deny himself the usual pleasures. But what is the status of corporate institutions that engage in such repression? How binding, for example, is the Shaker recruit's sworn allegiance to the Believers' Creed? How are the Four Noes enforced within the sect? Suppose two Shakers find themselves physically attracted to each other and decide to consummate—does the United Society of Believers have any right to place obstacles between them? These are vital questions that have yet to be answered by the Control authorities. But there are influential men in Washington who read the twenty-seventh amendment as an obligation on the government's part not merely to protect the individual's right to sensual pleasure but also to help him maximize it. And in the eyes of these broad constructionists the Shakers are on shaky ground.

TO: Stock, Ex-Ed., *I.I.*
FROM: Senter
(*WARNING: CONFIDENTIAL UNEDITED TAPE: NOT FOR PUBLICATION: CONTENTS WILL POWDER IF OPENED IMPROPERLY*)

FIRST VOICE: Bruce? Is that you?
SECOND VOICE: It's me.
FIRST: For God's sake, come in! Shut the door. My God, I thought you were locked up in that Prep Meeting. I thought—
SECOND: It's not a prison. When I heard you were prowling around town I knew I had to talk to you.
FIRST: You've changed your mind then?
SECOND: Don't believe it. I just wanted to make sure you didn't lie about everything.
FIRST: Do they know you're here?
SECOND: No one followed me, if that's what you mean. No one even knows who I am. I've redefined my set, as we say.
FIRST: But they check. They're not fools. They'll find out soon enough—if they haven't already.
SECOND: They don't check. That's another lie. And anyway, I'll tell them myself after Induction.
FIRST: Brucie—it's not too late. We want you to come home.
SECOND: You can tell Arlene that her little baby is safe and sound. How is she? Blubbering all over herself as usual?
FIRST: She's pretty broken up about your running away.
SECOND: Why? Is she worried they'll cut off her credit at the feel-o-mat? For letting another potential consumer get off the hook?

FIRST: You wouldn't have risked coming to me if you didn't have doubts. Don't make a terrible mistake.

SECOND: I came to see you because I know how you can twist other people's words. Are you recording this?

FIRST: Yes.

SECOND: Good. I'm asking you straight out—please leave us alone.

FIRST: Do you know they're tampering with your mind?

SECOND: Have you tasted your local drinking water lately?

FIRST: Come home with me.

SECOND: I am home.

FIRST: You haven't seen enough of the world to turn your back on it.

SECOND: I've seen you and Arlene.

FIRST: And is our life so awful?

SECOND: What you and Arlene have isn't life. It's the American Dream Come True. You're in despair and don't even know it. That's the worse kind.

FIRST: You repeat the slogans as if you believed them.

SECOND: What makes you think I don't?

FIRST: You're my flesh and blood. I know you.

SECOND: You don't. All you know is that your little pride and joy ran away to become a monk and took the family genes. And Arlene is too old to go back to the Big Board and beg for seconds.

FIRST: Look—I know a little something about rebellion, too. I've had a taste of it in my time. It's healthy, it's natural—I'm all for it. But not an overdose. When the jolt wears off, you'll be stuck here. And you're too smart to get trapped in a hole like this.

SECOND: It's my life, isn't it? In exactly one hour and ten minutes I'll be free, white, and fifteen—Independence Day, right? What a beautiful day to be born—it's the nicest thing you and Arlene did for me.

FIRST: Brucie, we want you back. Whatever you want—

just name it and if it's in my power I'll try to get it. I have friends who will help.

SECOND: I don't want anything from you. We're quits—can't you understand? The only thing we have in common now is this: (*sound of heavy breathing*). That's it. And if you want that back you can take it. Just hold your hand over my mouth and pinch my nose for about five minutes. That should do it.

FIRST: How can you joke about it?

SECOND: Why not? Haven't you heard? There're only two ways to go for my generation—the Shakers or the Ghetto. How do you think I'd look in black-face with bushy hair and a gorilla nose? Or do you prefer my first choice?

FIRST: I'm warning you, the country's not going to put up with either much longer. There's going to be trouble—and I want you out of here when it comes.

SECOND: What are the feebies going to do? Finish our job for us?

FIRST: Is that what you want then? To commit suicide?

SECOND: Not exactly. That's what the Bomb-throwers did. We want to commit your suicide.

FIRST: (*Words unintelligible.*)

SECOND: That really jolts you, doesn't it? You talk about rebellion as if you knew something about it because you wore beads once and ran around holding signs.

FIRST: We changed history.

SECOND: You didn't change anything. You were swallowed up, just like the Bomb-throwers. The only difference is, you were eaten alive.

FIRST: Bruce—

SECOND: Can you stretch the gray-stuff a little, and try to imagine what real rebellion would be like? Not just another chorus of "gimme, gimme, gimme—" But the absolute negation of what's come before? The Four Noes all rolled up into One Big No!

FIRST: Brucie—I'll make a deal—

SECOND: No one's ever put it all together before. I don't expect you to see it. Even around here, a lot of people don't know what's happening. Expiation! That's what rebellion is all about. The young living down the sins of the fathers and mothers! But the young are always so hungry for life they get distracted before they can finish the job. Look at all the poor, doomed rebels in history; whenever they got too big to be crushed the feebies bought them off with a piece of the action. The stick or the carrot and then—business as usual. Your generation was the biggest sellout of all. But the big laugh is, you really thought you won. So now you don't have any carrot left to offer, because you've already shared it all with us—before we got old. And we're strong enough to laugh at your sticks. Which is why the world is going to find out for the first time what total rebellion is.

FIRST: I thought you didn't believe in violence and hate?

SECOND: Oh, our strength is not of this world. You can forget all the tapes and bikes and dances—that's the impure shell that must be sloughed off. If you want to get the real picture, just imagine us—all your precious little gene-machines—standing around in a circle, our heads bowed in prayer, holding our breaths and clicking off one by one. Don't you think that's a beautiful way for your world to end? Not with a bang or a whimper—but with one long breathless Amen?

MORE TO COME

TO: Stock, Ex-Ed., *I.I.*
FROM: Senter
ENCLOSED: New first add on *"Shaker Revival"* (scratch earlier transmission; new lead upcoming).

JERUSALEM WEST, N.Y., Wednesday, July 4—An early critic of the Old Shakers, a robust pamphleteer who had actually been a member of the sect for ten months, wrote this prophetic appraisal of his former cohorts in the year 1782: "When we consider the infant state of civil power in America since the Revolution began, every infringement on the natural rights of humanity, every effort to undermine our original constitution, either in civil or ecclesiastical order, saps the foundation of Independency."

That winter, the Shaker foundress, Mother Ann, was seized in Petersham, Massachusetts, by a band of vigilantes who, according to a contemporary account, wanted "to find out whether she was a woman or not." Various other Shaker leaders were horse-whipped, thrown in jail, tarred and feathered, and driven out of one New England town after another by an aroused citizenry. These severe persecutions, which lasted through the turn of the century, were the almost inevitable outcome of a clash between the self-righteous, unnatural, uncompromising doctrines of the Shakers —and the pragmatic, democratic, forward-looking mentality of the struggling new nation, which would one day be summed up in that proud emblem: The American Way of Life.

This conflict is no less sharp today. So far the New Shakers have generally been given the benefit of the doubt as just another harmless fringe group. But there is evidence that the mood of the country is changing—and rapidly. Leading educators and political figures, respected clergymen and prominent consumer consultants have all become more outspoken in denouncing the disruptive effect of this new fanaticism on the country as a whole. Not since the heyday of the Bomb-throwers in the late seventies has a single issue shown such potential for galvanizing informed public opinion. And a chorus of distraught parents has only just begun to make itself heard—like the lamentations of Rachel in the wilderness.

Faced with the continuing precariousness of the international situation, and the unresolved dilemma of the Ghettoes, some Control authorities have started talking about new restrictions on all monastic sects—not out of any desire to curtail religious freedom but in an effort to preserve the constitutional guarantees of free expression and consumption. Some feel that if swift, firm governmental action is not forthcoming it will get harder and harder to prevent angry parents—and others with legitimate grievances—from taking the law into their own hands.

MORE TO COME